NEVER PLEASING TO THE WORLD

A Man and His Slaves

PEGGY PATTERSON GARLAND

Scripture taken from the King James Version of the Bible.

Archway Publishing books may be ordered through booksellers or by contacting:

Archway Publishing
1663 Liberty Drive
Bloomington, IN 47403
www.archwaypublishing.com
1 (888) 242-5904

ISBN: 978-1-4808-7520-3 (sc)
ISBN: 978-1-4808-7519-7 (e)

Library of Congress Control Number: 2019935007

Print information available on the last page.

Archway Publishing rev. date: 03/08/2019

This book is dedicated to the memory of Thomas Maund Arnest IV, of Nomini Hall, a direct descendent of Robert Carter and a good friend of my husband, E. B. Garland,

and to the memory of

my own dear "Rose," Marguerite Rose Carey Ball, a descendent of people freed by Robert Carter.

Foreward

The Northern Neck of Virginia is an amazing place, where the past still lives in the present. In the tiny, rural county of Westmoreland (2010 population 17,000), on the Northern Neck of Virginia were born two presidents, George Washington and James Monroe, two signers of the Declaration of Independence, the brothers Richard Henry Lee and Francis Lightfoot Lee, as well as the head of the Confederate armies during the Civil War, Robert E. Lee.

There was another man who made his home in that same small county. He was the grandson of an imperious colonial planter, Robert "King" Carter, who was probably the richest man in Virginia in his time. In his own right, Robert III was an accomplished musician, an avid reader and a largely self-educated judge and Councillor of Virginia, a successful businessman, manufacturer, and planter, a family man married to the daughter of a governor of Maryland and father of seventeen children, a friend of Virginia governors, a religious scholar and philosopher. He has remained obscure for two and a quarter centuries for the same reason he is most deserving of renown. In 1791, seventy-four years before the Emancipation Proclamation, Robert Carter, III set in motion the freeing of all of his slaves, approximately five hundred of them.

We must wonder why he did such a thing—a betrayal at the time of his class-- and how he got to that point. In order to figure it out, we must probe the life of an enigmatic personality. Robert Carter, unlike his contemporary and fellow musician, Thomas Jefferson, was not articulate about his thoughts. In fact, he was not much accustomed to explaining himself at all. To figure out why he did what he did, we must look, not to his thoughts written down, but to his actions. That is what *Never Pleasing to the World* is about.

The names of the characters in this book are almost entirely the names of the real people who lived in Robert Carter's world. The places are real. Contemporary natives of the Northern Neck will recognize the names. My good friends, Roberta and Ann Sanford, for instance, are married to men almost certainly related to Carter's overseer, John Sanford. My own late husband, E.B. Garland, was a direct descendant of William Garland, the surveyor that Carter used. The names Carter, Chinn, Ball, Beale, Henry, and Dixon, to name only a few, are still common names in the area. The name of the Billingsgate overseer, written as "Olive" in Carter's diary, is almost certainly the modern-day, "Oliff."

Most of the events in the book are also real, embellished with detail and conversation, and some speculation where necessary. For instance, there appears to be no record of where Robert Carter lived from the time he was six until he went to England, except for his time at the William and Mary Grammar School. One part of the story which is not based in fact is Tom Henry's temporary enslavement by Charles Thomas, and Charles Thomas himself is entirely fictional.

I love the Northern Neck and Westmoreland County. I trust that is obvious to the reader. I enjoyed getting to know

Robert Carter, III, **Tom Henry, Sam Harrison and all their contemporaries** through my research and I hope that those who read this book will come to appreciate the Neck, and particularly Robert Carter, III, as I do.

1

1731: Corotoman Plantation, Lancaster County, Virginia

Robert Carter III was three.

The sky was blue like the periwinkle flowers that grew behind the slave quarters, and soft clouds floated above. A breeze ruffled the curls of his grandfather's periwig and tickled Robert's face as he sat before him on his big horse. Robert could feel his grandfather's arm around his middle and smell tobacco and leather about him.

Grandfather bade the horse stop a moment. "Look, Robert." He pointed across the field. "See the Negroes working in the tobacco?"

Robert saw barefoot men and women sweating in the hot sun, the men naked to the waist, their backs beaded with sweat. The women wore loose dresses, stained with perspiration, and head rags that kept their hair out of their faces. They toiled slowly and rhythmically over the waist-high tobacco leaves, stripping away the fat tobacco worms by hand.

"Aren't they hot, Grandfather?"

"They don't feel the heat the same way as you and I do, Robert. They come from Africa, where it's always hot. That's why Negroes make good slaves. They are strong and stupid and slow, and their bodies are made to endure the sun."

Robert thought that Sam, his personal slave given to him at birth, was not stupid and slow, but he didn't ask anything more.

The child's attention was distracted by a beautiful buck standing still, its tail high and its eyes fixed on them. Robert held his breath, hoping the deer wouldn't start at the sight of them and run. Between the deer and them was the rolling land—the fields of great green leaves of tobacco—and beyond him were the cool woods. All of it, everything within sight, belonged to Grandfather.

On that Sunday, while the family was still visiting Grandfather, they all rode together to Christ Church in a carriage pulled by six sleek horses. The new building at Christ Church was not yet finished. On their ride around the plantation the day before, Grandfather and Robert watched some of Grandfather's Negroes under the white overseer laying the bricks in Flemish bond. King Carter provided the land and used his own money for the church because it was a pious thing for him to do.

The Negro postilion sat straight and tall on the lead horse, and the coachman sat on the seat of the coach, guiding. They were handsome. They looked proud, dressed in the sky-blue livery of the Carter family.

The three-mile road over which the coach traveled was lined on both sides by cedar trees, and it went directly from the great house of Grandfather's plantation, Corotoman, to the church. As they approached, they could see everyone standing outside. Church did not begin until King Carter arrived. That's what people called Robert's grandfather—King Carter.

Grandfather had sat on the seat across from Robert in the carriage. His white wig curled at his shoulders, and he wore a purple silk waistcoat, coat, and britches. He winked across at his grandson and smiled. To Robert, he seemed like a king indeed.

The coachman had gotten down from his seat as they arrived and handed down the family.

Then he lifted young Robert out, and as he set him on his feet, he smiled a toothy smile and said, "There you goes, young master."

Grandfather took the boy by the hand and led him into the cool church, and people began to file in behind them.

Grandfather had also built Nomony Hall, the house on a hill in Westmoreland County, where Robert, his parents, and his sister lived. The main house and its dependencies were surrounded by many acres of dark rich farmland, and there were many Negroes to work the soil and keep the house, but Robert loved most of all being at his grandfather's, riding out with him on horseback.

2

1732: Nomony Hall Plantation Westmoreland County, Virginia

It happened one day, less than a year later, when everything began to change. It was warm for February, and Robert was playing outside with his Negro servant, Sam.

"Robert," his mother shouted, "come right away."

The doctor who had come earlier was mounting his horse to leave.

His mother did not wait for him to come but hurried out to meet him in the yard, grabbing his arm and pulling him along with her.

Sam stood there, wondering what to do.

"It's your father," Mama said.

They went quickly upstairs to the big bedroom where Papa slept. Robert tripped over the stairs as he went, following in his mother's hasty footsteps.

Mama left him at the door to the room and hurried to the slave, Kate, who was giving Papa some medicine in a spoon. "Stand there, Robert," she said, pointing.

His older sister Betty was already standing in the doorway.

To Kate Mama said, "Should you be giving him so much of the opium?"

"It be exactly what the doctor say, Mistress. It do seem to ease his pain."

Papa saw Robert standing by the door and reached out a pale, shaking hand.

Robert never knew his father as a strong man. Though he was only twenty-eight, he seemed older to him than Grandfather. But he was good to Robert, often taking him into his lap as he sat in front of the fire, a blanket over his knees, reading to him.

Robert had never seen him this weak and sick, however, lying in bed, his head propped up with pillows. He wore no wig, and his face was as white as his linen nightgown.

He grunted from the effort to raise his head and lean forward.

"Son, come to your papa."

His blue eyes were dull and listless, his voice rasping and hesitant. His breath smelled of the opium.

"You're a fine young man." He paused to catch his breath as he took Robert's hand. "I'm proud of you. Remember that." Another pause. "You will grow up to be a great planter and a great man in the colony."

Robert was shocked by how cold his father's hand felt. *Why is Papa talking this way?* He said, "Yes, sir."

"Listen to your grandfather. I love you, Son."

Tears filled his eyes, though he didn't know exactly why. "I love you too, Papa."

"Don't cry, Robert. Be strong, and you will be well. Always remember you are a Carter."

That was the last time he saw Papa alive.

The funeral was at Nomini Church, a small white building, located on a bluff above Nomini Creek. That day it was being assaulted by rough, cold winds, and outside the windows, biting snowflakes flew in the dark sky.

Inside, the church smelled of melted candle wax and the musty odor of people in wool clothing.

Robert squirmed on the hard bench in their accustomed pew, and Mama gave him a piece of taffy. His sister, Betty, sat quietly on Mama's other side.

"You must sit still, Robert. It shows respect for your father."

"I love my papa," he whispered. "But it is such a long time to sit still."

"Hush, child. It won't be much longer."

The grown-up Negro house servants sat in the last pews at the back of the small building, behind everyone else, but Sam didn't have to come to church at all. Lucky Sam.

The service finally at an end, the procession of coaches and carriages made a slow process following the hearse along the rough roads, through the landscape of naked trees, and up the poplar-lined lane that came from the road to Nomony Hall.

Robert had to struggle to match his mother's pace walking to the graveyard on top of the same hill as the great house. He watched the pallbearers pull the heavy casket off the hearse wagon and carry it to a hole already dug beneath a tree. As the family approached the grave, Robert could smell the freshly dug earth. The Reverend Walter Jones, rector of the parish, spoke again at the graveside as the mourners stood all around, the white people close and the Negroes in an outer ring. The wind was still blowing snow, and he shivered. His legs ached as he held onto his mother's hand. Betty was as exhausted as he. Finally, they watched as the coffin was lowered into the hole, and slaves covered it with dirt, each shovelful falling with a dull *thump*. Robert struggled to understand what life would be like now.

———

Six Months Later
Nomony Hall

"Don't forget to pack Robert's new suit of clothes," Mama reminded the slave Kate. "Father Carter will want to show him off at Christ Church."

"Yes, Mistress. I remembers."

Kate, slender and quick, dropped a ruffled shirt over Robert's head and pulled up his britches. When she finished, she gently tousled his hair and proclaimed him finished. Sam had meanwhile dressed himself in his usual plain clothes.

Kate proceeded to pack clothes for them in a small trunk.

They had not been to Grandfather's since Papa's funeral. A brief chill came over Robert as he thought about Papa, lying weak and old in that bed, lying now in the ground. But it would be good to go to Grandfather's. Grandmother would have treats for them at the big house, and he would get to ride out with Grandfather again. Good to get away from the gloomy atmosphere at Nomony Hall.

Since Papa's death, Robert's mother had moved distractedly around the house and only perfunctorily dealt with the house servants, leaving most household decisions to Mrs. Sanders, the housekeeper. When she was not called upon, she sat and worked at her embroidery, saying little to anyone.

They piled into the carriage: Mama, Betty, Sam, Robert, and all their things. It was a hot day, but there was a breeze, and Robert enjoyed feeling it blow through his hair as he watched the wooded countryside go by on either side of the narrow road. It was a long way to Corotoman: out to the road to Northumberland Courthouse, across the ferry at Hampton Hall, and down into Lancaster Courthouse. Houses were sparse along the way in between.

Late in the day, they came to the lane that led to Corotoman.

When they arrived, Grandmother came out on the porch to greet them, a servant standing just behind her. It was unusual for Grandfather not to be standing there with her.

"Welcome, my dears. We'll have some supper directly."

She hugged the family and then indicated the door with a sweep of her hand. "Come in."

They entered the large main hall, which served as sort of a parlor as well as a dining room. There was Grandfather, sitting in a wingback chair. He did not get up but simply smiled broadly and held out his arms.

"Welcome, welcome. Children, come to your grandpa and give me a kiss."

The children did so. Sam went into the kitchen.

"Tell me, Robert," Grandfather said, holding on to his hand, "what have you been doing with yourself these sweltering days?"

At Grandfather's, they all ate meals at one big table, and soon they were enjoying a supper of cold meats, fresh fruit, and sweets for dessert.

"Is Father Carter all right?" Robert's mother asked Grandmother as the dishes were being cleared.

"Oh, yes, dear; it's just this cursed heat. He doesn't handle it as well as he once did."

They all sat together in the hall after dinner and talked until they went to bed. There was little formality at Grandfather's except on special occasions, and the children were not sent away.

The next morning, Grandfather was up and around early. He seemed like his old self.

"How about a ride out over the fields, Robert? I'd like to see how the crops come along."

Robert was ready to go in an instant.

He sat as usual in front of Grandfather on his large white horse. Because of the heat, he was allowed to wear only his shirt and britches, and he was content.

They jogged along in silence for a time.

Finally, Grandfather said, "Well, Robert, you are the head of your household now, eh?"

Robert turned to look up at him, puzzled. "Yes, sir. I suppose so." He didn't know what it meant to be the head of a household.

"Do not suppose, Robert." Grandfather laid the reins on the horse's neck and halted. "You are a son of a great family. Since your father has passed, you will have to prepare yourself for what lies ahead. When you come of age, you will be master of Nomony Hall and many other properties. As a leading landowner, you will be expected to serve on the vestry of Cople Parish. You will likely be chosen as a justice for Westmoreland County and a burgess, or perhaps as I am, a member of the King's Council. You will lead your community by Christian example. You must step up and take your place. Be strong and certain in your actions. This is your destiny."

All this talk confused and frightened Robert. He was just less than five years old, and a lot of what Grandfather said was completely bewildering to him. He did understand, however, that Grandfather was telling him about responsibilities he must take seriously. He believed his grandfather to be the wisest and best person on earth, and he was determined to be just like him.

"How shall I do all those things, Grandfather?"

"You must have a good education, Robert. I will see to it that you have that education as I saw to that of your father and uncles. I'll be here to guide you."

The thought of Grandfather's being there reassured him.

The next morning, Robert's mother awakened him. Her eyes were red from weeping.

"Your grandfather died in the night," she said. "I do not know what we shall do."

The shock of it silenced Robert. He could not imagine life without his grandfather.

He was still numb, trying to find a way to fill the hole left by Father's death six months before.

3

1734: Nomony Hall
Robert Carter, Age Six

Chilly October rain pelted against the window of the bedroom where I was snuggled down in warm covers. I did not want to get up, but Mrs. Sanders, the housekeeper, insisted.

"You children must put on your best. You are going to see your mother."

That made all the difference. I threw back the covers and set my feet on the floor. I longed to see my mother. I could remember her saying goodbye and driving away in a coach with all her clothes packed in boxes on the top. I stood at the top of the poplar lane that day, months ago, watching the coach disappear, my stomach aching with loneliness, wondering whether Mama would ever come home.

"Will Mama come home now?" I asked.

"Oh, no, child, she can't do that. She must live with her new husband, but now you will live there too."

I didn't really understand. *Wasn't I the master of Nomony Hall as Grandfather said? How could I live somewhere else? I did know that wives lived with their husbands. But what about me?*

A terrible thought assailed me. "Is Sam going?"

I looked at him across the room, in his usual happy mood, already up and dressed, already assuming he would go wherever I did.

Mrs. Sanders paused. "Your mother's letter said nothing about Sam."

My heart sank.

Sam's smile faded.

Then she stood taller, sweeping imaginary wrinkles from her apron. "Poor child," she said. "I will not see you cut off from everything you know. I will send him. Let them send him back if they must."

Shaking her head, she said to Kate. "I do not understand why she doesn't come to get them herself, poor orphans."

We were loaded up by Mrs. Sanders; Kate; and the manservant, Henry, into a coach, leaving just as Mama had done. As we traveled down the poplar lane, I looked back. I could see the three of them, standing in the rain at the top of the drive—Kate and Henry and Mrs. Sanders—the women's white caps dripping with the wet. I waved until I could no longer see them. I wondered what awaited me.

As we clopped along the road toward Richmond Courthouse, I peered out the rain-soaked windows of the coach, saying nothing. We were going, Mrs. Sanders said, to a place called Warner Hall, the home of the Lewis family in Gloucester County, because my mother had married a man named John Lewis. Warner Hall was farther than Grandfather's house, she told me, and it would take us all day to get there.

The narrow road was muddy, the fallen leaves being crushed into the ground as we went. Constant damp chilled me in spite of the warm blankets wrapped around me. I was grateful for Sam beside me on the seat. It seemed this trip was going to last forever.

We came to a dock on the Rappahannock River outside Richmond Courthouse, where we were told we would have to wait for the ferry across to Hobbs Hole. I shivered at the sight of the whitecaps blown up by the wind over the surface of the water. At last, we were able to cross the river, and, afterward, leaving the village of Hobbs Hole, we continued through heavy woods on the other side.

It was the edge of dark as we approached the lane to Warner Hall. I could just make out a white pale fence on either side of the gate, and at the end of a lane lined with tall boxwoods, the house. It was a story-and-a-half brick house, washed white with limestone, like Nomony Hall. It was a fine enough house, I supposed, but dread came over me. I did not want to live there. I wanted to go home, and I wanted my mother to come with me, but there was a cold feeling in the pit of my stomach that told me it no longer mattered what I wanted.

A somber servant opened the door and bid us enter. Inside, a tall, dark man stood before us, his old-fashioned red velvet waistcoat covering a slight paunch at his middle. He came forward as we entered a large hall. He looked older than Mama, unsmiling, intimidating. Mama was standing beside and slightly behind him, her hands clasped before her.

I wanted to run to her and hug her, but as I started to move toward her, a look on Lewis's face held me back. I felt stunned and confused. *Was this man going to keep me away from my mother?*

"So, pretty Miss Betty, we meet at last," Lewis said, stepping forward and smiling down at her. She curtseyed prettily, and he bent to kiss the hand she shyly offered.

"And Robert ..." Lewis turned to me, the smile on his face fading. He made a bow, and I tried to respond appropriately, making a bow of my own. I could not remember such formality among family at home or at Corotoman, but this was a different place. Lewis ignored Sam altogether.

Finally, Mama stepped forward hesitantly and kissed Betty and me on our cheeks and then went quickly back to her place beside her husband.

The entry hall in which we were standing was large and contained only a settee and a small table. On either side, a doorway led into other rooms; on the left I could see a dish cabinet, and beyond it, a long dining table. On the other side was a neat room with comfortable chairs and little tables with bric-a-brac on them, *not a place for running or playing.*

Finally, Lewis's eye settled on Sam, standing there, patiently waiting for someone to direct him.

"What is this?" Lewis asked.

Sam's expression quickly became inscrutable.

"That is Sam," my mother told him. "He is Robert's personal servant, given to him at birth. They have always been together."

Lewis looked angrily at Sam. "I did not anticipate another Negro in my household to support. No one cared to ask me if I would have him here."

I drew in a breath. I did not want to be in this strange place without Sam. I did not want to be without Sam at all.

After a late supper, set just for Betty and me, we went to bed, and I finally had a moment alone with my mother. She came to tuck me in. How beautiful and soft she seemed in her pale blue bodice and gown. The stiffness of our greeting in the hall was gone. She was a link with my old life, always quiet, always perfectly groomed. She smelled of lavender. Mother was a lady, a child of the distinguished Churchill family.

"I do not feel good here, Mama."

"You will come to be happy here," she said. She was sitting on the side of the bed, stroking my hair from my eyes with her delicate hand. "Your stepfather is a very important man, just as important as the Carters. You must remember that. He owns much land, and a gristmill and several ships."

It mattered not at all to me how many ships Lewis had, but I said, "Yes, Mama."

"Now, Robert, you know that your uncles have made sure that you will get your father's share of Grandfather Carter's inheritance when you come of age, as well as your full inheritance from your father. Your uncles will manage it for you until then. In the meantime, you will live here at Warner Hall, and my husband will take care of you."

"I don't think he likes me, Mama."

"Don't be silly, child. He doesn't even know you."

"He likes Betty better."

"Nonsense. He had a daughter about the same age as Betty who died. I'm sure she reminds him of that child. But she will inherit no fortune and is completely dependent upon Mr. Lewis's good graces. You are more fortunate. Now, you go to sleep, and tomorrow everything will seem better."

"Will Mr. Lewis let Sam stay with me?" I asked.

"I don't know, dear. You'll find out tomorrow."

There was a tap at the bedroom door. Mama turned her head.

"Priscilla," came Lewis's voice, "it is time to come downstairs."

Mama kissed my forehead and went out.

At breakfast the next day, Lewis told me he was going to let Sam stay. "As long as he behaves properly. If he does anything wrong, it will be you I hold responsible."

"Yes, sir. Thank you, sir." So great was my gratitude, I almost broke into tears.

At dinner that afternoon, Betty and I ate at the table in the small room behind the main dining room along with Lewis's sons. It was the first time I had seen them. Lewis's oldest son, Warner, being fifteen, was allowed to eat at the adult table. Around our table were Fielding, who was nine, Charles, who was five, my sister Betty, eight, and blond-haired John, just my age, six.

A brown-skinned waiter brought in platters of food and spooned it onto our plates. He was dressed in the usual brown knee britches, wool stockings, and open-necked shirt, a boy not much older than I. He was directed by a full-bodied female kitchen servant in a brown and white striped bodice and brown skirt. She wore a white apron and a neat white cap. She told Betty and me that her name was Hannah, and part of her job was to mind us children at the dinner table. Her step was certain and her voice firm, but she did smile at me, and I smiled back.

Young John Lewis said, "I hope we shall go back to Rosewell soon. Matthew Page is so much fun to visit. There will be enough of us to play stickball there."

"Yes," said Fielding, "and I am the best player."

"You are not," said John. "You're just the biggest."

"I would like to go to Rosewell," I interjected. "That's where Judith Page, my aunt, lives, and I have not seen her in a long time."

"Oh, really?" John asked. "I have never heard her speak of you or your family. She is a Page."

Hannah shook her head.

The Lewis boys continued to carry on their conversation, ignoring Betty and me completely.

After dinner, all the boys but Warner were sent out to play in the high grass of the yard. We played tag awhile, but suddenly young John Lewis stopped running and turned to look at me.

"My father says you are called Robert Carter III."

Fielding and Charles moved to stand close behind him.

"Yes, I am," I said, drawing myself up to my full height, which made me slightly taller than John.

"You Carters think you are better than anyone else, don't you?"

"That's not so."

"Then why did they call your grandfather King?"

"I don't know. Because he was a great man, I suppose."

John laughed at that.

He continued. "And your father. He's dead isn't he?"

"Yes," I said, beginning to feel threatened.

"Well, I heard all about him, too. He was an opium addict, and that's why he's dead. They found him drugged, down in the slave quarters, didn't they? He was not much of a man."

"Liar!" I had heard hints about my father's being addicted to opium, but I was sure no one ever found him lying down in the quarters. My face grew suddenly hot, and I leaped forward, thrusting my hands against John's chest, knocking him to the ground. I was just raising a fist to strike him when the other two brothers jumped into the fray.

Fielding grabbed my arm and twisted it behind me. I winced in pain, but I would not cry out. Then I felt a sharp kick into my side—Charles with his buckled shoes.

Sam moved forward to intervene, his usually happy face contorted with anger.

"No, Sam. It's all right," I managed to say. I didn't know what sort of punishment Sam might suffer if he struck one of these white boys. Sam looked as if he was inclined to intervene anyway but finally stood back, hands in fists at his sides.

With an effort, I shook myself loose from Fielding's grip, twisting around so that I stood with my back to them.

"You are just like your father," John said after me as I moved away. "A weakling, a wastrel, and a coward. You are a disgrace."

"Let's go, Sam," I said, grabbing his arm and pulling him with me. For the rest of the day, we stayed to ourselves.

At suppertime, we all returned to the great house. Lewis took one look at all of us—tousled hair, dirty clothes—and asked what had happened.

"Robert started a fight," said John.

"Robert, I am shocked. Your behavior is disgraceful. Here only one day, and already causing trouble with your stepbrothers. You must learn to get along with them. Have you anything to say for yourself?"

I was not going to explain myself to this man. I was sure he wouldn't believe me if I did. "No, sir," I said.

"I will not punish you this time, Robert, but this must never happen again. Do you hear me?"

4

1734: Warner Hall

"The problem with the boy is that he is proud and arrogant," I could hear Lewis telling my mother one evening when I had been at Warner Hall a month or so.

They were sitting in the large room that overlooked the Severn River. Supper was over, and they sat in wingback chairs on either side of the fireplace, sipping sherry.

I had been waiting to come into that part of the room from the sitting room to the right of the entryway. The two rooms were divided by a wall, with an archway in the middle. Lewis's library was in the room overlooking the river, and I was headed there to find a book to look at, wanting to practice the reading skills Mama had been trying to teach me.

I glimpsed them from the side, but they did not see me. Before speaking, Lewis had taken a small snuff box from his waistcoat pocket, opened it, drawn out a pinch, and closed the box. He carefully placed a dab on the back of his hand, and, after sniffing deeply, shook his hand slightly, showing the ruffle at the end of his shirt sleeve.

I stopped dead still when I heard his voice and quickly slipped behind the dividing wall.

Lewis continued. "He's just like his grandfather. You know they called him 'King' Carter for a reason, and it wasn't out of great esteem. He may have been the richest man in the colony, but the Carters are no better than the Lewises or the Warners. Now this child is in my household, with his own fortune, greater than mine, and two uncles who want to tell me what I must do with him, and a slave of his own." He made a slight snorting noise, wrinkling his nose as the snuff took effect. "Who has ever heard of giving a newborn a slave of his own? He does not give me proper respect. Oh, he says 'Yes, sir' and 'No, sir,' but he hangs about with his Negro, doing whatever he likes. He does not treat me as I expect a son to treat me."

"John," Mama said, her voice soft and pleading, "he is just a boy."

I had noticed how pretty she looked in her cream-colored bodice and skirt with flowers embroidered on it, her dark curls protruding from under her cap, but if Lewis noticed her beauty, it wasn't apparent.

"He respects you," she told him, "but you do not treat him as you do your sons. He doesn't know what he is expected to do. And he misses his grandfather. You know they were very close. Perhaps if you let him attend classes with the tutor ..."

"I would treat him as I treat my sons if I could, but my sons did not inherit an independent fortune. They did not receive a personal Negro at birth. They will have to make their way in society without the advantages that your Robert has."

"You are a great man in Gloucester County, and in this country, John. You will have a fine fortune to pass on to your sons, and they will be upstanding men themselves one day. I only wish you would be as kind to Robert as you are to Betty."

"I will be kind to him in proportion to his respect for me. I expect you to instill that respect in him, Priscilla. There is nothing more to say."

I could feel tears welling in my eyes as I heard Lewis's words but stifled them immediately. What Lewis said was proof that I was right about him. He didn't like me. I could not recall Lewis ever saying a kind word to me. But I would not cry. I was a Carter, and I would behave like a Carter. My chin tipped up a little. I turned away, back toward the entry hall, my heart filled with anger and determination.

Some part of what my mother said must have penetrated Lewis's thoughts, though, for within a week, I was ushered into the large schoolroom located in a dependency building to the right of the main house, the same dependency that housed Lewis's office.

I entered the room and looked around. It was furnished with a long wooden table and chairs. On the table before each chair were a slate writing board and chalk, an inkwell and a quill. In the front of the room was a desk and a podium, and on the wall behind the desk, a larger writing slate hung. Also on the wall hung a stout pointer.

Along one side wall were shelves of books and supplies; on the other side, a fire burned in the fireplace. *At last,* I thought. *I'm going to school.*

I sat down where I was directed by a tall shank-boned man with a long nose. He was not handsome. He had a sort of lumpy face, but his eyes were kind.

"I am Mr. Johnson," he said, "and I understand that you are Robert Carter."

"Yes, sir."

"How old are you, Master Carter?"

"I will be seven in February."

I remember he smiled at that. "I see. Can you read?"

"Very little, sir, ... but I like books."

"Good. How about your numbers?"

"I can count to a hundred."

"What have they been teaching you, then?"

"I have not been to school. My mother helps me sometimes."

"Well, we will see what we can do, shall we?"

As soon as the tutor's back was turned, Fielding bent forward to look down the table at me. He whispered, "You're not so smart, are you, Carter boy?"

"I am smart," I retorted, a little too loudly.

The tutor looked around at me. "What did you say, Master Carter?"

"I am smart."

The tutor looked puzzled. "We do not talk in class unless we are called upon."

"Yes, sir."

As soon as his back was turned again, John, who was seated next to me, picked up his writing quill and tickled my neck with it.

"Don't," I whispered, trying not to be heard.

He did it again.

I glanced at the tutor to be sure we had not gotten his attention and said more forcefully, "Stop it."

As soon as I turned away from him, John tickled my neck again.

This time, I grabbed his hand and wrenched the quill away, surprised at how easily I got it. I was quicker and stronger than he was. That thought gave me some small satisfaction.

The tutor, hearing something, turned around. To my dismay, what he saw was not John tickling my neck, but my taking away the quill.

It earned me a smack on the hand with the pointer.

Several incidents of the Lewis boys taunting me in the classroom had occurred when one day weeks later, I saw the tutor approach John Lewis in the hall between the schoolroom and the office.

"May I have a moment to speak to you?" he asked.

Oh, no! Given the way Lewis felt about me, I was bound to be in some sort of trouble.

"Yes, what is it?" Lewis frowned, directing a side glance over at me.

John smirked.

The tutor cleared his throat. "I should like you to understand the situation in the classroom, Mr. Lewis. May we speak in a more private place?"

Lewis shrugged and led the way into his office. I waited anxiously outside in the hall.

When the tutor came back out of Lewis's office, he saw me still standing there. His face bore a sad expression.

"I am most sorry, Master Carter," he said, looking at me. "This outcome is not what I intended. I thought I could help the matter, but it seems I've done the opposite."

In a short time, Lewis came out. His arms were crossed, and when he saw me, he glared down at me.

"What are you doing standing there, boy?" I turned to go, but he stopped me. "Well, since you are there, I suppose you need to know that I am removing you from the tutor's instruction. Your presence is disrupting the lessons."

"Then how shall I learn to read and write and cipher, sir?"

"I do not know. We shall ask your uncles about it. They are critical of the instruction I provide in any case."

"But, sir," I groped for something persuasive to say, to change his mind, "Grandfather said I must have a proper education."

I received no answer from my stepfather. *I cannot stay here forever and never go to school. What will become of me?*

To make matters worse, John Lewis then began telling everyone he spoke to that my unruliness had made a sustained course of learning for me impossible. Desolation and loneliness overtook me. Never knowing who had heard what Lewis said about me made me uncomfortable with each new visitor at the Lewis household.

Christmas 1734

Icy snowflakes pelted the windows overlooking the Severn while the wind brushed the branches of the cedar trees against them. I walked from the windows back toward the entry hall when I heard a knock at the door. The door was opened by Lewis's servant, and the next thing I saw was my Uncle Landon Carter, pushing into the room ahead of the servant. He wished Lewis a perfunctory, "Merry Christmas," bowed to my mother, and stated immediately that it was time I learned to ride.

"He'll be seven come February," he said. My uncle was only twenty-four, but everything about him bespoke strength and assurance. He reminded me of Grandfather.

Lewis had a sour expression on his face, but before he could speak, Landon reached out his hand to me and said, "Come with me, Robert. I have something to show you." He turned to my mother and said, "He'll need his coat, Priscilla."

Then, to Lewis, he said with a slight bow, "You'll excuse us." It wasn't a question.

As soon as my coat was on, he took my hand and led me to the door. We went out into the blowing snow and around to the stables. There, before us stood a great chestnut stallion. Even with his shaggy winter coat, he was a beautiful thing to behold.

"He has Arabian blood," Landon said. "You can see it in the shape of his head."

I stood transfixed.

"He is yours, Robert, but you must not ride him until you have been taught by an adult."

"May I touch him?"

I could just reach his neck, and Landon stood by as I gingerly approached him. I had never ridden by myself, but I had been around horses all my life, and I had ridden with Grandfather. I was not intimidated. I reached my hand out slowly, so as not to spook him. He snuffled at the hand and studied me with large, liquid eyes, but he did not move away. I knew we would be friends.

When I was called back to the house for dinner, Landon went back into the house only to deposit me. And Lewis did not ask him to stay. I was taught that it was a breach of manners not to invite a guest to dinner. Uncle Landon, however, seemed perfectly content with the arrangement.

"I will see you soon again, Robert." He bowed once more to Lewis, then to my mother, went out, mounted his own horse, and rode away.

I heard Lewis say to my mother, "The self-importance of young Landon Carter is too much to bear." Then he told me that, since I had received such an extravagant gift, I would not be allowed to take part in the family pageant that evening.

I had done nothing wrong. I had been practicing for my part in the pageant. A protest rose in my throat, but then I thought better of it. He would not pay any attention to what I said in any case.

My Aunt Judith and her family came to dinner that day from Rosewell. Judith was a daughter of Grandfather's first wife, an older half sister to my father. She was a big woman, though not fat, dressed in dark colors, and she held herself with a dignity softened only by her smile. I was looking forward to spending some time in her company (and proving to John that she was my aunt indeed.)

Upon seeing me standing in the hall, Aunt Judith lifted my chin in her hand and smiled down at me. "You know, Robert, you have the look of the Carters—that shiny dark hair and brown eyes. You are a handsome lad. You'll surely grow up to be big and strong like my father."

She kissed me on the forehead.

I saw a brief frown darken Lewis's face.

Aunt Judith was a widow, her husband, Mann Page, having died before Betty and I came to Warner Hall, but she brought my cousins. Marie was twenty; Mann II, nineteen; John, eighteen; and Matthew, nine.

I ate dinner at the children's table that afternoon, feeling too uneasy about what was to follow to enjoy my meal.

After dinner, a fire crackled in the fireplace in the room overlooking the Severn. Holly leaves decorated the mantle, and the whole room smelled of wood smoke and greenery. The odor of turkey, venison, oysters, and all the other meats of our meal lingered in the air. As a special treat, all the children were allowed to have a glass of sherry, and each of us was given an orange and some candies that came from London.

The whole company gathered around the fireplace, Lewis and Mama sitting up front, and the so-called pageant, which was a Christmas tradition in the household, began.

Warner read a poem of his own composition.

"You are very clever," Mama said. Everyone applauded. I burned with envy.

Fielding recited John Dryden's "Alexander's Feast," all seven verses, by heart. Everyone clapped again and acknowledged it as a great accomplishment.

John and Charles took turns reciting the Christmas story as it was told in the Gospels of Luke and Matthew in the Bible. John gave me a self-satisfied look as he finished.

Betty played the small stringed spinet. Lewis smiled at her indulgently and told her that she was becoming a fine little musician. Everyone clapped and laughed. I was proud of my sister, too, but dreaded what was to come. I wanted to leave, but there was no escape.

I sat and watched it all with my head held high. The Pages looked at me expectantly. I noticed my mother looking at me with worried eyes, but she said nothing. I was glad. I did not want any pity shown me in front of my relatives. Lewis did not explain why I did not come forward to perform.

When it was apparent I would not come forward, Aunt Judith looked puzzled.

I could see her lean over toward the chair of her son, Mann II, and hear her whisper to her him. "'Tis strange, is it not? I cannot imagine what would account for John's treating Robert the way he does. Is there something amiss?"

"Warner tells me that Robert does not deport himself properly." He looked over at me, and I pretended not to be listening. "He had to be put out of the schoolroom. He consorts with the slaves. He is incorrigible."

"Why he never seemed so to me. What a shame."

I decided that in my own time, in my own way, I would make them all see that Lewis was wrong.

Winter 1735

The first time Hannah gave me refuge from John Lewis and his sons, it was one of those days when the dampness in the air makes it seem even colder than it is, though it was not cold enough to snow. Sam and I had gone to the stable together to see my horse, which I had named Corotoman in honor of Grandfather's plantation. It had become our daily habit.

After visiting Corotoman, I sat down on a stump outside the kitchen house. The weather drove Sam into the big house, but I could not bring myself to go there. I pulled my great-coat close around me, bowed my head, and thought about the unhappy situation in which I found myself, living in my stepfather's house.

I picked up a stick and started drawing aimless circles in the sand at my feet. Then I heard Hannah's voice.

When I looked up, she was standing outside the kitchen, wiping her hands on her apron. "Young Master, what is you doing out here?"

"There is nothing to do in the great house, so I decided to sit here."

She glanced briefly at the overcast sky. "Come in the kitchen 'fore the rain come. I just make ginger cookies."

She held out her hand to me. Still feeling very solemn, I accepted the offer. Her hand was big and comfortable, and I followed her inside.

The warm, fragrant kitchen filled half the first floor of the square dependency, the other half being a washhouse.

Hannah invited me to sit on a high stool next to a rough wooden table that dominated the center of the room. On it were various items in preparation for the day's dinner:

vegetables, poultry and meat, herbs and spices, a cone of sugar, knives and spoons.

I looked around. The walls and floor were brick, and a huge fireplace was built into one end of the room, almost taking up the whole wall. It was much larger than the fireplaces in the house. Attached to the wall inside the fireplace above the fire were swinging iron arms, and upon one of them hung an iron pot with something cooking inside. Built into the walls on either side of the fireplace were ovens from which emanated the most heavenly smells. A large iron pot, topped with hot coals, sat on the brick floor before the fireplace. What held my attention, though, was a plain crockery plate filled with ginger cookies.

"Go ahead on, Young Master," Hannah said nodding toward the cookies.

I reached for a cookie and was soon enjoying watching Hannah and the other kitchen slaves bustling about the wooden table, making dinner preparations. My sadness and anger evaporated amid the delicious smells and the sweet, sharp tang of the ginger cookies.

A kitchen helper said, "Hannah, ain't you afraid what Master do if he find that child in here?"

Hannah gave a little snort. "Master never told me that child couldn't be in here."

<hr/>

Spring 1735

Early on a sunny morning, Sam and I followed a long path that led from the riverfront of the great house toward the Severn River. Since I was no longer allowed in the schoolroom, I felt free to ramble with Sam over the plantation. I noticed all the new spring growth as we walked about: flowers, buds on the trees, a new fresh smell in the air. As we came closer to the river, we could hear the rushing of water. What we heard was the mill race of Lewis's gristmill. It flowed from the Severn through a sluice gate under a creaking waterwheel, which the weight of the water turned. I had known for some time that the mill was there, but it took my annual spring fever to make me dare to go inside.

We entered what seemed to be the main floor of the mill. Inside, it was cool and dark. It took a moment for my eyes to become accustomed to the darkness. I watched and saw that the waterwheel outside was connected to a smaller wheel on the inside. That smaller wheel drove a gear wheel on a metal pole that stretched all the way from the top to the bottom of the building.

The white miller watched Sam and me warily but did not speak to us.

He finally went outside to smoke his pipe, and then one of his Negro helpers, who had been looking at me critically, asked, "You Master's stepson, ain't you?"

"Yes, I am Robert Carter, and this is Sam." I motioned in his direction. What's your name?"

"They calls me Enoch."

I was marveling at the rough stone wheels, each three or four feet in diameter and nearly a foot thick.

"Is it those big wheels that grind the grain?"

"The wheels be heavy, so they crushes the grain between them."

Enoch seemed both surprised and pleased at my interest. He stroked his chin with his hand thoughtfully and smiled at us.

"The top wheel called the runner. It be turned by the shaft you sees. The wheel on the floor called the bed. Sacks of grain be taken upstairs on the sack floor by the hoist yonder." He pointed to the hoist. "Upstairs the grain be poured into the slipper." Here he indicated a wooden tub with slanting side walls, the diameter being larger at the top than the bottom. "The grain come down the slipper and go through a hole in the runner. It fall between the two wheels and be crushed as they turn. You controls the size of the meal by how close the wheels be placed. The meal slip out the sides between the stones and get collected and be fed down a chute to the meal floor. He pointed to a floor below.

"Is that where the flour comes from that Hannah uses in the kitchen?"

"Yes, indeed. Sometime we makes flour and sometime we makes cornmeal, just depend on what grain we puts in the slipper."

After the miller left for the day, we gave no thought to being missed at the great house. Enoch began to beguile us with vivid tales of striped horses called zebras and green lizards as big as a man, with sharp teeth in their long snouts—crocodiles. He said his daddy told him about these wonders from Africa, where his daddy came from.

It was very late when we finally got back to the great house. We had missed dinner altogether, and John Lewis was seething, waiting for us.

"Robert, what do you think you have been doing all day? Account for your absence."

"We went to see the mill work, sir."

Lewis glowered down at me. "You do not have permission to go to the mill—or anywhere else without asking me first. I never know where you are or what you are doing."

I felt my face grow hot. I wanted to strike him. Lewis gave me no hint as to what he wanted me to do with my time now that he had put me out of the classroom, and he did not want me to ask him. He was unhappy with anything I did. And I knew I needed to be learning somehow to be the man my grandfather expected me to be. If it were not for my mother attempting to teach me when she could, I would know nothing, and she was always busy with the running of the household.

In as respectful a voice as I could muster, I stated, "I need to know how a plantation works, sir."

Lewis frowned. "Nonsense; you are nothing but a child—a spoiled child."

Then he brought out the switch he had been holding behind his back. He bade me lower my britches and bend over, right there in front of the house Negroes.

"This will teach you to keep your place."

The beating stung my backside and legs, but that was nothing to the humiliation I felt. But I would not give Lewis the satisfaction of seeing me shed the tears I could feel coming to my eyes.

At least there was no punishment for Sam. As he had said in the beginning, Lewis considered anything Sam did wrong to be my responsibility.

Sam and I stayed away from the mill for a month or more, until the siren call of Enoch's stories became too compelling to ignore.

Summer 1735

Prince was Lewis's hostler and postilion, a broad-shouldered man with heavily knotted muscles in his arms, black as midnight. He was the son of parents both born in Africa.

"Master say don't let you get hurt. That be all he say 'bout you and that horse."

Sam and I came every day to see Corotoman. The stable was warm and close with the smell of horseflesh, manure, and straw. On this day, there was no hesitation on either Sam's part or mine as Prince brought Corotoman in from the pasture. We knew each other quite well now. Corotoman lowered his head and pawed the ground until I gave him the apple I'd brought.

"Ain't a horse for nay child," Prince muttered, shaking his head.

The truth was the horse had been well-ridden and was manageable. In any case, we had taken to each other immediately.

"He do like you, though," Prince continued. "Ain't no use having a horse if you ain't gone ride him."

"You could teach me to ride, couldn't you, Prince?"

He started to say something but stopped. He paused a moment, thinking. Then suddenly he walked into the stable and took down a saddle and bridle. He put them on Corotoman, showing me how it was done. "Come on, then," he said, and lifted me to the horse's back while Sam watched. "It time you ride him."

I squirmed around in the saddle to get comfortable. Prince shortened the stirrup straps, and I stood up to try them out. At first Prince led the horse while I got the feel of him. Within an hour, I was walking him on my own. It was a powerful sensation to be in the saddle, like riding with Grandfather. I felt free for the first time in a long time.

"You a natural horseman," Prince commented, a small smile betraying his usually impassive demeanor.

Over my next few visits to Corotoman, Prince continued to watch and help me become secure in my control of the horse. I learned how to use my legs and the reins to let the horse know what I expected. Corotoman responded well, seeming glad to actually go somewhere for a change. Soon I began to teach Sam while Prince watched.

If Prince thought this was unusual or inappropriate, he did not say so. I didn't care whether it was appropriate or not.

Then Sam and I began to ride double on Corotoman, leaving without telling anyone where we were going. Most days, we simply rode through the woods and explored what lay down the roads, but on a particular Saturday, we let Corotoman have his head, and we rode with abandon. As the wind blew through my hair, I experienced a thrill of exhilaration.

I knew Lewis would not approve, and I assumed I would eventually be caught and punished, but I didn't care. He didn't pay much attention to me, anyway, unless I annoyed or embarrassed him.

Sam and I could always return to the kitchen, awash in delicious smells and warm with the person of big-breasted, big-hearted Hannah. We learned we could say anything to Hannah, who always offered treats to eat, and hugs. It was a temporary escape from my unhappy situation.

"You mama scared to stand up for you," Hannah told me one afternoon. "You stepdaddy mean to you. You uncles come and go. Ain't nay way to raise a child."

"You love me though, don't you?"

She smiled, tears in her eyes. "Yes, child, for all the good it do you."

"And so does Sam," I added.

5

August 1737: Warner Hall

I was greeted by the sight of my Uncle Charles Carter riding up the lane at a canter. Charles was more slender, genteel, and more soft-spoken than Landon, but he still had that distinct air of self-confidence about him.

Uncle Charles was coming from Aunt Judith's, and I wondered if he had heard from her or anyone else about my troubles with Lewis. *Would my uncles be disappointed in me?*

I was in the house because the humidity that day was so heavy that sweat ran down my cheeks just sitting still. I was dressed in a ruffled white shirt and unbuttoned waistcoat, even Lewis having acknowledged it was too hot for absolute formality. I did not want to exercise Corotoman in the hot sun, nor go anywhere on the plantation. At least the house benefited from the shade of trees.

My first impulse was to run downstairs to greet my uncle as he came in the door, but I knew I was supposed to wait until he and Lewis had greeted one another.

A servant answered the door, and Charles asked Lewis to go with him to Lewis's office. As he moved again toward the door, I could see Charles was frowning, and he walked purposefully. Lewis did not look any happier.

The tension was unbearable as I waited for them to reenter the house.

Only Charles returned. Looking down from the top of the stairs, I saw him approach my mother. He spoke to her too softly for me to hear, but after she heard what he had to say, she touched her handkerchief to her eyes. Then she stood on her toes to kiss his cheek.

My uncle turned from her and walked over to me, now at the bottom of the steps, motioning me to take a seat beside him on the settee in the entry hall. He sat down himself, sighed, and took a handkerchief from his waistcoat to wipe his forehead.

He looked down at me. "You need a proper education, Robert. You will have responsibilities when you reach your majority. Your other uncles and I want you to bring honor to the Carter name. Your grandfather specifically demanded that we see to it that you get a proper education."

I waited breathlessly for what would come next. I dreamed of having a tutor of my own. I would work very hard at my studies.

"Your stepfather refuses to take care of your education as he should, so we have decided to send you to the grammar school at William and Mary College."

"Where is that, Uncle?"

"In the capital, in Williamsburg. You would live there while you study."

I glanced up at him. "Live in Williamsburg?" It sounded far away, although I knew it did not take Lewis a whole day to ride there.

"Yes, Robert. It will do you a deal of good to be exposed to the people and the activities there."

"Will Mama go?"

"No, she must stay here and run John Lewis's household. Maybe she will be able to visit you there. All the boys there will be away from home, some of them a great deal farther than you."

"Will Sam go with me?"

"Yes. Many of the boys will have manservants with them."

Williamsburg sounded exciting. I wanted to go to school, but it was also intimidating. I remembered how it felt being behind in my studies when I was with the Lewis's tutor. But I was glad to be leaving Warner Hall. I would overcome any difficulty there.

"Come, Robert," Uncle Charles said. "Now show me your horse. Landon says he is quite impressive."

I led the way to the stable.

September

Once again, Sam's things and mine were packed into trunks, this time carried on a wagon behind us as we rode horseback over the hard, dry road toward Gloucester Point. Charles had been pleased to find out that I had learned to ride, and he allowed Sam to ride double with me on Corotoman.

The weather was mild, and the ride pleasant, but my mind was whirling. *What would it be like at the grammar school? How would the boys there treat me? How far behind would I be in my work?*

We had a short wait at Gloucester Point for the ferry that would take us to the village of York across the river of the same name. As I looked across the river, I thought that York reminded me of Hobbs Hole, a village sitting low along the river, but then, unlike Hobbs Hole, the town rose quickly uphill.

We had a small meal at an ordinary, Sam having to get his meal at the kitchen door and eat it outside.

We continued on toward Williamsburg, following the river for a time and then turning inland, arriving just before dark.

The college sat at one end of the town's main street, Duke of Gloucester, and there was just enough light to make it possible to see all the way to the other end where the capital building was located. That building was where both my grandfathers, King Carter and William Churchill, Mama's father, went to serve on the Governor's Council, and where Lewis went to serve in the House of Burgesses and to conduct business at the General Court. Uncle Charles was also a burgess, from King George County where he lived.

The street was sandy, but there were wooden walks on either side for people to walk on. There were small houses and shops, and an open marketplace, along the street, now all largely empty of traffic on foot or in carriages. I could see a church, grander than the one we went to in Gloucester, and a brick public building about halfway between the college and the capital. This was larger than any town I had seen before.

The college itself consisted of three buildings built around a grassy square. The grammar school was housed in the central building, an enormous brick building consisting of two-and-a-half stories with a cupola on the top. The half-story contained a row of dormer windows that overlooked the square.

We went up the front steps of the central building and passed under the arches of the porch. As we entered the door of the building, a fair-skinned man wearing a white wig came out to greet us. He was of medium height and weight, but what struck me about him were his long slender fingers.

I gaped at the entry hall, with its high ceiling and wooden paneling on the walls, but my attention was drawn back to the man who greeted us.

"Dr. Blair," said my Uncle Charles, "allow me to introduce my nephew, Robert Carter, the third of that name."

Dr. Blair smiled. "Welcome, Master Carter. I believe I had the pleasure of knowing both your father and your grandfather, did I not?"

I loved the sound of Dr. Blair's accent, the way he said, "Masterr Carrterr," with his Scots burr. "Yes, sir," I said.

Dr. Blair told us that classes were over for the day, and the boys were studying, as he directed Sam and me to the dormitory at the top of the building, a long room lined with beds, and at the foot of each bed a trunk similar to mine. Sam would sleep on a pallet beside my assigned bed.

Once we had put our things in the dormitory, Dr. Blair took Uncle Charles and me to a tavern for a late supper, and then Uncle Charles took his leave of us. I brought food back from the tavern for Sam. When he and I finally settled into our beds, the other boys were already in bed and asleep. The night was cool, a comfortable breeze blowing in through the windows. The events of the day had been overwhelming, and I dropped into an exhausted sleep.

The next day after breakfast, I was taken to the classroom where I would be studying. It was a large room with bare wooden floors and paneled walls, not unlike the schoolroom at Warner Hall except for its size. Here there were separate desks for the students, and in the front were a podium and a desk for the schoolmaster. Next to the classroom was a sort of office, which I supposed was for the teaching master.

As I sat down and looked around, I realized that most of the boys in the room were older than I. I lifted my chin and sat straight in my chair.

Each of us there for our first year was asked how much Latin and Greek we had. My heart was in my throat as I admitted I had none. The master made no comment, only making a notation on a paper before him on his desk. We began our studies with Latin.

Since I had very little practice reading English aloud, reading Latin was a challenge, but like everyone else, I was asked to read in my turn.

When I faltered, the master said, "Latin is pronounced just as it is spelled, Master Carter. Try again."

The day continued, tightly structured—breakfast in the great hall and morning prayer in the chapel. The day's teaching session lasted from then until dinner at 3:00. After dinner, we went into the great hall for supervised study, followed by supper, evening prayer, and bed.

I had paid close attention all day, and by the time we got to the dormitory, I was exhausted.

"Robert Carter is a fool," chimed one of the boys as I slipped into bed. "He never even went to school."

Too tired and discouraged to get into a fight, I curled up on my bed and tried to shut out the sound.

To my great surprise, an older boy, tall, with blond hair that fell lightly over his forehead, chastised him. "Leave him alone, Harry. It is hard enough to be new in school without being younger than most."

He came to stand beside my bed and made a bow, "William Rozell of Caroline County, at your service."

"Robert Carter," I said, bowing from my bed. *And where was I supposed to say I was from? Westmoreland? Gloucester? I left it at my name.*

"Carter? Are you any kin to the famous King Carter from Lancaster County?"

That got the attention of those in the room.

"He was my grandfather, and I am his namesake."

⟶

April 1738

One night, I waited until I thought everyone was asleep, and then I nudged Sam.

During the winter I had managed to catch up with the others, earning their grudging respect and greatly increasing my own self-confidence. Now, spring had come to Williamsburg, and a glorious spring it was. The wild redbud and dogwood appeared ubiquitous in the woods. In the town proper, the gardens were full of all kinds of flowers: yellow daffodils, tulips of many colors, flowering bushes and trees like catalpa and bright yellow forsythia. The air felt good on my skin, the cold that caused us to huddle before the fireplaces now a distant memory. Spring fever had caught me.

"What you doing?" Sam whispered.

"I thought we would see the town."

"You sure you should do this?"

"Are you scared to go?"

He shrugged, and we slipped noiselessly into our clothes. We left the dormitory with its many windows and had to feel our way down the stairs into the entry hall. There moonlight through the large paneled windows lit our way clearly.

There were few candles lit in the windows of the houses, and the shops along the street were dark, but the moon was full. We could see quite clearly as we walked up Duke of Gloucester Street, breathing in the sweet air.

We turned off Duke of Gloucester Street at the church and from there strolled along the palace green. The palace was all alight on this night with candles in every visible window. Wonderful measured tones of music came from inside. I was enthralled by the music.

"A ball must be going on," I told Sam.

We couldn't get close enough to the windows to see inside because there was a high brick wall around the building, and we were afraid to go through the wrought iron gates. Nevertheless, I imagined the dancers inside, going through elegant steps in time with the music.

"Someday, Sam, I will go to the palace, like Grandfather."

"I wishes we could go in now."

The last house along the green to the left of the palace was a long, two-story white house that had a long porch along the front.

"We could live there, Sam, when we come to Williamsburg. Uncle Charles told me that Grandfather built that house."

"That would be fine!"

We continued on our way back down the palace green and back to the college. As we approached the center building, I noticed a light burning in the entry hall. We went inside, and there was Dr. Blair himself. My exhilaration evaporated immediately.

"Master Carter, where have you been?"

"We went to see the palace," I said simply, not knowing what else to say. "We heard a ball going on there."

Dr. Blair's face was hard. "I am certain that you know that such behavior is unacceptable, Master Carter. The young men of this Grammar School do not wander about the city at night alone. I am very disappointed in you."

Disappointing Dr. Blair, for whom I had a great deal of respect, was an entirely different matter from disappointing John Lewis.

Dr. Blair went on. "What would your friend, William Rozell, think of you if he knew you had done this?"

The last hit me like a stout stick to my stomach. "I am truly sorry. I was wrong. I pray he won't have to know."

Dr. Blair raised a birch rod and gave me five stinging lashes on the back of my legs.

"The next time," he said, "the punishment will be much more severe."

He reached for Sam, still holding the rod in his hand.

"Dr. Blair," I said, "I made Sam go with me. I wish that he did not have to be punished."

"And will you take his punishment for him, then, Master Carter?"

"Yes, sir."

I received ten lashes this time. What hurt worse than the sting on my legs was the thought that I had disrespected Dr. Blair and dishonored my friend.

6

May 1739: William & Mary

The door of the office by the classroom was open, and unbeknownst to them, I could hear a conversation between my Uncle Charles and Dr. Blair.

I happened to be in the classroom, poring over my Latin to prepare for the next day. Since my second year's session at the grammar school was nearly over, I expected to have to go to Warner Hall for the summer, glad that I would only have to endure it until I could come back to the college in the fall.

"The boy has struggled, Mr. Carter," Dr. Blair was saying to my uncle. "He came to Williamsburg without a sound background in reading and writing, and he hardly knew at all about ciphering. He has a quick mind and has learned those basic skills as he has begun to master his Latin. Next session, he will be ready to work on his Greek. His curiosity and unbending pride sometimes get him in trouble, but, for the most part, his behavior has been exemplary. He is a hungry student. I pray you will not take him out of the school at this important juncture. He has had but two of the four years of the course of study here."

My chest tightened. My heart cried out for Uncle Charles to listen to Dr. Blair.

"As you may know, Dr. Blair," Charles said, "Robert is enrolled here with his own income, derived from the tobacco grown at Nomony Hall and the other plantations he will inherit when he comes of age. Athawes, his agent in London, tells me that his income does not justify the expense of his going to school here."

"Master Carter must be prepared to take his place in society, sir. He will doubtless serve in the government in due time, and in the church, like his father and grandfathers before him. He needs an adequate education to do that. Surely the grandson of the great Robert Carter of Corotoman can afford it."

"We will see that his education continues, but I am afraid we must remove him from school at the end of this session."

Within a fortnight, he took me, at eleven, away from my formal education, and I was choking back tears I dared not cry. "I don't want to leave," I said. "This is what Grandfather intended for me."

"I understand, Robert. You seem to love it here, and you are doing well. Still, I believe we are doing the right thing to preserve your property. Surely your Uncle Landon and I can see you provided with an adequate education."

We made our way to York, on the ferry over to Gloucester County, and back to Warner Hall. The heat of the late spring day seemed to me to be melting away any hopes for my future.

As we started up the boxwood-lined lane to the house at Warner Hall, I pulled up Corotoman and turned to Uncle Charles. "Must Sam and I go back to Warner Hall? I want to visit my mother and see some of the people on the plantation, but I do not want to stay."

"We will see first if John Lewis will do his duty by you."

I was certain that he would not.

7

1739: King George County

Uncle Charles said to Mama, "Have his things packed, Priscilla. Robert is going with me to King George."

He had come to check on the progress of my education at Warner Hall. No one was surprised that there simply wasn't any.

Just after dawn the next morning, Sam and I mounted Corotoman to ride double alongside Uncle Charles. We were followed by a wagon carrying our belongings. We traveled all the way to Westmoreland County without stopping. Fortunately, the weather was fine and the roads dry. Still, we were exhausted by the time we reached Nomony Hall to spend the night. Mistress Sanders had a late supper prepared for us. She and Kate fussed and cried over Sam and me and marveled at how we had grown.

Before Sam and I lay down for the night, I stood with him at a river side window, overlooking the Nomini.

"Someday, Sam, this will all be mine, and I will make it a great plantation. I will do things my way then."

"Yes, I believes you will. But you looks at things different from most folks, and I thinks life ain't going to be easy for you."

The next morning early, we continued to Uncle Charles's plantation in King George County. The house was a simple one set in the woods on a beautiful spot overlooking the Rappahannock River, which was much narrower here than at Hobbs Hole. This house was not the one he planned to build for his young family. He intended to call his new home Cleve after it was finished.

A petite pretty woman with dark hair under her cap and a warm smile greeted us upon our entrance to the house. Four little Carters peeked out from behind her soft gray skirts as she reached out both her arms. I could not help smiling at the children.

"Welcome Robert," she said.

She held me at arm's length and looked me over carefully.

"Charles did not tell me what a fine, tall, handsome young man you were."

Though her words embarrassed me, I smiled at her, drawing myself up to my full height and allowing myself to be hugged and kissed on the cheek by this new aunt.

There was a harpsichord in the sitting area of Charles's small home. One day, seeing no one around, I sat at the stool and placed my hands on the keys. I was just getting ready to press my fingers down when I heard someone behind me. I nearly jumped out of my skin and turned around to see my Aunt Mary. I stood up, embarrassed, expecting to be reprimanded, but she was smiling at me.

"Do you play?"

"No, Ma'm. I just love the sound of music."

"Well, then, you must learn to play."

She pulled a chair beside me, showing me how to place my fingers and how to use my feet.

Whenever we had a chance, Aunt Mary and I would play the harpsichord, and it soon became apparent that I had some talent for music. What a feeling! To actually hear coming from the instrument the sounds I could hear in my head or of the notes I saw on sheets of music.

Charles's two eldest children, my cousins Mary and Eliza, respectively eight and six years old, came dancing into the hall one day while we were at the harpsichord. They were laughing as they flitted around the room, causing their skirts to swirl.

"Cousin Robert, is it not wonderful?" young Mary said. "Papa is going to hire a dancing master for us."

"Yes," Eliza said, coming and taking my hand. "You must learn with us."

The dancing master, a prissy little man named Forsythe, came to stay for a month. In spite of the man's appearance and manner, I came to respect the slap of his stick whenever I missed a step. Nor did he spare the girls. He drilled us for two hours a day while Aunt Mary, and sometimes Uncle Charles, watched.

"Dancing is a part of the education of ladies and gentlemen," Uncle Charles told me.

At the end of the month, my uncle invited his neighbors to come and enjoy a ball. The two girls were allowed to show off their steps, but they were afterward whisked off to bed.

"You are eleven now," he said to me, "becoming a young man. You must stay downstairs and attend the ball."

I was tall for my age. I thought myself painfully skinny, and I did not want to dress up. Aunt Mary, nevertheless, insisted Sam dress me in a blue silk waistcoat and coat, with white knee britches. My hair was pulled back with a ribbon at my neck, and my new shoes had real brass buckles. I came slowly down the steps on the evening of the ball, hoping no one would notice me, thereafter standing on the sidelines. When anyone did speak to me, my face grew hot.

I loved the music, of course, and Forsythe said I danced well "for a novice," but I could not imagine asking a young lady to dance.

It was not that I didn't like young ladies, mind. They just flustered me. I never knew what to say around them, and I tripped all over myself.

The ball went very well, so far as my aunt and uncle were concerned, and afterward, I settled down with the tutor uncle had hired for me, to continue my Latin and Greek.

⁓

"Master Carter," the tutor McKenzie said to me with a burr like Dr. Blair's, but without the kindness, "what have you been doing with your time?" He frowned. "You must read four hours a day, either in Greek or Latin. Write down your translations. I will check them each morning. They must be exactly correct, so take care as you work."

As I worked at my translations, I glanced up and looked out the window over the river. I longed to be outside on Corotoman with Sam, especially when the sun sparkled on the Rappahannock, but I was also glad of the instruction I was receiving. Incorrect translations resulted in a smart smack on the back of my legs with McKenzie's pointer, but that only bothered me momentarily. I wanted to learn—had to learn.

⁓

Uncle Charles walked in as I was working under Mr. McKenzie's watchful eye, practicing my Greek.

"How does it go with Robert?"

"He does passably well, sir." Mr. McKenzie was not one for high compliments. "I have been meaning to talk to you, Mr. Carter." He turned away from me to face my uncle directly. "I do not mean to be impertinent, but I do not wish to be exposed to dancing again. It is wicked. If you will forgive me, sir, I will absent myself from future festivities of the kind."

"Good God, man! Everyone dances. It is a mark of polite society. How else are we supposed to socialize with our neighbors?"

"It is not only the dancing, sir. Balls encourage the ladies to dress in extravagant clothing that exposes their shoulders and necks. And then there is the gambling at cards that accompanies these fetes, and the excessive drinking of strong alcohol ... all supported on the backs of enslaved men and women—a wicked thing indeed."

Uncle Charles's expression was exasperated. McKenzie's eyes were on fire. For a second, I thought McKenzie was going to shake a finger in my uncle's face. Tension was palpable in the air. Gentleman or not, it was not in Uncle Charles's nature to allow himself to be scolded, especially by a mere employee. He was a Carter, after all. I prayed McKenzie's attitude would not interfere with my studies. The Latin and Greek were going well, and I seemed to have a knack for mathematics.

The moment passed. Uncle Charles left the room.

～⌐

At Uncle Charles's, I saw little of the activity outside the house. Unlike at Warner Hall, Sam and I felt welcome in the house and were kept busy with things to do, not the least of which was playing on the harpsichord. We did ride horseback, and walked through the woods, but we did not do any independent adventuring. As a result, I saw very little of the lives of Charles's field slaves or how he managed them.

I was reading one day, when my attention was drawn to the breaking of china in the dining room. I went in to see what was the matter.

"You clumsy girl," my Aunt Mary shouted at a child, a house slave of about seven or eight.

The girl had been setting the places for dinner at the table, and dropped a cup and saucer, which shattered on the floor. Her eyes were wide with fear, and she drew back from my aunt.

"I told you to be careful. Now look what you have done." Aunt Mary drew a strap from her skirt. Waving the strap at the girl, she said, "Go get a broom and sweep it up, and be quick about it."

Aunt Mary shook the strap in the girl's face. Sam looked at her in surprise. The girl flinched, but Mary did not actually hit her.

The scene puzzled me because Aunt Mary was very patient and understanding with me and her children, but clearly she did not consider this child worthy of such consideration.

I looked carefully at the girl's face. I could see hurt and resentment there as she left to get the broom. She came back with the broom and swept up the shards of china, and once Mary put the strap back in her skirt, the girl gave her head a barely perceptible haughty toss as she left. Aunt Mary missed the movement, but I did not.

A few days later, I was again in the schoolroom with Mr. McKenzie when Uncle Charles came. This time his eyes were ablaze.

"Mr. McKenzie, my children tell me that you have been preaching to them. I pray this is not true." He paused.

McKenzie stiffened but neither admitted nor denied the allegation.

"I see. Well, you are entitled to your opinion in religious matters, and I do not wish to interfere with your rights in that regard. However, I demand that you refrain from trying to inculcate your beliefs in my children, telling them that dancing and gambling are the work of the devil and that the institution that provides their maintenance is evil."

McKenzie said nothing, but it was clear that he was not volunteering to change his ways.

Charles said, "If I hear of your preaching to my children again, you will be gone from this place."

In three months' time, McKenzie was gone.

A new, less adamant tutor was engaged to teach my young cousins Eliza and Mary their basic skills, but he was not qualified to teach Latin and Greek.

"We do not really need a tutor, Robert," my uncle told me. "I have Latin and Greek. I shall set you on a course of study myself. I can check your translations and correct you when you falter."

His intentions were good, but between the building of his house, the running of his plantation, and his service as a delegate to the House of Burgesses from King George County, there was little time left to supervise my studies. I just kept reading and practicing.

8

Spring 1742: Sabine Hall

I drew my cloak around me as Sam and I traveled down the Rappahannock to Sabine Hall, Uncle Landon Carter's home in Richmond County. The boat was loaded with my possessions, including Corotoman. It was cold, with a drizzling rain falling.

In the winter, Uncle Charles's wife, Mary, had died suddenly. Charles was distracted with grief, trying to take care of his young children. He told me he thought I would be better served by living with Landon for awhile.

The truth was, I mourned Mary, too. She had been like a mother to me, both strict and kind. Her passing left yet another hole in my life.

We arrived at Sabine Hall at the edge of dark. The weather had cleared somewhat by the time we came up to the dock. Through the gray mist, I could see the house—a long two stories of brick with seven windows, or seven lights, as people like to say, across. On the river side, as I first saw it, was a columned porch running the full length of the house, with a dependency on each end, connected to the house by covered breezeways. The main house had four chimney stacks, like Nomony Hall—a sign of a residence of substance.

In spite of the weather, Uncle Landon came down to the dock to meet us. At thirty-two, he gave the impression of being a much bigger man than he actually was because of his bravado and sense of self-importance, always reminding me of Grandfather. He was accompanied by a delicate-looking girl with dark curly hair.

"Dear Robert," boomed Landon, "You are most welcome here. Come." He held out his arm toward the girl beside him. "You must meet my new wife, Maria."

I knew that his first wife had died two years earlier and that he had remarried, but I expected an older woman. I tried to hide my surprise. *This girl could not be more than a year or two older than I am myself.* "My pleasure, Madam," I said, bowing to kiss her hand.

Maria smiled shyly.

"You must call her Aunt Maria. We are all family."

Family included four children: Robert Wormley, who was nine; Landon, Jr., who was four; and John and Elizabeth, born at different ends of the same year. They were a little older than three and two-and-a-half, respectively. I could see why Uncle Landon felt the need to remarry.

Sam and I were fed supper in our separate places and settled in for the night.

The next day, Uncle Landon made his library available to me. He set up the school desk I had brought from Uncle Charles's house. Robert Wormley had a tutor, but he was not qualified to teach me Latin and Greek at the level I was reading. Once again, I was set to study on my own.

"Come, Robert," Uncle Landon said the first week, "let us ride out to see how things progress on the plantation."

I was anxious for my first real exposure to the way a plantation was run. I was fourteen, old enough, I thought, to be learning such things. We set out, Landon on a tall white horse, and I on Corotoman.

"Tobacco, Robert. It is a challenge to raise—takes a lot of Negro labor all the year through—but it is like money to us. In fact, we pay many of our debts in tobacco."

Landon pulled his horse to a halt upon seeing a slave plowing, getting ready for the planting of wheat. As we watched, the Negro, who Landon called Manuel, guided the oxen carefully, making the furrows deep and straight. I could smell the pungent odor of the freshly turned earth.

"He does well most of the time," said Landon, "until he takes a mind to abuse the oxen. He caused one ox to be mired in the marsh last month."

"Did he?"

"I do not tolerate the mistreatment of animals. I had Manuel whipped until his back bled. Then I threatened to sell him away from his wife." He settled himself into a more comfortable position in his saddle. "I would do it, too," he continued, "if it weren't for the good work he does when he's inclined. You'd think he would be grateful for the kind treatment he receives at my hands. I brought his wife, Sukey, from another quarter for him. Then he took a fancy to some little wench on the Beale place.

"The life of a planter is not easy. The Negroes must be kept in line because they are temperamentally lazy and dishonest. The overseers are not much better, so it is necessary to follow up on everything they do. My middling neighbors let their stock wander onto my land and eat my crops. The price of tobacco fluctuates from month to month so that I must keep up with the changes in order to sell at the right time, and the factors in London charge too much for their services. It is always something that needs to be dealt with."

Landon started again, walking his mount slowly. We made our way around the field and looked out over the marsh toward the Rappahannock. The river was tranquil, seeming to belie all the turmoil described by Landon. In the river was a johnboat with two Negroes fishing.

"We'll have fish for dinner," Landon said.

When we got back to the house, before he dismounted, Landon ordered postilion Tom released from the irons that had held him all night. "Whip him and turn him loose," Landon told the overseer. "That should cure him."

"What did he do?" I asked.

"He was working in the garden with Johnny. He pulled some of the bush beans we had just planted and left the weeds. The boy's too saucy to follow orders and too weak to command others."

Tom was taken in hand by the overseer and a Negro, his expression defiant. His hands were tied before him, and he was stripped of his shirt. They dragged him, pulling and twisting, to a pole with a large hook attached. They then pulled up his tied hands and secured them to the hook so that his back was to the overseer. The whip made a sharp crack as the overseer made a test strike. He then commenced laying lashes on Tom's back, counting each stroke. Tom could not help but wince, but set his jaw and did not cry out.

Each sharp crack of the whip drove a shock through my own body, a fact which I tried to hide from my uncle. Finally, the overseer reached thirty. Tom was cut down, bleeding and weak, and taken away to the quarters where I supposed someone would try to ease his suffering.

It occurred to me that postilion Tom was unlikely to be too stupid not to know the difference between bush beans and weeds. *Was the destruction of the beans retaliation for something Landon had done to him previously? If so, what sort of subtle retaliation would result from this beating?*

"That's done," said Uncle Landon. "We'd best be getting in to dinner."

I talked to Sam about my day as we prepared for bed.

"They was whippings at Warner Hall and at you Uncle Charles's, too. Prob'ly even at Nomony Hall. This ain't nothing you doesn't know about."

"Knowing and seeing are two different things, Sam. I never saw anybody get thirty lashes before."

The hall had been stripped of furniture, and the Negro fiddler and banjo players were setting up. In the dining room, the table was covered with a huge array of food—venison and beef, turkey, chicken, ham and rockfish, not to mention fried apples, puddings, pies, and several kinds of bread. The sideboards were burdened with rum punch, cider, grog, and wine.

Everyone was dressed in their finest, including me. Landon had me fitted in a new suit of patterned lavender silk—britches, waistcoat, and long coat—buttoned with black buttons all the way down the front. The ruffles of my shirt showed at the ends of my sleeves and at my neck. Uncle Landon made it clear that I, now fourteen, was expected to sit at the adult table, engage in polite conversation, and dance with the ladies. I was expected to be a proper gentleman.

As the coaches began to arrive, I recognized the family of Thomas Lee, who brought his three eldest children: Phillip Ludwell, Hannah, and Thomas, all of whom I had met at Uncle Charles's. Hannah was just my age.

John Tayloe, a pleasant-looking man of twenty-two, brought his visiting sister, Ann Tayloe Page, who happened to be married to my first cousin, Mann Page II. This fact caused me some concern, but no mention was made of John Lewis's claims about me. *Perhaps it was only because courtesy forbad insulting the host's kin.*

When the dancing began, I forgot to be shy. Carried along by the music, I danced with Aunt Maria first, then with Hannah Lee. Hannah was a plain-looking girl, but she was very clever. Her conversation revealed the good education Thomas Lee afforded all his children. I admired her and envied her learning. As the night wore on, I tried to dance with every lady available, and much to my surprise, I enjoyed it.

During the course of the evening, I managed to sip a little grog, too, without Uncle Landon's notice. Or, so I believed.

I went to bed exhausted, but by the next morning I was ready to go again, as Uncle Landon's balls lasted several days.

Maria Ball Carter died two years after her marriage to Uncle Landon, leaving yet another child behind, born the year her mother died. The child was also named Maria.

While the house was in mourning, Sam and I were sent back to Warner Hall.

The servant answered the door when we knocked. Only Mama was there to greet me. She stood, shifting from foot to foot, glancing over her shoulder. She hugged me and said, "I'm glad to see you." She kissed me on the cheek.

In a moment, John Lewis came into the entry hall. "Robert," he said, acknowledging me. Then he turned to Mama. "Is all ready for our guests at dinner, Priscilla? John tells me something is amiss with his shirt. Will you see that it is taken care of?"

I could see that Mama was torn, as always, between her attachment to me and the duties John Lewis believed were owed to him and his sons. I resented John Lewis as much as ever, but now I pitied my mother, too, for I could see the situation she was in as I had never seen it before. Sam and I made the rounds to see old friends: Enoch, Prince, and Hannah. After a month, we were gone, back to Uncle Charles's Cleve, the new home that he had built on his property in King George.

From sixteen on, I was a constant visitor, welcome at Cleve and Sabine Hall but not so much at Warner Hall.

9

1749: (five years later) The North Atlantic Robert Carter

I was free, in control of my inheritance, and free of uncles and stepfather. Though there was no one to introduce me or to ease my way, I was anxious to be in London. I could not be still, thinking about what lay ahead.

The air on the deck, as I looked out over the Atlantic Ocean from the *Everton*, was cool. The wind blew freshly through my hair, but the sea was calm and the sun warm on my skin. It was July, five months after my twenty-first birthday, and Sam and I were on our way to England, leaving the overseer, Simon Sallard, to run Nomony Hall Plantation.

Sam was standing by my side, nearly as tall as I, wearing a gentleman's waistcoat of silk, ruffled linen shirt, and matching britches, his hair pulled back in a neat queue at the nape of his neck, very much the way I was dressed myself. It behooved me, I thought, to have my manservant looking well. He was gazing over the rail at the placid sea.

Turning to him, I said, "Now I can make up for my lack of learning. All young gentlemen go to London as a part of their education. Grandfather expected it. He told me he would make sure that I had the best education possible, but now it is up to me. I will have my due, and I will not disappoint the memory of my grandfather."

Sam faced me, his mobile face wondering, and said, "You own all you daddy and you granddaddy owned, now you twenty-one?"

"Most of it, but only because my uncles assured my receiving my father's part of Grandfather's estate. I owe them a great debt of gratitude. Because Papa died before Grandfather, my uncles could have divided his share among them, but instead, they honored my grandfather's wishes. They went to the House of Burgesses along with my mother to arrange for much of Grandfather's estate and all of my father's estate to come to me. So, on my twenty-first birthday, I suddenly owned eighty thousand acres of land in the Northern Neck and elsewhere in Virginia, along with houses, woodlands, crops and stock, and over one hundred Negroes."

"Including me."

I looked at him, a little surprised. "I do not think of you that way, Sam. I don't feel like a master to you."

"But you is. I reckon sometime you gone to have to figure out what you does think about that."

A gentleman older than I approached us as we stood at the rail talking. His face seemed vaguely familiar, but I could not precisely place him.

He held out his hand, "Lawrence Washington, at your service."

Oh, I thought to myself. Lawrence was the master of a plantation, which he renamed Mount Vernon after he inherited it from his father. It was located several miles upriver from Westmoreland County in the new county of Fairfax. The reason he looked familiar to me was that I knew his half brothers. This Washington was older, not as tall or imposing as his younger brother, George. I noticed that he did not look well. "Your name is quite familiar to me. I have known your brothers, George and John Augustine, most of my life. They spent much of their time at Popes Creek Plantation in Westmoreland County when they were young. That is close to the homes of two of my uncles. My name is Robert Carter III."

"Who are your uncles?"

"Landon Carter of Sabine Hall and Charles Carter of Cleve in King George County."

"Of course. I should have known from your Carter name. Your grandfather had holdings in Fairfax County, if I am not mistaken."

"He did. They have now come to me."

"I see. And you have just come of age, I understand."

"Yes."

"I go to London for the Ohio Company," Washington told me, taking me by the elbow and turning away, leaving Sam standing alone.

"And I also hope to consult a physician. I seem to have some sort of weakness in my chest that just will not leave me."

I looked back briefly at Sam.

"That is most unfortunate. I hope you will find what you need in London," I said to Washington.

I felt resentful—not of Washington himself, but his company reminded me of my lack of formal education. Here was an oldest son who had been well-educated, properly sent to school in England, and prepared for his life of a planter and businessman. The Carter family's pattern had always been to prepare its sons well. My grandfather was adamant about it. If he had lived, I would have had tutors and then been sent to London to finish my studies as had my father and uncles before me. Instead, in spite of the lack of education, I was being criticized, mainly by my stepfather, John Lewis, for going to England at a time I should be taking over management of my own plantations. Lawrence Washington suffered no such difficulties.

I wondered what Washington might have heard about me. "I am going to London to complete my education," I told him.

He seemed to accept this statement without question. He gave no indication he had heard gossip about me that originated with John Lewis. *Had he not heard the rumors? Was he just being courteous? Did he intend to make his own judgment?* I tried to act as if it were not an issue.

As we walked along the deck in the pleasant weather, we talked about his purpose in going to England. He said that, like most Virginia planters, he frequently did business with merchants in London.

"You will soon learn that such men make their living entirely from Virginia planters. They arrange for the purchase in England and the Continent of Virginia products, particularly tobacco, and then either send the money to the planter or, more often, invest the money for him and send the returns. In order to grow the tobacco that sustains our economy, we must have slaves. The English government wants us to provide them with tobacco, and they also want the income made by the ship's captains and shipbuilding that the slave trade provides, but now many Englishmen have the audacity to claim they do not approve of slavery."

I recalled that, during the time I had lived with Uncle Landon, he liked to complain about his dealings with Virginia merchants from time to time, but Washington was more explicit.

"These so-called 'Virginia merchants' frequently make loans or arrange loans for planters during hard years. Since we in the colonies are not permitted to trade with anyone except through England, the merchants also purchase for us clothing and household furnishings we may wish to buy in England and countries on the Continent. In effect, they conduct business for us in exchange for a handsome fee for themselves." He frowned. "Planters are at a disadvantage in the arrangement, but we are dependent upon the contacts of the merchants. No one in the colonies can do for us what the merchants are able to do."

I could see that I had a lot to learn about the business of tobacco.

⁓

From the deck I watched the furling and unfurling of the sails, as the bare-chested sailors worked up and down the creaking ropes, responding to commands from below. The common sailors, both Negro and white, worked together as equals. The officers were, of course, all white. I supposed that these Negroes must be free men. Though the sailors were a foul-smelling, dirty, hard-looking lot, I was struck by their courage and efficiency at the jobs they were about.

The *Everton* was a square-masted schooner out of Liverpool.

"What are the sails called?" I asked the captain, James Kelly.

"The foremast, main, and mizzen," he said.

"How do they work?"

"I'll let you watch for yourself."

He shouted out orders, which were in turn shouted out from the deck. He even allowed me into the wheelhouse to watch the helmsman as he guided the ship, using a fascinating instrument called a floating compass.

I persuaded Captain Kelly to show me where the tobacco was stored deep in the dark bowels of the ship.

We descended the ladder below the hatch and quickly saw hundreds of brass-bound wooden barrels that I knew had been packed tightly, carefully, back in Virginia with the dried leaves. The Negroes had gingerly packed them into barrels at Uncle Landon's during the time I lived with him at Sabine Hall, always aware that any crushed leaves would earn them a beating.

The sweet smell of the tobacco was overwhelming in that confined space.

I asked questions wherever I went on the ship, and the rough sailors likely thought me more than a little strange, but I didn't care. I wanted to know everything in the world.

I was pestering Captain Kelly about the ship's routes, the items traded, and how profits were made as Washington and I dined with him. The sea was calm and the dining room most comfortable, the light sconces swaying gently with the movement of the ship.

I had never been on a ship before, but I did know that many of the ships that plied the water between the American colonies and Liverpool also carried slaves from Africa. My own grandfather had traded slaves from time to time, selling them straight off ships anchored in the Chesapeake Bay. It seemed to me that made me—and all like me—businessmen as well as planters.

"Slaves are carried in the holds of ships, are they not?" I asked.

Washington looked uncomfortable at this turn of conversation but said nothing.

"Yes," said Captain Kelly, without any hesitation, looking pleased with himself.

"Those ships must be bigger than the *Everton*."

"Not necessarily." Captain Kelly paused to take a sip of his wine. "In fact, the *Everton* does carry slaves. Why would you not think so?"

"I am just thinking of the size of the hold below." I tried to imagine human beings crowded into the space I had seen. "How many slaves do you carry on a single trip?"

"It depends. We usually start out with three hundred or four hundred," Captain Kelly said. He lifted a forkful of food to his mouth and then dabbed at his mouth with a napkin. "Of course," he shrugged, "we lose 15 percent or so on each voyage."

I took in a sharp breath. No one had ever told me that happened.

"How is it possible to get that many people into the hold?"

He set down the napkin and looked at me. "They are placed, one directly in front of the other, legs chained to planks, one row tight against the next. They are confined in hatchways, usually two per ship."

I struggled to picture this. "How do they lie down?"

"Well, we generally allow a space six feet long and one foot, four inches wide for men, a space five feet ten inches long and one foot, four inches wide for women, and a space five feet long and one foot wide for children. Most of them can lie down."

"How do they stand up, then?"

"Oh, they cannot stand up in the hold, Mr. Carter. Each hatchway is about three feet high, but they are taken out on deck for eight hours a day."

"Still chained?"

"Of course."

"And," I paused to find the right words, "how do they take care of their necessary functions?"

"They have to do that when they are on deck."

"But if they cannot wait, or they are sick when they are in the hold?"

Kelly simply shrugged.

"It must be filthy."

I had seen whipping and mistreatment, but I had never seen Negroes live in such horrible conditions as the captain described. I lay down my fork and knife. I was feeling a little queasy.

"It is not pleasant, I will grant," Kelly said, "but the holds are cleaned out with buckets and water when the cargo is on deck."

"By cargo, you mean slaves?"

"Yes." Seeing my expression, he added, "Let me remind you, Mr. Carter, that's what it takes to keep your tobacco plantations thriving."

That day on the Everton I realized just how bad the conditions were for slaves crossing the Atlantic. *What had I supposed it was like?* It was not possible to put aside the images I saw of them packed into the hold of a ship under such conditions. Thanks be to God that Sam and Enoch and Hannah were born in Virginia and didn't travel on such ships.

10

Seven weeks later London

The chair is a clever wheeled conveyance pulled through the streets by a single man with the largest calves on his legs that have ever been seen. I bounced about in the chair, but it was faster than walking. The chair man maneuvered his way through the throngs while I gazed all around me at the amazing things to see. My destination was the home of Edward Athawes, where I had been invited to dine. It was located in the financial district of London near the Exchange.

Dressed in clothes made of the finest wool by a tailor in Fleet Street, I had spared no expense to look proper and prosperous, including having livery made for Sam of the Carter blue with red trim, though I came alone on this evening. Washington had kindly helped us find rooms to let for Sam— and north of the Thames.

The house of Edward Athawes was a three-story brick affair, the front steps of which went up directly from the sidewalk. The front door was in a recessed arch. It was only one of a row of similar houses, standing wall to wall with each other and all fronting on the street.

I entered through an ornate door into an entry hall where I was greeted by an extremely courteous, unsmiling servant dressed in livery as fine as clothing I'd seen worn by any gentleman in Virginia.

The dour servant said, "Please wait here a moment, sir," and disappeared through a door to the back of the house. Shortly, a sixtyish, somewhat stout gentleman came through the same door, dressed in a fine gray silk waistcoat and dark coat of the new narrower style, decorated with a silver braid. He wore a spotless ruffled white cravat and ruffles at the end of his shirtsleeves. He wore no wig, but his hair was lightly powdered. His appearance was rich, and, at the same time, subdued. *So this is Edward Athawes, of whom I have heard my uncles speak.*

"Mr. Carter," he said bowing, smiling warmly. "May I call you Robert?"

The man's attitude belied everything I had heard about him from my uncles and everything Washington said about Virginia agents.

I bowed in return. "Of course."

"And you must call me Edward. I am so happy to finally meet the grandson of my dear friend Robert Carter. He was very proud of you, a favorite grandson named for him. He visited here in London from time to time, you know. I hope you and I will also do much business together."

Athawes put his hand gently behind my elbow and led me into a dining room, which was already occupied by other young Virginia planters. A few ladies were present, as most of the Virginians were not accompanied. I was introduced to Mrs. Athawes, a woman younger than her husband, wearing a gown of gold flowered chintz over an embroidered silk petticoat, her dark hair lightly powdered under her cap. She was quite pretty.

The dining room was intimate in its appearance. The walls were dark blue and hung with portraits all around.

The large fireplace was topped by a marble mantle and two matching sconces for candles. Wide floorboards were almost completely covered by thick Wilton carpet. Along the walls were small tables and straight chairs upholstered with striped damask at either side. A long table lavishly set, surrounded by chairs, dominated the middle of the room. Washington was correct when he said that the tobacco trade was profitable for agents.

Among the guests I saw Phillip Ludwell Lee, Phil, as he was called at home. He was a slender man with a prominent nose and sharp features. I crossed the room to greet him. Lee's manner always let one know that he considered himself a man of consequence. I thought him as brilliant as his five brothers but not as personable. The eldest son of Thomas Lee of Stratford Hall in Westmoreland County, he would one day be master of Stratford, a close neighbor to Nomony Hall. Like Washington, Lee seemed unaffected by the gossip of John Lewis and Gloucester County, and I relaxed a bit.

"Well, Robert," he said, "I did not think to see you here. What a pleasure. I am here to join the Honorable Society of the Inner Temple to study law. What will you do while you are here?"

"I have not yet decided. I am seeking to complete my education in some way."

"You should enter the Inner Temple then."

I thought that the Inner Temple would be a proper use of my time in London. My Carter name would assure me entry, but my lack of formal education made me pause. I would have to think about it.

"I would not, of course, let my legal studies prevent me from enjoying the many other delights of London," Lee continued, drawing a handkerchief from his sleeve, dabbing at his nose and returning it to his sleeve.

He continued. "You must shop at the Jasmine Tree in Pall Mall, when you have the chance, and see *Richard III* played in Drury Lane. Richard III was such a delightfully wicked man. There is much to do here."

The conversation around the table after we sat to dine intrigued me. What Athawes and his guests had to say awakened in me a great hunger to understand the world of business. The talk turned to tobacco's reliability as a primary crop. Although prices were good at the moment, the planters around the table were lamenting that the prices went up and down—and their fortunes with them. It was a common complaint in Virginia.

"You truthfully say that the price of tobacco is unpredictable," I said. "I know this to be true from my time at Sabine Hall. As we all know, tobacco destroys the soil as well, so that it is necessary to move the tobacco fields every few years, leaving the land fallow where the tobacco last was. It seems to me that it would be prudent to develop other crops along with the tobacco."

The faces around me looked at me in puzzlement. "But wheat and barley do not fetch nearly the prices that tobacco brings."

"Would they not make up in reliability what they lack in short-turn profit?" I asked. "It would allow us to use more of our land each year. Better to make something than nothing in the bad years. Perhaps if we grew other crops, we would not be so dependent upon slavery for our labor."

An uncomfortable silence fell over the table, and I suddenly realized that slavery was not a topic for polite conversation here. I was also learning that slavery, though brought to the Colonies by the English, was now frowned upon by many in London.

Athawes stood, smiling, and broke the silence, saving me from further embarrassment. "Well, gentlemen, I suggest we retire to the drawing room."

As I was preparing to leave at the end of the evening, Athawes drew me aside. I was afraid he was going to reprimand me for raising the subject of slavery during the dinner conversation.

Instead he said, "Your grandfather had a reputation for being imperious, as I am sure you know, but I was truly fond of him. He was an honest gentleman, and I considered him a friend, and I valued his esteem as well as his business. I ascertain that, in spite of good intentions, your property has been ill-managed. Your uncles have understandably been busy with their own affairs, and I am sorry your lot has fallen as it has."

Athawes continued. "There are many temptations and pitfalls for a young man in London. Be careful. I can see that you have a good mind, but you have many lessons to learn about life. For your grandfather's sake, I want to see you prosper here. Please come to me if I can help you."

I thanked him, but my mind was on seeing all that there was in London, and I was sure I could handle anything that came my way.

11

1749

London was a banquet! Nothing in the Northern Neck or Williamsburg could have prepared me for the sheer excitement of the London of 1749. Lee was right. In spite of the warning given to me by Athawes, I was determined to see everything in the colorful streets of King George II's capital city. It was a city of brick and stone. Many of the streets were grand, lined with shops whose bowed windows displayed books and pottery, poultry, meats and bread, perfume, tobacco and fine cloth—all things imaginable.

Strolling the cobblestone streets, I found that a series of four streets—the Strand, Fleet Street, Cheapside, and Cornhill—together, seemed to offer everything that anyone could possibly want to buy.

And the smells. Perfume from the ladies, the delicious odors of baked goods, coffee, flowers, spices from some shops, and ale and grog from others filled the air. Not infrequently, my senses were also assaulted by the stench of garbage, dead animals, and human waste that lay in open sewers along the streets. The odor of London was quite putrid in the summer, but I was undeterred by it.

Gazing into the windows of the shops, I had Sam beside me to carry whatever I might purchase. On Cornhill Street, I noticed that I was not the only one looking. Pretty young female shoppers occasionally glanced up, just momentarily, from their perusal of gloves or material, and smiled coyly at the skinny young Colonial trying not to look out of place.

Equally fascinating to me were the rabbit's warren of narrow streets where I was assured a gentleman could not safely walk. The city was endlessly fascinating to me, and although I did join the Inner Temple, I seldom attended.

On other days, in other parts of the city, I saw noisy public houses and alehouses and whorehouses, quiet during the day, as well as marvelous theaters and places of entertainment with brightly painted signs, especially near Covent Garden.

Richard III was not all that was playing in London.

The streets everywhere were full of creaking wagons and fine coaches pulled by sleek horses whose hooves made sharp clicking sounds on the cobblestone pavement. Many people were in the streets—some dressed in finery, walking quietly along with their heads held high, the ladies carrying parasols to protect their delicate complexions; others wearing rags so wretched no self-respecting planter would let his slaves dress in them. Everywhere, at all times of the night and day, I could hear street sellers crying their wares. I wanted to embrace it all.

One evening, when the fog lay low over the Thames, I walked out alone to St. James Park. I had seen well-dressed Londoners strolling there, and I decided I must join them. Dressed in my best, I began to walk slowly along the paths, pretending an interest in the various trees and flowers. I paused to watch an acrobat doing his routine for pennies from the crowd.

As I stood there, I was approached by three well-dressed gentlemen.

One said to me, "We have not seen you before. Come walk with us and make an accounting of yourself."

They seemed quite friendly, and, flattered to be noticed, I said, "I am Robert Carter, sir, at your service," and gave a bow.

"I am John Ashton," the young gentleman replied, "and these are my friends."

Introductions were made all around.

"From your accent, sir, I take you to be a Colonial."

It was said with no hint of malice or condescension.

"I am."

"Well, let us introduce you, then, to London."

We went together to a public house. St. George's was warm and crowded. The large main room had a stone floor, and on one wall, a huge fireplace. The walls were of either stone or brick, covered with a coating not unlike Nomony Hall's limestone. There was a long wooden bar beside the fireplace, but we sat together around one of several rough wooden tables.

We ordered tankards of ale and papers of fish and chips, paid for, in part, by me. The gentlemen regaled me with stories of the life of well-to-do Londoners and the merits of various places of entertainment in the city. I was feeling quite genial.

We soon moved on to another establishment, where we enjoyed still more ale. At some point, we began to play cards. I considered myself a passable player, cards being a frequent pastime at both my uncles' houses. The wagers were, however, higher here than at home.

As the evening wore on, I seemed to have a little more trouble than usual following which cards had been played, but the tankard of ale at my side gave me confidence.

"I will see your bet, sir, and raise you."

By some whim of fate, I continued to win at cards that night and earned enough to pay for the evening. I finally staggered through the streets and home to Sam, quite well satisfied with myself and my skill at cards.

Sam greeted me, frowning, hands on hips.

"You treadin' in dang'rous territory, Master. You come here to learn. What you gone learn in the public houses ain't worth knowin'."

The next evening, I went again to St. James Park and met the same group of young gallants. Again, we went to the public houses. They were all over the city. Again, I ended up playing cards. This time I did not win. I was not deterred. Given the skill I had demonstrated on my first evening out, I was confident I would win back all I had lost another evening, and the camaraderie was addictive.

One afternoon, I paid my penny to enter at the lion's head that symbolized the place called Buttons, a coffeehouse near Covent Garden. The room inside was large with tables set all around, most accommodating four to six people. The walls themselves were covered with amusing prints by an artist named Hogarth, as well as advertisements of various kinds. Large windows allowed in light, and the smell in the place was delicious. I could see that it was possible to buy almost anything to drink and something to eat as well.

Men sat in pairs and groups, drinking coffee or whatever else they desired, some smoking their pipes contentedly, others talking or arguing. Others sat alone, reading periodicals or writing with their quill pens. At several tables, men seemed to be conducting business. No one hurried them. Buttons was apparently as much a place to meet as to drink coffee.

I seated myself in a corner, out of the way, so that I could see and hear, for many animated conversations were plenty loud enough to hear. From their dress and conversation, it was evident that many of these were men of substance and education.

My attention was drawn to an unusually tall gentleman with rumpled and unkempt clothing. In spite of his appearance, his speech was cultured, and he spoke with authority. He made reference to a dictionary that he had just published.

None of the men at the table with the tall man paid any attention to me but continued talking about philosophy and government in their proper accents.

"Have you read the new book *The Spirit of the Laws* by the Frenchman, Montesquieu?" one portly, bewigged gentleman was saying.

"Yes," said a leaner companion with a great hooked nose, leaning across the table to make himself heard. "He supposes to analyze the relationship between government and the governed."

I had never thought to question whether one sort of government was better than any other. In fact, I had never really thought about the differences in government from country to country, or of the effect of government on the life of the individual.

"'Tis remarkable, is it not, that Montesquieu, a French baron himself, would come to such conclusions?" the portly man asked. "Where must he have learned to see things as he does?"

"He makes reference to our revolution of the last century, suggesting that France would benefit from a constitution similar to that we English have developed over time," said a third gentleman, sweeping his arm as if to indicate the passing of years. "He admires the many restraints put on the royal power after the Stuarts. Since William II came to the throne, our monarchs rule with the consent and advice of a parliament elected by the people."

"Yes, yes, he is very complimentary of our form of government," the portly man said. He smiled. "It is no wonder he is not greatly admired in his own country."

The other gentlemen laughed.

"He says no man should be afraid of another," the hook-nosed gentleman said, leaning close again.

"The implication, I suppose, is that the law should replace the whims of an individual ruler and should thereby protect all men," said the third companion, "and also that the law should protect men from an overbearing government. He argues for three separate parts of administration in order to balance the power of government."

"So it would seem." The portly man looked doubtful. "But where, then, does he believe this power of law comes from? Does he not believe the sovereign is anointed by God?"

"Is that not exactly what the Stuarts thought?" gentleman number three asked. "I thought we discarded that notion during the last century."

"He says he believes the power does come from God, or that it is the way God meant government to be," Hook-nose said, looking at each of the others in turn. "That natural law favors man in general, and not just a monarch. I think that in order to agree with Baron Montesquieu, one must believe in elected government."

What I was hearing impressed me greatly.

The portly gentleman looked appalled. "Do you mean to say that you believe all men draw rights equally from God?"

"John Locke has also written that all men do have certain rights," Hook-nose insisted.

"Pooh, Locke. Think, my friend, of the implication of what you are saying. Do you really mean that every human being, regardless of his place in society, is entitled to have a part in his government? Are you espousing democracy?"

"Is that not what it means to allow a man to vote for members of Parliament?"

"Men of property, to be sure, but what about lesser men—and slaves—a revolutionary idea indeed!"

That is the logical extension of what the man named Locke said, I thought to myself.

"He does not say that all men ought to be able to vote," the third man interjected, "but the baron says slaves are entitled to rights simply based on the fact of their humanity, and that is why he is opposed to slavery. Perhaps it is true that he would advocate that people now held in slavery, if they were not so held, be able to vote for their government."

The portly gentleman sat back in his seat, shook his head, and laughed. "I think that would be a hard case to sell to our colonies in America. They are quite addicted to slavery."

At that, I felt compelled to speak. Though I had seen things in my own country that made me wonder about slavery, my country had been insulted. I walked over to their table.

"I am a Virginian, sir. May I remind you that there are still slaves in England as well as in America? As for Virginia, slavery is a necessity imposed on us by the mother country."

I had spoken before I realized that, by doing so, I revealed that I had been eavesdropping. They all looked up at me, but if they were offended by my having listened, it was not evident.

I continued. "We are not only allowed but encouraged by the king to hold slaves."

"Whatever do you mean, young man," said the portly gentleman, frowning.

Now irretrievably into the conversation, I cleared my throat and spoke without hesitation. "The king allows the importation of slaves—and profits from it. The city of Liverpool depends for its economy upon it. We are expected to grow tobacco, to send to the mother country and to pay our taxes. Consider the profits the mother country derives from tobacco. Tobacco requires a great deal of hand labor in the hot sun for long hours at a time. Only slave labor makes the production of large quantities of tobacco profitable."

"But how can you justify holding human beings as chattel—property?"

"We did not choose the institution, but now we are chained to it whether we like it or not," I went on, making the arguments I had heard all my life. "We treat our people as children. We must take care of them. Being a slaveholder obligates us to feed them, clothe them, give them a living, support them when they are old, minister to them when they are sick."

As I said it, I fought back the memory of Postillion Tom at my Uncle Landon's.

The third man shook his head and brought me out of my reverie. "But you have the power of life and death over them."

"It would be foolish to needlessly destroy one's own property." I said, being now trapped in my position. "Besides, a landholder who abuses his people loses his good name among his neighbors, and, in the end, he answers to God."

"I believe you are very naïve, sir," said the third man. "There is no guarantee for the slaves that they will have a compassionate and responsible master."

On firmer ground, I said, "I ask you to consider whether life is much better for Negroes in London. Some are slaves. Those who are free are nearly all servants, doing the most menial of work. They are considered inferior to whites, inherently members of a lower order than whites. And what of the ragged beggars, white and Negro, who I see in the streets, their bodies emaciated and filthy. Are they better off than the slaves in Virginia? They are less than real citizens, unable to vote, with no guarantees concerning their condition, and no masters to care for them. But finally, gentlemen, if slavery is evil, then our king is complicit in that evil."

The third gentleman looked thoughtful. "I do not agree with you, young man, but you put your argument well. Let's just say that there is sufficient hypocrisy to go round, eh?"

I had occasionally wondered what life would be like if there were no slavery in Virginia but always set aside the thought as unrealistic. Nevertheless, I did determine on the spot to buy a copy of this book they talked about, *The Spirit of the Laws,* and also to see what this man Locke had to say.

12

1750

"You look fine this evening, Gov'ner," the man said, with a smile that revealed missing and blackened teeth.

Less than an hour before, a glance in the glass at the rooms I shared with Sam assured me that I did cut a fine figure. I was dressed in a fine new coat and waistcoat, good woolen britches, silk stockings, and shoes with silver buckles.

Walking out into the foggy evening, as I was wont to do, I found a chair to take me to St. James Park where I expected to encounter some dandies interested in drinking and gambling. The chair man stopped in an area where there were not many people about, but I could see the usual strollers only a short distance away. I wasn't worried. I paid the chair man, but stepping down, I noticed two disreputable-looking men loitering in the shadows. As I set out in the direction of the strollers, I could smell the stench of unwashed body about the men. It was the darker of the two who had spoken.

I said nothing in response but tried to walk quickly away. I was immediately blocked by the dark man's companion, a younger version of the first, with a deep scar across his face. He was leering at me. He reached out and grabbed my arm.

"No need to be in such a hurry, your grace. Come walk with us awhile."

I twisted away only to be struck in the mouth by the first man's fist. I struck out at my assailant, but he ducked, and the attempt only earned me a crack on the head that knocked me to the filthy street. For a moment, I felt kicks to my ribs and legs and blows to my head. Then I felt nothing.

~~~

Sam Harrison

I looks out the window at the drizzling rain. The sun be up, as much as it ever be up in London on a rainy morning. Master Robert accustomed to coming home late, but I thinks he never come in last night at all. He never stay out 'til dawn before. I checks his bed one more time. I can't sit still nay longer.

I remembers what Master Robert tell me about Master Athawes' offering to help him. I dresses myself in my best clothes and sets out through a steady rain to the address of Master Athawes. I comes to the place, scared of what they gone say, scared of what they gone think. The pillars and the windows on the front of the house looks so grand. I doesn't know how this gentleman, Athawes, gone receive me, but I knows I has to try.

I knocks at the front door because I can't figure out how to get to the back, and a serious-looking man come to the door. He dressed in livery, so I s'pose he be a servant, but he white. He have a cold look on his face but be polite in his words. He allow me to step inside after I tell him I be Master Robert's servant. He say to wait and go off to the back of the house.

It take Master Athawes a half hour to come to where I be, and I think he musta not been outa bed yet when I come.

"I's very sorry to disturb you so early, Master Athawes, but Master Robert didn't come home last night. He sometime come home late, but I never known him to not come home at all. I's afraid something bad happen to him. He tol' me you say come to you if he need help."

"Well, then, we must take a carriage and go find him. Where do you think he went last night?"

"He go walking in St. James Park, and then go off with young gentlemen to the public houses."

Master Athawes and me together rode through the streets. Fog lays everywhere over the ground, and I feels the cold creeping into me. We starts close to the park, stopping at every public house, asking if they see Master there. A lot of the owners knows him, because that the kind of low place where Master be hanging about, but they didn't see him last night.

We finally gets to a bad part of town, on a side street, not too far from the park. There we sees a place called the Red Rooster. It be so rundown and filthy, I don' want to go there, but Mr. Athawes say we needs to check everywhere we can.

When we gets out of the carriage and goes toward the door, a fat white lady step out from inside wearing a dirty apron.

"Would you be lookin' for a young gentleman?" she ask.

She show us inside to a dark room where people drinking, even though it be early in the day. The room smell of piss, rotten meat, and vomit. I notices Master Athawes put a perfumed handkerchief to his nose. I sniffs to blow away the smell. The fat lady lead us upstairs. In a room up there, we sees a man lying on a filthy bed, a thin blanket over top of him. I could not help from crying when I see the man be Master Robert.

Master's shirt and britches was torn; his buckles been wrenched off his shoes; his coat and waistcoat gone altogether. He covered with dirt, blood, and bruises.

"Found him outside me door this morning in the rain, I did," the lady tell us. "I run a honest place here. Can't have bodies layin' in the street in front of me place."

I was not sure whether Master dead or alive.

The lady said, "I brung him inside, looked after him."

Not much looking after going on here, I thinks to myself.

Master Robert still not moving, but looking closer, we could see he be breathing. He either be asleep or knocked out.

"He a friend of yours, gov'ner?" the lady ask Master Athawes.

"Yes, madam, he is, and I will take him from this place as soon as we can have him removed."

"Beggin' your pardon, sir, but I took him up from the street, gave him a bed, and took care of him. I'm entitled to a little something for me pains."

Master Athawes look at her with a spression on his face like he eat something bad. "He's obviously been robbed. How do I know that you didn't have something to do with it?" Anyway, he pull out a few coins from his purse and put them in the lady's hand.

Robert

I arrived at the home of Edward Athawes late in the morning, as I was requested to do in the letter that Athawes left for me. I felt much better after rest and a bath, but I still had a black eye, a sore head, and too many bruises to count, but no broken bones.

The same sober-faced servant I saw at dinner, pointedly pretending to take no notice of my appearance, met me at the door and took me directly to the paneled office just off the foyer. There was a very large desk stacked high with paper, presumably involving the financial well-being of some of my fellow planters. A long window let in sunlight that shone across the floor. The shelves, which reached from floor to ceiling, were filled with classics in Greek and Latin, and though I had learned less than I should of those languages, I did recognize names like Socrates and Herodotus and Tacitus that I had read at the grammar school and at my uncles'. There were also leather-bound books in English about the law and agriculture and business. Some of the names of the books I had heard mentioned at the coffee house. I searched for *The Spirit of the Laws*, specifically. I did not see it, but it could have been there. I longed to be able to sit and read all those books.

Athawes arose from his spacious desk to greet me and then motioned for me to sit in a comfortable chair. Athawes himself took another chair close by, not returning to the desk. He offered me whiskey.

"Thank you, sir, for helping Sam and for your kind care of me. I am most grateful."

"You should thank your manservant. It may be that he saved your life. He is very loyal—and courageous. You are very fortunate."

Bowing my head, I said, "Yes, sir." I knew it was true.

"As I have told you before," Athawes continued, leaning toward me, "I had a high regard for your grandfather. I find you to be an agreeable and intelligent young man. However, I do not think your grandfather would be particularly proud of your behavior these last months, do you?"

"No, sir." *Of course, Athawes is right. I am wasting my time and my fortune.*

"You have considerable property to manage and not a lot of formal education, as I understand from your uncles. You have had a difficult upbringing. Though you have done nothing to indicate you expect it, I feel somewhat responsible for making your stay in London pleasant and productive."

"Sir, what you say is most generous, but there is something I must know. Why did you advise my uncles to take me out of the grammar school at William and Mary? I had only had two of the four years' course of study there."

After I met Athawes, I wondered why he would have done such a thing. I believed he had interrupted my only chance at a formal education.

He sat back in his chair. "I would never have advised such a thing. Your grandfather would turn over in his grave. Why would you think it?"

"I overheard Uncle Charles tell Dr. Blair at the grammar school that he was removing me because you had told him that I could not afford it, based on what Nomony Hall and my other plantations were producing."

"Your uncle was mistaken, Robert. I did often chide both your uncles for not using your money more wisely, but I certainly did not recommend cutting short your education. I am sorry indeed if they mistook my meaning."

"Thank you for telling me that, Mr. Athawes."

"As I was about to say, I would be honored if you and your serving man would stay in my home and be a part of my family while you remain in London."

Overwhelmed by his generosity, I could not speak for a moment. I would have to live differently if I stayed in his home, but I was ready now to do that.

"I am humbly grateful for your offer, sir. I accept joyfully, and I promise that you will not regret your generosity toward me."

From that moment, I resolved that my education would take place in the home of Edward Athawes instead of at the Inner Temple.

13

1750

A muted sun through the window in my bedroom at the Athawes home woke me on my first morning there. Though the bed was comfortable and warm, I was anxious to start the day. Sam came from the servants' quarters where he was staying, to lay out my clothes and light the fire.

What was on my mind were all those books I had seen in Athawes's office.

Downstairs in the dining room, a shining table was set with fine china and silverware, the candelabra lit, as the room had no windows. On a sideboard were displayed a variety of breakfast foods, including kidneys, a delicacy I had not yet learned to appreciate. The tea was hot and strong. I filled my plate and cup and sat down at the table.

Athawes came in, dressed for the day in all but his coat.

"How did you sleep, Robert?"

"The room is most commodious. I thank you."

"Good, good. And what do you plan to do today?"

"I would really like to spend time among your books in the library."

"That's a splendid idea. Suppose you do that this evening? I would like very much for you to come with me to the Exchange this morning."

After eating, he went into his office, and I went to get my coat. Sam grinned as he helped me into it.

"Now you gone learn something worth knowing."

I strode with Athawes along the streets from his home among more purposeful walkers than I had seen elsewhere. The London that Athawes inhabited was more reserved, more serious than I had seen up until this time. We soon came to the Exchange, on the south side, which fronted on Cornhill Street. I immediately found myself surrounded by men dressed as gentlemen, standing in groups in a large courtyard, talking, arguing, and exchanging documents. The building itself was two stories, but each was quite tall. I was amazed at the pillared arches—the height of four men—and that was just the ground floor of the Exchange.

Athawes, unimpressed, I suppose because it was ordinary to him, led the way to an area where the gentlemen all seemed to be engaged with Virginia planters and tobacco.

"There are no official divisions here," Athawes told me, "but those conducting like businesses tend to assemble together. This area is called the Virginia Walk; that is, the place where the business has to do with Virginia trade."

We approached a well-dressed gentleman.

Athawes said, "I would like to introduce you to my young friend from Virginia, Robert Carter."

I bowed.

"He is the grandson of my good friend of the same name, who has unfortunately been gone for several years past."

"I do believe," the gentleman said, turning toward me, "I have heard of your grandfather. A rather large landholder, if I am not mistaken. A man of some parts."

We spent about two hours at the Exchange, where Athawes negotiated the sale of tobacco, talking of bills of lading, invoices, contracts, bills of exchange, insurance, weights and measures, all the while seeking the best prices he could obtain.

Engrossed in the conversation, I found I was developing an appreciation for what the Virginia merchants actually did for the money we paid them.

By the time we broke off from the Exchange and proceeded to a coffeehouse called Jonathan's, I was ravenous. Athawes claimed a table and ordered us ale and a meal, after which we sat for the rest of the afternoon, drinking coffee, continuing to conduct business with the various gentlemen who approached us. It was quite as if the table was Athawes's own office. I could look around and see that other gentlemen were doing the same thing.

Supper that evening included only the two of us and Mrs. Athawes, their children being grown. Afterward, Athawes and I retired to the library, where he offered me sherry. It was a great improvement over the grog and small beer to which I had become accustomed.

"What is it you are interested in reading, Robert?"

"Everything, sir." (I could not bring myself to address the older gentleman as Edward.) "But tell me first what I must read to help me understand trade."

Chuckling a little in the back of his throat, he said, "You planters are supposed to be above that sort of thing."

"That may be what they pretend, but I do not believe that it is really true. Successful planters must understand business. My grandfather did, or he would not have acquired the property he did."

Athawes smiled. "You are quite right, and he knew a great deal about methods of agriculture as well. He never tired of learning."

I took a sip of the fine sherry and thought about the conversation I had interjected myself into at Buttons some days earlier.

"Do you think it is possible to manage large plantations without slavery?"

"That I cannot answer, Son," he said, leaning forward, "In Virginia, your system of agriculture is so dependent on the institution, I don't see how it is possible to become disentangled from it. Maybe you will learn something here that will answer that question for you."

"I did not want to leave London without saying goodbye," Lawrence Washington said.

He had found me at the Exchange with Athawes one wintry day. His appearance was shocking, much paler and thinner than when we last parted.

We went together to Jonathan's, where we talked over a drink of claret. I noticed that he coughed more frequently and had begun carrying a handkerchief constantly in his hand. I thought I saw blood in it.

When we were settled, I asked, "Did you see a physician as you planned?"

"I did."

"And has he helped you?"

Washington sighed heavily. "He tried several treatments, but he now says that I need to go to a warmer climate—that the dampness and chill aggravate my condition."

"Will you go home, then?"

"He advises that I go to the Indies."

"What will you do?"

"I have connections on Barbados. I hope I can talk my brother George into going there with me."

"When will you leave?"

"I leave within the month to go to Virginia. Then I will go on to Barbados as quickly as I can arrange it."

"I wish you well. I hope I will hear of your cure."

Sam and I had each made our own adjustment to living in the home of Edward Athawes. The days I spent at business. In the evenings I read and discussed what I read with Athawes. I played on the harpsichord. Sometimes I even had an audience of family and guests. The harpsichord was my second greatest delight after learning business. I was quite content.

I didn't monitor Sam's activities closely, but I noticed that he got on well with Athawes's servants and that he occasionally went out into the city on his own. He was absorbing all that he could just as I was.

Gradually, Athawes began to have me check prices, talk to people on his behalf, draft documents, and generally run errands, so that I was able in some small way to return his kindness, but I knew this idyllic life could not go on forever.

14

1751: Williamsburg

A bewigged gentleman said, "I have just read a new English novel called *History of the Life and Adventures of Mr. Billingsley.*"

He was sitting with other gentlemen similarly wigged and dressed, at a long wooden table, drinking from a pewter mug. Seated at a table by myself, I could hear them, all strangers to me as far as I knew. Wearing my well-tailored English clothes, in soft colors that went with my dark hair and brown eyes, I was feeling altogether good about myself as I enjoyed fresh cornbread and she-crab soup. The soup was a treat I had not had since leaving Virginia two years earlier.

A small fire burned in the hearth of Christina Campbell's Tavern in Williamsburg where I had decided to stop before making my journey to Nomony Hall. The only thing that annoyed me was that Sam was, of necessity, at the kitchen door in back of the building where he was forced to go in order to be fed.

The gentleman continued. "The villain in the novel is a young American slaveholder that the author calls 'the richest heir in the colony.' He is described as uneducated and a man without manners."

I slowly lifted a spoonful of the rich, steaming soup to my mouth and thought how welcoming the cozy tavern seemed after the long sea journey.

"Oh, yes," said the speaker's companion. "I have heard of it. The villain is named Carter, is he not? And at the end, he is murdered by his own slaves."

At the sound of my own name, I almost spat out my soup.

"Do you think the author was thinking of young Robert Carter, old King Carter's grandson?" asked a third gentleman.

"Of course," said another. He waved his hand dismissively, the ruffle at his wrist just missing his plate of roast and gravy. "Who else could it be? And I have heard his own cousin, John Page, say that he is an illiterate."

My heart pounded, and my face felt hot, but the gentlemen took no notice of me.

"And vicious—a profligate," added the first gentleman.

"They say that he has been ruined by London."

A fifth gentleman looked thoughtful. "It seems to me that every family complains of a young offspring who goes to London and carouses and wastes the family's fortune."

"That is true," said the man with the roast beef, "but this one inherited a great fortune indeed and never did behave properly. His stepfather, John Lewis, declares that when he was a child, he was incorrigible."

"If it is so, 'tis a pity. Poor wretched young Carter."

I had lost my appetite. I forced myself to lay down my napkin without slamming it on the table. *Damn John Lewis. Damn John Page.* I left my soup to pay and walk out. *Is there to be no relief from my stepfather and his gossip?*

The Next Day

"Sam, I am more than ready to take over the management of Nomony Hall and my other properties, but now I am not sure I will be accepted here."

"What do that mean?"

"Based purely on gossip, five gentlemen at Christina Campbell's yesterday evening assumed I am the inspiration for a character named Carter in a book. That man was rich and went to England as I did. He wasted his money and his time there, as I did at first. But their main reason for deciding the character was me was that my own family calls me a profligate, uncontrollable, illiterate. My own cousin, John Page, says that—illiterate. It all sounds like John Lewis. Just the thought of the man makes bile rise in my mouth. He deprived me of my mother and my education, and now I fear he will deprive me of my good name forever."

"'Member Lawrence Washington, and Phillip Lee, they ain't heard nothing bad about you. You gone prove youself. You is who you is, and John Lewis can't change that."

I was on Corotoman, and Sam was on a bay I had ordered brought from Nomony, and we were jogging on our way to Nomony Hall. It was a humid day, and the warm spring air seemed stifling after we had been two years in England. All the material possessions that the two of us had acquired in England had been shipped directly to the port at Hobbs Hole to be conveyed by wagon to Nomony.

Moving along at a fair pace, I continued. "Edward Athawes treated me more like family than John Lewis ever did, and I was no kin to him at all. He welcomed me into his family and served as a mentor to me. He encouraged me to learn about his merchant business. He opened up his library to me, and we spent hours in that room talking and reading. I learned so much. He gave me the kind of advice usually passed from father to son."

"He a good man for sure."

It all brought to my mind the day I left the Athawes family. About to go on board the ship home, I suddenly realized that I would likely not see them again. The memory made me sad all over again. Suddenly I felt the need to embrace the man and kiss him on the cheek. Athawes must have felt it, too, for I believe I saw tears in his eyes on that day.

"I told him, when I left, there was no way I could ever express my thanks, and I was so right. You know what his answer was, Sam? He said, 'Just prosper. That will be thanks enough.'"

"And that what you needs to do—prosper."

After the long ride across the Middle Neck, over the ferry at Hobbs Hole, and up from the Rappahannock, we approached Nomony Hall. We made the ride straight through, so anxious was I to get there, though my body ached with exhaustion. I had not done this kind of riding in London. Nomony Hall was a welcome sight. In spite of all my time away, it was home.

The house sat like a great white monument on a high spot of ground at the top of its long lane of poplar trees coming from the east off the road. Though it was at a point where the Nomini forked, the river was not visible from the road at all. I hurried to get to the top of the hill, so that I could look out from the west side of the house, where I could see the Nomini again. There it all was: the house itself, the dependencies at its corners, the fields, the woods, some fifteen hundred acres surrounding it—home.

Several of the Negroes came out into the late evening twilight to greet us as we rode up from the road. I was touched by their welcome.

"They knows you in charge now, Master," Sam said. "They wants to know how you gone run this place."

The house inside was just as I remembered—some six thousand square feet, three stories, with four dependencies—but it was the land itself and the Negroes and the crops that would sustain all that was now mine. It was here that I would prove myself as a successful planter. I would show people that I was not the person John Lewis said I was.

———

The first day after my return to Nomony Hall, I rode out into a chilly March day on Corotoman, pulling up the collar of my great coat around my ears. Corotoman's hooves sloshed through icy water, and he picked his way through the woods.

I had reviewed the extent of my estate on paper on the first occasion available. It included about nine thousand acres in the lower Northern Neck and three thousand acres in Prince William County that I had inherited directly from Grandfather. From my father, I inherited the fifteen hundred acres with Nomony Hall, which was only part of the sixty-five thousand acres he had owned in the upper Northern Neck. Each of my plantations had its own stock and its own Negroes. Most had at least an overseer's house. Today began my inspection of that property.

Out in the fields, I sought out the overseer, Jack England, who had taken over from Simon Sallard in my absence. I knew him only through letters we had exchanged while I was in England.

"Welcome home, Mr. Carter."

I had to get used to a mature man calling me, at twenty-three, Mister. "I am mighty glad to be here, Jack."

Watching the hands planting the hills of tobacco in the field, I took particular notice whether manure was being added to each hill as I had instructed. The Negroes worked slowly and rhythmically, the way I remembered their doing during my childhood. Uncle Landon always claimed Negroes worked slowly because they were lazy, but I reasoned that they worked at the only pace that they could maintain in order to endure the long hours at a time in all kinds of weather.

I left them, guiding Corotoman across the fields to the Westmoreland/Richmond County road and across it to the path that led from the poplar lane on one side to the field on the other. The rutted path wound its way to the edge of the woods where the quarters formed a small village. There were the brick cabins with their rough board floors. They each contained two rooms downstairs and a loft above, which was reached by a ladder. The largest room downstairs had a fireplace at the end, which was used for both cooking and heat. Grandfather had prided himself that his Negroes had elevated bed frames, so that the sleeping pallets did not lie directly on the floor. He had followed that pattern when he built the quarters at Nomony Hall.

Since most of the workers were in the fields, few were left in the quarters—only small children and those left to mind them. Wide curious eyes peered out from behind doors and skirts at me, riding between the cabins on my fine chestnut stallion. *What were they thinking about their new master?* The curious children made me smile. I dismounted and walked about to look at the cabins.

The yards around them were swept clean of debris and grass; at least, that was the intention. The moist, fertile soil of the Tidewater did not allow ground to remain bare for long. There were few chickens in the yards and little evidence of patches for vegetable gardens behind the cabins. I resolved to change that. What I wanted to see were happy, well-fed Negroes, who had some control over their own lives. They would be more content that way.

I would not revolutionize everything at my plantations, but some changes did need to be made.

As my tours of the various plantations continued, I had long conversations with each of the overseers, listening to them and letting them know what I expected from them. In England, discussing the matters with Athawes, I had given the running of my plantations a lot of thought. I knew the overseers were not accustomed to some of the rules I would impose. After all, they had been virtually on their own for years. Their opinions mattered to me because of their experience, but some things I would insist on. It would be a gradual process. For instance, I decided that it was important not to move Negroes from one plantation to another, thus avoiding dividing families unless absolutely necessary. Respecting family connections would create more stability.

Something in my manner must have emboldened my slaves because while I was at the plantation called Gemini, a middle-aged Negro named Willoughby approached slowly, holding his battered hat in both hands before him, his head respectfully bowed.

The gesture made me reflect that I was the owner of this humble man and all the others I saw around me. It was a strange feeling after being in England for two years where I was in charge of nothing really.

"Master, Overseer John Simpson, yonder, come into my house and take a pound of yarn that belong to me."

"How did he come to be in your house?"

"He say he looking for some tobacco that gone missing."

"Did he find the tobacco there?"

"No, sir," he said, sounding hurt. "I never took nay tobacco."

I knew this would be only the first of many disputes to settle and was keenly aware that my handling of it would set a precedent. *What would Grandfather have done? What would Uncle Landon do?* I was setting the pattern for order among the Negroes from that day on. Finally, I took aside John Simpson, telling Willoughby I would get back to him.

Simpson, having heard my conversation with Willoughby, was immediately on the defensive.

"Is it true the tobacco was not in Willoughby's house?"

The overseer answered slowly, in a voice so low I could hardly hear him.

"Yessir," he finally said.

"And did you take a pound of yarn from his house?"

"I took it because it was good quality. I figured it musta been stolen."

"Had you been told of missing yarn?"

"No, but I thought it mighta been stolen anyway."

"What made you think that?"

"You know how these niggers are. It just looked too good to be there."

"Fetch the yarn back to him, today. I'm sure I will hear from Willoughby if you don't."

Simpson made a sort of grunting noise, plunked his hat on his head with some force, and turned to go, but he did not say anything more.

I returned to Nomony Hall only to hear another complaint.

"Overseer Jack England whupped me for nothing."

"What happened."

"I be in my cabin, minding my own business when he come along, pounding on my door and hollering to let him in or he gone knock it down. I lets him in, and he say, 'Come outside.' So I goes outside, and he commence to whup me, every single blow so hard it lift me off my feet. When he done, my back all cut and bleeding."

"Why did he come to your cabin?"

"I don' know."

"Well, what did he say?"

"He accuse me of beating my girl."

"Did you beat her?"

"I smack her with a willa branch like I always do when she misbehave."

"What did she do to cause you to do that?"

"She slip outta the house at night when she s'posed to be sleeping."

"Let me talk to your daughter."

She was a comely girl of thirteen or so, a fact which caused me to speculate on what might have caused England to take her side against her father, but I did not remark on it.

"Did your father beat you?"

She lowered her eyes and looked sidelong at her father.

"Tell the truth, girl," he said.

"Yessir, Master, he whup me with a willa stick."

"Did he injure you?"

"It hurt mighty bad … and I had red marks on my behind."

"What did you do that caused him to beat you?"

"Tell Master what you done, child."

She looked even more sheepish. "I snuck out at night."

I then went back and talked to England out of the hearing of father and daughter. "Jack, I do not know what you have been accustomed to do in the past, but a father has a right to discipline his own daughter, even if he is a slave. What happens in a Negro's home is his own business."

England looked inclined to argue but then thought better of it.

Unsmiling, he said, "Yes, Mr. Carter," made a curt bow and walked away.

I heaved a sigh. It was not going to be easy, but at least I had made a start.

15

1752: Nomony Hall

The tall oaks and sweet-smelling pines made the air cool as I traveled the long lane from the main road, which had brought me from Richmond Courthouse, through the woods to Sabine Hall, the home of my uncle, Landon Carter. At the clearing, the long house was visible before me. It seemed a long time since I had last seen this house.

Uncle Landon welcomed me with his usual loud heartiness. He was eighteen years older than I, and he had put on weight since I had lived with him. He still exuded absolute confidence and warmth. Landon Carter was the undoubted king of his world.

"Robert," he expostulated, "so much has happened I want to talk to you about! Come, have a glass of good Madeira, and I will tell you all."

Uncle Landon had been elected to the House of Burgesses from Richmond County in 1752 at the age of forty-two.

"It was my fourth attempt at election, Robert. Can you believe it?"

"Why do you think you were not elected earlier, Uncle?"

"I do not, and will not, kiss the ass of the electorate. You ran yourself this year, did you not?"

"I did."

It had hurt me more deeply than I was willing to admit. I did not know whether John Lewis's gossip had had anything to do with it.

"Don't worry, Robert. You are young and unmarried. Your time will come."

Uncle Landon let me know that the responsibility of being a burgess weighed heavily on him.

"Our country," he said, "is being ill-used by the mother country."

He was talking as he led me into the main hall of the house. As we sat down in the wide hall that extended from the river front to the road front, he directed his manservant, Nassau, to bring us wine and fruit.

"Welcome, Master Robert. It be good to see you again," Nassau exclaimed when he saw me. "You grown up to be a fine man."

"Thank you, Nassau. It's good to be home."

Landon ignored this side conversation and continued his own. "When you do get elected, you must watch out for our rights. London merchants have always had the advantage in their negotiations with us. They control all our trade and are not fair in what they pay us for tobacco and what they make us pay for the goods we get through them. We would be better off if we could trade freely with the countries of Europe ourselves."

I didn't disagree with him, but it seemed to me that the mother country had a right to impose some restrictions on us in exchange for the protection she provided.

"Do you believe that London interferes with our individual rights as Englishmen, Uncle?"

"No, I will not say that." He took a substantial drink of his Madeira. "Tell me, Robert, how do you find Nomony Hall after all this time, and how do you get along?"

"I am learning as I go. I try to balance the need to get the work done with fair treatment of my employees and the Negroes."

Landon laughed lightly. "Well, you're young yet. You will soon learn not to waste time worrying about the feelings of Negroes. You need to worry more about the feelings of your landed neighbors. They are the ones who count."

I disagreed. Although I yearned for respect and strove to get along with my neighbors, it seemed to me that my relationship with them had little to do with the success of my plantations, but I did not say so.

───✦───

Riding Corotoman on my first court date over the slippery, muddy roads of April, I was about to fulfill one of my grandfather's predictions. Like many sons of leading families in Virginia, though I had not been elected to the House of Burgesses, I had been appointed one of the justices of the county's court.

After more than a year, I was used to taking charge on my own property and dealing with businessmen concerning matters on my own plantation. My bad reputation in Williamsburg seemed to have no effect on the people of Westmoreland County and its environs. Today, it would be my job to pass judgment on those before the court. I spent the time as I rode thinking about how I would approach this new task. In preparation, I had ordered law books and spent the weeks prior reading them to refresh my memory.

The square brick courthouse sat in the middle of the small village of Westmoreland. Off to the side and behind it stood the two-story jail, also brick, with its barred windows, and in front of that, a stocks. In spite of the dampness of the weather, people were stirring restlessly in and around the yard that surrounded the courthouse waiting for the session to begin.

Inside, the courthouse consisted of one large room and one small side room where attorneys, clients, and witnesses could talk with a modicum of privacy. The main entrance was at the rear of the building, and upon entering, I could look up between the rows of wooden pews on either side of the center aisle, directly at a large stove meant to provide heat. Behind that was a space where litigants could stand, and in front of them a rail. Behind the rail was a desk for the clerk to record the outcome of the various hearings, and behind the desk an elevated platform where the justices sat. Three justices together decided the cases brought before them.

I quickly ascended to the bench, as the raised platform was called, bowing to the other two justices, one of whom was Phil Lee, also back from England. His father had died since I had seen him, and he was now the master of Stratford Hall.

This morning, one issue was the supposed assault and battery by a white middling farmer named Sisson, upon his neighbor. Sisson stood before the rail clothed in his plain open-necked work shirt and rough linen pants, his hat held respectfully in his hand at his side.

The aggrieved neighbor, the plaintiff, dressed in similar fashion, shifted restlessly from foot to foot as he testified. His story was that Sisson had struck him for no reason. However, when we questioned Sisson, he claimed that the neighbor had first insulted his wife.

"What exactly did he say?" I asked Sisson.

"He said that she was a ... (he bowed his head) a cow."

"I should be mightily offended if someone called my wife a cow," I remarked. Turning to the neighbor, I asked, "How would you feel if Mr. Sisson called your wife a cow?"

The neighbor looked at his feet a minute. "I don't have nay wife, your honor."

"How about your sister then?"

"I don't have nay one of those neither, sir."

The other justices each hid a smile behind their hands.

"What about your mother, then? I suppose you do have one of those?"

"Yessir."

"Well, what about it then?"

"I wouldn't like it."

"Might you strike him?"

"Could be."

"Were you injured?"

He paused a long time. "No, sir."

I turned to Mr. Sisson, still waiting patiently with his hat at his side. "The law says that no words, however grievous, suffice to justify laying hands on someone else. Do you understand?"

"Yessir."

"However," I paused and looked at the other justices for confirmation. They each nodded. "This time we find you not guilty, but do not come before this court again for the same offense."

He happily plunked his hat upon his head and turned to go.

We spent the day trying other misdemeanors and minor civil disputes. The felonies and more serious civil matters were tried by the General Court in Williamsburg. It struck me that the justices had a heavy bearing on the everyday lives of the county people. The thought humbled me. It was dawning on me that the Virginia gentry, who were those exclusively named as justices, members of the vestry of the established church, leaders of local militia, and members of the House of Burgesses and the Governor's Council, had absolute control of their whole world. It was not so in England where the civil and criminal powers were divided among many different entities.

16

1753: Annapolis, Maryland

Everywhere Sam and I passed, I noticed the green of late spring. There was the welcome sound of the birds, tobacco and corn poking their heads above the ground in the fields, the winter wheat having come up earlier, making their fields a carpet of green. The fresh smell of the season was in the air, and all was well with the world. It was May, and I was feeling my usual spring fever. The purpose of our trip to Annapolis was to arrange to have a small ship built to carry my own goods.

We took the ferry across the Potomac and continued our trip overland toward Annapolis. We went directly to the tavern called Middleton's down at the City Dock.

Middleton's was a long two-and-a-half-story tavern that served mostly the bounty of river and bay and whatever a man might want to drink. I arranged for us to spend the night. As I sat before the stone fireplace, I looked around. The place was full even late in the evening. I had a plate of crabcakes and then ordered another to take to Sam.

I rose early the next day to look around. My first stop was the City Dock, of course, which surrounded a long, narrow harbor. I was fascinated to watch the loading and unloading of goods from all over the world, as I enjoyed a mild breeze coming off the water. Like Liverpool, Annapolis's economy had benefited from the traffic in slaves, but on this day, I was grateful to see no sign of them.

After breakfast, I met with the shipbuilder at his yard. I found him surrounded by ships in various stages of completion, a large skeleton of a hull dominating. The workers, black and white, worked at huge steamers bending large planks for hulls. The wood appeared to be mostly oak, and more sat in piles ready to be used. The place smelled of the heated wood, as well as pitch and a kind of hemp fiber called oakum. We agreed to meet the next morning to talk about the schooner I proposed to have built. I would like to have stayed all day, but there was so much more to see in the city.

Annapolis was much smaller—and cleaner—than London, but it was cultivated and urbane for a Colonial city, and it had a fine harbor. Its cobblestone streets radiated out like spokes from two wheels. The center of one wheel was the Maryland Statehouse, sadly neglected in spite of its importance to the colony. The center of the other was St. Anne's Church, which I learned the locals called "the barn," probably because the main body was large and rectangular, and it had a square bell tower. There were fine houses and prosperous-looking shops.

In the afternoon, my attention was drawn to the local horse races. The horses looked fine, and, although I had significantly cut back my gambling from the time I went to live with Edward Athawes, I reckoned that a good race would be enjoyable.

I was standing around the track, admiring the horses and wondering whether to make a wager when a gentleman of sixty or so approached me. He was about my height, a little on the plump side, dressed in a fine frock coat of wool and silk fabric. Very confident in his bearing, he was obviously a man of some consequence.

I offered my hand. "Robert Carter of Nomony Hall in Virginia, at your service, sir."

"Benjamin Tasker of Annapolis."

"I have heard of you. Present acting governor of Maryland, are you not?"

"I am."

"I cannot decide, sir, whether to make a wager or simply watch."

"And I cannot decide how to wager," Tasker said. "The bay is reputed to be the fastest, but I like the looks of the chestnut."

"May I suggest that you wager on the chestnut, and I will wager on the bay and one of us is certain to win."

Tasker laughed. "Done."

We fell into conversation, soon finding out that we each had our own racehorses, I one and Tasker many.

After several races, Tasker said, "Shall we go across to Middleton's for something to drink?"

We continued talking.

"I agree with you that the growing of tobacco is not the best use of the land," Tasker said as we waited for our ale. "I cultivate several thousand acres in Maryland, and I am looking for new crops that are profitable and that will make the use of the same land sustainable over time. I do not like being totally dependent on tobacco. Manufacturing businesses also interest me."

"Several gentlemen in our Northern Neck, including my uncle Landon Carter, are invested in a venture called the Ohio Company. They hope to expand into western lands. I'm also acquainted with men who have interests in mining and the smelting of iron."

"As a matter of fact," Tasker said, "I happen to own a one-fifth interest in a company called the Baltimore Iron Works." Tasker paused to light his pipe. "I spent several years in the lower house of the Maryland legislature, and I am, as you know, presently a member of the upper house, the Council. As president of the Council, I serve as the provincial governor of Maryland. My position in government affords me many opportunities to meet people and learn of profitable investments."

The Iron Works particularly intrigued me. I listened closely to all that Tasker had to say.

He took a puff on his pipe and said, "I admire your common sense and your willingness to try new things. I believe your ideas about the humane treatment of slaves is quite wise. It is not only the Christian thing to do, it is more productive of good work from them."

We talked until suppertime.

"Well, Robert," said Tasker, standing and putting his hand on my back, "you must come home with me to supper and then stay the night."

I went to fetch Sam.

The home of Benjamin Tasker was a large, commodious house, on a sprawling piece of land on Market Street. Behind the house lay Spa Creek.

Tasker showed me around.

"I believe this house is older than many of the downtown houses, I've seen, is it not?" I asked him.

"The house was built by my father-in-law, William Bladen, a founder of this city. When my wife, Anne and I married, we came to live here. Then, when her father died, we bought the house from the estate."

Like the outside, the inside of the Tasker residence was fine without being ostentatious. The furniture was English of solid quality as were the damask drapes and chair coverings.

A Negro showed me to a room where I could refresh myself before the meal. Sam was sent to stay with Tasker's house slaves.

I completed my toilet and started downstairs. Turning in to the dining room, I was pleasantly taken aback by what I saw.

A young woman was standing near the table, half-turned away from me. She was slender, with dark, shiny hair falling gracefully from under a white cap. Her flowered satin gown flowed out from her neck in a matching sack. Even from this angle, I could see that the skirt of her gown belled out from a slender waist. When she finally turned to face me, I could see that her bodice revealed a lovely creamy neck and throat, but what struck me most were her gray eyes.

As I approached her, her father came into the room. Smiling, he said, "Robert Carter, may I present my daughter Fanny."

I bowed.

"Fanny," Tasker said, "this is my new friend, Robert Carter from Virginia."

I bent to kiss the soft delicate hand she offered. Lifting my head slightly, I was able to look into those eyes that so caught my attention.

She was fifteen as I learned, but there was something deeper in her eyes than in women much older. She did not look away shyly, as young women of her age were wont to do, but just smiled up at me with perfect composure and perhaps a touch of irony. A sudden warmth overtook me.

At the supper table, the talk was of books. Fanny talked not only about poetry and the new novels as many young ladies did, but of ancient Greek and Roman philosophy. She was also familiar with the writers of the Enlightenment, including Montesquieu.

"Montesquieu is right about slavery, of course," she said. "There is no justification for it. We must find a way to change our system of planting."

Her mother shook her head slightly and looked daggers at Fanny. Fanny pretended not to notice her mother. The young lady had opinions and did not mind expressing them. She was much like Hannah Lee, whom I knew growing up, except that she was beautiful, too.

"How do you propose that we do that, Miss Tasker?" I asked.

"I do not know exactly, but there must be a way to convert forced laborers to paid ones, gradually, over time."

Her mother, Anne, finally intervened. She was clearly trying to steer her errant daughter away from what she considered her unladylike and controversial expressions of opinion. Fanny's father, on the other hand, appeared to be amused.

"Fanny," said Mrs. Tasker, "You are going to bore Mr. Carter with all your talk of philosophy."

"Not at all," I said. "I find Miss Tasker's conversation quite fascinating."

I had met several well-read and attractive young ladies in London but none so clever as this one.

After supper, Fanny asked if I would like to see the family library.

"Very much indeed, Miss Tasker."

"Call me Fanny."

I could sense Tasker smiling after us as we walked toward the library, with Fanny's arm on mine. Her touch excited me.

"I have just read a novel called *Moll Flanders,*" Fanny was saying as we entered the library, looking back to be sure that her mother did not hear her.

"It is about the adventures of a rather exceptional woman. Although the novel, and the woman, are English, part of it takes place in your own Westmoreland County, in Virginia."

"That is remarkable, but, if you do not mind my impertinence in saying so, I am surprised that a woman of your intelligence would bother with novels."

A slight look of defiance came into her eyes.

"Novels are all the rage in London, as I am certain you know. And this one is popular because it is considered quite naughty. I only have it because my cousin there keeps up with all the fashions. Mother would be appalled if she knew I had it. However, I must say that it is thought-provoking as well as amusing. The author, Daniel DeFoe, writes deftly and humorously, but he speaks of the very real uncertainty of life for a woman in English society without a man's protection. DeFoe has much to say about society."

Yes, I am familiar with Defoe's reputation. Tell me, do you believe a woman such as Moll Flanders would fare better in the Colonies?"

"As a matter of fact, Moll, in the book, does fare somewhat better in the Colonies, although I observe that life is no easy matter for an uneducated woman without male family connections even here, especially a woman of the lower classes. Neither women nor Negroes are treated fairly in this world."

What a remarkable woman was this Fanny Tasker.

The second day of my visit to Annapolis, I was to travel with Tasker to see the Iron Works. Much to my surprise and pleasure, Fanny showed up in a forest green riding habit to accompany us. The habit had a bodice much like any gown, but what appeared at first to be an ordinary skirt was actually slit and sewn into two legs. It was intoxicating to touch her boot, to help her mount onto the horse's back, ready to ride astride. She turned out to be a fine horsewoman. I was struck again with how much this lady was different from any other I had ever met.

The Baltimore Iron Works were a distance outside the city, in the direction of Baltimore, on land which extended from Gwynne's Falls to a little village called Johnnycake. The overland ride took a day, and on the first night we made a stopover at a country ordinary.

The Iron Works was as intriguing as I had imagined it would be. The works actually consisted of two furnaces and three forges, plus a bellows house and a casting house, all set about in a large field. The furnaces were built from local stone and lined inside with another type of stone that Tasker said was imported from England. I walked closer and closer to one of the furnaces, trying to gain a better look inside, until finally the intense heat drove me back. The iron ore was melted inside and then poured into molds to produce bars of iron called pigs. Robert Coxall, who managed the Works for the partners, explained that the pigs were taken elsewhere to make such things as skillets and pots.

Tasker said, "I formed the Iron Works in 1731, along with four other men. I believe it was the earliest of its kind in Maryland. The Works are manned by ninety-four men, both black and white, about half free and half slave."

"And they all work together?"

"Yes, yes, no problems. The foreman, of course, is a white man."

"Where are the pots and skillets made?"

"We ship the pigs to factories in Baltimore and Philadelphia."

"Why are the final products not made here?"

"There are no artisans available out here in the country."

Almost immediately I began thinking what it would take to bring artisans to the site. Slaves could be trained to do the work. I was distracted from my thoughts by Fanny, who had brought a picnic lunch from the inn where we stayed the night before.

"The Iron Works is a good business," she said. "As the Colonies grow, people will need more and more iron. If we have the ability to make our own products, we will not be dependent on the slow and expensive shipping of those products from England. We will eliminate the middle men who take their share of the price for bringing them here."

How observant she is. My, but she is beautiful this day! I was suddenly quite hungry.

When we returned to Annapolis, I went again to Middleton's, where I made final arrangements with the shipbuilder for a small ship, but I did not leave the city without asking permission to call on Fanny in the future.

As we began our ride back, I said to Sam, "You always know what is going on."

"Yessir, you prob'ly right about that."

"Here is what I want to know, then. What do the Tasker servants think of Miss Fanny?"

"She a fine lady."

"Is she kind, to the slaves?"

"Oh, yes, sir. They say she expect things to be just right, but she treat people good."

Sam fell silent, but I could see him grinning at me, showing the slight gap between his two front teeth.

"You think I admire her, don't you?"

"Yes, Master, I can see that you does. You been smiling all over youself ever since you met her."

"Do you think she admires me, too?"

"Yes, Master, I tell you what I thinks. I thinks the lady pretty, smart, and rich. I thinks she make a good wife for a young gentleman with lots of land and a pretty house in Virginia."

"Do you suppose that I should court the lady, then?"

I watched Sam's smile grow wider. "Yessir."

17

1754: Nomony Hall

I had never awaited the birth of a child before, and I was finding it very disconcerting. I was pacing in front of the fireplace in my office, wearing my shirt, and britches, and a warm banyan over all. Sarah Henry, the cook, was in her eighteenth hour of labor, in the cook's quarters above the kitchen on a frigid January day. I was fond of Sarah, and this child would be the first born on the plantation since my return.

Mama Gumby was acting as midwife. She and her husband Thomas, whom we all called Dada, lived in a little cabin near the kitchen garden. Their age and long service, beginning long before my birth at Grandfather's, earned them special status.

Mama came to report, sweat drenching her wrinkled forehead. "Sarah mighty tired, Master. Joseph need to come and stay close by. The fire burning hot, and Sarah been moved close, but she real cold. I's afraid we have to pull the baby out. Sarah just can't push no more."

Mama went back to the kitchen, leaving me even more agitated and uncertain. I sent Joseph, the baby's father, after her.

At last, though, Mama came to me, smiling, carrying a healthy boy, wrapped in a blanket.

"Sarah sleeping, Master. She take one look at that child, smile, and go right off to sleep. She need rest bad, but she gone be all right."

I looked down at the bundle Mama held. I was relieved and grateful that Sarah and the child were well. The baby was incredibly wrinkled and red but stretched his arms and legs. He appeared to be light-skinned like his mother, though it was difficult to tell.

"What you gone call him?" Mama asked.

"That is for his parents to do. I will not be naming other people's children."

His parents named him Tom Henry.

After Mama took him back to his mother, I could not get him off my mind.

Annapolis, April 1754

I walked the quiet morning streets with Sam up the hill from Middleton's to St. Anne's Church. I was dressed in new satin britches, waistcoat, and coat, a carefully tailored wig and shining shoes, much more dandified than my usual attire. In the vestibule of the church, the marriage party assembled while Sam went upstairs into the gallery to watch. I gazed at Fanny in a gown of pale pink silk, brocaded with flowers in a slightly darker color. Truthfully, however, what drew the greater part of my attention was the triangular opening of her bodice, which revealed her long, lovely neck.

I was glad to be marrying for love, although, truthfully, the marriage could not have been better for both our families.

We lined up: first the rector of St. Anne's; then Fanny and me; followed by Benjamin and Anne Tasker; then my mother,

Priscilla; and finally the young bridesmaids dressed in their finery. John Lewis did not deign to come, nor did I miss him.

After the vows were made, we all went to the Tasker home. A lavish feast awaited us. Candles and flowers were everywhere. Tables were set with quantities of food, and wine flowed freely. Though I wished nothing more than to be alone with my long-awaited bride, that was not to be for several hours. We were toasted, teased, and celebrated. Everyone ate, drank, played cards, and danced. Finally, at suppertime, we were allowed to leave.

We set out as quickly as we could decently get away for Nomony Hall, leaving the others to continue the celebration without us. We traveled on my boat loaded with Fanny' belongings.

Fanny looked out from the rail as the boat made its way down the Bay, her skirt moving with the wind, turning her head this way and that. "What a great expanse of water, Robert. Are you in the habit of traveling often by boat?"

She continued to watch, fascinated, until dark.

We continued to sail overnight and arrived in the morning. As I watched her, back at the rail, my mind drifted to what was to come. *How would Nomony Hall appear to her, as it had changed in my three years at home?* That was not the first thing on my mind, but it ran a close second.

The plantation that would be home to Fanny Ann Tasker Carter now had on it oxen, horned cattle, hogs, sheep, and poultry. There were horses of all kinds, both for riding and for working. My most-prized possession was a racing mare who was the offspring of Yorrick, a famous thoroughbred stallion owned by John Tayloe and a mare owned by the Prince of Wales.

The fields were now planted not only in tobacco, but barley, wheat and corn, as well as flax and hemp, all now spiking their sharp green spears above the ground. At my instruction, care had been taken to enrich the ground with manure before plowing. In the quarters—and this would perhaps impress my bride the most—the people now had chickens and were preparing their gardens for their own use.

When we reached the Potomac, it was choppy, stirred by a stiff breeze. At King Copsico Point, we turned into the calmer Nomini and traveled southeast. By the time we reached the wharf at Nomony Hall, the water was still and green, the river narrow, crowded on both sides by heavy growth.

Fanny insisted on walking from the wharf to the great house. It was cold for early April, but she was undeterred. Smiling at her as she laughed and wrapped her cloak more tightly about her, I walked briskly to keep up with her. She took long strides that carried her easily up the incline, away from the river. She looked back and forth as the road took her past the woods, now blooming with redbud and dogwood, along a street of sorts, past the storehouse, the dairy, and, finally, the kitchen house. I enjoyed watching her taking it all in, this city girl I had married. Sam followed us up the hill, and I looked back at him. He was grinning happily. The house servants and others not in the fields lined the walk from the kitchen to the house.

Fanny saw Sarah Henry holding her young baby.

She stopped and looked into the baby's face. "What a fine child," I heard her say. "What is his name?"

"Tom Henry, Mistress."

"May I hold him?"

As Sarah handed over the five-month-old, I could not help smiling. "Sarah, this is your new mistress, my beautiful wife, Fanny. You will be taking direction from her from now on."

Sarah curtsied, keeping her eyes respectfully lowered. "Pleased to meet you, Mistress."

Fanny gave the baby gently back into his mother's arms. She smiled and looked Sarah in the eyes, which made Sarah nervous. "I am most pleased to be here, Sarah."

The other servants were introduced and bowed or curtsied each in turn. Fanny looked into the face of each of them and called them by name. The slaves smiled shyly at her, and I could tell that they were favorably impressed by her attention.

When we arrived at the long pillared west porch, I lifted Fanny into my arms, kissed her in spite of the watching servants, and carried her into the house.

We entered the first-floor hall on the river side. Fanny turned into the ballroom. She gazed around the room, thirty feet long, with its seventeen-foot ceilings and broad board floors. It had no rug. Suddenly, I realized how empty it looked, how neglected. The only piece of furniture I had purchased for it was a harpsichord, which I loved to play. I had neglected the inside of the house. *What had I been thinking?*

We went into the large dining room. There was also the second, smaller dining room intended for children. With new eyes, I saw that the rooms contained the barest essential furniture and that the drapes were old and worn.

"Although there has been a housekeeper here, Fanny, there has been no woman really in charge of this household since my mother married John Lewis nineteen years ago. It needs a mistress's touch."

"Yes, it does. And I am most delighted to be that mistress."

My heart beat fast as Fanny entered the office/library. The room had a worn carpet, a sofa, chairs, and a large desk in need of polishing, but it wasn't the appearance that concerned me now. I was afraid the library would be a disappointment to her. Fanny, however, spent several minutes looking at the titles of the books. She noticed that I had a list of them by shelf and number, several hundred of them.

"You have an eclectic taste in subject matter, Robert. Have you read all of these?"

"I am not quite through reading all of them ... but I am working on it daily."

Fanny just laughed, the soft playful laugh I loved. Then I realized she was teasing me.

After looking for a time at the books, we went upstairs while the Negroes stayed at a respectful distance below. I had told Sam to see that we were alone when we went upstairs. I had also decided that it was time Sam had his own rooms on the third floor, complete with bed, chest, rugs, and fireplaces, because he would no longer sleep in my room.

At the top of the stairs, Fanny and I arrived in the central hall. On one side of the hall was a very large bedroom, appropriate for a dormitory. The furnishings were plain.

"We seldom used this room when I was a child. I suppose my parents planned on a larger family than they had."

Beside that room on the same side of the hall was a small bedroom.

"This is where my sister, Betty, slept."

Fanny dutifully allowed herself to be shown into each room in turn, but I began to sense a certain impatience in her manner. I was nervous about just how to handle what was to come after we finished our tour, so I continued. On the other side of the hall was a third bedroom comfortably large. A four-poster bed dominated the room in spite of its size. A tall dresser stood along one wall, and easy chairs were set on either side of the fireplace. The furniture here was of the best quality, bought by my parents in preparation for their own marriage.

"This room was used by guests during my childhood here."

"Where did you sleep, Robert?"

"I left this house when I was six years old. I still slept in my parents' room, in a small bed near their bed. I had just turned four when my father died. Here is the room."

The room I saved for Fanny to see last was the master bedroom. It had a fine four-poster bed made of walnut, the bed where my father died. A cradle still sat in the corner of the room, and a small child's bed was near the larger one.

Fanny went over to touch the white, lacy coverlet on the bed and bent to smell it. I held my breath.

"It smells like sunshine, nice and fresh," she said. "I will be sure to tell the servant who made this bed."

I dared to breathe again.

There were two upholstered wing chairs, placed on either side of the fireplace here as in the guest room, a large chest for folded clothes, and two tall dressers. Each of the second-floor rooms had a fireplace, and the one in the master bedroom was now filled with a glowing fire. Fanny went to it and warmed her hands briefly.

She sat down on one of the chairs by the fire. She appeared to be entirely composed, immediately slipping off her shoes and cap, looking up at me with a smile.

Smiling back, I removed my wig, coat, waistcoat, and shoes. My hands were shaking slightly.

Fanny took out hair pins and let her long dark hair fall onto her shoulders.

She was beautiful. I went to her, held out a hand for her to stand, and kissed her tenderly on the lips.

She returned the kiss sweetly.

We had managed quick embraces and kisses here and there during the times I had visited in Annapolis during our courtship. Her father had actually given us remarkable leeway.

She was so young. I was determined not to rush her, although my pulse was racing, and I could feel an insistent stiffening in my britches.

I kissed her again, this time holding her in a close and enticing embrace, feeling the softness of her breasts above her stays. It was maddening.

She stepped a little away from me, and I was afraid I had done something wrong, but she merely unfastened her skirt and let it fall to the floor. She smiled at me again. Next, she opened her bodice and let it fall, then her petticoat. She stood before me in her stays and shift.

I stood in britches, stockings, and shirt, transfixed.

Fanny unfastened the stays and let them fall away. I didn't think women, even married women, usually behaved this way. Moreover, I was certain this was not something her mother taught her. Maybe it was all those novels she read, such as *Moll Flanders*.

She paused and looked at me. "Will you undress, then, Husband?" she asked, a little smile teasing at the corners of her mouth and her eyes sparkling.

I flushed at this. I was not yet used to Fanny's loving teasing. Nevertheless, I fumbled as quickly as I could, unlacing britches, pulling off stockings, unbuttoning shirt. Soon, all were in a pile on the floor.

There I stood, in my drawers, horribly conscious of the bulge.

I felt Fanny's eyes move over me slowly, and then she looked me directly in the eyes as she calmly took off her shift and stood before me. I thought perhaps I should look away, but I could not take my eyes from her. Her breasts were round and firm, the nipples dark, her complexion creamy and fine. I ached for her. I could bear it no longer. I took off my drawers at last and finally stood as exposed as she.

I took her hand in mine, and we slipped into bed together, naked. Fanny was trembling now. As I pulled her close to me, I could smell the lavender scent she wore. Her hair fell against my shoulder. I felt the soft pressure of her bare breasts against my chest.

By this time raging with desire, I kissed her again, slowly, deeply. She responded with a soft moan in the back of her throat, arched her back, and pressed herself tightly against me. The passion of her response surprised me.

I kissed her breasts, her neck, and her ears. I lost all sense of time and place. Hungrily, we explored each other. Then feeling a joy I had never known, I came up between her legs and slowly but insistently penetrated her. She drew in her breath momentarily, but then thrust her body against mine. We began to move in rhythm with each other, slowly, then more quickly, more intensely, over and over, until we lay sated and exhausted beside each other on the big bed.

Our night clothes lay untouched, folded neatly over a chair.

———

Sweeping from room to room at Nomony Hall, with a slave to do her measuring, Fanny was exclaiming, "Robert, I am so excited!"

She came to me and kissed me. Then she returned to making notes for the size and design and color of wallpaper. Her searches of London catalogues led to lists of rugs and drapes, furniture, china and silver. She ordered mundane kitchen needs not made on the plantation and a quantity of tea and sugar, precious commodities.

It was a pleasure for me to indulge her. Her dowry was ample, including, among other things, a one-fifth interest in the Baltimore Iron Works, and I let her order whatever she wanted. For my part, I ordered books, as always, music, some material for the slaves' clothing, and a few tools. The large order was sent to Edward Athawes in London.

Fanny went about bringing the household into an order that suited her. Though she was young, she managed the house servants with a mature balance of firmness and gentleness. I was pleased to see that she gave respect to each person according to his or her abilities. She quickly acknowledged good work and duly noted less desirable work, but Fanny was slower to punish than to explain. What she did not tolerate was deliberate insubordination. She did not carry a strap like Aunt Mary, Uncle Charles's wife, had done, and, it really wasn't necessary. The servants seem to enjoy pleasing her.

Next, Fanny turned her attention to the kitchen garden, and then the flower gardens, something I had neglected almost entirely. Soon daylilies and China yellow roses appeared in open areas and lilac bushes and quince among the trees. The boxwoods were trimmed, and the bowling green was repaired.

She set Negro carpenters to making benches to set in the shade. On the day the first were finished, she brought me to sit down beside her and kissed me unabashedly in front of the slaves who were working there. "I like this place of ours," she said.

18

1754

It was Sunday, the first after we got settled. I had the carriage brought around by Ned, who was our coachman. Fanny was wearing a yellow flowered gown and cream-colored petticoat that showed off her skin and dark hair to perfection. She had on a flat, wide-brimmed straw hat, held on by a white scarf. She carried her own personal *Book of Common Prayer*. Nat handed her up into the carriage. She smiled and settled herself into the carriage, adjusting her dress.

"I'm anxious to go to church, Robert," she said, "curious to meet our neighbors. Sarah is ready to have guests for dinner. I thought to invite the Reverend Mr. Rose and his wife. What do you think?

"I think it is a splendid idea, my dear," I said, grinning at her sitting beside me. "I'm sure you want to show off the house. You have done beautifully."

I had attended the churches of Cople Parish on and off through my childhood, depending on where I happened to be on a Sunday. Whether I was at Nomony Hall or not, money had always been sent to the parish on my behalf because my plantation was located within it. Everyone within the parish was required to attend and to contribute to the church, and the wealthy especially were expected to support it and care for the poor within its area.

To tell the truth, I was no more or less religious than many others of my time and class. I regarded the Anglican Church as a quasi-governmental entity, since it was the established church in the colony. It was a beneficial institution tasked with teaching people to live together in peace and dispensing charity to those in need. Over my childhood, my own curiosity had driven me to read the Bible, and I knew it rather well, but the sermons I heard did little to add to that except to teach me my duty to the church as a member of my class. I expected little from the church in any spiritual way.

We set off down the road southeast and toward the Potomac, into the countryside where the road eventually brought us to a quiet clearing in which was located the small church called Yeocomico, the church building of the parish in the southern part of the county. This building had been built around the time I had left Westmoreland to live at Warner Hall, although the church body was older. There was a carefully maintained cemetery behind it and a low brick wall surrounding it all.

Before going inside, I walked among the gentlemen of the parish who were talking in small groups, mostly about business. I proudly introduced Fanny as I passed among them and noticed with pleasure their quietly appreciative attitude toward her. For her part, Fanny was assured without being haughty—a fine lady.

Inside the church was simple and elegant. The brick aisles were laid out in a cross, but the wicket entrance door did not bring parishioners on to the upright of the cross, but to the side of it. We walked past the raised platform upon which stood the pulpit and the clerk's and reader's desks. To our left was a gallery and to our right, at the end of the crossbar of the cross, was the chancel on another raised platform. The pulpit, but not the chancel, was at the top of the cross.

I directed Fanny to the pew on the left, facing the pulpit, where I had sat with my mother, father, and sister as a small child. People acknowledged us as we passed to our place. The gentry sat in the front in their box pews, the middling sort farther back. Nat, along with all the slaves who were there, sat in the balcony at the back, facing the pulpit.

After kneeling and saying a brief silent prayer, Fanny sat down and looked around, holding her prayer book in her hand.

"This is an unusual layout for a parish church," she whispered. "I've never seen one quite like it."

I nodded.

I did love the music of the service that filled the building, but I was not impressed as the Reverend Mr. Rose, a short, kindly looking man, gave a neat little message discouraging controversy among church members. His gospel text was from 1 Corinthians 12, and he reminded each person that he or she had a particular place in society, and that by carrying out the duties of the class to which he or she belonged, that harmoniously constituted the whole. I did not think that was precisely what Paul had in mind when he wrote the letter to the Corinthian church, but I supposed that it tended to keep the peace.

"Reverend Rose," Fanny said as we passed out the door to leave, "I hope you and your wife will do us the honor of dining with us today."

"We would be most delighted, Mistress Carter."

And I was certain he was. The good reverend was curious to see what we had made of Nomony Hall, and since pastors were not paid overmuch by the church, he was sure to be looking forward to a good meal.

I resolved not to be argumentative at dinner, no matter what I thought. I now knew Fanny well enough to know that she would also curb her thoughts and remain a pleasant hostess.

I was sitting on the sofa in the office, head in hands, when Fanny came in softly. The 1754 election for burgess from Westmoreland County was over. It had been a disaster for me.

As she sat down quietly beside me, I asked, "Why do they not like me, Fanny? I do not understand. I lost by an even greater margin than I did back in '52. Could it be the gossip of John Lewis has reached Westmoreland at last?"

"I don't think so, dear. I have not heard any such gossip."

"What could it be, then?"

She took both my hands in hers. "Robert, you do not dissemble or flatter. You do not go about the shops and taverns and gossip or hang about the courthouse after your business there is done and talk away the afternoon at the inn across the road. Nor do you promote yourself. Though you are the most democratic man I know in your heart, you may not appear so to the middling folk because you hardly speak to them. What's more, you have been away from here most of your life. You are not well-suited to be a politician."

I was a little taken aback. "You are very hard on me, my dear."

"Not at all. You are a quiet, sincere, and caring man. You are devoted to your home and plantations. All the reasons you are not suited to be a politician are reasons why I love and respect you."

Fanny lifted my chin so that I was looking into her eyes.

"I have met many politicians at my father's table, Robert, but you are unique among men. You are a very special person."

"But Fanny, how am I to do my duty to my county if I cannot be elected to office?"

"You must be yourself, whatever betide, but you will find a way to be of service. I'm sure of it."

I was not greatly comforted.

During the next year, I continued to make changes to the plantations. I used more of my tobacco land for wheat, flax, and hemp. I slowly acquired more and better livestock. Keeping my own accounts finally allowed me to take control of overseers who had had too much independence, and I continued to put in place strict rules for the treatment of my Negroes, many of whom I began to have trained in artisan skills. All possible work of that kind, I believed, should be done by my own people on my own properties. The Negroes usually responded by working hard.

James Thomas, a blacksmith on Nomony, approached me one afternoon.

"Master, my Horace just turn twelve. I wants to teach him the blacksmithing trade."

"What is he doing now?"

"He work in the fields, Master."

"It will be fine, then, for him to learn smithing from you."

"But, Master, he stay at Coles Point."

"He will need to come to Nomony Hall, then. Is that what you mean?"

"Yessir."

"Very well. Go and get him. I will give you a letter for the overseer there."

James grinned wide. "Yes, Master. Right away."

19

1756

I was pacing up and down the upstairs hall, wringing my sweating hands. *What would I do if something happened to Fanny?*

Fanny finally took to her bed with the first pangs of childbirth on a raw, windy day in January. Mama Gumby saw to it that the fire in the bedroom was well made and that the room was comfortably warm.

Fanny was lying quietly between spasms and patiently enduring them when they came. She was maddeningly calm.

Mama bustled about in the master bedroom with absolute confidence. She fluffed up pillows and propped up Fanny's head. She then lifted the covers to examine her patient to see how far along the baby had come. She replaced the covers and smiled at Fanny, laying her hand gently on the place where the baby waited.

"You gone be a good mama. This no big job for you at all. You made for birthing babies."

She made final preparations of the room, making sure everything was clean. She ordered hovering servants to get this or that, as much to keep them busy as anything.

Seeing my pale face, I suppose, Mama said, "Best thing for you is sit in you office. Sam bring you something to calm you nerves."

I obeyed reluctantly, going down to the office as if in a dream, sitting awhile in a comfortable chair and then getting up and pacing awhile. I gulped down the grog brought by Sam and asked for more. I tried to read, but my mind refused to focus on the words before me.

Twelve interminable hours later, after screams of agony from Fanny, each of which cut into me like a sharp knife, a new cry came from the bedroom. As soon as I heard it, I left the office and leaped the stairs two at a time to get to the bedroom.

"It be a boy," Mama said, "but he a little scrawny."

Those words chilled me. So many children died young. But I pushed the thought out of my mind as soon as I saw Fanny lying in the middle of the bed. She looked exhausted, and her face and hair were damp from effort, but she was beaming. I thought she had never been more beautiful.

"Thank God," I said. "And it's a boy, a boy!"

I took the bundle from Mama Gumby. I kissed Fanny gently on the forehead.

"Wonderful," Fanny said and smiled. Then she went promptly to sleep. I was thoroughly happy.

What more could any man want?

20

1758: Tom Henry

I be out in the stable with Nat. I only be five at the time, but I likes being round the horses. They doesn't scare me none. I stays close beside Nat, currying the horses, hoping he send me on some errand, let me stay around the stable.

Then Master Robert come into the stable. Master a tall gentleman with dark hair and a kind face. I sees him all the time in the big house when I be there with Mama. The man always speak to me. He don't speak right away today, though. He just stand by and watch me and Nat work.

I always move round the horses slow. You got to be careful not to spook them. You never walks behind a horse less you lets him know you there. That what Nat say. Sometime, Nat get a little hasty with the curry brush, and I talks soft to the horses. They likes that.

Master call to me and tells me come to him.

I goes and stands right in front of him, but he take me in his lap, even though I be covered with stable dirt and all. He smell of the soap Sam Harrison use to shave him.

He say, "Tom Henry, you likes horses, don't you?"

"Yes, Master. I surely does."

"Well," he say, "then I got a proposal for you. You come spend time in the big house with me, and you learn manners, and I make sure you can spend time with the horses. What do you think?"

I be old enough to know that I has no choice. White folks' suggestions be orders for folks like me. The idea of being in the big house to learn manners don't sound so special to me, but I likes Master's way of doing things."

I say, "I think that be fine, Master."

Master smile at me and set me down.

"Tom Henry a special child, Nat," he say. "You take good care of him when he out here in the stable."

"Yes, Master," says Nat. "He do have a way with the horses, and I look out for him."

———⌒

Second only to being around the horses, I likes to follow Dadda Gumby around. Dadda dark-skinned. He walk a little bent over, and he have deep wrinkles in his face. Dadda's own father be a real African, who come over the ocean long ago. No one know how old Dadda be.

One thing sure. He old enough to be allowed to spend his time any way he want. He putter round with his chickens and his garden. Sometimes he go fishin', but mostly he love to hunt in the woods for his medicine herbs.

Dadda Gumby take me with him to look for them.

We walks along, and Dadda swing the bucket in his hand.

He say, "I's from the Igbo tribe. My daddy a priest in the old country, till he was snatched away by the English. If I be in Africa now, I be a priest too.

"Chukwa be the supreme spirit, the god like the white folks' god. He be here just like he be in Africa. He live in the sun and make all the things on earth do what they does. He teach the priests to make magic and about herbs for healing. Chukwa a good spirit. In Virginia, the herbs be different than in Africa, but they still for healing if you knows them. You just got to learn them. I gone teach you about them because you got the way of a healer."

Dadda press deep into the trees. The woods feels wet and cool on my skin. We walks between the tall oaks and the sweet gum trees. I follows along, smelling the dark woods earth. Dadda find some pretty little white flowers with yellow middles.

"This be chamomile, Tom Henry. You makes tea, and it help folks sleep, or you can 'still out the oil and make a salve. It good for skeeter bites and wounds."

He put the flowers and stems in his basket. He reach for a plant with green, pointy leaves.

"This be peppermint."

He break a leaf and stick it under my nose.

"Smell that? It smell good, don't it? It good for making folks stop throwing up. They be other kinds of mint. They mostly tastes good, makes good tea to drink. You can tell mint because it have a strong smell, and it got square stems."

Dadda cut off lots of leaves from the peppermint.

We spends a long time digging up roots and gathering all kinds of flowers and leaves.

Then he sit me down on a rise. "I wants to tell you something, Tom Henry."

"What, Dadda?"

"Last night I have a vision, plain as day. It be about you. You was grown into a big, strong man. You not wearing slave clothes; you dressed like a white man, a gentleman. The spirits tell me you gone learn things most Negroes don't learn in this here country. That be good. Mind you learn all you can because I seed you the leader of the Negro people in a future time when lots of things be changed. The people come to you for a wise man and a healer."

"What does I need to do, Dadda?"

"Jus' you listen and learn, Tom Henry, from black folks and from white folks too. Master Robert Carter a good man—better than he know his ownself. You trust him."

After we talks awhile longer, Dadda pick up his herb basket and walk back to his cabin next to the garden. I hurries to keep up.

Dadda take me to the woods lots of times, and he make me learn the plants, and he teach me to make tea and 'coctions and balms. He make me promise to take care of my people.

21

1758: Williamsburg

Robert Carter

It was not yet real to me. Only a few months earlier, I had been at my desk, reading the *Virginia Gazette*. I looked up from my paper at Fanny, sitting on the sofa, reading. "Fanny, it seems our new governor is interested in music and science as well as business, and holds a sympathetic view to the concerns of Virginia citizens. Perhaps he will establish a better relationship for us with the mother country."

"He sounds very much like you, my dear."

In Williamsburg, his coming meant a changing of the guard. Fauquier would actually be lieutenant governor, but since the governor appointee had no intention of coming to the wilds of Virginia, he would be governor in all but name. That had become the pattern.

With his coming, there were openings on the Governor's Council.

I was interested, and I had expressed my interest to Fanny and her father. "I think I have something to offer."

"Uncle Thomas agrees," Fanny had assured me. "And he seems to think the king is positively disposed toward you."

Fanny's Uncle Thomas Bladen lived in London and was highly regarded at the court of George II. I was chosen, but so were John Page, son of Mann Page II, and Warner Lewis, which gave me some pause.

So on a warm October day, we traveled to the capital for my swearing in.

I had allowed Tom Henry to sit on the seat beside Nat. He was learning his manners very well and was quickly adapting to the speech of white folks in the great house. He was a natural mimic. I congratulated myself that the child was as exceptionally bright as I first imagined.

"Sam," I called out over the noise of the horses and the rattle of the carriage, "do you recall the night we went to the Governor's Palace?"

"Oh, yes, I surely does. You say we go inside someday."

"I did, didn't I? Now it could really happen."

The capital was in a great state of anticipation with the arrival of the new governor. Crowds had gathered outside the capital building as I approached it. I strolled from the rooming house on Nicholas Street over a block and then up Duke of Gloucester Street. Sam had gone on ahead in hopes of finding a place to watch.

The capital stood at the opposite end of the street from the college, and I turned and looked for a moment before I entered the building, down the length of the street, past the Commons and the James City County Courthouse, the shops and houses, at the place I had received what formal education I had been able to manage. It had been a long journey for me, down Duke of Gloucester Street. I remembered how uncertain I had felt then, younger, filled with fear that my fellow students would see me as John Lewis and my Page cousins did. During the years in London and at Nomony Hall, I had not thought much about them, but now I was faced with their specter once again.

The building I approached was not the same as it had been when I was at school. This building had been erected on the same spot just five years ago after a fire that destroyed the old capital building. The new building was brick, two stories with a porch at its first-floor entrance and a balcony on the second floor. I had been here to the General Court a few times since coming back from England.

Today, I entered the General Court, on the West side of the first floor for a different purpose. After the swearing in, I made my way upstairs to see the room where the council met. I had never been upstairs before. A long polished walnut table dominated the center of the room, surrounded by thirteen chairs, one for each councillor, and one for the governor himself.

Pausing at the door before entering, I was suddenly struck by the thought that both my grandfathers, Carter and Churchill, had served on the council. Councillor was the highest office that could be held by a Virginian, and I did, in spite of John Lewis or his cronies, belong here. I resolved to keep that fact in mind.

A slender and dignified gentleman approached me. He was perhaps twenty years my senior and was, by his dress, undeniably English. He had a narrow, handsome face and discerning hazel eyes. He wore a fine periwig and on his right hand a ring with a large diamond. *A man of expensive and refined tastes.*

He held out his hand with a smile and said in an accent I had not heard since leaving London, "I am Francis Fauquier. Do I have the pleasure of addressing Robert Carter of Nomony Hall?"

Bowing, I said, "At your service, your excellency."

He smiled, "Francis will do. May I call you Robert?"

I liked his manner.

I already knew most of the members of the council. In addition to John Page and Warner Lewis, Phil Lee, once more one step ahead of me in my progress; Uncle Landon's neighbor and friend, John Tayloe; and John Blair, nephew of Dr. James Blair of my school days. John Blair was one who had been derisive of me when I returned from London, but today he could not be gracious enough.

After we had gathered, we all retired to the palace for some Madeira.

I passed through the iron gates that had discouraged Sam and me all those years ago. It was set between brick pillars topped on one side by a lion and on the other by a unicorn. We then walked through a courtyard flanked by two advance buildings and into the entry hall of the main house.

The white paneled walls were hung with a powerful statement of British supremacy: weapons of all sorts—muskets one above the other on one side, pistols arranged in a semicircle on another, swords crossed and hung in rows on either side of the firearms. The palace was not only a residence but part of the armory of the colony. The building was not actually so grand as many of the country homes in England, nor was it even as impressive as some in Virginia, but there was no question it represented the might of the British.

We walked past rooms on either side of the entry hall—one an office, the other behind a locked door. An archway divided the entry hall from a room with curved staircases rising on either side. Finally, we came to a rather intimate dining room, probably usually used by the governor's family. We were invited to sit.

Mrs. Fauquier, Catherine, an attractive woman of forty or so, came to greet us. Then she left us to the servants' ministrations. We had very fine Madeira and some small cakes. The new governor was very personable, and the atmosphere was relaxed. He told us that he drank no hard spirits, but was quite addicted to wine. He liked intelligent company, the implication being that those of us in the room fit that description. I felt perfectly at ease in his company.

One by one the other councillors left, and I was preparing to leave as well, when the governor stopped me.

"Robert, please stay a moment. I understand you are a musician." As he spoke, he took me gently by the elbow and directed me up the stairs to a sort of parlor on the second floor, where there were a harpsichord and other smaller stringed instruments.

I dared to ask, "May I try the harpsichord?"

"You are my guest."

I sat down and ran my fingers slowly over the keys, picking out a simple melody. The instrument was superb, as I had expected.

"The tone is beautiful."

"I enjoy music in the evenings," Fauquier said. "George Wythe and Dr. Small come from the college from time to time, and Wythe promises to bring a young student named Jefferson, who plays the violin. Perhaps you would join us."

"I would be delighted." I couldn't believe my good fortune.

"What are they wearing in Williamsburg?" Fanny wanted to know when I got home. "Do you like the governor? What of the Pages and Lewises? What is the political gossip? How were you received?"

"Let me catch my breath, and I will tell you all."

22

1761

"We have much to order from London," Fanny was saying. "The Williamsburg house must be fit for a member of the Governor's Council. We will have many guests."

She immediately set Joseph to measuring, and following her around as she gave directions and wrote things down. I had not seen her this excited since she decorated Nomony Hall.

She also engaged six-year-old Tom Henry in her projects, and he was now holding the other end of a measuring stick for his father, Joseph.

"We need wallpaper, crimson for this room: fifty-five feet from floor to ceiling; white with green leaf decorations in that room; yellow flowers on a blue background for this one. The staircases and passages must be papered as well. We should not take shortcuts. For window hangings, we shall need yellow silk, and for seat covers, worsted damask. We need one marble hearth, Wilton carpets in the rooms downstairs, a mahogany tea chest, silver and plate with the Carter crest ... the rest we will find here in the colonies."

We had brought little from Nomony Hall other than books.

I had been uncertain about my position on the council when George II died, but I was appointed by George III, and then Fanny and I had resolved to move the family to Williamsburg. We had prospered, and I believed we could afford to maintain both houses.

By this time, we had two more children, Robert Bladen, born in 1759, and Priscilla, born in 1760.

I had purchased the Williamsburg house from my cousin, Robert Carter Nicholas, son of Elizabeth, a daughter of my grandfather by his first wife. It was the very same white frame house I had pointed out to Sam when we made our nighttime expedition while I was a student. It was a long house, a two-story main section and an attached office, all facing the Palace Green and a short walk from the palace itself. It had a deep backyard with a kitchen, coach house, and orchard.

I must say that I enjoyed little in my life more than taking possession of that house. I smiled at Sam, and he smiled back. He remembered.

From Nomony we brought Sarah; Joseph and Tom Henry; Sam Harrison and his new wife, Judith; two other housemaids and all their children; and Nat, the coachman. Sam and Nat would dress in livery.

I had briefly met Peyton Randolph, a friend of Fauquier's and the speaker of the House of Burgesses. Within a few days of our moving to Williamsburg, a group of men who had just finished a fine dinner at the Governor's Palace retired upstairs to what I now called the music room, and that is when I got to know the man.

He was a big man, both tall and heavy, and clearly used to being deferred to, a man who valued his own importance. He was, after all, the speaker of the House of Burgesses.

He looked at me as he held his wine glass to his lips. "Well, Robert, how do you find the Governor's Council?"

"I am learning a great deal. I am most glad to be living here in Williamsburg so that I can attend every meeting and court session."

"A wise course, young man. Your first duty is to serve the king and make sure his work is carried on in Virginia."

"Yes, I believe that is true."

Daring to go on, I said, "I feel I must also represent the people of Virginia to the king. It seems to me it is a reciprocal requirement. On the other hand, I believe you have a primary duty to Virginians and a reciprocal duty to the king."

Randolph was somewhat taken aback, but he smiled. "I see my duty as carrying out, on a day-to-day basis, the work of the colony within the framework of the king's authority."

"Are you not elected by the people as their representative to the House of Burgesses?"

"Of course."

"And suppose the king proposes a thing that is directly against the welfare of the people of Virginia?"

"The king is the law. I would try to reconcile as best I could any difference between the crown and the colony."

"I understand that the king is the supreme law, but Englishmen have rights, granted to them over the centuries, in particular those granted by William II when he came to the throne. Our monarchs are bound by those rights."

"What you are really asking is what would happen if the king violated the English Constitution."

"Exactly."

"I hope it shall never come to that. I should think the Parliament would have something to say about it."

"The Revolution against the Stuarts established that monarchs are subject to the law, and King William specifically promised us no less."

"Surely you do not advocate violence if we should disagree with the king."

"I abhor violence. I just believe that Englishmen, including those of us in Virginia, have rights that supersede the rule of any monarch."

"Where do you suppose these rights originate?"

"In our Constitution and from the Creator."

"Aha, now I have you out. You are an advocate of the so-called Enlightenment."

"Do you disagree?"

"I pray that the king himself is too enlightened, and too bound by Parliament, to cause it to ever become an issue. I do not necessarily agree with you, Robert, but I can see you are a very thoughtful young man. I think you will do well as a member of the Governor's Council."

I was ecstatic. "Fanny," I said when I got home, "I have come to understand that I can hold an intelligent conversation with no less a man than Peyton Randolph. He said I would do well as a member of the council."

"I am not surprised, Robert. You severely underrate yourself. I believe that you will realize not only that you have learned a great deal from all your reading but that your ability to reason is second to none."

"You are always my greatest supporter. Perhaps that is why I love you so passionately."

She gave me an impish smile, her eyes dancing. "Oh, my dear, I do not think that is the only reason."

I no longer blushed when she said such things. They just brought me a sense of pleasurable warmth. I was briefly distracted by the thought of how long it would be until bedtime.

I said, "You have seen Peyton Randolph's manservant, Johnny, have you not?"

"Yes, but I have not paid a lot of attention to him."

"He impresses me—his manner, his speech. I believe such a servant enhances his master's standing in a place such as Williamsburg. Peyton tells me that Johnny attends a school here in Williamsburg called the Bray's School. It is designed for both free and enslaved Negroes."

"That is most unusual. Tell me more about it."

"I asked Randolph who ran the school and what they taught the children. It turns out that my own cousin, Robert Carter Nicholas, is a trustee, as well as Randolph himself. A gentleman named Thomas Bray, an Englishman, had the idea to spread religion—Anglicanism precisely—to those of the Negro race in the colonies. Benjamin Franklin, of Philadelphia, became interested in the project, not so much because of religion, not being an Anglican himself, but because of the educational possibilities. William and Mary College is sponsoring the school because of the friendship that exists between Dr. Bray and our Dr. Blair."

"What sort of thing do they teach? Catechism, I suppose?"

"Indeed, I am sure they teach catechism, but I also understand that the children—boys and girls alike—learn reading, writing, and ciphering, as well as deportment. The girls also learn sewing."

"Aha, as I suspected, you are not so much interested in the spread of the Anglican catechism. It is the other subjects that intrigue you."

"You know me too well, my dear. The mistress of the school is a widow who has taught in several of the colony's leading homes. She cannot fail to be well-qualified. The school attracts as many as thirty students each session."

"And allow me to speculate ... You propose to send Tom Henry there."

"Do you approve?"

She laughed.

"Would it make any difference if I did not?"

⁓

I was on the harpsichord, red-headed Thomas Jefferson and Dr. Small on the violin, George Wythe on the flute, and Fauquier on the cello, sitting around the governor's music room. This playing required close attention. It was challenging to play along with others. We finished a sonata by William Boyce and began a Corelli concerto. These sessions were always intense.

Afterward we enjoyed glasses of fine sherry. As we sat back in comfortable chairs, the subject turned to religion. Wythe, whose mother was a member of the strange sect called Quakers, believed in what he called the free exercise of religion.

"What about the established church?" asked Dr. Small, his dark eyes inviting response. "What do you suppose would happen if there were no longer an official church supported by the government?"

"I believe it would continue to serve a purpose," said Fauquier. He set down his glass thoughtfully. "If people followed their true spiritual inclinations, then those who remained Anglicans would do so because it satisfied their spiritual needs. Accordingly, they should be willing to support it through their own efforts, without the help of the crown. It is my belief that the freedom to choose would actually improve the church. I consider myself a godly man, but I do not accept all of the things the Church of England teaches."

We all knew that Fauquier refused to recite the Apostles Creed, which he was required to do by the rector of Bruton Parish. Like many men of the Enlightenment, Fauquier did not agree with all the statements in the creed. It was a bone of contention between him and Dr. Blair, but he was the governor, after all, so nothing was done about it.

"Is it not hypocritical to practice a religion that is not felt in the heart?" asked Jefferson. "And does it not follow that forcing a man to follow a particular religion results in his being a hypocrite?"

"Would you propose to have the established church dissolved?" I asked, genuinely curious.

Before Jefferson could answer, Fauquier said, "Not necessarily. It ought only to be up to the individual how he should worship."

"And he should be allowed an exemption from having to contribute to the established church should he choose not to worship there," Wythe said.

These conversations always made me sort through my own beliefs—and why I held them.

23

1762: Tom Henry

Master Robert took me by my hand and walked me down the Palace Green. He told me we were on our way to school.

It was the first Monday after Twelfth Night, a few weeks before my seventh birthday. We kept walking until we got to a small white house on Ireland Street.

My heart beat fast as we approached. It was a story-and-a-half wooden house, surrounded by a white picket fence. It looked just like any small house, but Master said it was really a school. I had never set foot inside a schoolhouse and certainly not one for Negroes. But that is what Master said this was. I had never met any free Negroes up close, either, but Master said I would meet some here.

Master read books all the time, and I was curious about the words that were in them. I tried to work out the words in them sometimes. It would be fun to go to school, dressed up as I was today, like a gentleman, and learn about such things.

Mistress Anne Wager, the schoolmistress, was a pleasant, plump white lady, older than Mistress Fanny. She had on a brown bodice and gown, with a white petticoat, very plain, like a shopkeeper. A scarf was draped over her shoulders, the ends tucked into her bodice. Everything about her was prim and proper, but she had a sweet face. I decided I liked her.

"I am Robert Carter, madam," said Master, "and this youngster is Tom Henry. I think you will find him a willing and apt pupil."

"Yes. Councillor Carter, I was expecting you and Tom."

She looked at me. "Welcome, Tom. Come let me show you the school and introduce you to the other children."

Mistress Ann took me by the hand, and when I looked around, Master was slipping away.

First we walked into a wide hall. On one side was a small parlor where there was a sofa and some chairs. On small tables, I saw sewing things. On the other was a larger room with a long table around which chairs were set. Slates and slate pencils sat on the table in front of each chair. Along the side of the room was a bookshelf lined with books, but on the top shelf were quills and bottles of ink. The room smelled of paper and ink. At the end of the table was a speaking podium and a large slate board hanging on the wall. I always supposed that these things were only for white children. I felt as if I had suddenly been carried away into a magical world.

The other children, who had been coming to school since September, filed into the room quietly and sat down at the table. They watched me with curious eyes.

There was something about Mistress Ann that discouraged any kind of misbehavior. She held my shoulders and stood me in front of her facing the children.

"Children, this is Tom Henry. He is joining us starting today. I expect you all to be courteous to him and to help him catch up on what he has missed."

She paused, "And now, let us say our opening prayer."

Everything we did was closely supervised, with lessons in reading, writing, and ciphering. Mistress Ann said a lot about the Anglican Church, and I also began to learn the catechism, which we would say every day. Master was a member of the Anglican Church, but he had never pressed me, or his own children, either, to learn the catechism at home. Mistress Ann also taught us good manners, especially correct table manners, and the importance of being humble and obedient. She told us that it would make our lives easier.

We did have a few minutes of free time, to go outside into the backyard, about midway through the school day.

Walking out into the chilly January air that first day, I tried to act confident although I felt very unsure of myself among all these new children. There was a small boy, a free Negro, who wore shoes with nice brass buckles and a spotless white shirt.

"You think you better than the rest of us, Nigger Boy," said a large, dark-skinned boy dressed in the usual unbleached muslin shirt and oznaburg pants with shoes that sported no buckles.

He picked up a handful of dirt and hurled it at the clean shirt of the smaller boy. Mistress Ann was not in sight.

"See how you uppity mama like that," he said.

It made me angry and caused me to forget that I felt awkward and new. I grabbed the large boy's arm. I was pretty big myself. "Leave him alone!"

The larger boy turned his attention to me. Jerking his arm away, he said, "You be just as uppity as him, talking all fancy like white folks," but he went away without doing anything more.

The free Negro boy and I walked along and talked. Dadda Gumby had told me to listen and learn from everyone, and that is what I was going to do.

The boy told me he lived just outside of town with his mother, father, sisters and brother, and some cousins who had just come to live with them.

"Why do your cousins stay with you?" I asked him.

He shrugged. "They daddy pass. Nobody else take care of them."

"If your father and mother are free, what do they do? I mean how do you live?"

"My daddy a carpenter. My mama take in wash and sewing. They got a good name in town, do work for lots of folks."

We went home in time for dinner at three o'clock. On the way home, I thought over the day. I was interested in how life could be lived without a master. I learned that free Negroes paid rent and bought things they need with money they earned.

Master Robert lets his slaves sell things they raise or make. Sometimes he buys them himself, and they do not have to pay for a place to live or their basic needs. They would not be left homeless like the boy's cousins. Their work is whatever the master says it is.

On the other hand, free Negroes can move wherever they want and be with whomever they want, and do whatever work they want—just like white folks. There would be more to learn from my new friend.

Robert

"How is my lovely godchild doing?" Fauquier asked as we greeted him at the door.

Early that year, Anne Tasker Carter had been born. She was a healthy child, and when she was christened at Bruton Parish Church, the governor stood as her godfather.

I reflected how far I had come from the little boy disregarded by John Lewis.

"She is quite fat and sassy, thank you," Fanny told him. "You shall have to see her before you leave."

On this evening, the company sat around our table, lingering after having eaten. Fanny loved holding these intimate dinners among close friends. Besides the governor, Peyton and Betty Randolph, George and Elizabeth Wythe, and the young law student Thomas Jefferson were there.

Wythe was about my age, but his wisdom and studiousness made him seem older. Probably because of his Quaker mother, he held views very much opposed to slavery, although he owned a few slaves himself. Always the teacher, he initiated a new subject to the after dinner conversation.

"We have read that the rights of man flow directly from God." He looked around the table. "If that is so, then should the Negroes be held as slaves?"

I smiled at Wythe's diving so quickly into a controversial conversation.

"My belief," said young, red-haired Jefferson, an heir himself to over a hundred slaves, "is that all human beings are meant to control their own destinies. Slavery is not good for slave or master."

"Certainly, slavery carries with it great responsibility for the master," the hook-nosed Wythe said, egging him on.

"I mean more than that," Jefferson said, sipping his wine and setting down the glass gently. "Slavery encourages tyranny in the master. The natural inclination of uncontrolled power is to exercise it excessively. It encourages our children, seeing the actions of their parents, to be equally arrogant, lording it over all their inferiors."

He paused for effect. "It also makes us dependent on the labor of others and disinclines us to wholesome effort."

It was hard for me to believe Jefferson was just a student. *What a mind he has.*

"It is all well and good to speak of the evils of slavery," said Peyton Randolph, shaking his head, "but what would the consequence be of turning loose hundreds—no, thousands—of Negroes without employment or land or direction, and with no love for their former masters, either. Do we not have a tiger by the throat?"

"They need a settlement of their own, perhaps in the West or in Africa, away from their former masters," said Jefferson.

"But that would force them to leave the places that have long been their homes ..." I said, thinking aloud.

Betty Randolph sat forward in her chair and placed her napkin firmly on the table.

"Oh, pooh, Robert. Negroes are lazy and unruly and have not one whit of sense. Surely you and Tom cannot believe they could govern themselves without masters."

"We do not really know what the Negro is capable of with training and education and a chance at self-direction. My Tom Henry, for instance, is a clever lad."

I turned to Peyton Randolph. "Your manservant, Johnny, is a very competent man. You sent him to the Bray school to learn, and I can see that you trust him."

"Perhaps so, but I do not believe Johnny could function on his own. I certainly would not trust him to run free over the Virginia countryside without any control from me."

None of us could actually conceive of Johnny or any other slave being so tested.

Fanny saw that both Jefferson and I were poised to answer. Betty Randolph was shaking her head emphatically. Fanny gave me a sidelong glance that told me to say no more.

"Governor," she said, turning to him, "I have been told that you have grand plans for the king's birth night. Would you be so kind as to tell us about it?"

24

1763: Savannah, Georgia

Francis Fauquier and I sailed into the Savannah River in October, the weather unseasonably warm—hot and cloying. The sides of the river were lined with trees and brush and marshland. Along the sides of the river, on both banks, were low wet fields. Perhaps ten miles from the sea, the river made a half-moon, and on its south side was a bluff perhaps forty feet above the water.

It was at the foot of this bluff that our ship came to rest in an area of many wharfs.

I was tired and wanted nothing so much as a bath and a glass of wine. We both stood looking around and, seeing no one to greet us, proceeded up a set of wooden steps that led to the top of the bluff.

There, spread out before us was the city, if it could be called such, neatly laid out in a regular pattern. I saw no brick buildings; even those that appeared to be substantial were made of wood, most painted either blue or red.

There was a stockade around three sides of the whole; that is, every side except the river side, with a gate in each. There were also forts at the edges of the city for defense.

As we determined to find someone to ask for directions, we were approached by a Negro, dressed in finer clothes than most of the residents of the place. He sat on one horse and held the reins of two others.

"Gentlemen," he said, dismounting and bowing, "Do you be Governor Fauquier and his traveling companion?"

"Yes."

"I is here to direct you to the governor's house."

And so we mounted and rode away from the river a short distance, which we could easily have walked. The city was nothing if not diverse. Savannah was obviously a developing town, full of people of all sorts. We had learned a little of its unusual history in preparation for the trip. I assumed that it was due to the founder's establishment of freedom of religion that the city had attracted Jews, Lutherans, Moravians, and Anglicans. There were Scottish Highlanders, Germans, Dutch, Welsh, and Irish. Catholics had only recently been permitted to come because of fear of the Spanish in Florida. There were also both Negroes and red Indians.

The city was laid out in squares, each having a name, the center of each a park. The residences and other buildings were built around them. We arrived shortly at a square that was called St. James. Across from the park of this square was a well-built house, far better than most.

"This be the governor's house," said our companion.

He gave the reins of all the horses to another Negro who came out as we approached and then led us into the house. He bade us sit down in the richly furnished front parlor of the place.

"Governor Wright be here to see you directly."

"Francis," I said, "I am amazed. This is the colonial capital, but it is so raw, almost no more than a country village. Just when I had decided that was what we had come to, I see this house and the servants, as well trained as any in Williamsburg or Annapolis—a strange place of contrasts."

An affable man of medium height came through the door to the parlor. He was dressed in a white shirt with ruffles and a blue waistcoat trimmed in gold braid. He wore no wig but instead tied back his naturally reddish hair at the neck.

"I am Governor James Wright," he said. "Welcome, gentlemen, to Savannah."

He led us to a more comfortable room where he sat across from us on a Windsor chair. A Negro followed us in with the obligatory wine and a sweet treat Wright called benne wafers.

"I am most glad to welcome you to Georgia. You must find us quite unrefined. I think I need to tell you something about our history. James Oglethorpe established Savannah, on the Yamacraw Bluff over the Savannah River only thirty years ago. Oglethorpe himself laid out the squares that you see and designated lots, common areas, public buildings, and the forts that lie at the edges of the city. The walls surrounding the city were built later, to protect us from the Indians, the French, and the Spanish, and the king has garrisoned troops here.

"Oglethorpe forbad rum, slavery, and lawyers in his new colony, but that did not last. The ban on slavery ended in 1748, but the ban on lawyers continued until 1755—an interesting commentary, I think, on the particularities of our settlers.

"Oglethorpe also had close relations with the Yamacraw, the natives of this place, and we continue to be on generally good terms with them."

He paused a moment to take a wafer and eat it. "I had the good fortune to come here at a time when, given that we have won the Seven Years' War, the French and Spanish are less of a threat than they were formerly. In fact, our constant strife with them is the reason the city and the colony have not prospered in the past. The large rice fields—the low, wet fields on either side of the river, which you may have noticed on your way—are a result of the peace and of the use of slavery."

I was dismayed at this last, but I said nothing.

"As you know," Fauquier began, "we have come to participate in the negotiations with the native tribes. It is indeed our understanding that in Georgia you have maintained good relations with them and hope now to open up fresh lands for settlement."

"Yes, and the peace between the mother country and the French and Spanish has finally allowed Georgia to flourish, so now we must establish a lasting relationship with the natives that takes into account those factions being absent."

Wright modestly looked down at his hands a moment.

Then he continued. "I inherited office in a colony where the settlers and the Indians have lived in peace. The king is amenable to dealing with the tribes in a respectful manner, and the tribal leaders, for their part, are willing to listen and negotiate in good faith as well."

I was thinking that this was not, unfortunately, the case on Virginia's western frontier, but the outcome of these talks was supposed to apply to Virginia and the Carolinas as well as Georgia.

"Are you saying that the key to your success has been a respectful attitude on both sides?" I asked.

"Most definitely. What the colonial settlers want is land on which to settle and protection from raids. What the Indians want are European trade goods, such as pots and pans, knives, guns, cloth, some foodstuffs, and other things. There is therefore a basis for negotiation. What the king wants, I want, is a continuation of peace in the colony."

The next morning we set out together with Wright for the inland and Fort Augusta. We were advised to wear boots and to prepare for rough country.

Leaving Wright's home, we traveled northwest from the settled area around Savannah along the Cherokee Trading Trail. The trail more or less followed the Savannah upriver, and most of the time, we could see the river through the trees on our right. It was a wilderness, the trees, mostly pines, tall. The underbrush was not thick but was constant and filled with various kinds of vines and sharp thorns that pulled at the horses' legs. In places it was swampy, and we had to carefully pick our way around water. Along the way, there was the occasional primitive homestead, and the thought crossed my mind that the white encroachment (as the Indians saw it) on their lands was not nearly as advanced as in Virginia. I had never been in a place so wild. Now I understood why we were accompanied by armed men, part of the British garrison at Savannah. This was the frontier, less tame than that of Virginia even beyond the Blue Ridge.

Soon we reached Fort Augusta, which was located on the south side of the river and which formed the border with the South Carolina colony. This fort had been the site of a trading post with the Indians since James Oglethorpe. It had been built in 1735 as a place of meeting with the Indians and a place of protection for white settlers.

Now, with the Seven Years War just over, it was time to secure British rule over the formerly disputed territory in Western Georgia. During the war, the Choctaw had sided with the French, but the Cherokee and Chicksaw had sided with the English. Today, they were all willing to meet with the English governors.

Outside the walls of the fort itself but close by was an Anglican church, the only sign I saw of the established religion in this wilderness. Inside, the fort was simple and utilitarian. In a large building in the enclosure, chiefs of the various tribes were present: Cherokee, Catala, Creek, Chickasaw, and Choctaw. They were seated at a long table.

The appearance of the Indians was disconcerting to me since I had never been to the West, even in my own native Virginia. They were even a little frightening—wild-looking men in a wild land. I was much taken aback at first, but Wright seemed to think nothing of what he saw.

The Indians were dressed in long shirts of linen, decorated with colorful badges, and cloth leggings that fitted over their legs from thigh to ankle. The cloth for these items of clothing must have come to the Indians as a result of the trade of which Wright spoke. On the Indians' feet were shoes of deerskin, which they called moccasins, and over all, they wore long robes or blankets, draped over their shoulders and reaching the ground. Their faces had been tattooed, and their hair was mostly hidden by hats or decorations.

Their skin was copper, darker than that of whites, but lighter than most Negroes, and what showed of their hair was black as jet and straight. They had no facial hair. They made an exotic show and were vastly different from any human beings I had ever seen. However, when the negotiations began, I had occasion to look into their faces and into their eyes, and there I saw simply men, very serious, and, if anything, more dignified than most.

Governor Wright began the meeting. "My brothers," he said, "I have come to establish a lasting peace between your people and ours."

He told them that he represented the authority of the Georgia Colony and George, the king of England. He asked them to speak frankly about any concerns that they had.

"We have sold land to the white man, and we have ceded land to the chief of the whites," said a solemn Creek, who appeared to be the main spokesman for the group.

"The white chief George promised to us protection of our other lands against new settlement by the whites, but still they come. We now claim that protection if ever again a violation of our property be attempted." The Creek spokesman continued. "The trade of the whites has been a blessing to us. We receive supplies of goods from the English, which we ask may be continued forever."

"These are reasonable terms," said Wright, "but we must have some assurance in exchange for our agreement. There have been hostilities and atrocities committed by your people against his majesty's white subjects. This cannot be."

"It is true that our people, when they have been invaded, have attacked the whites. If the whites do not come where they are not allowed, there will be no attacks."

The requests of the Indians were granted in full, but only in exchange for a million more acres of Indian land to be ceded to the Colony of Georgia. Wright did agree that encroachment (or settlement as he called it) would stop at the Appalachian Divide, as promised by the king. It was a good deal for Georgia. I wasn't at all certain it was such a good bargain for the Indians—a high price paid for trade goods and a promise of restriction on settlement.

The meeting ended with a peaceful settlement between the southern tribes and the Georgia and South Carolina Colonies. A proclamation would later be signed by the king, which related not only to Georgia but to all the coastal colonies. Unfortunately, the agreement did nothing for the relations between the northern tribes who were not included in the negotiation and thus had little effect on the more northern colonies, including Virginia, except that the king would no longer protect the settlers beyond the Blue Ridge. That would not sit well with settlers who had already made homes in lands beyond the mountains.

The people; the hot, humid weather; the geography; the swamps and forests fascinated me, as new things always did. However, I was most struck with the freedom of worship in the colony, and the many diverse settlers, and most of all, the fact that, at least for a time, slavery had been forbidden.

As we boarded the ship for home, Fauquier and I discussed what we had observed.

"The Enlightenment tells us that all men are essentially equal," I said. "That would mean that the red Indians are entitled to the same rights as you and I. We will get along better with them if we treat them accordingly."

"I do not disagree with your philosophy, Robert, but I am not optimistic. Even the Creeks hold Negro slaves. What sort of equality is that? And Virginians insist on moving westward, regardless of what the king says. They need the land to grow tobacco when their old land has run out. How long will it be until that drives them to take land beyond the mountains? Where will equality and this agreement be then? I am not as confident as you of man's capacity for equal treatment."

"I can see that there was a time when the Indians in the south could play the French and Spanish against the English, but now they are greatly at our mercy. Still, I hope we can work out a way to live together in peace over the long term."

"You are very optimistic, Robert."

25

1765: Williamsburg

"By God, Robert," Richard Henry Lee, a younger brother of Phil Lee, my neighbor, and currently a delegate from Westmoreland County, was saying, "This is intolerable!"

I had been trying to avoid the situations in which the rising discontent—and perhaps worse—was discussed. I had such mixed feelings about the state of the colony. Nevertheless, I now found myself at Raleigh Tavern at a time when I would rather have been elsewhere.

Richard Henry Lee and his brother, Francis Lightfoot Lee, also a delegate, and a group of their friends, had come into the tavern after the October meeting of the House of Burgesses. I was sitting nearby, and R. H., as I called him, included me in their conversation.

By this time, my young family had expanded by two more children, the first no doubt as a result of Fanny's enthusiastic welcome of me after the trip to the South, but I was beginning to wonder what sort of country our children would inherit.

The Lees and their associates from the House were discussing a new law known as the Stamp Act. "We all agree, but what must we do?" a delegate asked R. H.

Another said, "I think Patrick Henry's response is too extreme. We will only alienate Parliament and the king. We do not want to go to war. We just want to preserve our rights."

"It's just a tax, like many others," said a third delegate.

"No, it is not," R. H. told them, waving his injured hand in the air.

"We have been taxed to regulate commerce in the past. This tax is to actually raise revenue for the mother country, a tax imposed upon us without our prior consent. Englishmen do not pay taxes legislated without their consent. That was the promise King William made to us. If we allow this tax to go unchallenged, it sets a precedent. We will forever lose the right to determine our own taxes."

Young Tom Jefferson and his friend, Dabney Carr, nodded in enthusiastic agreement.

I did not comment, but the conversation made me very uneasy. Objections in the past had been made respectfully to the king and the Parliament.

The resolutions that these men were discussing had been proposed in response to the March 22, 1765, act that placed a tax on every piece of printed paper in the colonies.

The Stamp Act Resolutions proposed by the burgesses constituted an angrier statement than any prior resolutions. I was aware of their content. Although beginning with a declaration of loyalty to the king, they were not merely complaints, but an outright refusal to pay the taxes.

The truth is that I was sympathetic to the complaints of the delegates and felt that in a larger way it had to do with all the rights of the colonists. However, I was a member of the Governor's Council, and Francis Fauquier was my dearest friend. And I disliked strife.

Clearly, the consensus at the next table favored the resolutions, or some of them, at least.

Being quite skilled at political maneuvering, Patrick Henry eventually managed to get five of the Stamp Act Resolutions passed while some of the more conservative burgesses, including my friend Peyton Randolph, were away from Williamsburg.

At the palace a few days later, over a glass of Madeira, Fauquier and I discussed what was going on.

He said, "There are two more resolutions that Henry wrote but did not propose. I have reported to my superiors that the burgesses have two more resolutions in their pocket. These are treacherous times, my friend." His expression was one of deep concern, and he looked tired. I knew he was not entirely unsympathetic to the complaints either, but he had a job to do.

I sighed and set down my glass. "Yes, I know, Francis."

"What do you think of these resolutions of Henry's?"

I thought very carefully how to answer. My friend the governor was a good man and a good administrator. On the other hand, I was a citizen of Virginia first, and I agreed with the basic premise of the resolutions. I knew my history well enough to know that the English king was bound by the promise of King William, almost a hundred years ago, that no Englishman would be taxed without having representation in Parliament. The question, it seemed to me, was whether the king considered colonists in the New World Englishmen as we had always assumed he did.

"You are in a most difficult spot, Francis, not as a result of anything you have done or would have wanted done. It is the Parliament that has put you in this position. As for the resolutions, even Patrick Henry does not really wish to alienate Virginia from the mother country." *I hope.* "Though he speaks in a manner calculated to stir the rabble, what he seeks is to have recognition of the rights we have always enjoyed as Englishmen. I cannot say that I disagree with that."

I paused to look into Fauquier's eyes to measure his response to my words. He looked down.

"We are unique among nations, we English," I continued, intentionally changing my point of view from colonist to Englishman. "We have allowed our colonies self-government as nowhere else, and that is especially true of the North American colonies. We in the colonies have always been proud of that heritage. This is a matter worth working out, not a matter worth fighting over. And I can tell you that these resolutions are enthusiastically received in many parts."

Fauquier nodded at that. "I prayed it would not come to this." He sighed deeply. "As the king's representative, whatever my personal feelings might be, I must dissolve the House of Burgesses over Henry's resolutions. They sound like treason to the crown."

I flinched. "An awful word, *treason*. I am most sorry to hear you use it, but I do know you must do your duty."

Fauquier's expression revealed great unhappiness. It hurt me to see him so.

"You know I love you well, Francis," I said.

He smiled. "And I you."

I returned home a very troubled man. *What rights could the colonies count on now? Will these resolutions cause a schism among Virginians? And if we whites insisted on our rights, what does that mean for Indians and slaves?*

26

1766

Colonel Chiswell and a man named Robert Routledge were at Mosby's Tavern in Cumberland Courthouse, a place on the edge of the wilderness. Routledge arrived first, dressed in the habitual costume of the West—buckskins and moccasins. He was among a group of neighborhood men, middling farmers and artisans, who sat at an unvarnished plank table and talked, peaceably drinking their tankards of ale together.

Chiswell came in, dressed as a gentleman.

Routledge knew him. "Come join us," he said.

Chiswell sat down with them and ordered wine.

After drinking awhile, and appearing to be agreeable, Chiswell suddenly said, "Damn me if the country isn't going to hell. We are overrun these days with men from the West."

He looked pointedly at Routledge. "Such men stir up trouble for peaceful people. They are bloody uncivilized."

"Chiswell," said Routledge, "I think the drink has gone to your head." He waved his hand around the room. "You are among good men here. No need to curse or hurl insults."

"By God, Routledge, you are nothing but one of those fugitive rebels who come here to defraud honest men of their property."

That was too much for Routledge, who stood and threw a full tankard of ale across the table directly into Chiswell's eyes.

In response, Chiswell tried to throw first a bowl, and then a candlestick, and then a pair of tongs, but others in the company grabbed his hand each time and prevented him.

"Goddamn you all. Let me go!"

He wriggled himself free.

"You, Anthony," Chiswell said to his slave, "go to my room and bring my sword. We shall see how you all like that!"

When the servant returned, Chiswell took up his sword. One of the others tried to take it from him, but he hung on, pushing the man away and pointing the tip of the sword at his throat. The man backed away with his hands in the air.

Chiswell then turned to Routledge and shouted, "Get out. I order you to leave this place, or I will surely kill you!"

Routledge held his ground, saying nothing. Then, before anyone could stop him, Chiswell thrust with his sword forward across the table, and stabbed Routledge in the heart. While everyone stood speechless, Chiswell withdrew the bloody sword. Routledge's shirt slowly grew red with blood, and he looked down, an astonished expression on his face. Then he slid to the floor, dead.

Chiswell turned to the men standing there. "He deserved his fate, damn him. I aimed for his heart, and I have hit it."

When Chiswell first came before the General Court, of which I was a member, since I was a councillor, it was to decide whether he should be released pending his trial. The man seemed to me to have little self-control, and to therefore be a danger to society, but over my strong objections, because his father was a distinguished member of the Burgesses, he was released.

Three of the councillors sitting that day also declared that the killing must have been Routledge's fault.

"Robert," William Byrd said to me, "you must realize Colonel Chiswell is a gentleman. Routledge is just a rough Presbyterian fellow. Surely the assault was justified."

"We have no evidence to that effect," I said. "If I understand correctly, after their initial disagreement, Chiswell sent his slave after a sword. Then Chiswell deliberately attacked Routledge and afterward said he intended to do it. Rough or not, Presbyterian or not, Routledge had a sacred right to his life. I suppose he is just as dead as if he were a gentleman."

"Chiswell had a chance to leave, Byrd said. Such Dissenters put themselves in harm's way by their unruly behavior."

I did not argue further at the time, but eventually Chiswell was locked up.

Before he could be tried, however, he died in jail under mysterious circumstances. Bruton Parish would not bury him because they suspected his death was a suicide, and he was finally buried at Scotchtown, his family home, with a mob following determined to make sure it really was Chiswell who was being buried.

George Mason, a burgess from Fairfax County, caught up with me after a few days.

"That was well done, Robert," he said of the incident between Byrd and me. You are a man of good common sense and courage. Either the law applies to all men equally or it is of no use to us."

I was later told of a conversation between Tom Jefferson and his friend, my cousin, John Page, son of Mann II. "You have remarked from time to time upon the ignorance of your cousin, Robert Carter," Jefferson is reputed to have said.

"However, he seems to be developing a good reputation as councillor."

Page answered, "I admit he has gained from his association with our highly enlightened governor, Fauquier, and Professor Small."

Jefferson persisted. "To what do you credit his ability to converse with such learned men? I myself have found him quite thoughtful in his discourse."

"Well," Page said, "I suppose that Robert may have benefited from all that reading that he does. He is not the man he used to be."

It did me good to hear the story. I had accomplished my stated goal of winning the respect of my peers in spite of John Lewis. But somehow, it was not enough. There was something more I needed to do to be at ease in my mind. I did not know what it was. I only knew that Virginia and the American colonies were very likely heading on a hard course.

27

1766

"What do you think of this?" Fauquier asked me.

He handed me a document that I had heard about but not seen. It was signed at Leedstown, on the Rappahannock in upper Westmoreland County, by some 121 landholders of my county and neighboring counties.

It was actually written by Richard Henry Lee at his home, Chantilly, and what it said was that the Stamp Act violated Virginians' rights as Englishmen. It called for not only an outright refusal to pay the tax, but retribution against anyone who attempted to sell the stamps.

I said, "I think this should convince the king and the Parliament of the strength of the opposition to the Stamp Act. Each colony has done some act of rebellion against it. This is only Virginia's contribution."

Fauquier was speechless for a moment. Then he said, "What do you know of these people, Robert?"

"I know them, and you know many of them, too. Look at the names. The signers include most of the men of substance from those parts. Two are brothers of George Washington, who distinguished himself in the late war with the French and Indians. Four of them are brothers of Phil Lee, who serves on your council. The Lees are the most influential family in our county. One is my own first cousin, Robert Wormley Carter, son of my uncle Landon. They are all men of great respectability. They are not rabble-rousers."

His brow was knitted. "Why, then, did you not sign these Resolves, as they are called?"

"To begin with, I was not offered the opportunity. I am a member of his majesty's Governor's Council. That is probably why you do not see Phil Lee's name, either. And, even though I confess to you that I believe R. H. is correct in what he says in the Resolves, except for his call for retaliation, I happen to have a very high regard for my friend Francis Fauquier, who might suffer by his close association with me were I to sign such a thing."

Fauquier did smile at that in spite of his concern.

"Do you think they will actually carry out such Resolves?"

"Let me explain what I know of the background of Lee's call for retaliation. Archibald Ritchie is a wealthy Scots merchant in Hobbs Hole who has never been known as a friend of the large planters on either side of the Rappahannock. He is a great shipper of goods and a tightfisted businessman." I was hoping to impress on Fauquier the strength of the feeling against the Stamp Act and its purveyors. "My uncle Landon and his neighbor, John Tayloe, among others, have had serious disputes with Ritchie at various times over the years. This February past, Ritchie attended the court at Richmond County Courthouse, across from Hobbs Hole.

"'My ship carrying grain to the Indies will sail from Hobbs Hole with stamped paper,' Ritchie told the men at court, 'and I know where I may buy the stamps.' The landowners present exploded at his statement.

"That is what caused Richard Henry Lee to vow that Ritchie must be stopped. He then began a campaign of verbal attack on Ritchie. He said that 'on this occasion everyone should think alike; everyone should look on Ritchie as the greatest enemy of his country, and who should be punished, unless he immediately gives up his intention ... and publicly informs us of his change of opinion.' Such, my friend," I said, "is the fever and the anger surrounding the issuing of stamps. Ritchie did make a small concession to a delegation of Essex men, but he was unwilling to give up the idea of selling the stamps. After Lee published these Resolves that you have read, a greater confrontation seems to me to be inevitable."

"Robert, I am appalled that it has come so far. I hope you are mistaken."

Soon after our conversation, I had occasion to tell the governor about what happened next.

"A group of men slipped across the Rappahannock from Richmond County early in the morning while the fog lay on the river. By the time they reached Ritchie's house in town, an angry crowd had already grown to over a hundred. The crowd demanded that Ritchie desist from selling the stamps and issue a public apology for supporting the Stamp Act.

"Ritchie was standing in the doorway to his home, I hear, still in his nightshirt, barefooted and wigless, but the crowd would grant him no time to dress himself. They stood outside the door, cursing and waving their fists. Some were armed. It was an alarming situation. The crowd was threatening to strip Ritchie to the waist, tie him to a cart, and parade him through the town. They then planned, they told him, to strap him to a pillory for an hour, after which, if he did not apologize, they would throw him into Leedstown jail to await further punishment."

Fauquier looked amazed.

"Ritchie looked to the gentlemen who had come across the river for protection from the mob, but the gentlemen only assured him that if he did not apologize and vow not to sell any of his stamps, he would suffer the consequences. Ritchie's face turned pale, and he was actually trembling. He finally consented to make a written apology and to refrain from using or selling the stamps.

"The gentlemen then helped disperse the crowd. Their leader told the crowd, 'You have won the battle. Now go to your homes in peace.' They departed, but reluctantly. And I thank God for it. It troubles me deeply that Ritchie and the others came so close to violence. Whatever you do, Francis, do not underestimate the strength of feeling about this issue in Virginia. Please communicate that to the king."

"Who were these gentlemen who crossed the river, Robert? Do you know?"

"I know, but, in spite of our friendship, I don't feel comfortable exposing their names at this moment."

Fauquier was not happy with that, but he said, "I can understand your reluctance."

The Stamp Act was ultimately withdrawn by the king, but he reiterated Parliament's right to have passed it in the first place.

⌐

I motioned to my friend Peyton Randolph, to sit in a comfortable chair. Sam brought refreshments. Randolph looked quite serious.

"I come to you in my capacity as speaker of the House," he said.

"I am glad to see you, Peyton, but I can see in your face that this visit is not a casual one."

"You did not sign Richard Henry Lee's Resolves," he said, "although I know he is your friend and neighbor. It is also

known, however, that you condoned resistance to the Stamp
Act. You are close to the governor. We all agree that you are
the appropriate person to write to the king thanking him for
withdrawing the Stamp Tax. I am hopeful we may retrieve
our rights without any resort to violence."

"Of course, I will be pleased to write the king. And I assure you, I will be most gracious."

This time Fauquier himself approached me. "The king's wife
has borne another child. Would you do me the courtesy of
making a public address to congratulate the king and his
family?"

"I'll be most pleased to do so. Everyone can celebrate the
birth of an innocent child. Maybe it will calm the waters."

It was my Fanny's idea, though, to hold a ball in honor of
the child.

She was soon supervising the cleaning and polishing of
every item in the house and picking out recipes and instruct-
ing Sarah and the cooks in the preparation of food. She found
the best fruits and meats. She kept the entire household busy
for weeks.

The first guests to arrive when the day finally came began
to arrive at seven. Fanny and I stood at the door to greet each
one as he or she came. Fanny's gown was so blue that it was
almost purple, very becoming to her. I was dressed in my
finest as well. I even wore a wig for the occasion. The house
was alight with a hundred candles.

The governor arrived dressed impeccably, as always. He
came alone since his wife and children had found Virginia
too provincial and gone home. Bowing, he kissed Fanny's

hand. "I am delighted to see you, fair lady. We needed this reprieve from the recent tension."

Benjamin Tasker came all the way from Maryland to help us celebrate. "Fanny," he said, "you have outdone yourself."

The Peyton Randolphs were both there, and so were his brother, John, and his wife. John did not hold with the action of the Burgesses in resisting the Stamp Act. John Tayloe, by now long married and a father, brought his three oldest daughters, including fifteen-year-old Rebecca. The girls wore gowns all alike except for the color—silk with petticoats of flowered chintz. Rebecca, resplendent in yellow, slipped a demure look at Frank Lee.

"Poor girl," I thought to myself, "she is smitten." Frank was a good bit older than she, a bachelor, considered to be quite eligible, but reputed to be as fickle as he was charming.

It was warm for October, perfect weather, and it was during the session of the House of Burgesses. Everyone was in town. Phil Lee came, as did Richard Henry Lee, Tom Jefferson, Dabney Carr, and, to my surprise, John Page. George Wythe came with his wife, Elizabeth, and Dr. Small.

The house sparkled from candles in the windows and in candelabra and wall sconces. The food was delicious and plentiful, dishes of every kind spread on the groaning table. There was plenty of wine and rum punch, ale, cider, and grog. After dinner, the Negro fiddlers and banjo players kept the company lively, first with formal dances, then country reels. We danced until three. Everyone seemed to be smiling.

As the evening progressed, I noticed that Frank Lee spent most of his time dancing with Rebecca Tayloe. *Perhaps the perennial bachelor was snagged at last.* It made me smile. I hardly had a chance to dance with my own wife, so sought after was she as a partner. I must say, I danced with a few ladies myself. Sam, passing around the room, making sure everyone was taken care of, dressed in his livery, gave me a congratulatory smile.

This ball I would remember with nostalgia as the differences between king and colony grew worse.

28

1767

Fauquier looked pale. He crossed to a chair with his glass of claret in hand and sat down with a sigh. He took a sip and fixed his eyes on me.

We were in the music room at the palace, but there was no music on this evening.

"Robert," he said, "I have not had good news this day. My physician tells me that I suffer from something called schirhus testicles, whatever that may be. He tells me that it is often fatal. I know that I am in a great deal of pain."

"My God, Francis. My God, what a shock!"

Truly, the news struck me like a knife in the belly. "I am so sorry. What must be done?"

"There is nothing that can be done, my friend. Spend time with me as you always have, and, should I become unable to handle my personal affairs, I pray you will help me."

1768

Francis Fauquier died on March 3, 1768.

"I cannot imagine life in Williamsburg without him," I told Fanny. "All our deep conversations. There is no one else except you that I can talk to that way. His humor, the wine and music in the evenings, the trips to new places ... My life is changed forever."

I thought for a moment.

"There is just one good thing. He will not live to see Virginia come apart at the seams. "He has asked that I be one of the executors of his will. I want to read you something from his will that affects me strongly."

"It is now expedient that I should dispose of my slaves, a part of my estate in its nature disagreeable to me, but which my situation made necessary for me; the disposal of which has constantly given me uneasiness whenever the thought has occurred to me. I hope I shall be found to have been a merciful master to them and that no one of them will rise up in judgment against me in that great day when all my actions are exposed to public view. For, with what face can I expect mercy from an offended God, if I have not shown mercy to those dependent on me? But, it is not sufficient that I have been this master in my life, I must provide for them at my death by using my utmost endeavors that they experience as little misery during their lives as their very unhappy and pitiable condition will allow. Therefore, I will that they shall have liberty to choose their own masters ..."

I felt my voice crack as I read. "He owned twelve slaves, Fanny. We own hundreds. Am I a master who can be forgiven at the hour of judgment? Am I merciful? Is that enough?"

"I can answer, Robert, that you are a merciful master. I have never believed that slavery was right, but I do not know what can be done by those of us whose families depend on it for their living."

"If there is a revolution coming, perhaps it will create an answer for us."

"Perhaps." She seemed doubtful.

On the day of Francis Fauquier's funeral, I stood near to his burial place with the others who were close to him in the last years of his life. According to his wishes, we made sure that his burial was carried out with as little ceremony as decency permitted. Fauquier said he believed that ostentatious funerals were contrary to the spirit of Christ's religion. I believed he was right. As shovels full of dirt were thrown upon the casket, I could not help but think of the loss of my father and grandfather, and the loss of three of my own small children who lay in this very same graveyard at Bruton Parish.

On a soft April day, always so sweet in Williamsburg, Fanny and I had strolled out together along the palace green. We lingered awhile at the market on Duke of Gloucester Street, looking around, purchasing nothing. Finally, we made our way toward home.

"What a perfectly lovely day," she said as she bent to smell the late daffodils that were growing in front of the home of George and Elizabeth Wythe.

"It makes me feel that the world is better in spite of the world's troubles. Spring always has that effect on me."

"Yes, and it is hopeful to be expecting another child. I feel quite well. Lord Botetourt seems a pleasant governor—though he is no Francis Fauquier—and our relations with the mother country are calm. And I am beginning to make a nice profit sending our wheat to Madeira to buy wine to sell in New York."

"Life is good to us."

"It is, but I find that I am not quite content, Fanny. I feel there is something I should be doing, but I don't know exactly what it is."

We had reached the house. I kissed Fanny on the cheek as I turned to go to the children's dining room.

"Now, let me see if I can find any of our children."

I entered the room just in time to see the Negro seamstress, Mary Ann, beating seven-year-old Priscilla on her back and head with a stick. The child was cringing, holding her hands in front of her to protect her face. Tears were streaming down her face. Priscilla was a gentle child, inclined to do what she was told, so I was doubly shocked. I had never experienced a slave beating one of my children, and I could not imagine what had precipitated the beating.

Without even thinking, I snatched the stick from Mary Ann and turned on her in anger. She shrank back, shocked. She had never seen me strike a servant, but she was afraid.

"Please, Master, don' beat me. I won't never hit that child again."

I had been on the verge of striking Mary Ann with the same stick she used on Priscilla. Then I thought better of it. *Violence begets violence. Besides, I would never be able to trust her again.* "No," I said. "I won't beat you, but you will never strike a child of mine again."

I turned and walked away and I am sure she thought that was an end to it, but she was wrong.

I spoke as soon as I could to the ship captain who was shortly leaving to take the next wheat shipment to Madeira.

"Take Mary Ann with you," I told him. "When you arrive there, contact Scott, Pringle and Associates. I will send a letter with you, telling them to sell her to the highest bidder. You can tell them that she was banished for beating one of my children."

Just over nine weeks later, I saw Fanny walk slowly into the hall and drop onto a bench, a letter hanging from her hand. It was unlike her to look so broken.

"What is it, my dear? Surely not more bad news."

"Father is dead," she said, the tears dropping from her eyes and onto her bodice.

I went to her and sat down beside her, pulling her to me and stroking her soft hair. "He was a father to me, too. He believed in me when others did not."

"Mother has been appointed executor of his estate, but she wants you to help her carry out her duties."

"Of course, I will."

Fanny sighed. "He never knew about his latest grandchild."

She had written to her parents in Annapolis when Harriet Lucy was born. She received this letter back almost immediately. She realized this letter had been sent before hers reached them.

There was little time for reflection. I received a letter from a Mr. Lowndes of Bladensburg, Maryland, informing me that Benjamin Tasker, Fanny's father, who at the time of his death was handling the estate of his son, Benjamin Tasker Jr., had asked that the settlement of the son's estate be turned over to Tasker's other daughter, Anne Tasker Ogle; Lowndes; and me. I now was involved in three estates.

As a part of my duties, I wrote to Daniel Delaney, who was acting on Fanny's behalf regarding her inheritance from her father:

"Mistress Carter and I rejoice at your great humanity, and hope that the Negroes who have alliances at Bel-Air may not be sold till those slaves be, and that the Negroes then be sold with wife and husband. We desire that you will draw for us the allotment of slaves (those who are not to be sold) that shall be agreed on ... and inform me how many of said male and female slaves belong to us. My wife and I had rather let those slaves chose masters in Maryland than send them to any of our plantations, for we cannot employ them in our family."

We could learn that much from Fauquier.

29

April 1769

"Robert, whatever is the matter?"

My pacing in front of the fireplace in the office had roused Fanny from her reading.

"What must I do?" I asked. "I feel desperate. What am I to think? As a member of the council, I am sworn to uphold the king in all things, but I do not agree with him."

My despair arose out of the regular April meeting of the House of Burgesses, held downstairs from the council. They passed resolutions declaring the colony's right to control its own taxation. This was a reaction to the law called the Townshend Acts, the first of which had been passed by Parliament two years earlier, but which were becoming ever more odious. I was not surprised at the actions of the burgesses given the talk I had been hearing in the taverns.

"What the burgesses refused to do in response to the Stamp Act," I told Fanny, "they have now done. They resolved that they had the right to freely correspond with other colonies, a determination in direct conflict with the crown's orders. I myself have agreed to serve on the committees of correspondence for Virginia. I do not believe it is treason to work along with the other colonies to try to address our mutual problems. The council was in a meeting upstairs when word of their action officially reached us. The governor immediately dissolved the burgesses as his position required him to do. The burgesses simply went down the street to the Raleigh Tavern and reconvened as an 'association.'

"Fanny, our rights as Englishmen surely include the right to communicate with people of whatever stripe in other colonies. It is also clear to me that English law allows us to tax ourselves, but we now have taxes imposed entirely without our consent. We have no representation in Parliament. Worst of all, I have read that the king has sent troops to Boston and quartered them in people's houses. He could do the same in Virginia, in the capital, or in Portsmouth. Botetourt is a man in an impossible situation. I like him well enough, but I like my cousin Robert Wormley Carter, and Jefferson, and Mason, and the Lees, too. Where do I stand in this?"

"You must follow your conscience, Robert, as you always have."

As if to put icing on the cake, Parliament, shortly after my conversation with Fanny, declared that anyone in the colonies accused of treason would be tried in the mother country. I recognized that as a denial of the right to trial by our peers, another of the sacred rights of Englishmen.

How could the king be so blind? He was turning more and more of the colonists against him. The affability of Governor Botetourt would not maintain this uneasy peace forever. I thought about the conversation I had with Peyton Randolph when I first came to Williamsburg. Randolph had asked me whether I would advocate violence if the king disregarded the rights of the people. Now, Randolph himself was a member of the outlaw assembly who met at Raleigh Tavern.

I had refused to take sides, but I could now see that my position was untenable.

30

1771: Tom Henry

The idea of going to the country seemed welcome to me after the heavy Christmas social season in Williamsburg was over. It had been dull and wintry since January. This day, even though spring had come, was unusually cold and overcast. It would be good to see summer come at Nomony.

I was pleased with myself. I had just been made a postilion and coachman, a great honor for someone only nineteen years old, and a token of Master's fondness and faith in me.

I was entrusted this day by Master Robert with the task of getting the vehicles ready for the trip to Nomony Hall. Master said that we would all go down to Westmoreland County.

All of Mistress's china and bric-a-brac was being packed, wrapped in cloth and put into barrels. My mother, Sarah, and Sam's wife, Judith, were folding all the clothes for Master and the family and putting them into trunks. Sam and Joseph were packing some of the books from the library. Master did love his books!

They must be leaving the furniture because I had heard nothing about it being loaded. Master was keeping the house in Williamsburg. I was just glad I didn't have to do all the packing. My job was to supervise the loading of the wagons and getting them down to the port. Then I busied myself getting the carriages ready to take the family home.

Well, I reckoned that Nomony Hall had plenty of furniture, and I wished we were already there. Though Master had gone there periodically while we were in Williamsburg, it had been a long time since I had seen the wide green fields and tall poplar trees. I wanted to tell folks I had known as a child about my new position.

Master did not share with me his reasons for going back to the country, but I had a pretty good idea what they were. Master's official explanation for leaving was that his family had grown too big for the house in Williamsburg. It was true that Mistress had borne eight children during the time we were here—five of whom survived—but I was sure that was not the reason they were leaving.

I had overheard the dinner table talk about the writers with new ideas about government—the Enlightenment. One writer they talked about was a fellow named Voltaire, and another was an Englishman named John Locke. Locke was the one who said that all people have rights just by being born. Montesquieu said the best kind of government was self-government. He also said there was no justification for slavery. *Did he mean that rights were for Negroes too?* I wondered as I listened to them. Master, like some of the others, thought slavery was wrong, but that had not changed the condition of slaves. I do not think Master knew what to do about slavery.

On the other hand, I could feel the change in the politics in Williamsburg. The law called the Stamp Act had caused a great stir. Some of the gentlemen in the House of Burgesses had made petitions and resolves objecting to what the king did. I had never heard of such a thing. Then the king repealed the Stamp Act, but more trouble was coming.

The gentlemen like Master were less adamant than men like Patrick Henry. He was a redhead, full of fire! It became fashionable to be a Patriot, and those who were not Whigs were called Tories. Everyone became suddenly serious about politics. Master said, "A new system of politics in North America began to prevail."

I listened and learned, just as Dadda Gumby had told me to do. More acts, called the Townshend Acts, were passed by Parliament in 1767, and two more regiments of troops were sent by the king to keep the peace in Boston. They were even allowed to stay in people's houses, whether the people wanted them or not. Since the colonies had started to write back and forth to each other, what happened in one colony became news in all the colonies. Master was on what was called a Committee of Correspondence. What was to keep the king from sending troops to Virginia?

When the new governor, Botetourt, came in October of 1768, people liked him. Master liked him. Still, when Botetourt shut down the House of Burgesses, instead of petitioning the king, the members just went on down Duke of Gloucester Street and kept holding their meetings at the tavern. They intentionally disobeyed the orders of the governor and the council. That put Master right in the middle. He said the king was just wrong, especially for trying people accused of treason committed here, in England. I know what trial by your peers means, and it means they should have been tried by other colonists.

What is funny is that the colonists, white folks complaining about the king's laws, used that word, slavery, to describe their condition. Well, they don't know what it is to be a slave. Still, their thinking might be a beginning of understanding what it is like to be a slave. A man can hope.

Then there were the deaths of three babies. That was devastating to Master and Mistress. And Master had lost the two men he loved best in the world, Governor Fauquier and Benjamin Tasker. I could see it all took a toll on Master and Mistress.

It seemed to me, though, that the final blow came when Lord Dunmore sailed into Virginia and took over as governor. Governor Botetourt had died suddenly after only two years in office.

I distrusted Dunmore the first time I laid eyes on him. He is a cold man with dark hair and eyes who looks down upon all the people of Virginia, even the gentry. Word is that he told the people in New York when he left for Virginia that Virginians were backward, ignorant people, and he could not stand to live among them.

Master Robert did not like him, either. In fact, I do not know of anyone who liked him. The slaves heard all the talk, of course. Dunmore has slaves, himself, and unlike Governor Fauquier, he treats them arrogantly and sometimes cruelly. He is not a man to be trusted.

After Dunmore came, Master no longer passed happily between home and the governor's Palace, and from the palace to the Capitol. He didn't have a warm personal friendship with the governor any more. Lately, Master drags himself to meetings of the council, and he never voluntarily goes to the palace.

Master is torn. He does not like violence, but he must surely see it coming. He is not a man who wants to rebel against government, and yet he believes that the king and the governor are wrong. What will be the outcome? Whatever it is, life is going to change. Because I know that Master, and young red-headed Tom Jefferson, and wise George Wythe, and tall George Washington, and hot-blooded Richard Henry

Lee and his brother William have all said slavery is wrong, I can hope the coming revolution will change the lives of slaves too.

In any case, I believe Master's going back to Nomony Hall is his way of rebelling.

31

Summer 1771: Nomony Hall Tom Henry

I had never heard of this man, Charles Thomas. He had lately come with his wife to the county. In any case, there was a light wind blowing; it was a pleasant drive to his house, and I was enjoying myself.

Thomas' so-called plantation, Greenfields, was really nothing more than a farm. The house sat at the top of a hill and commanded a view of anyone coming up the drive, which ran up through planted fields and curved into a circle as it reached the house. It was a typical story-and-a-half frame farm house, and I knew without seeing inside that it would have a central hall with rooms on either side of it. I had heard from the slaves at Nomony Hall that Thomas had come into some money by inheritance and was anxious to be thought of as genteel. A visit from Master would increase his status in the community. That could even have been Master's reason for this visit. Master was like that.

Charles Thomas came out to greet Master and Mistress as we came into the circle at the top of the drive. He turned out to be a short, round little man with a red face. The man's demeanor told me that the master of Greenfields was neither a proper gentleman nor a kind person.

After handing Mistress out of the coach, I led the horses around to the back, to rest them. I had been away from Westmoreland a long time, and I wondered whether I would know any of Thomas's slaves. At least I was hoping to catch up on the news from around the county.

Then suddenly, she caught my eye. She was coming up from the clothesline behind the kitchen house with a basket of clothes in her hands. She had on a little white cap and a white apron over a plain skirt. Everything about her was neat and orderly.

She was not uppity. That wasn't exactly it. She was serene, tall and slender, but full in the breast. Her skin was the color of coffee and cream, with high cheekbones that suggested she might have some Indian blood. Her eyes were deep green and her full lips pursed slightly as if she was displeased. She was a beauty. There was no nonsense about her, either. That was plain to see. She knew just who she was.

I had learned that I had a certain quality that drew people to me. I could not say that I was especially handsome, but I reckoned that I was pleasant-looking enough, because I had never had any trouble attracting the ladies. So I was very sure of myself.

I slowly looked this beauty up and down. I meant it to be an appreciative look, but I could see right away that it was a mistake. The coolness that emanated from her gave me a chill. The girl made me wonder whether everything was in order with me and my fine clothes after all. My livery, which should have let her know that I held an important position, was sky blue with red trim, made up of a good light wool coat, waistcoat, and britches, all of which fit me perfectly and showed off a physique I was proud of. My hair was tied back in a braid. Like my master, I took pride in my appearance.

This beauty, however, pretended to ignore me. Still, I thought I caught just a little side glance. That was all the encouragement I needed. I fell right in beside her as she walked toward the great house. She or the clothes—or both—smelled of sunshine.

"You have the most beautiful eyes I've ever seen," I told her as I tried to keep up with her.

She said nothing, nor did she look at me. Lifting her pretty chin a little with a movement that said "hymph," she let me know she was no woman for trifling. The fact that she deigned to communicate this attitude to me only further encouraged me. If she really had no interest in me, she would have truly ignored me. Or so I believed.

"I beg your pardon, Madamoiselle," I finally said in my best cultured voice, coming around in front of her with a slight bow, to try another tack. "My name is Tom Henry. I am coachman for Councillor Robert Carter of Nomony Hall." I paused to let that sink in. That usually got some respect. Then I said, "We've lately come from the capital. Come home to stay."

She finally looked directly at me with her clear eyes, and I thought my heart would stop.

"What is your name?" I dared to ask.

"I be called Rose," she said. She was not flirtatious at all, but she did smile a little. It was like the sun suddenly shining through on a cloudy day. The smile warmed me all over.

"May I help you?" I offered to take the basket of clothes she carried.

"If you likes, Tom Henry."

She passed me the basket, smiling again.

Oh, glory! I said to myself.

The back door of the house came too soon.

"I'll be coming again," I said as I handed back the basket.

"I be here," Rose replied.

———

Later that summer
Robert

The day after the birth of our latest child—finally another boy, whom we named John Tasker—I was riding home from a day at Richmond County Court.

The slaves were tending the tobacco plants, cutting off suckers. I could not give up the cultivation of tobacco altogether because it was still profitable, and I needed it to pay my taxes.

Nomony was beginning to show the effects of my renewed close attention. People came just to see my new double mill at Nomony, and I had found factors in Alexandria and New York to help me conduct my business. I was feeling quite content.

Tom Henry came to take my horse. It was such a beautiful day that I decided to sit on one of Fanny's benches underneath a maple tree to enjoy the breeze before going into the house.

Tom had been gone long enough to direct the currying and putting up of my horse, and I saw him come from the stable and turn toward the place where I was sitting. He walked slowly, hesitated, and then began again. It was not like Tom to be hesitant. When he arrived before my seat, to my surprise, he dropped to his knees and looked up at me.

I could not imagine what would cause such behavior. I really did not like my slaves to beg.

"Master Robert, you have always been kind to me. I am grateful to you." Then he swallowed hard and said, "I have something to beg of you."

I smiled at him. Fanny accused me of doting on Tom Henry. "Stand up, Tom, and tell me what it is."

"I have found the woman of my desiring. I want to marry her."

"Oh, who is this lucky girl?"

"Her name is Rose. She lives at Greenfields."

"Yes, I believe I saw her the day we went there. She is quite comely. Does she want to marry you?"

"She says so."

"Now I see why you have been asking for passes to go to Greenfields on Sundays. Are you seeking my permission to marry her? Is that it?"

"Yes, Master, but that's not all."

"Yes?"

"I do not mean to be forward or to ask too much, but ... well, we want to live at Nomony Hall."

"You mean you want me to buy her from Thomas?"

Tom began to talk quickly. "She is an excellent house servant, Master. She sews beautifully. Her mother is a seamstress. She has good manners. She helps her mistress prepare for and serve company. She is not silly like so many girls. You would be pleased with her."

Fanny was right. I was a fool when it came to Tom Henry, but he was just so capable and intelligent and willing to work. He had exceeded all my expectations.

I said, "The question is whether Thomas will let her go— and at what price."

~⁓~

I arrived at Greenfields, alone on horseback, two days after my conversation with Tom. It had turned windy and cloudy, and it was not a pleasant ride—nor an errand I was looking forward to. I had decided what I thought was a fair price for a young house servant such as Rose. I knew Thomas to be a greedy man and reasoned that money was the only way to persuade him to sell. That meant that I would likely have to pay too much.

Charles Thomas came out to meet me. "What an unexpected surprise. Come in out of this wind," he said.

He was dressed in a manner too formal for every day and too warm for the weather. The man did not impress me favorably.

We walked together into the front hall. The house was a typical center-hall farmhouse, the hall being about twelve or fourteen feet across. Half its width ran from front door, where we had entered, to a back door. The other half was taken up with a staircase to the second floor. To our right was a dining room and to our left a formal sitting room, where Fanny and I had sat on our visit here. This time, however, Thomas drew me past the staircase to another, more comfortable room that smelled of whiskey and tobacco.

"Would you like something to drink?" Thomas asked as he settled his roundness into a leather chair. "Some grog? A lemonade?"

I sat across from him. "No, thank you, Charles. This is really a business call."

"Really?" He brightened.

"I think you know my coachman, Tom Henry?"

"Oh, yes, an uppity young dandy, if you ask me."

"Well, he is a very valuable servant to me," I told him a little curtly. "I have found him to be extraordinarily responsible."

"I wish I could say as much for any of my niggers."

I ignored the use of a word I did not permit the use of in my family.

"Tom Henry wants to marry one of your servants."

At this Thomas threw back his head and laughed out loud.

"Marry? You know that the law does not recognize marriage among slaves. What do niggers know of marriage? I don't care who they lie with or how many babies they make, but marriage? Don't be foolish, Mr. Carter."

I was growing angry, but I held my temper. I was on a mission. "Well, that is the way Tom Henry looks at it. In any case, it is your Rose that he fancies."

"Rose, the seamstress? She is a beauty, I must say."

He leered at me. "Would I not have hell to pay with my wife, I could fancy her in bed myself."

I tried valiantly not to look as disgusted as I felt. I cleared my throat. "So you have no objection to their marrying?"

"Not unless they expect a wedding." Thomas clearly considered this a fine joke. "I won't have Rose missing any time from work, mind."

"That is the other thing I want to talk to you about ..."

"What?"

"I am prepared to buy Rose from you."

Thomas started a little. Recovering, he changed his tone. "Rose is very valuable to our household. Mistress Thomas depends upon her."

I knew at once I had made a mistake. *I should have just offered to buy the girl.*

"You don't have to build her up, Charles. I am willing to pay a fair price."

"I am not sure I want to sell her at any price."

I mentioned the price I had in mind, which I thought was generous enough to pull him in while still leaving me an option to raise the offer later if necessary.

"I don't know."

"That is my first and last offer." I lied.

"Let me think about it for a week."

Solomon Dixon came back to check around the gristmill before going to bed. Though he was a slave, he was in charge of the new double mill as he had been of the old mill.

Solomon always wore a battered hat, which he took off to fan himself. The evening was hot for spring. He wiped his brow with the back of his arm.

He then noticed two scruffy-looking white men inside the millhouse. He saw them filling sacks with freshly ground grain. He watched for a minute, then came into the doorway, and saw them quickly try to put the partially filled sacks out of sight.

Solomon pretended he hadn't noticed the sacks. He was thinking that there were two of them and only one of him. "What you doing here?" he asked them. "You not from around here."

"Just traveling, looking for work, and something to eat."

"Well," said Solomon, "I could use a little company. Come on to my cabin, and my wife get you something to eat."

At the house, they had some cornbread left over from supper. While they were eating, Solomon brought out a stone jar of grog and took a sip. "Have a little drink?" he asked, holding out the jar in their direction.

"Sure." The first one wiped the top of the jar with a filthy sleeve, took a gulp, and passed it to his friend.

Solomon took another drink, pretending to take a big swallow, but in fact swallowing none of it. He passed the bottle around again. This continued for an hour or so while Solomon kept up a pleasant conversation. It wasn't long until the two men got sleepy. Solomon made them each a pallet on the floor and gave them each a blanket.

"Now, Isaac," he said to his son, when he was sure they were asleep, "you go get George Dawson; tell him get the sheriff."

Next thing the would-be thieves knew, they were in custody.

When Solomon told me his story, I laughed. "You are a good man, Solomon." And I sent a hog over for him and his family to enjoy.

32

Summer 1772: Tom Henry

All that was on my mind was Rose, and when Master Thomas would make up his mind, but Master sent me to Annapolis to show the way to the new steward, William Taylor.

After a three-day stay in Annapolis, we were on our way home on two young geldings, and I was anxious to get there. The heat was stifling, and, for whatever reason, Taylor was also in a hurry.

I knew it would be best not to hurry in spite of the way I felt. "Can't push the horses, Mr. Taylor, in this heat."

"What did you say?"

Taylor was frowning. "I am not in the habit of taking advice from slaves. Let us be on our way." He mounted and began to move forward, using the whip to slap the fine young chestnut gelding, West Wind, that Master had loaned him.

I had no choice but to follow. We quickly made it to Port Tobacco, pushing hard. West Wind began to pant and refused to go forward without urging. By the time we stopped for the night, I was worried about him.

"Stubborn beast," Taylor said. "What is the matter with him?"

"He needs a rest. Let me get him water, and give him a shot of whiskey to relax him. Then we need to allow him time to recover."

"That is not going to help him, you fool. You are no doctor."

"I always see to Master's horses," I insisted. "What this one needs is a day off to rest."

"Well, it may suit your master to rely on you, but it doesn't suit me."

"I am responsible for this horse." I was used to being in charge of the horses, and my concern for West Wind was increasing. "I know him."

"As I said before, I do not rely on the opinion of slaves. We will leave first thing in the morning."

I knew I had no choice without Master there to intervene.

The next day, we got up early, and, by the time we stopped for dinner, West Wind was in distress again. He panted and kept trying to stop. Each time, Taylor struck him with the whip until he began again.

West Wind stopped several times, but over my objections, Taylor pushed him on. Then, suddenly, West Wind stopped still and fell forward on his knees. It hurt me to see him suffer. I jumped down from my horse and took hold of the reins.

"Let him rest, please."

Taylor pulled the reins back from me and made him get up, but he immediately fell again. I went to him, but it was too late. In a few minutes, he was dead there in the road. I could not say what I wanted to say. Instead, without saying a word to Taylor, I took the other horse back to the ordinary where we had stayed and got a shovel.

As I began to dig a grave for the brave animal, Taylor cursed and paced, but since I kept him from getting the other horse, he had to wait for me to finish.

"Your master will hear about this," Taylor said.

We finally got home with the other gelding, this time at a slower pace.

"Where is West Wind?" Master Robert asked.

"There was something wrong with him," Taylor said before I could speak. "Took sick and died on the road."

Master Robert looked doubtful. He turned to me.

"Is that so, Tom? It does not sound right. He was a healthy gelding."

"No, Master, Mr. Taylor wanted to get home fast. West Wind started acting weak before we got to Port Tobacco. We spent the night, but Mr. Taylor wanted to push on in the morning. West Wind was in distress, but he wouldn't let him stop. Finally, West Wind fell down and died right there in the road."

Master grew red in the face. He held Taylor with a firm gaze.

"Mr. Taylor, I realize that you don't know us well, but Tom Henry has been taking care of my horses since he was a youngster. He loves them, and he takes good care of them. In this place, he is the expert on horses. Never again let me hear that you have argued with him about the care of any horse of mine. Do you understand?"

"Yessir," Taylor said, but he was not smiling. He stomped away.

Steward Taylor did not last long at Nomony Hall.

<hr />

Robert

"Master," Sam said, coming into the office, "Charles Thomas here to see you."

"Show him in. This must be happy news."

Thomas entered the room, holding his hat in his hand.

"I am glad to see you, Charles. Have you thought over my offer for the little seamstress?"

"I have thought about it. Give me a pound more than you offered, and I will do it."

I knew he would ask for more, so I had held back a bit on my offer. I now paused. I did not want to seem too anxious. "All right," I said finally, "but it is more than I expected to pay."

"Good. There is just one condition."

"What is that?"

"They can be together right away, but they must live for awhile at Greenfields, both of them."

"Are you suggesting that you rent Tom from me for a period of time?"

"Oh, no, I want him to work for me for a time, but not for rent. I mean it to be part of the price for the little wench. This was your idea, after all."

"That is outrageous! How long did you mean to keep him?"

"Five years. You know, like Jacob and Rachel in the Bible."

"Five years, indeed!" I stood up and slammed my fist on the desk so hard it made the inkwell jump.

Thomas gave his parting shot, "No Tom Henry, no Rose. And I will no longer allow him to visit at Greenfields."

I had to restrain myself to avoid throwing a book at his departing rear.

Telling Tom was very hard.

"Master, I cannot bear to be cut off from Rose completely. Please do something. I will do anything to make it up to you. I'll work there and here—anything."

"Much as I love you, Tom, I cannot do what you ask. It is too much."

A month later

"That Charles Thomas back, Master."

"Show him in, Sam. Let's see what he's got to say."

"Councillor Carter," said a smiling Thomas, holding out his hand. "I think perhaps I was a bit unreasonable."

"You think so, Mr. Thomas?" I tried to keep the sarcasm out of my voice.

"Suppose Tom Henry works for me for two years instead of five."

I thought about how, if I did not accept, I would feel in Tom's place, forbidden to marry, or even see the woman I loved. I did not like being manipulated by the little red-faced man, Thomas. "If I were to agree to that, Mr. Thomas, I would pay you half for Rose at the beginning of our bargain and the other half when she and Tom come back here to live permanently. And I don't know what I will do without Tom Henry for that period of time. Further, you must acknowledge that Rose is mine, on loan to you, as is Tom for the entire time. But I have a few conditions of my own. I insist upon my slaves being well-treated. Tom and Rose may not be beaten or whipped without my prior permission—and I can assure you that permission will not be easily forthcoming. You and your overseer shall not lay hands on either of them, unless you confer with me first. If you fail these conditions, they will both immediately come to Nomony Hall as my property, and the rest of the contract will thereafter be null and void."

"You drive a hard bargain, Councillor."

"I do not think so, sir. I only do it at all because of the value I place on Tom Henry's happiness."

We shook hands, and I had the bargain drawn up, and we signed it with witnesses. I did not trust the man.

Tom was joyous.

"I can't wait to have that uppity nigger under my control," Thomas had said after we signed the contract, and I had a very bad feeling about what I had just done.

33

Late September, 1771: Greenfields

Tom Henry

"The weather is threatening, my dear," Thomas said to his wife. "Don't you think you should wait and go another day?"

The morning sky had been blue, but now, off to the west, black clouds were gathering.

Mistress Thomas was pacing impatiently, dressed for visiting in a green silk bodice and overskirt over her ample bulk, with a quilted petticoat underneath.

"My heart is set on going to visit my sister in Westmoreland Courthouse, as you very well know, Charles. Her baby will be here anytime now, and I want to take her the blanket and booties I have knitted. Rose has folded it all, and everything is set to go. The clouds will blow away. I'm certain of it."

Thomas sighed. His wife became extremely irritable and occasionally violent when she did not have her way. I had seen her beat him with a stick of wood from the fireplace.

I wanted to strengthen his resolve. "It looks like a bad storm coming. The wind is already picking up. The coach will get muddy, and the horses are afraid of lightning and thunder."

"I did not ask your opinion in the matter. Take her, and you best be certain she does not come to any harm."

I opened the door to the coach I had just cleaned and shined and gave Mistress a hand up as she raised her plump body into it. It was already loaded with her gifts. I had hitched up the two steadiest horses, mares named Zepher and Bonnie. The coach was a new one, which looked suspiciously similar to Master Robert Carter's, painted a subdued green with black trim, and bright yellow wheels, but that was the only similarity this place bore to Nomony Hall.

I climbed atop the driver's seat, and we were on our way. The road to Westmoreland Courthouse from Greenfields was really just a narrow path through the trees. Today, it was still slippery from yesterday's rain and was treacherous for the horses.

Our journey began over a flat area. Then the road dipped toward a ford over a swamp. The horses shied at the water around their feet, but continued through the water without incident.

The road then curved, crossed another flat area, and curved again. As we came to the curve, the road began to drop off toward a second ford. Just then, there appeared a sudden zigzag of lightning, followed by a loud crack of thunder, and it began to rain heavily, a thorough, soaking Northern Neck rain.

The slippery descending road, the lightning, the thunder, and the rain combined to spook the horses. I slowed them down and managed to calm them, but Zepher balked at crossing the stream. I could feel the rain soaking into my hat, white shirt, and coat.

"Tom Henry," shouted Mistress, sitting in the relative dryness of the coach, "get me to my sister's and out of this storm right now."

"I'm doing my best, Mistress. The horses are skittish."

"Whip them. Get them moving." I realized now that she was as afraid of the storm as the horses.

"If I whip them, they will be worse. I have to keep them calm and under control."

"Nonsense! I order you to whip them."

All this talking went on while I was trying desperately to bring the lead mare, Zepher, back under my control. Every clap of thunder, every streak of lightning—and they were frequent now—made her more nervous. I was afraid she would bolt at any minute, away from the road. The ground was slippery under the horse's feet, and I could hardly see for the rain coming down.

Mistress's screaming made the horses worse. I managed to stop them and jump down from the seat to take Zepher by the harness in order to lead them through the swamp.

After I dismounted, I saw Mistress out of the corner of my eyes stand up in the coach and reach out the window to take the whip from its holder. Before I could say anything, she gave the whip a hard crack.

Zepher bolted immediately, causing the coach to careen off the road and into the swamp, taking Bonnie, Mistress, and me with it. The harness was forced out of my hand. The coach crashed into the murky water with Mistress inside.

Standing shin deep in the cold water, I looked around. Zepher was now standing still for the moment, shying at the water and mud swirling around her feet. Bonnie stood restlessly next to Zepher, looking confused. It could have been worse. The legs of the horses were sound, not broken.

The black and green paint of the coach was streaked with mud. It stood at a crazy angle, up to the front axle in mud. One of its fine yellow wheels was off its axle and lying in the muck stirred up by the wreck.

Mistress Thomas was trying to right herself on the seat, arms and legs askew. She screamed that her leg hurt.

I recovered the harness before the next clap of thunder could send the horses off running. I disconnected them from the coach and tied them to a tree.

Then, after the horses calmed somewhat, I turned to Mistress. Had the situation not been so fraught with dangerous consequences, it would have been funny. Mistress was sitting up against the side of the coach, one elbow down, one leg in the air, petticoat and overskirt partially covering her head.

I took off my coat and set it beside the road on a patch of grass. I half-pulled, half-lifted, Mistress Thomas bodily from the coach and to the relative safety of the road. It was not an easy task. I expected her to resist any attempt of mine to touch her, but she did not. She merely continued to scream and scold as I placed her, sitting, on my coat. All that concerned her was that she was getting soaking wet and was in pain.

The rain ran off Mistress's hat, and her curls drooped in the downpour. As I looked at her, I realized that, although it was she who had put us in this situation, I was the one who would be in trouble.

I had to push that thought to the back of my mind. Right now, I had to get the mistress to safety, hang on to the horses, and preserve the coach—if all that was possible.

Up on a hill nearby, I spotted the house of Abraham Anderson, a free black man who was married to a kitchen slave at Nomony Hall. I was sure that Mistress Thomas also knew Abraham. Smoke was coming from his chimney. It would be safe and dry in his cabin.

"Mistress, can you stand?" I asked.

"My ankle hurts too much."

"We must get to that house yonder." I pointed to the cabin.

"I will not set foot in that place," she said. "Negras live there."

"But, Mistress, surely it is better than sitting here in the pouring rain."

Nevertheless, with the rain pouring over her and frequent bursts of lightning and thunder, she insisted she could not go into the home of "those people."

"I want to go home," she said. "Now."

God preserve us, back across the swamp. I reckoned we had gone just about half the seven or eight miles from Greenfield to Westmoreland Courthouse.

"Try to stand," I said as I put my hand under Mistress's elbow. She was still fussing, but I got her to her feet. She attempted to put weight on the foot of her injured leg, but she crumpled, putting most of her weight on me. She really could not walk.

I had never seen her on horseback.

"Do you ride?" I asked.

Her answer surprised me. "When I was young."

"If I go to Greenfields to get someone to bring you there, you will have to wait here in the rain for my return. If you can get on one of the horses, I can lead you home."

Given the choice between waiting in the rain and the mud or riding horseback, Mistress reluctantly agreed to try the horse. Placing one hand under her muddy shoe to hoist her up on Bonnie, I gingerly used the other to push her rear. This was a touchy business indeed. When I first moved in that direction, Mistress turned and gave me a look that would cut rope, but she must have decided it was the only way. She closed her eyes and let me push on her through her petticoat and skirt. She grabbed the harness, and together we managed to get her on Bonnie's back.

Bonnie sidestepped a little. *Please let the thunder and lightning hold off until she's well seated.* Mistress sat sideways with her injured leg on the horse's neck. She bumped up and down, but she managed to stay on. I rode Zepher and led Bonnie. We made a soggy parade back to Greenfields.

As we traveled, it continued to rain, and there were occasional flashes of lightning and thunder. Finally, we approached the drive to the house. Out of the great house and into the rain with a whip in his hand came Master Thomas. His wig was askew, his waistcoat unbuttoned.

"What is this? I told you to be careful. How dare you come back here without the coach. What manner is this to treat your mistress? You uppity nigger! I always said Councillor Carter was too easy on his slaves—don't teach them right. Thinks he is such a great man. And you, you presume to insult my wife."

I knew the futility of arguing with him. No matter what I said, it would be even worse if I tried to contradict him. He had his house servants lift his wife off Bonnie and help her inside. She scolded and fussed the whole time.

Thomas pointed the whip at me. "You bring the coach back here, and then I will deal with you."

I gathered some tools from the coach house and walked the horses once again to the swamp. By now, there was no thunder or lightning, just a steady downpour of rain. I was wet through to the skin. Moving steadily and calmly, under my gentle reassurance, the horses pulled the main part of the coach from the swamp onto the road. It was dripping with mud and swamp plants. Then, I went back for the wheel. When it was freed from the mud, I could see that the wheel itself was not badly broken. It could be fixed. Temporarily attaching it to the coach, I hitched Bonnie and Zepher once again to the front to pull. I sat atop Zepher's back and guided the horses slowly so I could watch the wheel.

At last, the horses and I, soaking wet and exhausted, arrived at Greenfields.

When Master Thomas saw the coach, his round fat face grew redder than ever, and his eyes glinted. He struck the tip of the whip in his hand on the ground. He was standing legs apart inside the coach house, out of the rain. I could see that he wanted to use that whip, and as he approached me, I could smell grog on his breath. The man was furious and drunk as well.

"Good thing for you that Carter forbad my whipping you, but you will pay for this. The rest of your time here, you will be treated as a field slave. You will live and work with the field slaves, and get one peck of corn per week."

I never had been a field slave. A coachman was very high in the hierarchy of slaves, entitled to respect. I had been born a house slave, and, what is more, I had earned my position. This was impossible. This could not be happening. Hot rebellion rose in me at the thought of being treated as a field slave. All that meant nothing to the angry little man before me. Outwardly, I stood firm without flinching. I had no choice but to be strong.

Master Thomas thought a moment more, and a wicked smile came over his face.

"You insulted my wife," he said. He cracked the whip in his hand. "I will punish your nigger bitch."

I know my face changed then in spite of my willing it not to do so.

"Your little wench will work in the fields, too. She will have the hardest duty I can give her. She will get a field slave's rations and live in the quarters, but not with you. If it weren't for my agreement with Councillor Carter, I would teach you both your proper places."

Holding the whip in one hand, he ran the free end through his other hand and looked at it longingly.

"Tell me," he asked, "how long do you think your pretty little Rose will survive in the fields?"

I took a step toward him, fire burning in my chest. It took all the control I had to keep from pummeling the man. The thought crossed my mind that I could easily strangle him with my bare hands. My fists were clenched, but I managed to stand firm. I knew that Thomas would welcome any excuse to break his agreement with Master Carter.

"And one thing more," Thomas added. "You and Rose will not speak to each other until the end of your time here."

34

Fall 1772: Nomony Hall

Robert

Tom Henry always lurked somewhere in the back of my mind, but I had not seen him. I had expected to run into Charles Thomas out with Tom driving, but I did not. Today was no different, but I was busy. I was meeting with my stewards. The planting was mostly done, and the crops seemed to be coming along as they should. The problem was going to be selling them at a good price.

"I've observed some young hands," I told my stewards, "who seem likely for better things than field work. Priamus from Forest Quarter, for instance, I want to learn the trade of carter. Dennis from Old Ordinary and Dick from Libra, I will have learn the trade of miller. Simon from Nomony Hall is a good carpenter; he shall be trained as a cabinetmaker, and it's time Jesse, Baptist Billy's son, began working the seines with his father."

"Councillor, you are diverting workers from the fields into trades."

"Yes, that is my intention."

"Aren't you afraid they will run away if they get too skilled?"

"My experience is that they will like the skilled work better than working in the fields, and I no longer need so many in the fields."

The mills and the bakery were not making as much money as I had hoped, but it was a beginning. The Negroes assigned to them seemed pleased with their new responsibilities.

Sam and I made a trip to Baltimore by boat to visit the Iron Works before it got too cold. The Iron Works, at least, was making good money.

I took the time to go over to Annapolis to visit Benjamin Tasker's widow, Anne, taking gifts and letters from Fanny.

Back home, all seemed to be well with young John. He was growing apace, but I could see immediately on my return that Fanny was not her usual happy self. She hugged me and smiled, but it was a wan smile, and when she sat down on the sofa in the office, she did not speak.

I sat down beside her. "What in the world is the matter?"

"Ben has been sick—coughing. No one seems to know what it is. He gets very weak and pale and stays in bed. Soon he is up again, but then he is down again. I do not know what to do for him, and the doctor is really no help. And Bob. He leaves the house in anger, and stays out all night. He refuses to say where he goes. He pays no attention to me when I try to correct him."

"Surely, whatever Ben has will pass. We will call another doctor if you like. As for Bob, I will talk to him. What he needs is a good tutor and something useful to do."

I didn't tell her that Ben's illness sounded like that of Lawrence Washington; he coughed like Ben, became exhausted like Ben, and no one seemed to know what to do. He later went to Barbados as he had said he would, and he died there. I really did not want to tell Fanny that. I didn't even want to think about it.

～

There had still been no visit from Charles Thomas and no sight of Tom Henry out driving. I thought to see them at Nomony Hall or at court, but there was no sign of them.

It had been a busy time, but I felt I must ride out to see Charles Thomas regardless of what else had to be done. It had been a year.

I set off on a cool morning over the narrow road through the woods and up the lane to the house. Thomas came out to greet me, but he was not so jovial this time. In fact, he seemed quite ill at ease.

"How are you, Charles?" I asked.

He did not seem inclined to invite me into the house, instead remaining standing on the porch.

"I had thought to see you out and about before this," I said. "You must be very busy."

"Oh, yes, indeed I am."

Still he made no move to let me come into the house.

"I would like to talk to you," I said. "May we go inside?"

He shrugged but stepped aside and motioned me into the house. We went to the formal sitting room. Thomas could not seem to sit still. He sat on the edge of his chair, crossing first one leg and then the other. His hand lay tentatively on the arm of his chair.

I endured some pointless small talk about crops and weather. Finally, I could stand it no longer.

"How is Tom Henry working out for you, Charles?"

"He is somewhat insolent, to be blunt."

"Tom is an intelligent person," I said, a little put off by his remark. "I'm sure he has some ideas of his own about things. Nevertheless, I have never known him to be insolent. I will be glad to talk to him if you like."

Thomas shook his head quickly. "Oh, no, that is not necessary. He's gotten better these last weeks."

Strange. "And Rose, how is she doing?"

"She's fine. She's fine, learning to become a seamstress like her mother."

"Good. Good. If you don't mind, I would like to see them both, to say hello."

"I'm truly sorry, Mr. Carter." Thomas looked down and shifted in his chair. "They happen to be away at the moment. Perhaps you can come some other time."

"Away? Is that so?"

"Yes, yes. Tom has driven Mistress Thomas and Rose to my wife's sister's for a visit."

It seemed strange to me that Rose would go. It did not feel right. Still, it was a serious matter to call a man a liar. I determined to come another day.

⌁

October 1772
Greenfields
Tom Henry

The bell rang at sunrise, and I dragged myself out from under my thin blanket. Fall was coming on hard now. At Greenfields, the field slaves were expected to go barefoot until cold weather set in, and I still had not received my shoes for the winter. My feet had at first grown cut and sore before calluses finally began to form. I had labored under the rain and the sun during the hot spring and summer months with nothing but a straw hat for protection, and now we began to suffer from the cold.

I picked up my knife for cutting the tobacco from its stalks. This morning I was supposed to choose, as I went among the plants, which leaves were ready and which needed more ripening, a hard task for someone who had never cut tobacco before, but I fell back on Dadda Gumby's advice and listened and learned. The penalty for not knowing what to cut was the same as wanton disregard of duty.

So I began walking down the first row, watching the more experienced hands, trying to figure out what the leaves ready to cut looked like—yellower than the rest of the leaves, and wrinkled, kind of like alligator skin. I forced my sore hands to do what the others did. We all laid the cut leaves on the tobacco hill, all pointing the same way.

After it was full daylight, we stopped for a breakfast of bread made from the weekly ration of corn, which was one peck per slave. We received no meat at Greenfields. I was told we would get some at Christmas.

After breakfast, we worked until the sun was high in the sky at noon. Our dinner, which was a repeat of our breakfast, took place in the field. After dinner, we began picking up the piles of tobacco leaves, called "turns," which we had cut and piled earlier. The turns were heavy and awkward to carry, but work would not end for the day until all the tobacco cut that day was hung, regardless of how late it got.

I was aching in every muscle of my body, looking forward to going back to the quarters. I was sure I would never get used to the long hours of physical labor. Supper would have to wait until the workday was over. Maybe I would skip supper and just go to sleep.

I had always considered house slaves to be superior to field slaves—speaking better, dressing better. Working alongside the field hands for this time had taught me that, just as the men of the Enlightenment thought that the idea of equality ought to apply to all whites, it now seemed to me that it also ought to apply to all blacks. I spoke better and knew more than the field slaves about the greater world, but they knew about growing tobacco—and they knew about survival. They just managed to keep on and on, in good weather and bad.

We worked in a gang: another man, a woman named Kitt, and I. Rose worked in the other gang. The work of the women was identical to that of the men, and I had come to respect the field hands' strength and skill, as well as their composure under difficult circumstances. I let them know of my new respect.

"We blessed, now, man," Apollo said. "Harvesting the easiest part. Hard time planting in the spring, weeding and grubbing in the summer, suckering and topping and pruning. We lucky this time of year."

Henry Ross, the overseer, was riding on horseback, going back and forth among us, keeping us moving—and keeping Rose and me apart. He drove us hard, wielding a rawhide whip that had the butt end loaded with lead. He liked to crack it menacingly at anyone who paused in his or her work. I'd seen him strike out any number of times, cutting a person who displeased him wherever the whip-end landed. I had my head down, looking to pick up a turn.

Suddenly, I heard Ross's whip split the air with a sharp crack. "Goddammit, you clumsy nigger bitch," he shouted.

His words cut me to the heart. *Rose?*

But his wrath was directed at Kitt, who had tripped and fallen, dropping the turn she was carrying. Tobacco leaves littered the ground, and some were partially crushed.

"Master's gonna be mighty mad. I'll teach you to watch what you're doing!"

With that, he jumped down from his horse and grabbed Kitt by the arm. He dragged her kicking and screaming to the tobacco barn from which extended a beam of wood.

Thank God it was not Rose.

"Mercy, Master, no. Have mercy," Kitt was screaming, tears streaming down her face and onto her bodice.

"I didn't do it on purpose. It won't never happen again."

I watched in horror as Ross threw her to the ground, tied up his horse, and unwound a rope from his saddle. He stripped Kitt's dress all the way to her waist, leaving her back bare and her breasts exposed. She shivered, and I could see gooseflesh on her arms and chest. She bowed her head and tried to cover her breasts with her arms. Ross then threw the rope over the beam on the tobacco barn and tied Kitt's wrists together in front of her with the other end.

Terror showed in Kitt's eyes. "Oh, mercy, mercy."

She pulled at the ropes to no avail. The more she pulled, the tighter they held. Tears were streaming down her cheeks and over her neck and breasts, and her eyes were wide with terror.

Ross pulled the rope over the beam until Kitt was suspended by her arms, her feet just touching the ground. She kicked in vain, trying to get a foothold, but she could not, and the whole weight of her body was now suspended from her wrists.

Glancing around him to make sure no one would try to interfere, the overseer got himself into position and drew back the whip. The lead weight came down on Kitt's back with a crack. She screamed. Then another blow. Over and over. The lead cut her skin. After the third lash, blood began oozing out of the stripes on her back.

I instinctively started to move forward, but two others held me back. "You can't help her. Only get punished you ownself."

Ross counted his blows. Kitt continued to scream and cry until she could scream no more. When Ross reached thirty, he loosened the rope and let Kitt's body drop to the ground. Then he left her there, hands still bound, to bleed on the cold ground with nothing to cover her. No one dared touch her. He ordered us all back to work.

As I bent to pick up my turn, I saw Charles Thomas, astride his horse, smirking at me.

When work was finally over for the day, I went with Apollo in the dark to pick up Kitt. She was lying, weak and chilled, right where she had been left. I was afraid at first that she might be dead, but then she opened her eyes.

I had taken my remedies along. Not only did I have those Dadda Gumby had taught me about; I had learned about the remedies white folks used. Like Dadda before me, I had developed a reputation for healing and had been called upon by whites and blacks at Nomony Hall. Charles Thomas did not know or care.

Kitt drew in a breath when she first felt me clean her cuts. I used a soft cloth and soap to gently remove the dirt and dried blood from her skin. Then I applied an ointment I had made from violets and marigold blossoms.

As I worked, I thought about Master Carter. He would never have allowed such a beating to begin with, especially for something accidental. He always asked what really happened and was as likely to believe a slave as an overseer. He certainly would not have left her beaten on the cold ground. Master Robert was a different sort of master from Charles Thomas, but slaves did not choose their masters. All I could hope for was for Rose and me to survive until we could go home to Nomony Hall.

Having done what I could for Kitt, I told her family to keep her warm and keep the wounds clean. I left some of the ointment with them. She would be expected to be up and working in the morning.

Exhausted, I returned to the cabin I shared with a family. They were asleep on their straw pallets on the dirt floor in the single room of the cabin when I returned. I slid beneath my blanket and tried to sleep.

I thought of Rose. I missed the smell of her and the warmth of her body, and I knew she must be cold, too. While we worked, at least I could see her. She was growing thinner and more drawn as time went on, but she was beautiful to me. Night was the hardest time.

Even at Greenfields, Saturday night after the work was done, the men brought out their banjos, fiddles, and drums and played and sang. And on Sunday, I would go out to the circle beneath an old oak and listen to the preacher talk about Jesus. I had been taught Anglican catechism at Bray School, and the African religion of Dadda Gumby, but Rose listened to the Dissenter preachers, so I came, too.

As the slave preacher exhorted us to have faith in a God that could free our souls—if not our bodies—I could see Rose and judge her condition. We sang a hymn of hope, its hidden meaning clear to all of us:

"Go down, Moses,
Way down to Egypt's land.
Tell old Pharoah,
Let my people go."

I doubted we would ever see a Moses come along for us. That was that, just a dream.

After the service, I left the circle and went into the woods, looking for herbs.

35

January 1773: Nomony Hall

Robert

"It is time you learn something of dealing with people," I told Ben and Bob. Ben was feeling well, and Bob was being unusually cooperative, so I took them when I set off for Greenfields. They were now sixteen and fourteen, respectively, old enough.

We enjoyed the ride together in spite of the chill wind, joking and laughing.

As we rode up the lane to Greenfields, I saw Charles Thomas come out to meet us. I always had the feeling he stood at the front window of his house, keeping his eye on the drive.

His expression when we arrived told me that he was not glad to see us. However, he did have a servant, who was not Tom, I noticed, take our horses and invite us in. He did not offer any Christmas season cheer, although the Twelve Days were not yet up. Tom was right; the man was no gentleman.

We stood in the hall.

"Charles, I have come to see Tom Henry and Rose."

"I'm sorry," said Thomas, avoiding looking me in the eye, "but I sent Tom Henry off to take Mistress Thomas to her sister's for an after-Christmas visit. Rose went along. She is to teach the sister's seamstress some special stitching."

That struck me as very odd indeed. I looked at the boys, and they looked at me.

"When may we see them, then?"

Thomas hesitated. "I will have Tom Henry carry Rose to Nomony Hall one day."

"I will look forward to that happening very soon."

"Papa," said Ben as we were riding home, "don't you think Mr. Thomas is lying about Tom and Rose not being there?"

"I do not believe him, but I'm not prepared to call a man a liar without proof. Let's see if Tom and Rose come to us." *Why, I wonder, is he hiding them?*

———

I was off to Machodoc Plantation on my usual rounds to see overseer John Sanford. I was approaching Sanford's house when the slave named James limped toward me. James was usually a humble person, never caused any trouble, but today there was a small group of people coming behind him from the quarters.

James paused in front of me, looking down and shuffling about on his feet.

"Tell him, tell him," said a voice in the group behind him.

James looked up at me. "Master, John Sanford beat me for stealing a hog from his pen, but I never steal nay hog in my life."

"He right, Master." Several slaves nodded in agreement.

"One of you go tell Sanford I want to see him here."

Sanford came out of the house, looking surprised and a little bewildered.

"John," I said, "what is this I hear about a stolen hog?"

"Somebody took a hog from my pen two nights ago, Councillor. It was James."

"I've never known James to steal. What makes you think he took it?"

"He was roasting a hog in his yard yesterday."

"James, Mr. Sanford says that his hog went missing two nights ago and that yesterday you were roasting a hog in your yard. Is that so?"

"Yes, Master, but it be my own hog. I never took his'n."

"Can anyone verify that?"

Several slaves stepped forward. One said, "I knowed James used to have two hogs. Now only one be in his pen."

Another said, "James never stole nay thing from nobody."

A short man, who had been quietly listening, stepped forward. "Master Carter, I knows who taken that hog."

"Who was it, Henry?"

"Claude Beauchamp, Master. He have a little place just down the road."

"I know him. What makes you think he stole it?"

"I seed him take it from the pen."

"Really?"

"If you goes there right now, I bet you see that hog."

"Why didn't you tell Mr. Sanford this before now?"

He looked from me to Sanford and back to me. "I don't like to get mixed up in white folks' business."

Sanford and I rode to the Beauchamp place, and, sure enough, there in a muddy pen was the missing hog. Beauchamp was nowhere to be seen.

"Go see the sheriff about Beauchamp, John, and in the future, don't be so quick to jump to conclusions." There was no way, however, to take back the beating of an innocent man.

Fanny took to her bed about three in the afternoon. This would be our thirteenth child. I was forty, graying at the temples, carrying a little extra weight around the middle, but as she faced the familiar ordeal of childbirth, she was as beautiful as ever—and just as serene.

Childbirth always made me nervous, in spite of the many times Fanny had been through it without a problem. I remembered too well Aunt Maria and several others I had known over the years.

The house servants were scurrying this way and that under orders from Mama Gumby, who, bless her soul, was still in charge. I sent for Dr. Jones and a wet nurse and retired to the office with a bottle of grog.

Sarah Fairfax Carter came into the world—lusty and loud—and I went upstairs to see the bundle wrapped in a white blanket. All the children trooped in as well to greet their new sister.

I still had not seen hide nor hair of Tom Henry or Rose. Thomas didn't send them as he promised, and something always seemed to keep me at home.

March 1773
Greenfields
Tom Henry

I grabbed Charles Thomas by the throat with my bare hands. I saw the look of surprise on his face. He struggled, kicking his feet and clawing at my wrists with his hands, but to no avail. I had him tight. I heard him gasp for breath. Stark fear showed in his eyes. I squeezed harder, and I saw his eyes bulge. Finally, he stopped struggling.

Then I awoke. I had been tossing on my hard straw pallet, and though I had never been a violent person, this had become a recurring dream.

I despaired at the thought of another day at Greenfields. It wasn't the work. What kept me from returning to sleep on this night was worrying about what would happen to us. What would happen to Rose?

Even though Master had tried to protect us, the contract seemed to do us little good. We had not been physically beaten yet, but I was afraid Thomas might even cross that line. He certainly wanted to. I could see it in his eyes as he watched us, and he watched us all the time. I would catch him sitting on his horse, looking at us, and particularly at Rose, with that malignant smile of his.

I was familiar now with the beatings at Greenfields. They were both frequent and vicious, and though I was sure I could stand it myself, I didn't know about Rose. I could not bear the thought of the lead-tipped whip cutting into her delicate skin as it had Kitt's. What if she simply became too weak to go on?

During the winter, Thomas made Rose chop and carry firewood and every other heavy task he could think of. Then she had been sick, and he made her suffer without treatment and without letup in her work. I could picture her, as I lay on my pallet, thin and pale, the shine gone from her eyes, her clothes ragged, and her hands chaffed to the point of bleeding. I could do nothing to help her.

What would happen to her as spring drifted into hot summer, and we had to cut the tobacco blossoms in the hot sun, pull off the grubs and worms by hand, and pull weeds in heat and rain?

Would she even survive?

Why hadn't we seen Master Robert? We were only supposed to be loaned to Thomas after the first year—well, I always was. Why didn't Master check on us? Thomas was abusing Master's trust, but Master did not know it.

Running away wasn't possible. Rose didn't have the strength for it, and I would not leave her. I thought of trying to get a message to Master Carter, but no slave would carry it. They were all afraid of Thomas.

Our only hope was Master Carter, and he did not come.

36

March 1773: Nomony Hall

Robert

Nat brought my horse for the ride to Greenfields. After my last visit, I had seen nothing of Tom Henry or Rose, and I was going to find out what happened.

My anger grew as I mounted and began down the poplar lane, but before I got to the end of the lane, Sam called to me.

"Mistress say you need to come right now!"

Fanny was in the hall at the bottom of the stairs. "Ben is worse. I've never seen him this bad."

I went upstairs. Ben was back in bed again, horribly pale, coughing, sweating, and fighting for breath.

We sent for Dr. Jones. He insisted it was just a bad case of ague. He knew better; he just did not know what to call it.

"This cannot be the ague," I said. "It does not come and go this way."

"I recommend we bleed him," said Dr. Jones.

"No!" Fanny was adamant. "What is the logic in taking the blood of a person who is already weak? I will not have it. I wish Tom Henry was here."

I did not want to say that I did not believe Tom Henry could help either. I remembered Lawrence Washington.

"Very well, Madame," said Dr. Jones, frowning and pushing his glasses to the bridge of his nose. "Then I will leave him to your care."

We gave him honey in grog to ease his cough. I watched as Fanny administered the concoction. She tried to smile at me, but her face was almost as pale as Ben's. With a sigh, she sat down by his bedside and rubbed her forehead.

The day was ruined.

———

Before I could even think to leave the next day, a frantic messenger came to the door. Sam showed him to the office, and I went there to see what was the matter.

The man was too agitated to stand still. "You know John Sorrells," he said without introduction.

It was a statement, not a question. Sorrells was a middling farmer and a close neighbor of ours.

"Of course I know him. What has happened?"

"Well, Councillor, some niggers tried to kill him last night."

"What? How do you know this?"

"The sheriff sent me round to let everybody know."

"But he was not killed, you say? You said they tried to kill him."

"Yessir." The messenger shifted his weight to his other foot.

"Mrs. Sorrells seen them running away. They was caught this morning. They are in jail now in Westmoreland Courthouse. Everybody's in a state, sir. Might be the beginnings of an uprising. Sorrells never did nothing bad to nay niggers."

"Yes, yes, I understand what you are saying. Thank you for coming."

"Do you think it is an uprising, Robert?" Fanny asked me.

"I do not believe so. Still I will stay close to home until the panic subsides." I loaded my flintlock pistol and laid it on a table by the door and told Bob to load a weapon as well.

"Will they come to kill us, too, Papa?" Betty asked me.

"No, dear, no one in this house is going to be killed. I mean to stay here to be sure of it."

Two days later, I went to Westmoreland Courthouse to find out what was going on.

"What's going on, Sheriff?"

"Turns out the slaves belonged to Sorrells's brother, Councillor. They said he told them to kill Sorrells. Something about a land dispute between the Sorrellses. Anyway, John Sorrells's wife saw them running away—that's how they got caught. Lost their nerve, they said. Said they had nothing against John Sorrells."

"Will the brother be prosecuted?"

"Not likely. You know niggers can't testify in court. There ain't nay other evidence."

The justices ultimately decided the evidence was too weak to prosecute the Negroes for attempted murder, but they were ordered whipped and released.

The county breathed a sigh of relief, except, I supposed, for John Sorrells.

I had lost three days. Now, I must certainly go to Greenfields.

I was dressed for riding. Ned was bringing my horse and another around. Fanny came out of the office with a newspaper in her hand.

"Virginia has formed a permanent Committee of Correspondence, Robert. R. H. Lee and your cousin, Robert Carter Nicholas, are on it. You must read this."

"That is an important development, my dear. I imagine they will now behave as if they were an alternate government to the governor, but I'll read it later. I can wait no longer to go to Greenfields."

I went from the house and mounted my horse, leading the other. I set out for the Thomas place. Charles Thomas did not come to meet me, but I saw activity around the place. I did not believe Thomas was away.

I tied the horses to a tree, as no one came to get them, and knocked on the door. I was determined to see Tom and Rose. No answer came to my knock at first, but then an ancient Negro opened the door.

I recognized him from the visit Fanny and I made to the place. He was called Daniel.

"Master Carter, how you?" Not looking me in the eye, he said, "Master Thomas not here today."

"May I come in?"

Daniel stood aside to let me pass.

I stood in the hall.

"I will wait for your master to return. I want to see Tom Henry and Rose."

Daniel smiled and nodded. "Would you care to sit in the parlor?"

"No, Daniel. I will wait here. You might as well tell your master that I will not leave until I see him."

He smiled again and shuffled down the hall. I could hear him muttering to himself. "He know Master Carter here, but he scared to face him."

I waited a half hour or so. Just as I was about to invite myself to search the place, Charles Thomas appeared.

"I came to see Tom and Rose," I said, "and I won't be put off."

"They are not here just now.

"Where are they this time?" I did not even try to keep the irony from my voice.

I could see Daniel, standing behind Thomas, shaking his head ever so slightly. The air in the house was still and hot. It occurred to me that, although the hall lay open from the front straight through to the back door, the doors were not open to let in cool air. *What is Thomas trying to hide?*

"Well, where are they, then?"

Thomas took a minute before answering. "I don't know, exactly."

"Charles, I find that hard to believe. You just do not have so many slaves that you cannot keep track of them."

Daniel, still standing behind Thomas, nodded his head slightly toward the back of the house."

"Well, suppose we just go look for them." I started toward the closed back door.

"No need to do it ourselves." Thomas rushed to keep up with me. "I'll send Daniel."

Daniel opened the back door and started down the hill behind the house, and I followed him outside. Daniel shuffled down the hill toward the back fields. It seemed to me that he knew exactly where to look for them. *But what are they doing in the back fields?*

"Come on inside," Thomas said. "We can wait for them in the parlor."

"I prefer to stay right where I am."

After what seemed an eternity, Daniel came up from between the outbuildings, walking along the road from the fields. Just behind him were two Negroes, barefoot, their clothes dark with sweat and covered with dust. They were dressed in rags and terribly thin. The woman particularly looked wan.

At first, I did not comprehend that these two scarecrows were Tom and Rose. As I realized who they were, I was enraged. I had been intentionally deceived, and they looked terrible.

Tom swallowed hard, holding back tears as he approached. *Could this be my proud Tom Henry?*

Rose stood back, a stunned expression on her face.

My face was hot, and I felt my hands ball into fists.

"What have you done to my people, Thomas? Look at them."

"I needed help in the fields," Thomas said in a low voice.

Before I could stop myself, I grabbed Thomas by the front of his shirt. I was taller than him, and when I pulled him up, his feet barely touched the ground. I shook him, and his eyes went white with fear. We were nose to nose.

"They are not field slaves, you damned idiot! You can be glad I don't have a horsewhip to hand, or I would show you how I truly feel."

I let go of him with such suddenness that he landed on his buttocks on the ground.

I told Daniel, "Go get my horses. I am taking Tom and Rose from this place."

Thomas got up with as much dignity as he could muster under the circumstances and dusted himself off. "They are mine to do with as I please," he said. "You cannot take them."

"More than a year has passed, Thomas, and they are both mine. You have broken our contract. You have abused them sorely, and you have betrayed my trust."

Daniel returned. I helped Tom and then Rose onto one horse, and I mounted the other. Tom sat as straight as he could on the horse. Rose huddled wordlessly against him, arms around his middle. We started down the lane.

Tom said, "I thought you had forgotten us."

Thomas ran alongside us. "I'll call the sheriff on you for this."

"Do your damnedest."

I was almost as angry at myself as I was at Thomas. How could I let this happen to my people?

37

October 1773: Nomony Hall

I spotted a young man coming up the poplar lane on horseback. He was soberly dressed, a slight, pleasant-looking soul with brown hair pulled into a queue at the nape of his neck.

He smiled, and shouted to me from a distance, extending his hand as he came across to where I was. "Are you Robert Carter?"

"Yes, indeed, and you must be Phillip Fithian. We have been anxiously awaiting your arrival. You must be worn out from your journey. Come inside."

Tom Henry had sent someone to take his horse by the time we reached the door.

He got down stiffly from his mount. "I am glad to be here, indeed, Mr. Carter. I have ridden all the way from my home in Greenwich, New Jersey."

"Not all in one day, I trust."

He laughed. "No, sir, not all in one day."

As we entered the house, the older children all came into the hall to greet him. Of all of them, seventeen-year-old Ben, feeling well again, was most excited to meet him.

"All right, children, let Mr. Fithian catch his breath."

The next day, Sunday, Ben had Fithian ride with him to services at St. Johns Church in Richmond Courthouse.

"We heard a sermon by the Reverend Mr. Gibbern," Ben said when they returned. He laughed and looked at Fithian. "I do not think Mr. Fithian was favorably impressed."

Fithian colored at Ben's frankness.

I smiled.

"I am afraid, Mr. Fithian, that the reverend is less renowned for his sermons than for his propensity to drink and play cards. He is a very sociable fellow, you see."

"Robert!" Fanny said, shocked.

For his part, Fithian looked as though he did not know what to say.

The schoolroom downstairs in the schoolhouse building was large—bookshelves around the paneled walls, a fireplace on one wall, individual desks for the children—a place I would like to have studied as a boy. It was good to see it filled again.

The children filed in. Ben, dressed neatly in shirt, britches, and waistcoat, eagerly took his place at a desk in the front of the room. Bob slouched in a desk near him, frowning. Next to him sat my nephew, Harry, my sister Betty's son, already fidgeting. Priscilla was sitting up straight, smiling, eagerly placing herself as close to the front as the boys would allow. Anne Tasker looked around as she sat herself in her seat, crossing her legs at the ankles. My younger daughters, Fanny and Betty, sat demurely, hands folded in their laps, waiting to see what Fithian would say. All the girls were dressed in white on my orders. I thought it would set a certain sense of decorum.

Slender and dressed in his sober fashion, Fithian stood at the front of the room, a slate board behind him on the wall and a podium in front of him. I noticed that he had hung a switch in a prominent place next to the slate.

I thought it was a daunting task he was setting out to do, teaching Bob and Ben Latin and Greek, Harry and the girls ciphering (for Fanny and I intended our girls to be educated).

They were all to learn French as well. Each child, Fithian said, would be allowed to proceed at his own pace.

As I slipped quietly out of the room, I heard Fithian say, "Now, ladies and gentlemen, let me tell you what I expect."

Fithian rode with us to attend a horse race in Richmond Courthouse.

"I'm glad you accepted my invitation, Mr. Fithian," I told him as we trotted along the road from Nomony Hall. "I wasn't sure you would feel it was proper to attend."

"I want to learn all I can about the lives of my students. It is true that I don't believe in gambling, but then, I do not believe in slavery, either, and yet here I am."

The man was nothing if not direct. "Is slavery not still legal in your colony of New Jersey?"

"I am distressed to say that it is, and I am sure there are those there who gamble as well."

"Someday, Mr. Fithian, I would like to hear whether you think slavery can be peacefully and economically ended."

We were so distracted by our conversation that we seemed to arrive quickly at our destination. At Richmond Courthouse, the road from Westmoreland Courthouse made a T. At the intersection, on a slight rise, was the courthouse. To our right, a much wider road stretched toward St. John's Church and beyond. To our left, the road made a gradual turn toward the Rappahannock, where a ferry connected Richmond Courthouse to Hobbs Hole.

Today, that wide section of the road would serve as a racetrack, starting at St. John's Church and ending a mile away toward the river. Men of all stations were already standing along the sides of the road, milling around and laying bets.

"The real runners in today's race are Yorrick, who belongs to John Tayloe of Mount Airy, and Gift, who belongs to Dr. Flood, "I told Fithian. "Both are reputed to be swift, but my money is on Yorrick."

We took our places on the north side of the road as the horses were readied to start from the church. A gunshot was fired, and the race began.

Fithian had not placed a bet, of course, but I noticed him standing beside Ben, loudly shouting encouragement to Yorrick. And, in the end, it was Yorrick who won.

We congratulated John Tayloe, collected our winnings, and proceeded to the tavern to spend some of them.

It was one of those rare occasions when there were no guests at the family table at dinner. The day was overcast; the sconces were lit. Altogether, the atmosphere was intimate, and, as we drank our wine, conversation flowed.

"I was warned against coming to Virginia, you know," Fithian said.

Fithian was a quiet man, but I had learned that he did not shrink from speaking his mind.

"Why is that?" Fanny asked him.

"I was told that it was a sickly place, that the people were wicked and profane, and that I would spend more than my salary would cover while I was here."

"My goodness," said Fanny, "and did you find us to be wicked and profane indeed?"

Fithian hesitated just a moment.

"What I found was a delightful countryside, where people were civil and polite, and the family to which I came to be remarkable for their regularity and economy."

"That is very kind of you to say, Mr. Fithian," I said.

Fithian also revealed that he kept a diary, and I realized suddenly that we were under close, though friendly, observation.

"You do not approve of slavery, however. Is that not what you said?"

"No, I do not, but it is not my business to tell the people of Virginia how to conduct their lives."

"There are many of us, even in Virginia, Mr. Fithian, who wish there were a way out of slavery."

"If that is so, why do you let it continue?"

"Of course, there are others who are quite content with the institution as it is. The problem, for those of us who would change it, is not so much whether to end it, but how. I am very hopeful that if we separate from England, Virginia will pass laws that gradually end slavery."

"Could you not simply free your slaves on your own?"

"Alas, there are strict laws regarding manumission. The only way one may free his slaves is in his will, or a slave may buy his freedom or another buy it for him. If a slave is freed, he must leave Virginia."

"Why would there be such a law?"

"Think about it. There are thousands of slaves in Virginia. If they were freed and allowed to stay, they might have no means of support. Many of them do not have skills that would allow them to make a living. There is, of course, the fear that large numbers of former slaves without employment or direction might turn against their former owners."

"Why do you not sell your slaves?"

"In the first place, I would then have no way to get the work done on my plantations. I will be completely honest with you as you have been with us. If I were to free my slaves, I would lose my family's living entirely. Though the slaves themselves are worth thousands of pounds, like most large landowners, I have very little actual money. I could not afford to pay wages to the hundreds of people I now own.

"And there is another consideration, equally important. If I sold my slaves, I would not have the ownership of them on my conscience, but they would still be slaves, likely separated from their families and their homes. Selling slaves is very disruptive to their lives. Selling them does not really solve the problem, you see."

"I see," said Fithian.

"I do not know the answers, Mr. Fithian. I wish I did. In the meantime, I believe it is my duty to care for everyone, my family and my slaves, and hope for a better future."

Bob changed the subject. "You know how you say, Papa, that Negroes are capable of learning if they have the chance? Well, Mr. Fithian has introduced us to the poetry of a free Negro woman from up North. Her name is Phillis Wheatley, and I really like what she writes."

"Is that so?"

"Well, Bob," said Fithian, "I am most glad to hear you express such sensibility. I've always said that you are not without ability, but you are an uneven student. I heartily wish you would adapt the same attitude toward your other studies."

My thoughts wandered a moment. Bob was not a stupid child, but Fithian was right that he was unsettled. What's more, he had a quick and violent temper. Just a few days before our conversation, he had struck Anne Tasker, and I had ordered him whipped for it. He treated the house servants abominably. It was hard to believe that the boy who expressed an interest in poetry was the same one who could be so untamed. I really did not know what to do with my son, but I commented instead on Phillis Wheatley.

"She is proof indeed that Negroes are capable of learning, and of refined sentiments. Look at Tom Henry, who reads and writes and ciphers quite well. I trust him to help me conduct my business, and I have never had cause to regret it."

Fanny said, "The Baptists welcome Negroes into their meetings. They worship together, white and black, slave and free. Many people think ill of them for it and for their boisterous way of worship. On the other hand, the same people find fault with them for criticizing gaming and dancing and Sabbath-day diversions. Mr. Gibbern preaches against them."

"Some people do not even like Presbyterians," said Ben. "Mr. Fithian is a Presbyterian, and we all know what a fine man he is."

"I happen to like the litany of the established church," said Fanny. "It is spiritually fulfilling to me, and I am accustomed to it. I like my *Book of Common Prayer*. Nevertheless, I cannot agree with forbidding or discouraging people from worshipping in whatever way they see fit. In any case, it seems to me that the beliefs of the established church are not so different from those of the Presbyterians or the Baptists. It is wrong of Mr. Gibbern to preach against his fellow Christians."

"My sweet Fanny," I said, "I heartily agree with your sentiments. And more, I would bet ten pounds sterling that you are better read than either Mr. Gibbern or our own Mr. Smith, and certainly more pious than Mr. Gibbern."

38

1774: Robert

Fithian's mount was limping as he and Ben came up the path from the Nomini.

"What do you do about lame horses here, Mr. Carter?" Fithian asked as they approached me.

"Tom Henry will take care of him."

Fithian made a face.

"I think this is more than a stone in his hoof. I know Tom is good with horses, but I did not think he was a horse doctor."

"Tom does a lot of doctoring—of people as well as horses. And he has a special way with horses. You will see."

"I told you," Ben said.

Still, Fithian hesitated before going with me to the stable to find Tom.

"Tom Henry is a most unusual slave, Mr. Carter. I notice he does not speak like the other slaves."

"I sent him to school."

I made no further explanation, and we proceeded to the stable.

Tom was supervising the cleaning and polishing of harnesses. When he saw us approach, he looked up. He immediately came to the lame horse. Without any prompting from anyone, he gently took the horse's bridle, talking to him in a soothing voice.

The horse's muscles relaxed as Tom ran a hand across his withers and back.

Tom looked the animal over carefully, stroking him with sure hands so that when he finally stooped to examine the lame leg, the horse barely flinched.

Fithian watched carefully, beginning to relax as he saw the horse's reaction to Tom.

"The leg is not broken, Mr. Fithian. It is sprained. I will apply spirits of turpentine to the leg and wrap it. He needs to be kept quiet so he can heal. I'll see to it."

Fithian and I walked back toward the house and saw Morgan, George Lee's overseer, canter up the poplar lane. Morgan was a barrel-chested man accustomed to swaggering about with a plug of tobacco in his mouth and a whip on his belt.

His horse, which was, like the rider, big and coarse, clopped over to us. Morgan jerked the horse to a halt so hard the animal whinnied in pain.

Morgan then took a disparaging look back toward Tom Henry.

"Councillor Carter," he said, spitting a stream of tobacco, "Mr. Lee sent me to bring you this message."

He dismounted from the horse and held out a piece of paper.

I stepped forward and took it, then read what it said. "Thank you, Morgan."

Morgan did not move.

"The note requires no answer. You are free to go."

Instead of leaving, he said, "I see you all been talking to that nigger, Tom Henry." He laughed and spat again. Looking at Fithian, he said, "I know how to handle niggers, now. For obstinancy or idleness, what you got to do is strip the nigger down and tie him to a post. Then you take a nice sharp curry comb and curry him till he is well scraped, rub him with salt and turn him loose. Changes their attitude every time." He grinned, showing missing teeth.

Before I could interrupt, he shifted his weight to his other foot and continued. "To get a secret from a nigger, you put a thick plank on the floor with a peg in it about eight inches long. The peg has to be hard wood now, and real sharp at the upper end." He smirked at Fithian, whose face had now grown pale. "You strip him and hang him by a strong cord to a staple in the ceiling, so that his foot just rests on the peg, then you spin him around." Morgan slapped his knee. "Now if that ain't a sight to see."

I stared at Morgan as if he was demented. I could not believe he was regaling us with such a tale of cruelty. "We do not want to hear any more, Morgan. Get on your horse and leave—now."

I turned toward the door to the house, Fithian beside me.

Fithian's face was pale and his eyes wide.

"We are not all so crude, Mr. Fithian. I hope you know that."

Fithian nodded mutely, but the memory of the incident stayed in my mind. I felt somehow personally dirtied, though I would never have spoken or behaved as Morgan did. I certainly did not condone the behavior, nor did I allow my overseers to use such methods. I finally comforted myself with the thought that there were cruel and ignorant people everywhere, not just on Virginia plantations.

But it is the system that makes such behavior possible.

The cornfields were parched from the August drought, but we had been able to salvage most of the crop. I was reflecting on our good fortune as I rode to Westmoreland Courthouse to act as justice. I expected a dull day.

As I came into the village, I noticed that the courthouse and its surrounding green were alive with mingling men. Rumors were flying. It seemed Westmoreland's own R. H. Lee had been chosen to represent Virginia in a joint meeting of the colonies to be held in Philadelphia. They were calling the meeting the Continental Congress. R. H. and a Massachusetts man by the name of John Adams had worked hard to bring this meeting about. It was a direct result of the Committees of Correspondence in the various colonies. I was pleased to see us working together to address our problems with the English government.

I also learned that my friend Peyton Randolph, long a more conservative voice in the Assembly, had gone to the Continental Congress as well. If the king had any sense, he would take note.

When I got home and told Fanny, she said, "It does not surprise me that Peyton has joined the movement. Like you, Peyton loved Fauquier and supported him, but Virginia was always first in his heart. Also like you. It is unfortunate that now everyone is forced to take sides."

"Peyton will bring gravity and prestige to the Congress, but he acts at a high personal price. I understand that his brother, John, is very much the king's man. He is threatening to take his family to England to live. The brothers hardly speak, and Peyton's wife, Betty, is most unhappy with Peyton.

"I noticed a difference in the attitudes of the merchants and middling farmers at court, too. They are less deferential to the gentry. I suppose that is why John Tayloe and

Uncle Landon complain that good order has gone out of government."

"And what do you think, dear?" Fanny asked.

I considered the question for a moment.

"A rebellion against British rule would change many things. If we base our claim to our rights on the Enlightenment idea of the equality of man, we should not be surprised if men believe they should be treated as equals.

"It is so typical of you to answer with an analysis rather than an opinion. That was well put, Robert, but what I want to know is how you feel about the changes."

"To tell you the truth, dear, I believe I would be relieved if I were a middling farmer and did not have to worry so much about such things."

39

Autumn 1774

Mistress Stanhope, the housekeeper, dragged an unwilling Sukey after her into the dining room where I was having my breakfast. The early-morning sun shone in the windows of the room, and I was looking forward to a good day.

"Mr. Carter, something untoward is going on."

Sukey had round cheeks and bright eyes. She was a pretty Negro girl who was helping to care for our youngest child, Sarah Fairfax. Although she was only fourteen, I could not help noticing that she had a body unusually mature for her age, and at the moment, she was using all of the strength in that body to try to avoid being brought before me.

Mistress Stanhope held her with both hands.

"Tell Master Carter what you told me, Sukey."

The girl held back, head turned away from me, trying still to pull away from Mistress Stanhope's grasp.

The night before had been a hot September night, and there occurred one of those crackling, booming Northern Neck thunderstorms that always drove Fanny into a dark room. The thunder had sounded so close that we could feel the reverberation in our bodies. Lightning had lit up the sky.

And while the storm was going on, I thought that there was some sort of disturbance in the baby's room, but I wrote it off as restlessness caused by the storm.

Mistress Stanhope pulled Sukey around to face me, and the girl, now resigned, looked down at her feet.

"Tell him, Sukey. It is not you who are in trouble."

Still staring at the floor and speaking very softly, Sukey said, "Something came onto my pallet last night while the storm was going on. I was scared."

"Onto your pallet, child? What do you mean? What did it do?"

"It lie down beside me and touch me."

"Touched you? In what way?"

"You knows …"

She looked up at me. Her eyes beseeched me not to make her explain.

"Touched your body? You mean your private parts, as a man would do to a woman?"

She was barely audible.

"Yes, Master."

"Who did this to you?"

"I thinks it be a ghost."

"There are no ghosts in this house, Sukey. What did the ghost look like?"

"I doesn't know, Master."

I resolved to keep the house locked at night. That way, no one, including my own sons, who slept in the dormitory over the schoolroom, could get in.

Ben lapsed again into a fit of illness, his face chalky white. This time, for the first time, he coughed up blood.

"What can be done?" Fanny asked. "The doctor insists we must bleed him. Do you think that will help him when he is already so weak?"

"No, I do not. Tom Henry says it sounds like a disease they call consumption and that we should move him into the house, keep him warm, and let him rest when he has these fits."

"I think he is right—about keeping him in the house."

I was filled with that overwhelming impotence that I always felt when faced by any of my children's troubles that I could not solve. Once again, I thought of Lawrence Washington, but once again, I did not mention him to Fanny. In my office alone, I drank brandy and reflected upon the powerlessness of human beings over many of the great events of life. I stayed until the darkness made me go to bed.

———

Eight-year-old Dennis was setting the table for breakfast, his bright eyes intent on what he was doing, his small hands full of silverware. He laid each piece carefully and then looked at each place to make sure it was right. Very mature for an eight-year-old, I thought.

"Good morning, Dennis, how are you this morning?"

He looked up and a smile came over his face.

"I's good, Master."

Instead of going back to his work, he continued to look at me.

"Is there something on your mind, Dennis?"

"Yes, Master. I wonders ..."

"Out with it."

"Master Robert, do it be true that Tom Henry go to school in Williamsburg?"

"Yes, that's right. Why do you ask?"

"What you got to do to go to school?"

"It takes a desire to learn and a willingness to work hard. I thought Tom Henry was a special child, a very intelligent child, and that it would be wasteful for him not to know certain basic things like reading and writing."

"Is I intelligent, Master? I knows how to read and write some."

That impressed me. "Who taught you, Dennis?"

"Oh, nobody, Master." He bowed his head. "I hope you don't be mad at me, Master."

"Why would I be mad at you?"

"I picks up the books and the slates when I be cleaning up the schoolroom. I looks at them and copy what I sees."

"Show me what you know, Dennis."

His face shone. He ran off to the schoolroom and soon came back with a slate and a grammar book. He pointed to the letters in the book and named them each. Then he wrote his name on the slate, carefully working over each letter.

"That is very impressive indeed. Do you want to go to school?" I was thinking that it would not hurt for Ben to have a manservant who could read and write.

"Oh, yes indeed, Master. I surely does."

"Well then, I will tell Mr. Fithian to allow you to sit in on lessons whenever your work allows it."

"Thank you, Master. You won't be sorry."

"No, Dennis. I expect to be proud of you."

⌐⌐

I could not sleep. I got out of bed quietly so as to not disturb Fanny. Passing the window on my way out of the room, I looked out on the schoolhouse. The moon was nearly as bright as day. A movement caught my eye. It was Ben, who was supposed to be sleeping in the house because of his illness. He was walking toward the house.

I thought about calling to him but then thought better of it. I waited until I heard him come into the house and climb the stairs to go to bed. Then, drawing my banyan around me, I went quickly down the stairs and out to the schoolhouse.

There, on a pallet on the floor of the schoolroom was Sukey. As I came through the door, I saw her bury herself in the covers and pretend to be asleep.

"Sukey, what are you doing out here?"

She reluctantly came out from under the covers. She sat up straight and opened her eyes, but she would not look at me.

"I doesn't know, Master. I musta been walking in my sleep."

"You know that I do not believe that, don't you, Sukey?"

Her head was bowed. "Yes, Master."

"Well, get yourself and your pallet back to the baby's room. We will talk about this in the morning."

Next morning, when Fanny awoke, I said, "Last night I could not sleep. I found out who Sukey's ghost is."

We discussed the best way to deal with the situation. I did not know whether Sukey went willingly or not, but the blame lay primarily with Ben in any case.

I went to Ben's room. "I want you to dress and come to my office directly."

I sat at the desk and placed Ben in a straight-backed chair facing me.

"Son, your mother and I have always taught you to treat our servants with respect and to be aware of their personal feelings, have we not?"

Ben squirmed in his chair. He had been in the house for a week this time, and it occurred to me that he was looking well at the moment. He was tall, dark-haired, a good-looking young man, usually thoughtful and compliant.

"Yes, sir," he said, looking down at his hands in his lap.

"I found Sukey in the schoolroom last night, just after I saw you come into the house. She was lying on a pallet where you left her."

He did not try to contradict me.

"We believe that you have been lying with Sukey and that you are the ghost she complained about. Is that true?"

He squirmed a bit more but finally answered. "It was only this once, I lay with her."

I shook my head. It made me more sad than angry, though I was angry enough, that any child of mine would behave this way. *Here is another evil caused by the institution of slavery.*

"It is an understatement, Ben, to say that your mother and I are disappointed in you and ashamed of you. I might have expected this of Bob, but not of you. Such behavior is absolutely unacceptable in this household. Do you understand me?"

"But, Papa, it happens everywhere. Your friend, Squire Richard—"

"I have heard the rumors about Squire Richard, but, even if they are true, they do not justify your behavior. You know better."

"I don't understand why I cannot behave like everyone else."

"It is not everyone else who behaves that way, Ben. In any case, Son, everything other people do is not necessarily right. You must answer to your own conscience. You do know that what you did was wrong, do you not?"

Ben lowered his eyes from my steady gaze. He sat for a long time before he answered.

He finally said, "I suppose so, sir."

"You must promise me, now, that this will not happen again."

"Yes, Papa."

I had him whipped to make my point. Then I let him go.

How can I raise my children properly when the society in which we live conspires against it?

40

October 1774

Fithian came quietly into my office as I prepared to go to Williamsburg for business I had before the General Court.

"Mr. Carter, I will likely be gone when you return from Williamsburg. John Peck should be here, if not by that time, shortly thereafter. I will not likely see you again."

It made me sad to think so, but it was the arrangement we had made.

"I am sorely sorry to see you go. Fanny and the children will be sorry, as well. Can I not persuade you to change your plans and stay another year?"

"I will miss you and Mrs. Carter, and my lovely charge, as I will always think of them, but my life must be at home. I have learned a great deal here, but now I want to see my beloved Laura, and I feel I must be prepared to fight for New Jersey if it comes to war with England.

"You have been a great benefit to our family. If you must go, know that you do so with our love and gratitude. Be assured that you can always count on me for an excellent reference. I am hopeful that Mr. Peck will be a satisfactory tutor, but I cannot believe that he will come near you in that capacity."

I pulled some English money from my desk and handed it to him. It was more than I had promised for his service. I felt he had earned it.

"I thank you, sir, for all your consideration of me, for treating me like a member of your family. I hope Ben will come to visit me. In spite of his health, I pray he will have the bright future his mind and demeanor deserve." Fithian smiled. "Bob, now, has more capability than he is willing to exercise. I am hopeful he will mature. The girls are lovely and intelligent, especially Priscilla. I am confident about their futures. You will all be in my prayers."

Meeting John Peck upon my return from Williamsburg, I saw before me a very handsome young man with blue eyes and blond hair worn in a queue, curling around his face and above his collar. He appeared to be nothing like Fithian, although he had been trained at the same college as a Presbyterian minister.

My older daughters noticed Peck's good looks also. They were uncharacteristically giggly around him.

Winter 1774

Since I had come back from Williamsburg, I had worked hard at Nomony Hall and my other plantations, and, in spite of the hardships imposed by the mother country, I had prospered. But my spirit was restless, so when I was asked by the others on the vestry at Cople Parish to be warden, I accepted hopefully. Regardless of my opinion of the efficacy of the church as a whole, I could embrace the opportunity to actually help people who needed it.

Stephen Self approached the house at Nomony Hall, walking up between the poplars from the Westmoreland-Richmond County road. He carried with him a small child of about a year and a half or so.

Self was directed by Sam to sit in my office near the fire.

"Councillor Carter, begging your pardon, sir, but this child needs the help of the parish."

It was a chilly November day, with an overcast and threatening sky, but I noticed that Self had walked to my home without gloves or hat, in a threadbare cloak. The child he carried was wrapped in a blanket.

Self took off his cloak and then unwrapped the child and set him on the floor. The child did not have on any outer clothing to protect him from the cold.

Self drew close to the fire, pulling the child with him, and then sat back down with the child on his lap.

"What can the parish do for you, Mr. Self?"

"Sir, this is my daughter's child, Samuel. I have tried to care for him, but I just cannot keep on. My wife has passed, and I can barely feed my own children."

"Who is the child's father? Why are he and your daughter not caring for the child?"

"The father is Samuel Beale, the instructor at the school."

I was shocked at that, but I did not say so.

"You are talking about the school held at Cople Parish?"

"Yes, sir."

"How old is your daughter, Mr. Self?"

"She is thirteen."

I knew that Beale had a wife, but she was not Self's daughter, and she certainly was not thirteen.

"The child was born out of wedlock, then?"

Self bowed his head and said, "Yes, sir." He paused a minute, then continued. "I try to raise my children right, Mr. Carter. I take them to church, but it is hard without a wife."

He then raised his head and looked me straight in the eye. "How should I know that evil lurks in a school run by the church itself?"

"You are quite right, Mr. Self. You should be able to trust the church. I am sorry that your trust was betrayed. Why does Mr. Beale not provide support for the child?"

"He denies him."

"Very well. I will see to it that either Mr. Beale or the parish will provide for the support of the child."

Two days later, Mr. Beale came to Nomony to fetch the key to use the church's property for his school. He was a man in his thirties, pleasant-looking and plainly dressed. He looked like any other schoolmaster. Appearances, however, are deceiving.

I motioned Beale to sit.

"Mr. Beale, what do you know of Nancy Self and her child, Samuel?"

Beale was taken aback.

"She claims the child is mine, as you must have been told."

"Indeed I have, Mr. Beale, and is the child yours?"

Beale considered for a moment.

"Could be."

"Well, are there any other possible fathers that you are aware of?"

He said, "Not as I know of, sir."

"Then what do you intend to do about his care?"

A long pause ensued before Beale answered. "Well, if old Self won't keep and maintain him, I will have to take him to raise with my own family. I cannot afford to pay him money."

"Good. You can count on my checking on Samuel's welfare, Mr. Beale. I do presume you want to keep using parish property to conduct your school?"

Beale understood the threat.

The same day, I wrote a letter directing that the parish pay Thomas More six pounds per year for taking care of a bastard child of Squire Richard Lee's. Ben had not been wrong about the squire's proclivities, but, as it happened, this child was white.

A woman named Anne Browne Williams was ushered into my office by Sam a week later. Mistress Williams carried a toddler. There was obviously something wrong with the child. He was weak, almost to the point of being helpless.

Mistress Williams was not emotional, however. She was very matter-of-fact.

"Councillor, this here child belonged to Hampton Wilson. He used to give me money to take care of him. The boy has sore legs, as you can see. Now Hampton's dead; someone got to provide for Jamie. I can't do it by myself."

"Hampton Wilson was your husband, then?"

"No, sir, but he was Jamie's father—always claimed him. Everybody knew."

"Tell me more about Mr. Wilson. Did he have any family besides Jamie?"

"No other children, Councillor Carter. He lived by himself."

"Did he own the house?"

"I think so. He was a waterman, but he always had some money put by. He died last month, and I ain't had no money since."

"I will look into it. Come back in a week."

It was true that Jamie was Wilson's son. He had openly claimed him while he was alive. And, Jamie was Wilson's only child, and therefore his sole heir. I managed to arrange for Mistress Williams to have the house (in Jamie's name). If there had been any money, it was gone, so I arranged for Jamie to receive a small stipend from the parish each month.

December came in cold and stormy. Neighbors reported to me that John and Susanna Winters were both unable to work. They were sick and suffering in a rundown house and had no food. I sent Tom Henry to fetch them to the parish poor house to be fed and clothed.

Later that month, I was at the service at Nomini Church, the upper church of Cople Parish. The church stood on a bluff over Nomini Creek, and the wind was cold that day. I was anxious to get away and go home. As I entered our carriage, Dr. George Steptoe approached me.

"Councillor Carter, may I have a word?"

I stopped and turned away from the carriage, leaving Fanny and the older children bundled up and Tom Henry impatient to go. Dr. Steptoe was a good man. He would not keep us all in the cold for no reason.

"What's on your mind, George?"

"Young Samuel Mockridge is a patient of mine. He has a bad left leg—has had for some five years. I can do no more for him, but I have lately heard of a specialist in Baltimore that may be able to do so. But the care is costly, and Mockridge's family has no money. His mother and father are dead."

"And you wonder if the parish will pay the expense of his care?"

"I would be most grateful. He is a fine young man."

"I'll talk to the vestry about it."

I was very quiet on the way home.

Fanny asked, "What is on your mind, Robert?"

"I was just thinking; you and I and the children are going to our warm, comfortable home—a house cleaned and maintained and staffed by Negroes. We can always look forward to a plenteous meal. What a contrast there is between our lot and that of the people the parish assists."

Fanny could only agree.

"What is it that makes us different? Surely we are no more deserving than they."

"The practical answer is that the difference lies in our ownership of property and of slaves to wait on us. But why we were born into our circumstances and not they, I cannot answer. Some would say it's God's will, but I'm not sure I agree with them."

Later that month, I rode to visit the poorhouse. It was a mile or so beyond Westmoreland Courthouse. It was surrounded on all sides by fields, which were worked by the residents able to do so.

The poorhouse was a large, plain, clapboard building that sat on a rise above the road.

I went inside. The front hall was wide and served as an office as well as a sort of central gathering place. Off the hall were rooms of various sizes. The furniture was no more than barely serviceable, and the place was not adorned in any way. I found it depressing.

I asked to be allowed to roam through the place and talk to those I found there. The housekeeper, a Mistress Jones, looked a little surprised but raised no objection.

"Why, Councillor, I reckon you are welcome to go wherever you like."

First, I encountered Ann Stowers, who was quite well but was seventy years old and had no home, no family, and no means of support. She lived in the house and helped with the cooking and cleaning and other chores.

Then I came upon two young people sitting together. They were dressed in warm but shabby garments.

"Good morning," I said. "I am Robert Carter from the Cople Parish. I have come to see how people here are getting along."

"Good morning, Councillor," said the young man. "I am Willoughby Collensworth and this is my sister, Sarah."

"How old are you, and how did you come to be here?" I asked.

"I am seventeen," said young Willoughby. "Sarah is twenty."

"Tell me about yourselves and your family."

I noticed as he answered that Willoughby had to stop speaking every once in a while to catch his breath, and he laid his hand upon his chest as he spoke.

"We came here after our parents died when our house burned down. We have an uncle somewhere in the mountains. Went there a long time ago. No other family.

"And what is wrong? I can see it is difficult for you to breathe."

"Dropsy," Willoughby said, "both of us. Can't work."

"Are you well treated here?"

He nodded.

John Winters, whom Tom Henry had brought to the poorhouse, suffered from what was called "sore legs," which seemed to be a catchall phrase for any crippling in the legs. He was unable to walk without a cane. He was only thirty-five but looked fifty.

His wife, Susanna, had sore legs as well and dropsy. She was bedridden.

I talked to others, and to the housekeeper, Mistress Jones, and left before dinnertime.

Back at home, I sat at my desk and ordered things for the poorhouse from Fisher and Cunningham: blankets; waistcoats; petticoats; linen for shifts; shoes and stockings;

material for handkerchiefs, hats, britches, and shirts; an iron pot; a frying pan; and a hair sifter. I ordered three bedsteads with boarded bottoms to be made.

More importantly, as I saw it, I drafted a letter to the vestry recommending that a plot of land near the house be enclosed and planted with vegetables in the spring. I had a letter from Squire Richard, who, whatever his failings might be, was a generous man, assuring me that he would have some butchered hogs sent to the poorhouse this winter as he usually did.

"Master," said Tom Henry when he saw me attending to the parish poor, "who takes care of free Negroes in need?"

It was a good question, and I did not know the answer.

41

Spring 1775

"Governor Dunmore has seized the arsenal in Williamsburg!"

"What? Robert, how do you know this?"

"It is here in the *Virginia Gazette.* I suppose that he did so in response to the Minutemen firing on British soldiers in Lexington and Concord in the Massachusetts Colony."

"There is no longer any hope of peace."

"No, I do not believe so, Fanny. I am going to write Robert Prentiss in Williamsburg to lock all our valuables left in Williamsburg and put them in a secure place on his own property."

"Will you still send Dennis to Williamsburg to train as a manservant for Ben?"

"I will for the time being. If it becomes unsafe for him, I will have him brought home."

"Oh, my ..."

"What else, Robert?"

"As I read further, I see that all the weapons in Maryland have been seized by the royal governor there."

Sam came to say that R. H. Lee had come, and I put down my paper.

R. H. came into the room, wiping his forehead with a handkerchief.

"Welcome, neighbor, what brings you out on this hot day?"

"I have just come from a meeting in Williamsburg."

"Come, sit down."

I motioned him to a comfortable chair and asked Sam to bring us lemon punch.

R. H. caught his breath, and when the punch came, he held the cold glass to his forehead for a moment.

"We are all agreed, Robert. We need you and Robert Corbin to meet with Dunmore, to negotiate some sort of accommodation about the weapons from the arsenal. The English still do not think you such a radical, but you are also trusted by the members of the Assembly for your good sense."

"I am flattered, but I am not optimistic. Nevertheless, I will certainly try to talk to the man."

Back in March, Patrick Henry had made a fiery speech in Richmond, copies of which were disseminated throughout the colony. Then he had begun mustering men to march on Williamsburg. Dunmore had threatened martial law.

Before Corbin and I could even set up a meeting, on May 3, Dunmore and his family fled the Governor's Palace in the middle of the night. They were said to have gone to Dunmore's hunting lodge in York County.

The next thing we heard was that, on June 8, Dunmore had escaped to His Majesty's ship *Fowey,* which was anchored in the York River. He proposed to make war on the colony of Virginia from there.

Frank Lee was elected in August to join his brother in the Continental Congress meeting in Philadelphia. All those who joined the Congress, from every colony, were considered traitors by the English. They put their lives and fortunes on the line for what they believed. I feared for them, but I agreed with them. I no longer had any sympathy whatsoever for a king who blindly ignored the legitimate concerns of his colonial citizens and instead sent soldiers to live in their houses and threaten them. He left us with only the option to use force to protect ourselves.

October 1775

"What is the matter?" Fanny stepped back from my greeting embrace and looked at me with questioning eyes.

I had just come back from business in Williamsburg. I sat down on the bench in the hall. "Peyton Randolph has died in Philadelphia."

"I'm so sorry." Fanny said.

"The funeral has already been held in Philadelphia. The *Pennsylvania Gazette* says that hundreds of people came out to honor him. The king and the Parliament should be reminded that this former conservative and loyal Englishmen became a Revolutionary—and that he was much esteemed for it. But I do not suppose it will make any difference to them now."

"Yes, I fear the British have gone too far down the road to be moved to a peaceful solution now—unless we capitulate."

"That we will not do."

We rented out the house in Williamsburg, feeling safer in the country, but the fact was that Dunmore had begun sending raiding parties up the rivers, including the Potomac. Soldiers raided the plantations of the rebels, as they called us. The war was at our doorstep.

42

1775

The proclamation that Dunmore issued on November 14, 1775, formally offered freedom to any male slave who would join the British army. It sent an electric shock throughout the colony. Besides the economic consequences of losing slaves, there was always a latent fear among whites that the slaves would revolt. Certainly, there were slaves who would take him up on his offer. I did not think slavery was a moral institution, but I could not advocate the chaos that Dunmore's Proclamation was likely to cause. It had the intended effect of instilling fear in the white colonists, but it also had the unintended effect of pushing many reluctant patriots into the rebel camp.

I had reason to be glad I had always treated my people well. I sensed little change in the attitude of my slaves.

It was especially urgent now to have news as soon as possible, so when the post rider that brought the *Virginia Gazette* no longer came, I began to have it picked up at Hobbs Hole and have it delivered to my neighbors myself.

A few days after the proclamation, Dunmore won a skirmish at Kemp's Landing down near Portsmouth. Included among the soldiers were ex-slaves he called his Ethiopian Regiment. It was frightening news. Fighting had begun in Virginia, and former slaves were armed.

Then in December I read that we won a decisive battle against him at Great Bridge. Dunmore loaded many Virginia loyalists and his troops, including the Ethiopian Regiment, onto British ships and headed toward New York.

The next thing we heard was that smallpox had broken out in the cramped confines of the ships.

Tom Henry

It was Sunday, and I had just returned from taking the family to church. It was a cold day, so I wasted no time putting up the horses and cleaning the wheels of the coach before it was put in the shed.

Then I went and sat down in the stable awhile. The air was warm from the bodies of the horses, and I could sit and think without being disturbed.

After an hour or so, I was sure my first inclination had been correct. I climbed the stairs to our little home above the stables. I was ready to talk to Rose.

She was sitting at the fireplace, working on some mending for Mistress Fanny. She looked up when I came to the top of the steps.

"You know that the Englishman Lord Dunmore has offered slaves freedom if they will fight for his army?" I asked her.

She dropped what she was doing into her lap. "Yes, indeed, folks talking about it."

"I want to talk to you about it." I pulled up a chair from the table and sat facing her. "I am not afraid to fight, or to die, for something I believe in. And I believe in freedom. The idea of freedom is like a hunger. I have thought about what would happen if I joined the British."

Rose drew in her breath. She looked alarmed and started to speak.

I held up my hand.

"Hear me out, Rosie Girl. Here is what I know. The British frown on slavery in their own country, but their ships carry slaves to the colonies. We should not be deceived. They brought slavery to these shores in the first place and still allow it and profit from it, here and in the Indies. They do not make this offer of freedom out of any love for Negroes. They offer it to strike fear into the hearts of whites, and to find soldiers to do their fighting.

"The British do not respect the rights of their white colonists. They are not likely to respect the rights of Negroes. They are depriving the whites here of the right to tax themselves because they are not represented in Parliament. Now they are depriving them of their right to be tried by their peers, which the colonists have been doing since the beginning of these colonies. The British are breaking promises that their kings have made to British citizens who live here and violating the documents of their own constitution. They don't allow the colonies to trade except through the mother country."

"How you know all that, Tom Henry?"

"I have listened and learned like Dadda Gumby told me, and I have read whatever I could.

"I also know the man Dunmore. He came to Williamsburg before we left. He is arrogant, and he doesn't care for the welfare of slaves—or anyone else. He did not deal fairly with men like Master, and he did not treat his own slaves well. When he first proposed the idea of offering freedom to runaways who would fight for him, some slaves came to him, and they were turned away. He was not serious then. Now that he's been driven out of the palace and has to fight from ships in the ocean, he has to find new ways to control Virginians. And of course he is willing to have slaves for fodder for the American guns. I do not trust Dunmore."

Rose began to relax a little.

"What Dunmore is asking is that we leave our homes and our families and take up arms against people we have known all our lives. Maybe some have nothing to lose, except their lives, of course, but you and I have a lot to lose. We do not know how the British would treat us, and we do not know what will happen after the war. Would those who fought be free, if the English won, and the rest remain slaves? And if the colonists win, will the English protect those who fight or abandon them? But there is something else, Rosie." I felt tears begin to form in my eyes. Rose looked surprised. I do not think she had ever seen me cry.

"I remember when I was a very young boy, the tall man with the kind eyes who picked me up, stable dirt and all, and sat me in his lap, and told me I was special. And I remember walking down Duke of Gloucester Street to Mistress Ireland's, hand in hand with the same man on the day I started school. And I remember, though he did not want to send me to Charles Edwards's, and I wanted to go because of you, how he made the arrangements anyway and how he paid too much to buy you and how he did without his postilion and coachman, all because that is what I wanted. And I remember the day he rescued us from Edwards, how he said nothing about any sacrifices he made, but was angry at himself because you and I were mistreated.

"Rosie, we have a good master. He treats us with respect and looks after our needs. You and I have a lot of freedom. I love Master Robert, even if he is our master, and I believe he loves us. I also know that he believes slavery is wrong, although I don't think he knows what to do about it. For all these reasons, I choose not to follow Dunmore and the British."

Rose smiled. "Thanks be to Jesus for that! As for me, I chooses to stay right where I is."

43

February 1776: Robert

"I thought that Dunmore was going to New York, but now I hear that he has sailed up the Chesapeake and stopped at Tucker's Point," Fanny told me.

She had just come back from services at Cople Parish. I was indisposed, staying at home in the cold, rainy February weather.

"That cannot be good," I said. "If his ships carry people with the pox as we have been told, it may spread when he lands."

"Yes, and they also say that many of the Ethiopian Regiment have deserted."

I finished her sentence. "Taking the pox with them into the countryside."

———

March was cold and rainy with spitting snow—late for such cold weather.

Sam sent a messenger from Burgess Hall in Northumberland County to my office. He was a young man, with a wool cloak and woolen scarf, but he looked cold. I invited him to sit and warm himself by the fire.

"I have been asked to request that you have your blacksmith make fifty bayonets for the Northumberland County militia."

"Of course."

We discussed exactly what they wanted and when they were needed.

The young man did not seem inclined to go quickly and I couldn't blame him. Let him rest awhile before facing the cold again.

He asked, "Have you heard about Dunmore, Councillor?"

"What is he doing now?"

"His ship, the *Otter*, was seen about Annapolis doing reconnaissance two days since."

"Is that so? My ship, *Atwell*, has gone to Annapolis to deliver corn and pork to the Iron Works. Is Dunmore stopping ships?"

"I don't know, Councillor. I told you all I know. Are there slaves aboard your ship?"

"The captain, William Lawrence, is a free mulatto. Alexander Jones is on board. He's a free Negro, married to one of my house servants. David is the only slave on board. The rest are white. I believe they will come home unless Dunmore forces them."

I was more worried about their safety than their loyalty. As if to increase my worry, Matthew Leonard, the overseer from Coles Point, came to see me.

"Councillor Carter, I have two of John Tayloe's slaves at Coles Point. I need to know what to do with them."

"How did they come to be at Coles Point?"

"They told me six of them ran away from Mount Airy to join Dunmore. These two decided at the last minute that they did not want to go be soldiers for the British. They would like to stay with you."

"You know that I cannot keep someone else's slaves. Make sure they have a good meal and anything else they need to travel and then take them back to Mount Airy."

"Yes, sir."

"And, Mr. Leonard, be certain to tell John Tayloe that they decided for themselves not to go to Dunmore."

"Yessir."

He bowed out the door.

In April, the *Atwell* crew came back to Nomony Hall intact. Clement Brooke at the Iron Works had detained the ship and sent them home overland.

⌇

May 1776

I was at my desk, reading the *Virginia Gazette* as I had begun to do faithfully and with growing urgency. Fanny was on the sofa.

"They report that Dunmore left three hundred graves at Tucker's Point—many of them graves of the Ethiopian Regiment," I said.

"Those poor souls, Robert, hoping for freedom and dying in misery. Was there nothing Dunmore could have done for them?"

"I've heard that he was advised to inoculate them, since people here have little resistance to the pox. He refused because the process would put them out of service for a month or so."

"Horrible."

We soon heard that Dunmore had set up camp at Gwynne's Island, which was just off Middlesex County, near the southern side of the mouth of the Rappahannock. He was coming closer to us.

Tom Henry

"Ride with me to Coles Point," Master Robert said to me.

It was a hot day and not one I would have chosen to take a ride. It was unusual for Master to ask me to ride with him in any case. We first rode out in silence, Master deep in thought.

The roads were hard—no rain in the last few weeks—and I could hear the horses' hooves hitting the road with a kind of thumping sound as we passed head-high corn, and smelled the wheat fragrant in the heat.

Finally, Master said, "I trust you have heard of Dunmore's Proclamation made November last?"

"Yes, Master Robert. He said he would free any male slave who joined his army."

"What do you think about it?"

I frankly told him how I reasoned it out. I did not usually hesitate to be honest with Master, and I had never suffered for it.

"I was certain that you knew about the proclamation and that you had made a conscious decision about it. You are correct about what he said, of course. Dunmore now has control of the king's army in Virginia. I expect you are familiar with his raids on the Potomac and the Rappahannock. He has been burning crops and houses on both sides of the Potomac. He has also been recruiting Negroes to his cause. Now some sixty sail are to be seen off Ragged Point. Yesterday, his ship *Roebuck* was sighted at the St. Mary's River in Maryland, just across the river from Coles Point Plantation. Our militia is not capable of stopping him, and we are at his mercy."

"So, I have heard."

"I intend to talk to my people at Coles Point before he arrives. I hope to persuade them not to go with him. I trust you, Tom, and they trust you. I need your support. That is why I want you with me when I talk to them."

Master Robert stopped his horse and looked at me intently, waiting for an answer.

"You can trust me, Master."

Master's face relaxed. He said, "I am very grateful to you, Tom." Then he nudged his horse and rode on.

Matthew Leonard had already gathered the Coles Point people before we arrived. They stood in small groups in the heat, wiping their brows and talking among themselves. The summer sun was beating down. If nothing else, I thought they must appreciate the break from their work.

Master sat tall and still on his horse. He was wearing a straw hat, but sweat was running down his face and neck. As he faced the group of people, he took off his hat, wiped his brow with the back of his arm, and put the hat back on his head.

I sat tall on my horse beside him. *What other slaveholder comes out into the hot sun to talk to his slaves?*

The crowd grew quiet, and Master Robert spoke.

"The king of Great Britain has declared war against our people in the colonies …"

All attention was on Master.

"Our governor, Lord Dunmore, has now taken command of the king's forces in Virginia. Today, he has six ships off Ragged Point."

Some of those in the crowd shifted on their feet, but no one spoke.

"Many of the people in Great Britain do not approve of this dispute between them and the thirteen colonies … and have refused to enlist as soldiers. Therefore, the king has employed foreign soldiers to fight for him against us. Lord Dunmore, by a proclamation, has called upon the black people in North America to join him, and he has declared that all white indentured servants and slaves who run away from their masters and enter into the king's service shall be free, and their masters should have no future claim against them."

Master paused and fanned himself with his hat. There was a stirring in the crowd. Most had heard of the proclamation, but Master now confirmed its existence himself.

He held up his hand for their attention. When it grew quiet again, he said, "I ask you to think." He paused again. "If the king should be victorious in the present war, has Lord Dunmore honesty to perform his part of his declaration respecting the slaves, ... will he not sell them to the people living in the West Islands, who are friends and subjects of Great Britain? Since the publication of Lord Dunmore's Proclamation relative to slaves and servants, both sorts have joined him. Do any of you dislike your present condition of life as to wish to enter into Lord Dunmore's service and trust to the consequences?"

The hands shuffled about and talked among themselves.

Shortly Prince Johnson, a leader of the slaves at Coles Point, said, "We does not want to go to Lord Dunmore and fight against the white people of the colonies. We will stay with you, Master."

His statement did not surprise me. Like Rose and I, Prince Johnson was one of Master's most trusted servants. Besides, what else would they say to Master's face?

"Then," said Master Robert, "the only order I shall now give is that if any of Lord Dunmore's party shall land on Coles Point ... you men take your wives, children, male and female acquaintances, clothes, bedding and tools, removing all into private places away from the rivers Potomac and Machodoc, and send a person off to Nomony Hall immediately to advise me at what place you have gotten to. And I will give them directions tending to your immediate relief."

Master then turned to Matthew Leonard. "Mr. Leonard, attend to the growing crops at Coles Point Plantation as usual; keep a constant lookout, and if Lord Dunmore's fleet should move upwards, advise me thereof. If any of said party of men should land here and demand provisions, do not refuse, and refuse any money or other consideration that might be offered."

That is clever of Master, I thought. Dunmore will not know for sure whether he is a Loyalist or a Patriot.

The gathered slaves watched as we rode away.

"What will they do, Tom? Will they stay as they promise?"

I knew that Master was not just looking for a pleasing answer. "You ask the question as a man who wants the truth, and I will give you as honest an answer as I can. Your people know you to be a kind master. I certainly know what things some masters do, and so do they. Not only do you require that punishment be meted out fairly, but you keep families together. You make sure your people are fed and clothed and housed. You provide medical treatment when it is needed. You listen to what slaves have to say when disputes arise between them and whites. By your speaking to them today, you show them respect. Though I will not say that they do not wish to be free—because I believe most slaves wish freedom in their hearts—I do not believe most of them will take their chances with Dunmore and his army. Most will not trust Dunmore enough to leave home and family to risk their lives for the British."

"Are you saying that they prefer the devil they know to the one they do not know?"

"You are no devil, Master, but in a manner of speaking that is so."

"Well, I thank you, Tom, for standing with me."

"I did not do that just for you, Master. I did it for them too."

Dunmore's ships traveled on up the Potomac, beyond Coles Point, looting and burning. Among the slaves they took were three from George Washington's Mount Vernon while Washington was in New York, leading the American army.

No slaves from Coles Point went to join Dunmore.

We did not know on that day the horror that Dunmore had left behind on Gwynne's Island just four days earlier.

44

July 1776: Robert

"Fanny, it has come at last!" I stood up and lay the *Pennsylvania Gazette* I had been reading on the desk.

"What? It must be exciting indeed to judge by your face."

"Indeed, Fanny. R. H. proposed to the Congress that the colonies declare themselves independent from Great Britain. After much argument, the motion passed. Thomas Jefferson; R. H.'s longtime correspondent from Massachusetts, John Adams; and old Dr. Franklin from Philadelphia were tasked with writing the declaration. When it was ready to be presented, R. H. was absent because he had problems he needed to deal with at home. They have printed a copy of the declaration here. I recognize the style of Tom Jefferson.

"So, my dear, the deed is done at last! We are an independent country."

"Yes, now all we have to do is convince the British that we mean to remain independent, not an easy task."

"Well," I said, "we have declared our final separation from them. I'm pleased because I believe the new country will endorse the equality of man—that's what the declaration says: 'All men are created equal.' I wish, though, that it had specifically addressed the rights of slaves."

"Robert, do you believe that the Carolinas and Georgia would have endorsed a declaration that stated the equality of slaves?"

"No, no, I suppose not. And it would be a hard case in Virginia, as well. You are always right, and I am too naïve."

⟷

August 1776
Tom Henry

I found Master Robert pacing up and down the floor in the hall as I came into the house.

"Ride with me to Forest Quarter," he said. "I will explain why on the way. Bring your doctoring equipment."

We rode side by side toward Richmond County, over the road hardened by hot, dry weather.

"Those who found them said it was a pitiable sight, Tom. At Gwynne's Island, after Dunmore abandoned it in May. The Patriots who took back the island found five hundred there, the dead already in a state of putrefaction and others still dying, most of them from the Ethiopian Regiment."

I looked at him in alarm. I had not heard this. *If the slaves from Coles Point had joined Dunmore in May, the same could have happened to them.*

"Some were still at the edge of the water where they had crawled on their bellies to get a drink, too weak to walk. Bodies of the living and the dead were lying together in heaps on the ground. Many of them were contagious with smallpox and other diseases. There were 130 graves, some of them big enough to contain a corporal's guard. Then, they say, Dunmore continued up the rivers and continued to recruit slaves who contracted smallpox as well."

I felt a shiver run through my body.

"I am very much concerned about an outbreak of pox at Forest Quarter. Deserters have been spreading the pox all along both sides of the Rappahannock as well as on the Potomac. Today, I received word from the overseer at Forest Quarter of a sick boy there."

Leaving the hard surface of the heavily traveled road from Nomony Hall toward Richmond Courthouse, before we got to the Westmoreland/Richmond County line, we turned into the sandy lane that led to Forest Quarter. Amanda, the mother of a sixteen-year-old boy, ran out to meet us.

She was screaming as she came right up beside Master Robert's horse and grabbed at his leg in its stirrup.

"Oh, Lord, Master Carter, James got the pox."

Master stopped his horse. To the others standing around, gawking, he said, "Go on now. You will get sick, too, if it is the pox. Stay away."

Wide-eyed, they slowly dispersed, and we followed Amanda to her cabin.

Master and I dismounted. We covered our noses and mouths with handkerchiefs and went inside.

My nostrils were immediately assaulted by a sickening, rancid odor. When my eyes became accustomed to the dark, I saw a young field hand I knew as James, lying on a bed. Sweat covered his brow. In his mouth and nose were sores that were beginning to fill with puss. The boy was desperate for water, but I saw that it was hard for him to swallow.

"I think he have the ague," Amanda said, sniffling. "Then he seem to get better, but this morning, he all broke out in them sores."

She looked at me. "Do it be the pox, Tom Henry?"

"It likely is," I told her.

I found a rag, dipped it in water, and squeezed water into James's mouth to give him some relief from his thirst.

I had been learning all I could about the pox since I first heard talk of it in the countryside and had been planning how to use my skills to the best advantage. I knew of no cure.

"You need to keep everyone away from him," I told Amanda, for I understood that it spread by contact. "You have already been exposed, so you need to keep away from everyone else too. Tie a rag around your nose and mouth— all the time—in case you have not already caught it. Wipe James's head with a wet rag; keep him as cool and comfortable as you can. Get some water into him as I did. He is going to get sores on his hands and feet. Let them be. Do not touch the sores with your hands. The sores spread the disease. Burn all his clothes and bedclothes any time you change them. Master brought things for you to use. Do you understand all I'm telling you?"

"Yes, Tom Henry."

"Then I want you to repeat it all back to me."

Fairly soon, she was able to repeat back to me all that I had told her. When I was satisfied, we left the cabin, and Forest Quarter, and returned to Nomony Hall, where we bathed and burned our clothes.

⟶

Robert

We set up a makeshift hospital at Forest Quarter. I had a large military tent set up in a clearing.

The doctor came as soon as the hospital was set up. He was a slender young man, reputed to have studied medicine in Edinburgh. He dressed in a plain waistcoat and britches and wore a sort of apron. He also covered his mouth and nose with a kerchief, which I thought was a sign of his knowledge and care.

Tom Henry stood by to help, and to watch and learn all he could.

The doctor approached the first patient, lancet in hand. As he moved closer, the patient's eyes grew large, and he pulled away.

"Do me first," said Tom Henry.

He must have been afraid, had to be so, but he showed no outward signs of it. Truthfully, I was afraid myself. I did not want to lose Tom Henry.

The doctor made a small cut in Tom's upper arm. Then he retrieved a thread that he ran through a dish of pussy substance, which he told us was from an active smallpox wound.

I raised my hand to object, thinking of changing my mind about the whole business, but then I thought of how many of my people were vulnerable to the disease and could get a raging case. Everything I had read indicated this procedure saved lives. I dropped my hand.

Tom Henry sat rigid as a stone.

The doctor pulled the thread through the cut in Tom's arm and then bandaged it. The deed was done.

"See," said Tom to the crowd, "it is simple. It doesn't hurt. You will get sick," he said, "but you will be taken care of, and then you will get well. After that, you will never be able to get the pox no matter how many others around you may have it."

The others slowly allowed themselves to be inoculated.

It had been necessary to petition the General Court in order to inoculate my people. Unlike Maryland and Pennsylvania, the state of Virginia frowned on inoculation, believing it to be too dangerous. I was resolved, however, not to be as short-sighted as Dunmore had been in refusing to have his Ethiopian recruits inoculated.

Generally, I was told, of those who got the pox naturally, about 15 percent died. Of those inoculated, about 2 percent might die. We lost no one to the disease.

January 1777

It was cold. The pox was still rampant, and that fact aggravated my usual fears about childbirth, but our fifteenth child, George, came safely into the world.

As soon as I heard the cry from the bedroom, I rushed to see Fanny and the new child, as I always did. I looked into the face of a healthy child, red-faced, with his tiny fist raised in the air.

This time I developed the habit of going to our bedroom a few hours each day and reading to Fanny, or having her brought downstairs so that I could play the harpsichord for her. I often ate my meals with her in the bedroom. She was not recuperating as quickly as she had in the past.

As I sat by her bed one day, Tom Henry approached me.

"Master, come see my new son."

I went with him and climbed the steps to the second floor of the stable and found it transformed. I had not been there since Tom and Rose had come back from Greenfields.

In spite of the cold outside, the place was warm and smelled of fresh-baked bread. What had been one large room was now divided into smaller ones. The end of the original room where the fireplace was located was now the kitchen. It held a wooden table, several chairs, and a cupboard. One of the chairs was a rocking chair, I noticed, and sitting next to it was a cradle. The fireplace had on it or around it every implement of cooking imaginable.

From the main room a hallway extended, and bedrooms were on either side. The largest had a double bed with a handsome coverlet, no doubt made by Rose. It also held a chest for clothes. Tom had not built the walls of the rooms all the way to the ceiling, allowing the warmth that rose from the fireplace to flow to the other rooms.

Rose was up and about, dressed in a neat cotton dress, a white cap, and an equally white apron. She was smiling, and her eyes sparkled. It made me happy just to look at her.

"I wants Mistress to see the baby as soon as she be able."

"She would be delighted if you took him to see her." I bent over the cradle. "Who would this be?" I gently pulled aside the blanket to take a look at the new arrival. He was light-skinned like his parents and had a hint of high cheek bones like his mother.

"His name Edmund," said Rose.

"Edmund Henry. Well, that is a noble name indeed. He is a big boy. He'll be strong like his father and smart like his mother."

I winked at Rose.

"We not sure we gonna ever have children, Master. It take so long. This child a blessing from God."

The delay was no doubt because of the treatment Rose received at the hands of Charles Thomas, but today is a day for rejoicing.

45

October 1776: Robert

My resignation from the vestry at Cople Parish caused a stir, but I felt I had other things to do. Now that we had declared ourselves independent from the British, I had no time for the English church. Truly, I had been drifting away in any case. I felt the need of something more than it offered. Even the work in the parish no longer satisfied me. I was curious about the Dissenters and their ideas about equality. They seemed to fit with our political revolution. I knew I was not making my neighbors happy and I knew what it would do to my position in the community if I joined the Dissenters, but had Fanny and I not always told our own children to follow their consciences?

The war, on the other hand, consumed a lot of my thinking.

R. H. Lee came to see me. He bore the marks of strain and exhibited a restlessness.

"Sit down, please," I told him, "and have some good rum punch."

After a few sips, he relaxed into the chair. "I am involved in my work at the Continental Congress," he said, "but you know we are trying to organize our state government in Richmond at the same time. We need your help in Richmond.

"Our bakery is supplying bread to the Continental Army as well as to our neighbors," I said. "Our spinnery and fulling mill are supplying cloth for the cause and for the public. The gristmill supplies flour and cornmeal to the militia. My blacksmith makes swords for the Westmoreland militia, bayonets for Northumberland, and tools for me and my neighbors. The Iron Works in Maryland is turning out pig iron for the army, and my ships are used to ship it. I supply the greater part of their workers and most of the provisions to keep them going. Of course, my ships carry men and supplies to the Works as well. I cannot leave these endeavors without supervision. And, truthfully, I could not bear returning to politics.

"Ben and Bob are both registered for the militia, though neither has been called upon to fight. Still, they could be called at any time. It would not be good if they were. Ben is probably too sick to be in the army, and Bob is quite possibly just too ornery. And we have a new baby on the way."

R. H. looked surprised at the last, but he went on to say, "I know you are contributing in your own way, my friend."

He went away disappointed, and though my heart went out to him, I felt I had made the right choice.

46

June 1777

M oses was the leader, just like in the Bible.
Moses, a slave belonging to Landon Carter, told Postilion Tom and young Joe to sneak into the room of Billy Beale, Landon Carter's steward, and to take all the guns they could find. They found two. One belonged to Robert Wormley and the other to Landon himself. For good measure, they stole silver buckles and bullets that belonged to Robert Wormley's son, Landon. They took shirts, waistcoats, britches, and all the powder in the house. Then they met in the main hall.

As dawn began to break, they all went down to the landing on the river: Moses, Postilion Tom, Joe, and five others. They stood there awhile, waiting for some of the Robinson slaves to come meet them, swatting mosquitoes and looking warily at the house.

Soon the Robinson people came in a boat down the river. Moses crowded the Carter slaves into Landon's pettiauger canoe, and then the two boats were paddled slowly down the river, hugging the shore, the runaways looking over their shoulders.

What pumped Moses up was all the talk about men being equal. They heard it from the preachers who said that meant Negroes too. Then he heard about the proclamation that Dunmore made, and started talking up running away.

Finally, he heard that Dunmore was down in the bay, and today they were off to the Promised Land.

Moses had always been caught between Landon and Robert Wormley. If he pleased the one, he made the other mad. Either way, Moses ended up getting whipped. Robert Wormley, usually sent Moses running around the country doing his errands. Moses knew his way around.

Postilion Tom was always doing little things to Landon, and he always ended up getting punished for it.

Joe was just a boy, but he knew where everything was kept in the house, so he was the one to find the guns and powder. He had spent time locked in the damp and moldy cellar, handcuffed to the wall, more than once, for all the things he had done.

Manual was a hard case. He liked to drink and chase women. He was good with the oxen when he wanted to be, but sometimes he drove them too hard. Landon liked the oxen better than he liked Manual, so Manual was always punished severely for mistreating them. Manual's wife had let out a cow she was supposed to be caring for, and it died. Landon had her tied up and lashed for it. That didn't set well with Manuel. Landon often threatened to send Manual South, but he never did it.

Manual's son, Billy, just went because his father did.

Tom Pantico, who had once gotten a tobacco stick in his leg, was always beating his wife. So Landon brought her up to the big house to live and left Tom alone down in the quarters, but Landon did remove the tobacco stick.

Mulatto Peter was always taking off with Landon's horses and staying out all night. Of course, he was whipped till his back was raw every time.

Lancaster Sam was a thief. He got plenty of whippings. They all thought they had their reasons for leaving, but Landon, on the other hand, saw them as ungrateful, feeling that each of them owed him a particular debt of gratitude.

Robert

Not long after Uncle Landon complained to me about eight of his people running away, I watched as Priscilla and Ann Tasker came up from the wharf. They had taken a fishing trip on the Potomac with friends. Given all that was going on, I was glad to see them home safe.

Priscilla hitched up her skirts and ran up the hill to me, breathless.

"Papa, you will not believe what we heard!"

"What did you hear?"

"Louisa Lee told us she heard some minutemen at Mosquito Point saw nine Negroes in a pettiauger going fast on the Middlesex County shore of the Rappahannock. They chased them and fired at them, but the Negroes left the boat and took to the shore. The minutemen followed, but they didn't catch them." She took a minute to catch her breath. "Papa, do you think they could be Uncles Landon's people?"

"They certainly could be."

"Will some of our people run away too, Papa?"

"I do not know, child. I do not know."

"All the talk at Westmoreland Courthouse is about Negroes running to Dunmore," I reported to Fanny as I entered the house. I had just got home, and Tom had taken my horse.

"Dunmore's Proclamation continues to send shock waves running through the county."

Fanny and I sat down on the sofa in the office, and Sam brought us something cold to drink.

"I also heard news of Betty Randolph," I told Fanny.

"Oh?" Fanny looked concerned.

"Eight of the family's slaves took off, including Eva, her own maidservant, and Johnny, who was always so faithful to Peyton when he was living. Upon her widowhood, Betty took over control of the family's affairs. When I heard that the slaves left her, I was shocked, but you know, after I thought about it, I am not sure I am so surprised."

"Neither am I, frankly, dear."

"I thought of the time Betty loaned her house slave, Charlotte, to her nephew. Do you recall it?"

"Yes. Her nephew returned the girl a year later, and she was expecting a baby—turned out he was probably the nephew's child. And when the baby was born, Betty kept Charlotte and gave the baby away to her nephew."

"I thought that was a cruel thing for her to do."

"I do not think the slaves would have left if Peyton was still alive. I always did think Betty was too sharp with her people, but still I feel sorry for her. She must be terrified."

"She and many others besides."

"Remember our discussion so long ago about whether Johnny could make it on his own? Now he will find out whether or not he can."

"You know what? I believe he will."

47

May to July 1777: St. Mary's County, Maryland

A breeze blew, and the water smelled heavily brackish as I looked out across the Potomac toward the Maryland shore seven miles away. My ship, the *Betsy*, moved out of Nomini Creek at King Copsico Point. On the other side of the river I saw the trees that lined the St. Mary's shore.

I had finally convinced Fanny to let me take the older children to Maryland to be inoculated against smallpox. It was still rampant around the Northern Neck.

Tom Jefferson had the procedure done in Philadelphia. He said it was done there routinely. In Boston, there were mass inoculations, and I had good success with the inoculations of my own people at Forest Quarter. I felt secure about what I was doing.

After reading all I could get my hands on about the subject, I decided to take family members to a Dr. Brown in St. Mary's. A Mistress Ford and her daughter cared for the recovering patients at her home.

"Have things packed for a month's stay," I told Fanny. "We will leave at the break of day."

The next morning, we boarded the *Betsy*. This trip I was taking Priscilla, who was seventeen, Ann Tasker, who was fifteen, John Tasker, who was five, and Sam. We were worried about Ben's health and decided not to tempt fate. Bob flatly refused to come. Tom Henry came along though he was already inoculated, and Sukey came to help care for the girls.

We disembarked from the *Betsy* at the St. Mary's wharf before dinnertime. Our ride out from there took us through a pleasant pine woods, the fragrant needles underfoot softening the sound of the horses' hooves. After a short ride from the little village, we came upon the plain, white clapboard house that belonged to Mistress Ford. The place, in spite of its plainness, was large and commodious.

Mistress Ford herself was a pretty woman of middle age—a widow, as we learned. She wore a blue gown with a white scarf tucked modestly inside the neck of her bodice.

She and her daughter took pains to make us comfortable.

A sort of infirmary had been set up within a large room, which had likely been the parlor. There were five beds lined up side by side with just enough room between them to walk. To the side was a table with a cloth on top, for medical instruments, I supposed.

Mistress Ford led us to the dining room.

"Won't you have a meal? You've had a long journey."

We sat down to a dinner of steamed crabs and roast chicken, fried apples, potatoes, and bread.

On the next morning, May 30, Dr. Brown arrived. He was a man of small stature, with a confident bearing, and as soon as the formalities were dispensed with, he explained that the latest technique for inoculation was to use puss from the sores of inoculated patients rather than from those who had contracted the disease naturally.

"The new procedure causes a milder form of the disease," he said, then went on to explain the process that Tom Henry and I had witnessed at Forest Quarter.

Brown had a pan of soapy water brought into the room and set on the table. I noticed that he washed his hands, something other doctors did not always do. He then laid out his instruments on the table, a roll of thread, a scalpel, a small knife, and bandages. Each of us in turn lay on a bed made up with clean sheets.

Dr. Brown began with me.

I got sick. I had a fever and aching and pain. Running sores developed on my body and in my mouth and throat. Then the fever grew worse ...

The next thing I remember was waking up alone in a strange room in a strange bed. It was twilight. The bed was large and comfortable, with a light cover over it, but I could not remember how I got there. I looked around myself at the walls, the flowered wallpaper, the pictures, the curtains; not a thing did I recognize.

I tried to sit up but found that all the strength had drained from my body. My head was light. I felt unconnected to the world around me, as if I was a mere observer. *Is this a dream? Am I still alive, or have I passed over to the other side? Is this what death is like?*

I did not want to be dead. I wanted to live. Fanny came to my mind, and Sam, and my children. I did not want to leave them.

I thought to call out, but before I could do so, a small, glowing light seemed to appear and increase in intensity until it filled the room with a glorious warmth. The sight and feel of it made the hair stand up on the back of my neck.

I do not believe in the supernatural. And yet, this must be what it is like to be in the presence of something otherworldly. My heart pounded, and I began to tremble. I realized I was afraid. "If there is a God," I said aloud, "I pray that He will be here with me."

As the words left my mouth, I heard a voice, *or is it only in my mind?*

"Do not be afraid, Robert," said the voice.

The voice or thought, or whatever it was, was soothing. My heartbeat slowed; my body relaxed; a feeling of contentment came over me.

Suddenly a realization struck me as surely as the touch of a hand. *This is the voice of Christ.* I felt certain of it.

I thought of grace. I had heard a lot in my life about grace, even studied a bit about it. It was a strange, distant concept that was supposed to explain how sinners were allowed to go to heaven because Christ died for them. It had never seemed to have anything to do with me. But now, suddenly, I knew what grace was, and I was, miraculously, the recipient of it. I could feel it. It calmed me. It enveloped me in love—not the kind of love I had with family and friends, even Fanny, but something deeper, a reassurance, a certainty that I was a beloved child of God and part of a great spirit alive in the world.

I was overwhelmed by gratitude. "What shall I do now?" I asked aloud.

"When the time comes, you will know what you must do," said the soft, clear voice in the twilight.

I fell into a quiet sleep.

When I woke again, I remembered where I was, but I still remembered the encounter in the twilight. Surrounded by the faces of the doctor and Fanny and Sam and Tom Henry, I could see that Fanny and Sam had been crying.

"We all got sick," Sam said, "but you the sickest. Tom Henry take the children home when they get well, long time ago. The doctor, he tell Tom Henry to bring Mistress Fanny back. We been watching over you, worrying about you."

"I must tell you all," I said, "about what happened to me— about my gracious illumination."

<hr>

July 1777
Nomony Hall

I was dressed in a waistcoat, cutaway frock coat, and fresh shirt. I had gathered the whole family, including the house servants, in the ballroom.

"I want you all here to help me celebrate the first anniversary of our new country."

They all looked at me expectantly.

"I also want to celebrate my gracious illumination that I told you all about."

They continued to look expectant. It made me very nervous. Since the voice in the twilight did not tell me what to do, I had decided to preach a sermon.

I tried.

Fanny bowed her head and put her hand over her mouth, trying to cover a smile. The children looked away, and Bob shook his head. The servants were polite. Only Sam listened to what I said with close attention.

Oh, well, I never was articulate. I could read English and Latin with ease, even a little Greek, but, thanks to my lack of early education, my sentences often came out disjointed and clumsy. Perhaps this was a sign from God that I was not meant to be a preacher or a writer.

Praying aloud went a little better, but I quickly learned that my prayers were better kept between me and the Almighty, who already understood me.

The family, unmoved at this point by my conversion, were respectfully anxious to see how I would now behave.

I had so much to learn. Perhaps that was the lesson. I set myself upon a course of religious study, ordering books of all kinds from Philadelphia and New York. My desire to learn soon propelled me to ride with Sam all over the Northern Neck, to hear preachers of every stripe: Methodist, Baptist and Presbyterian. During the sixty days following my return from Maryland, we attended twenty-eight different religious services.

48

1777

Many times I had ridden over the road to the courthouse, but now it was the state's courthouse, not that of the king. The politics of the rebellion were not going to stop on account of my illumination, so, in spite of the hot sun beating down mercilessly on my back and my shirt sticking to my skin, I rode at a trot to Westmoreland Courthouse.

A crowd of all classes of men were moving about on the courthouse green when I arrived: large landholders and middling farmers in their osnaburg pants and open-necked shirts, all talking excitedly, smoking their pipes, chewing tobacco, arguing, and gesturing. Some staggered; probably they had had a little too much grog that day. It looked like court day or Election Day.

I walked up the steps and into the building with mixed feelings. I knew that what I was about to do would confirm me as a traitor in the eyes of the English. There would be no uncertainty now about which side I was on when the English sailed up the Potomac foraging. At the same time, I felt a great sense of pride and the excitement of a new beginning. Along with the others who served the county as justices, I swore that

I was renouncing my allegiance to King George III and giving my allegiance to the United States of America.

"The State of Virginia," I told the crowd, "requires that every free male over the age of eighteen must swear the oath you have just heard us swear."

Men began to line up. I read the oath to a middling farmer named Yeatman, who was first in line.

"Do you so swear?" I asked.

"I swear," he said.

I wrote down Yeatman's name and the date.

Then the next man stepped up.

Three of us administered the oath, but it took us well into the afternoon to finish the process. Now we had to ride out into the countryside, list in hand, to swear those who had not come to the courthouse because that is what the statute required.

We were not asked to administer the oath to slaves.

Tom Henry came in with the mail as I was sitting at my desk preparing to write the day's letters.

He handed me a letter from Coxall, the manager of the Iron Works. I unfolded it.

"I think that you should be informed," said the letter, "that a boat carrying slaves from Virginia to the Iron Works was stopped by the British. All the slaves defected to the British."

I was worried.

"However," the letter went on, "I am happy to say that they were not slaves from your plantations. Please send me more workers at your earliest convenience. Congress demands much ore from us."

My mind was not greatly eased. They could have been my slaves.

I finished writing my daily letters about midday. I stood and stretched and went into the dining room. There was Rose, directing the setting of the table for dinner. Her duties had grown steadily since she had come to Nomony. She was a fine person, almost as clever as her husband. We relied on her. She and Sam's wife, Judith, really had the running of the household.

At the moment of my arrival, Rose was happily humming to herself.

"Are you wearing your apron a little higher these days, Rose?"

She blushed.

"Yes, Master, another baby coming soon."

"I think that is wonderful."

That very evening, Fanny and I were preparing to go to bed. I was standing near the fire in the bedroom when she came in. Instead of beginning to undress, as she usually did, she sighed and eased herself slowly into one of the comfortable chairs flanking the fireplace, her hand on her lower back.

"Are you feeling unwell, my dear?"

"Perhaps I am, a little. We are going to have another baby."

"Another baby?"

I did not feel the happiness I usually did at such news. I recalled that Fanny took a long time recovering from George's birth. She was no longer a young woman like Rose. She would be forty on her next birthday, though she looked younger. I had already turned fifty. And what was more, Fanny worried constantly about Ben and Bob. It wore her down.

How passionately I had loved her that day I brought her up to this room for the first time. How passionately I loved her still. The only thing that had happened was that our love had grown much deeper. I went to her, to kiss her cheek, and she took my hand, looked at me with those deep-seeing gray eyes of hers, and smiled gently. I noticed a touch of gray in her hair. *Ah, well, I had more than a touch of gray in my own.*

"We must take better care of you, the slaves and I. You do too much."

"You'd best not spoil me, Robert Carter. You could live to regret it."

The thought crossed my mind that, without the help of the slaves, Fanny's burden would be much greater.

"The only thing I would regret, my sweet wife, is having you taken from me."

49

1778

The view from the office window presented a bleak winter landscape as I reflected on what I believed and what I must do.

I was distracted from my reverie by Fanny and Priscilla and Ann Tasker coming into the office, fresh from Cople Parish, which they still attended. Christmas and Twelfth Night had passed. I had not been to either of Cople's churches since I had had my gracious illumination in St. Mary's. With Sam at my side, I had attended various meetings, mostly Methodist and Baptist.

I looked up at Fanny, and she was frowning.

"What is it, my dear?"

"It's Reverend Smith, Robert. He has joined those who preach against the Dissenters. Everyone looked right at the girls and me when he did it. Everyone knows you go to Dissenter services. I do not blame you—or anyone—for practicing according to their beliefs. God knows you are more of a Christian than most, and I have always said that Christians should not preach against Christians. I must tell you that I am dismayed. What is this revolution for, if not for the freedom to worship as we choose? Not only is Reverend Smith, by his preaching, criticizing your choice, he is making it difficult for me to worship as I choose. I do not know if I can continue to go. He has the temerity to quote the Bible, 2 Timothy 4:3: "For the time will come when they will not endure sound doctrine, but after their own lusts shall they heap to themselves with itching ears." Their own lusts, indeed. What have lusts to do with worshipping God in a different way."

Rose, who had long followed Dissenter preachers, was passing the door to the hall. I heard her make a sort of huffing sound and saw her roll her eyes.

"Of course you are right, my sweet lady," I said. "And those who really think will agree with you. Do not let them deprive you of the privilege of worshipping as you choose. Though I would dearly love it if you accompanied Sam and me in our travels, you must follow your conscience. This revolution is changing our world in ways some do not want to acknowledge. How many who attended Cople today would truly agree that all men are created equal? Yet that is what the Declaration of Independence says."

I was sorry that my family suffered on account of my beliefs. *Shall I refrain from doing what I believe is right?*

"Well," said Fanny, "I am most put out with Reverend Smith. And I must tell you what else I heard at church."

"What is that?"

"On the tenth of this month, the British were on the river again. This time they took cattle, hogs, poultry, and slaves from some of the people who attend Cople. We are very fortunate that they have taken nothing from us."

"Indeed."

I rubbed my forehead and picked up my quill. I was preparing to draft a letter to accompany Bob to William and Mary. I sat with quill poised. Nothing we tried with the boy seemed to work. He stayed out all night. He was rude to family and servants alike. He became violent when he was angry. He had taken scant interest in anything the tutors had taught, and he was not inclined to learn on his own. He exhibited all the worst traits of the elite class. Fanny and I had no control over him. Now he was eighteen, soon to be of age, and we were in despair.

As I was thinking these things, still hesitating to put ink to paper, Fanny came to me and laid her hand on my back.

"Are you certain this is what you want to do?" I asked her.

"Robert, we have talked and talked, and tried and tried. I believe this is our best hope. Perhaps a person outside the family can reach him." She sighed heavily.

"If this does not work, I do not know what we shall do."

And so, I began my letter to the Reverend James Madison at the College of William and Mary:

"My wife and I send our son Robert Bladen Carter to you with hopeful hearts. Bob (as we call him) has taken little interest in learning, and his behavior has not been as it should be. However, he is not lacking in intelligence, and he has been taught right from wrong. We are trusting in the quality of the college and your own reputation as a fine man and a good teacher. We send him to you to learn mathematics, but more than that, we hope that your example will instill in him a more pious disposition."

We packed his things, and Bob and I set out early in the morning for Williamsburg on horseback. Bob was sullen, and hardly a word was spoken between us on the long ride.

"This reminds me," I said, "of my own journey to Williamsburg to go to the grammar school at William and Mary."

Bob made no reply.

"Of course," I continued, "I was only nine, so it was different."

Still Bob said nothing.

"I was very uneasy about being away from my mother and in a strange place, but everyone else was in the same situation. What I am trying to say, Bob, is that I know this must be hard for you."

"I'm not afraid, Papa. I just don't want to go."

I thought about asking what he did want to do, but we had had that conversation before. It always led to an argument. It seemed to me that he did not know, or care to know, what he wanted to do.

In Williamsburg, I delivered him to the reverend in his office in the college building with a heavy heart. I arranged to leave a horse with him so that he had the means to get home on his own.

The next morning Bob and I were standing outside the front of the college building.

"Bob," I said as I prepared to mount my horse to make the long return trip, "this is your chance to prove yourself and to learn what you need so that you can choose what to do with your life. Your mother and I love you very much. We will miss you."

I offered my hand, and Bob took it and shook it, but he did not look me in the eye.

"I will do my best, Papa," he mumbled, looking at his feet.

I wanted to believe him.

March 1778

The sky was overcast and the weather cool. Sam and I continued on horseback, riding on the narrow road through the woods, keeping our heads down and trying to get to the little church in Lancaster County before the rain came. We had been on the road since early morning.

At last we came to a building set in a clearing on a rise in the woods. It was the meeting place for a newly formed Baptist church, the first building of its kind in the Northern Neck. The church was led by a preacher named Lewis Lunsford.

As we approached, I saw several people, white and black, some on horseback, most on foot. We tied up our horses and went inside. The stove at the front of building put out welcome heat. We walked up and sat side by side on a pew not far from the stove.

A few people looked at me askance, but there was no other indication of their thinking it was strange to find me there. As I sat there, however, I was aware on some level that I had crossed a line. A person of my class, sitting on a seat next to, and in an equal position with, a slave held by my family, participating in a church service where race, family history, and status did not matter, was something new. I knew, without a doubt, that this would ultimately change the relationship between me and my people—and probably the relationship with my neighbors as well. *There will be no turning back from this point.*

⟶

October 1778

"I was most glad to read of your proposal for the banning of importation of slaves to Virginia," I wrote to Tom Jefferson, who was now in the Virginia General Assembly. It was the first act of its kind in the new United States, and I was proud of it.

Jefferson and I had had little correspondence since we had played music together in Williamsburg. We had agreed then about many things—that slavery was immoral and bad for the country and that church and state should be separate. I knew that he had proposed his "Statute for Religious Freedom," but that the Assembly had not acted on it.

I went on to write:

> "I have been studying these many years, what I should believe. You and I have discussed Deism, which you have said is your understanding of Christianity. You believe Christ was a great teacher but doubt His divinity. I have had the same doubts. I find that I am now content that Christ is divine. It is because of a spiritual experience which I had ..."

> I wished that Jefferson might understand what had happened to me. However, I never heard from him on the subject of religion again.

April 1778

On an evening that was warm and pleasant, Fanny went with me to the fulling mill on Aries Plantation. A slight breeze caught the hair that showed beneath her hat. I was pleased because she was going with me to hear Lewis Lunsford, whom I had invited to come speak.

The fulling mill was filling with people of all sorts. It was my practice to allow, but not require, my people to attend Dissenter services, and many of them were there on that evening.

The Negroes noticed my being there, of course. Apart from Fanny, there were no others of our class in attendance, though I did know that the irrepressible Hannah Lee Corbin had been a Baptist for some ten years past.

I liked Lunsford. I liked his preaching, and I liked that the Baptist Church had gone on record against slavery. Perhaps, I hoped, the enlightened people of Virginia would see their way clear to support a statute for manumission.

The crowd hushed as Lunsford stood to speak. Though he was a big man, he was young, about twenty-five or so. He began his sermon quietly in language that was not cultured, nor even, in some cases, grammatical. But as he proceeded, his voice increased in volume and emotion until he was speaking with great fire and conviction. His voice was astonishing, and his intensity and honesty were compelling. He was visibly moving the crowd as he spoke.

About midsermon, Sarah, a young laundress from Nomony Hall, began to quake, crying and moaning. She asked her mother, Teanor, to request a hymn about death and resurrection. I had never seen anyone react so strongly to a sermon.

Two days later, I invited a Methodist layman named John Turner to speak at Nomony Hall. This time, the whole family attended, including many of the Negroes. It was to them that Turner primarily directed his sermon. Tom from Coles Point broke down into tears and confessed his sinfulness and asked for forgiveness. Sarah was again moved to weeping and shaking.

⌒〜

"Come down from that stage," Captain Stewart Redman shouted, shaking a sword at Lewis Lunsford as he spoke.

He and a group of about sixty-five men had come to a farm in Westmoreland County where Lunsford was speaking outside before a large crowd, over a hundred in number.

Redman's men approached the platform, threatening and gesturing toward Lunsford. Lunsford stood his ground. He was well-built, and appeared to have the courage to match his strength.

"The Commonwealth of Virginia has granted me a license to preach," he shouted, facing them defiantly. "This is a new day and I am on private property, invited by the owner. You have no authority to remove me."

Redman grew red in the face. "I say you shall come down, or we will take you down."

He turned to his men, who raised clubs to any worshipper who objected to their treatment of the preacher. Several were knocked to the ground.

Before I could think what to do, a great ruckus ensued, as worshippers of all stripes resisted the blows of the vigilantes. Meanwhile, two of the largest members of the audience each grabbed Lunsford under an arm and pulled him into the owner's house, locking the door behind them.

Redman and his men went after them and beat on the door of the house, trying to get in. They were apparently reluctant to do actual damage to the house, owned by a white man.

They finally gave up and walked away, pushing and shoving their way through the crowd.

"There will be another time," Redman shouted. "We'll be back. And you," he said, waving a club at me, "will stay away from these preachings if you know what's good for you."

50

1779: Leo Plantation

Before the rider even spoke, Fanny turned pale. The messenger was exhausted, sweat covering his face and neck, water dripping from his hair. His horse was soaking wet as well.

"I've come from Loudon County, Mr. Carter. I came as fast as I could."

I was afraid Fanny would faint.

"Stay until you have rested. I'll have my people get you something to eat and drink. Mistress Carter and I are leaving immediately."

Tom brought the coach around. It would be a rough trip in the coach, but Fanny was no longer up to riding the distance on horseback.

The coach bumped and tossed its way over the rutted roads. Fortunately, they were dry.

"We should not have let him take on Leo. It is too far."

"He is of age, Fanny, and he wanted to manage the plantation. We cannot keep him a child."

She made no response, just wrung her handkerchief in her hands.

I looked out the window, deep in thought. It was May. May was Ben's favorite time of year. He always loved to ride out on horseback as the weather warmed. May meant fields of sweet-smelling young wheat; the first creamy flowering of the magnolia; May apples in the deep, pungent woods; and snowy laurel on the riverbanks. May was warmth and music and joy and hope and poetry. Ben, good Ben, always waxed poetic after his rides in May. But even Ben had been tainted by the system in which we lived.

We arrived at the main house, a simple one-bedroom affair. Ben's manservant, Dennis, the same one who went to school to learn, his face creased with worry, ushered us quickly to the bed where Ben lay.

"I don' think he gonna make it this time, Master. Doctor don't offer nay hope for him."

The bones in Ben's face showed prominently, and it was whiter and thinner than I had ever seen. His voice, when he tried to speak, was weak and hesitant, every breath an effort. His words were interrupted by fits of coughing that racked his whole body.

He struggled to speak. With a great effort, he lifted himself on one elbow and said, "Mama, Papa. I love you."

He took a deep, ragged breath and lay his head back down. His chest rose and fell with the exertion of speaking. He looked up at us, seeming to want to say something else. Then, suddenly, his whole body relaxed, and the words never came.

Fanny fell over his lifeless body, shaking with sobs. I held her for a while as she lay there. After some time, I lifted her gently and pulled her away.

"Come, my dear; we must take care of him."

Two of the field slaves built him a rough casket and dug a grave near the edge of the woods. There Tom Henry, Fanny, and I stood silently along with Dennis and all the people on the place, as Ben was lowered into the fertile soil. I did my best to say a prayer over him.

"Father, please welcome and comfort this good child."

In the coach on the way home, Fanny and I sat close together. We did not speak, just held hands as Fanny wept. I silently prayed for strength and understanding. Our most promising son was gone. It seemed too much to bear.

We arrived home to find that Rose had given birth to a baby girl, whom she named Betty. Death and birth, birth and death, the cycle of life, so apparent on a plantation.

Nomony Hall

The heat of the summer was upon us, and my outlook was morose. Ben was gone from our life. Fanny was not pursuing her usual summer planting of flowers and vegetables. She was suffering from her latest pregnancy as she had never done. The whole place seemed to be under a cloud.

I wiped my brow as I rode up the lane from the road. I approached the house and was preparing to dismount when Tom Henry came to me. His expression told me that he was not going to tell me anything that would improve my mood.

"Master, Bob has come home."

This cannot be good. Was he put out of school in Williamsburg?

"You left a gelding with him, didn't you, Master?"

"Yes, I did."

"Bob came home without it. He must have borrowed the one he rode home. I asked him what happened to the gelding, but he did not choose to answer."

I would not mention the horse to Fanny. Let her enjoy this visit of her second son.

Bob was in the schoolhouse, where he still slept whenever he was at home. He was wearing only his shirt and britches, and he did not have the grace to stand when I entered the room.

"Is there any particular reason why you have come home from school, Son?"

"I came to see you and Mama. I know that you are mourning Ben."

"If that is so, it is very considerate of you. Certainly your mother can use comfort. Does Reverend Madison know why you left Williamsburg?"

"Yes, Sir; I told him just as I told you."

"I see. Tom Henry tells me you came home without the gelding I left for you in Williamsburg. Where is he?"

Bob shifted his feet. He looked at the floor and then back at me. Then he spoke in a low voice. "I sold him."

I did have to give him credit. Cornered, Bob usually told the truth.

"Sold him? For what reason would you do a thing like that?"

"I needed the money."

I could feel my face becoming red. "And why, pray, did you need money? Your needs were well provided for."

"I overextended myself."

"In what way did you overextend yourself?"

"I made a few friendly wagers, you know, with the other gentlemen at school."

"Well, my son, you shall return to school immediately—and without a horse."

"But Papa ..."

"Immediately, and without a horse. You can ride back on the mount you borrowed to get here."

A letter from Reverend Madison arrived the next day. He informed me not only of Bob's gambling, but also of his traveling to Gloucester County for what the reverend termed "inappropriate recreation."

Well, the lack of a horse might also keep him away from Gloucester County.

I called John Peck, the children's tutor, to my office. I motioned for him to sit in a straight-backed chair facing my desk.

He smiled as if nothing was wrong, a lock of his blond hair falling over his forehead. He was a handsome young man and on the surface quite charming. I had learned during his time with us that he liked to flatter those from whom he sought advantage.

"I am going to have to let you go," I told him bluntly.

Before he could ask me why, I began.

"There are a number of reasons. I have learned that you have told our neighbors that you suffer from lack of funds even though I pay you more than the usual wage for your position. I have also learned that you are slow to pay your debts and that you are frequently dishonest in your dealings with people hereabouts. In short, you do not set a good example for my children, and you embarrass me. Finally, Mr. Peck, I have told you and I have told Anne Tasker that your attentions to her are not acceptable. Neither of you has paid attention to that, and so now I must insist that you leave this house and not come back, even to visit. I will give you a month's wages to tide you over until you can find another position. And, you are to have no contact whatsoever with Anne Tasker."

My greatest hope was that Peck would leave the area and go back to his native New Jersey.

Peck had other ideas.

Robert Mitchell's visit to my office was a surprise. He was dressed in his best and looked like a gentleman. I had not seen him since he had left my employment as a steward at Nomony Hall. He'd done an excellent job as steward and had saved money to farm for himself. I hated to see him go, but I admired his ambition.

I sent Sam for refreshments and invited Mitchell to have a comfortable seat.

"It is a pleasure to see you indeed," I said. "Tell me about your land and what you are doing with it."

He answered my question politely. Then he said, "Actually, sir," pausing to take the glass of lemon punch from Sam's hand, "I came for a particular purpose."

I straightened. I had noticed a growing attraction between him and Priscilla, but I did not know whether they had stayed in touch after he left.

"What is that?" I asked.

"I wish to marry your daughter Priscilla. She and I have grown quite attached over the years, and I am now in a position to support her, not as well as you, of course, but in a manner I believe will be congenial to her. My future prospects are good."

I was disappointed in the attachment. I could not say exactly why. I could not say that Mitchell was an undesirable suitor. Perhaps I just did not want to let Priscilla go.

Mitchell leaned forward and spoke with feeling. "I would cherish and care for her, Mr. Carter, as she matters more to me than anything in the world. She wishes for the marriage as much as I do, though I'm sure you will want to talk to her about that. I do have a letter with me that she wrote to tell you her wishes."

"This is something I will have to talk over with both Priscilla and her mother. I cannot give you an immediate answer."

"I understand." Disappointment showed in Mitchell's face. "I will anxiously await your answer."

I did talk to Priscilla, and to Fanny, but I never did give Mitchell a definite answer. I permitted him to come to Nomony Hall to court her, however. Finally, they took matters into their own hands and married without my permission but also without any objection from me.

I was not about to be deterred from my mission. Sam and I rode over the familiar Westmoreland/Richmond County Road until we reached the road that turned off to Totuskey Creek. The weather was fitful—cold for September—the wind was blowing, and a chilling drizzle was falling.

We proceeded toward the water where a large number of people were gathered. Lewis Lunsford was there to speak.

He stood tall on a high piece of ground, and with his melodious voice and eloquent gestures soon had all the gathering enthralled.

Afterward he invited those so inclined to become a part of his flock. In spite of the weather, several people made their way toward the water to be baptized.

I removed my hat, coat, and shoes, and approached the water, waiting my turn. I had made up my mind that it was time to make a commitment, and so I had told Sam as we rode over from Nomony Hall. Now, as I looked over my shoulder, I saw Sam remove his outer clothes to follow me into the water.

"Are you certain this is what you want to do, Sam? Is this what you believe?"

He just smiled that broad, gap-toothed grin of his. "Yes, indeed, Master, but I wonders, what take you so long to make up you mind?"

The water was cold. My head was lowered into it, and it covered my face so that for a moment I could not breathe. I came up gasping for air. The experience gave a new meaning to the phrase "born again."

I felt closer to Sam at that moment than I had ever felt. We rode home in silence, wrapped in blankets and deep in thought. It occurred to me then that we were more like brothers, as the church called us, than master and slave. There was still, however, one thing we did not talk about.

51

1780

Bob and I stood in my office at Nomony Hall—he sullen, and I angry.

When we sent Bob back to William and Mary after his impromptu visit, I wrote to Reverend Madison telling him that Bob was forbidden by me to go to Gloucester or anywhere else, including home, during the school term. Bob had refused to comply. So I finally gave up and had him removed from school entirely. That solved Reverend Madison's problem, but not mine or Bob's. I despaired for his future.

"My son, I have tried having you tutored at home. I have tried having you apprenticed. I have tried having you work here on the plantation with me, and I have tried sending you to William and Mary. One way or another, you have managed to make sure that all these efforts are in vain. You are no longer a child. You must do something useful in this world. What do you suggest that I do with you?"

"Give me a plantation to run on my own, as you did with Ben. I'm your oldest son now."

My initial reaction was to reject the idea out of hand. Ben had been a responsible young man and was willing to learn.

That did not describe Bob. I did not believe he had the disposition to run a plantation.

"I will think about it," I said.

I waited a week, during which time Bob was on his best behavior. I talked it over with Fanny. Our doubts remained, but what else could we do with him?

I called him into my office for another talk.

"Sit down, Son." I remained standing. "I have been thinking about your wanting to manage a plantation. Billingsgate is a small place, with a decent house and about ten slaves. It is close by. It has been well-cultivated, and the overseer there, Thomas Olive, has been there for some little time. He knows the place, though sometimes I think he is overharsh with the slaves. I would count on you to remedy that."

"I was thinking of something grander than Billingsgate."

The remark annoyed me, but I said, "If you prove yourself there, we may consider something larger. It is as fine a place, in any case, as Leo, which Ben managed. You will have to stop wasting money on gambling and riding out at all times of the day and night. You will need to apply yourself, but this is an opportunity for you."

"I will apply myself; you'll see."

The next day, we rode together to Billingsgate. The place was small, less than two hundred acres, and some of that was forested. Its entrance was off the road between Westmoreland and Richmond Courthouses.

The lane was lined with cedars, and fields were on either side. There was a small tobacco crop, but this plantation grew mostly wheat, and young green stalks waved peacefully in the wind as we approached. The main house was two stories, not elaborate but adequate for a family, and the overseer's house was nearby.

Thomas Olive was a short man with dark curly hair and a smiling visage. As we rode up, he came out to meet us.

Today Olive seemed quite content. Unbeknownst to Bob, I had gone to see him before my son and I rode to Billingsgate together. Olive, being used to having a fair amount of independence at the plantation, was less than pleased that an owner would be living on the property, but I stressed to him the honor and importance of teaching Bob the ropes. When I offered him an increase in wages as an inducement, he liked the idea much better.

For his part, Bob seemed to be quite enthusiastic and entered into the discussions about how things would be done.

I left him there while I went on to arrange for the necessary funds to be available for him to set up the house as he wished.

June 1781

Fanny and I were sitting at the dinner table at Nomony Hall with the older children. The house was much more peaceful with Bob at Billingsgate. I had heard nothing from Olive or anyone else that made me worry about how things were going there.

"It appears that the war continues to go poorly, my dear," I said to Fanny, "especially in Virginia. When the British approached Richmond, the government moved to Charlottesville; Tom Jefferson met with the General Assembly near Monticello. The last time the Assembly met in Charlottesville was May 28. Then on June 4, they adjourned to Staunton, trying to avoid the British."

"Where is Staunton?"

"It is a small settlement on the western frontier, hardly more than a trading center."

"What became of Tom? Did the British follow him to Monticello?"

"That is what I see the answer to in this week's *Gazette*. On June 4, a man named John Jouett rode to warn him and the General Assembly that the British were coming to Charlottesville. Tom sent his family to Poplar Forest, farther west. When troops arrived at Monticello, they demanded to know where Tom was. His manservant said he was not at home. While the servant was telling that to the British officers, Tom was leaving out the back door. He was leaving to go to Poplar Forest himself. The British did not catch him.

"What is unfortunate is that Tom's term as governor was supposed to end on June 2, and he assumed he was a private citizen. However, because the General Assembly left for Staunton without electing his successor, he was still governor until they did meet again on June 12. Now Tom is being called a coward for running from the British. I do not know what they think he could have done to help the situation."

"Poor Tom. I'm glad he was not captured. What will happen, Robert, if the British win this war?"

"I do not know, my dear, but many of us will suffer for rebelling. I can only guess what could happen to us and our people. I just pray that they do not win."

52

1781: Tom Henry

"Tom," Master said to me, "these are some of the same people we talked to at Coles Point five years ago, who chose not to run to Dunmore." He put his hand to his forehead, closing his eyes.

I had come into the office to tell him what I knew of the events on the Potomac. It was true that since we talked to the people at Coles Point, the British had been back in that vicinity in both 1776 and 1778, and none of the slaves had defected to the British. Sometime between March 31 and April 8 just past, British privateers were on the river again. They made three raids. The first two times, none of Master's slaves left. They hid out as they had been told. The third time, however, the *Atwell* was in the river with thirty-three of Master's people on board. All of them went to the British, who had promptly taken them on board their own ship and sunk the *Atwell*.

"Gone, then? Why, Tom? After all this time, why would they go? Do they mislike me so much and I not aware of it?" He looked at me beseechingly. "Have I not looked to their needs in these hard times?"

"We do not know that they went willingly, Master."

"They always managed to avoid the British before."

I had no answer for him, though I was not certain they were not compelled to go.

"I will divide the land at Coles Point into parcels and rent it out until the end of the year. I will move the livestock and store produce away from the river. I can use my own sloop to move corn from plantation to plantation, and I shall remove the remaining people from Coles Point to other places. We must continue to make a living."

53

October 1781: Tom Henry

The first thing I noticed as I approached Hobb's Hole was that people of all stripes were standing around, some with the *Virginia Gazette* in hand, talking in animated tones. The air was alive with excitement. I had gone to get the mail.

"Surrendered?" I heard a merchant say to his neighbor. "Surrendered, you say? General Cornwallis? I thought he was supposed to be a very able soldier. Are you sure?"

"Read it for yourself, my friend. Surrendered his whole army to George Washington and the French."

"They say," said a gentleman holding his own copy of the *Gazette*, "that Cornwallis was not pleased to surrender to the Americans. He would not come out to deliver his sword. He sent his second-in-command to do it. First they tried to deliver the sword to Rochambeau and the French army, but Rochambeau refused to accept it. So Cornwallis's man tried to deliver it to Washington. And Washington told the man to give it to the American's second-in-command."

They all had a good laugh about that.

I rode home over the cold roads, anxious to tell the news.

November 1781

The sun was shining and, as I brought out Master's horse, I saw six ragged-looking figures on foot beginning the climb up the poplar lane. I watched as they came toward the house. A sickening smell of urine and unwashed bodies preceded them, but when I made out their faces, I recognized Tom, Daniel, Fanny, George, and two others who had gone missing from Coles Point. I sent them to the kitchen. "Cook will give you something to eat. I will tell Master you are here."

"Will he whup us?"

"I do not know what he may do."

"Will he let us stay?"

"You will have to wait to hear that from him."

Master Robert himself came back to the kitchen with me. The head cook, my mother Sarah, was keeping her distance from the prodigals, holding her apron over her nose. They reeked with the smell of stale urine and sweat, but they were eating voraciously from plates of cornbread with gravy, picking up the bread in their fingers and stuffing it into their mouths as fast as they could. They were reluctant to stop, but they stood up when Master walked into the room.

"Finish eating," Master said. "When you are done, Sarah will see that you get some soap and a tub of hot water. I will send Rose with some decent clothes. Then straight away, I want you all to come to my office in the big house."

George did the talking when they arrived in Master's office.

They stood gathered around Master's desk, heads down, hands clasped in front of them.

"We run away from the British back in the summertime, Master."

"Where were you?"

"We at a place they call Portsmouth. They boat take us there after they sink the *Atwell*. We sneak away after we get on the shore. We be trying to get home ever since. We never wanted to leave, Master. They say they kill us if we don't go. The rest of them musta stayed at Portsmouth. The British talking about sending them to someplace called Yorktown. I knows for sure that Tom Cooper, Nanny, Betty, and Judy still be there when we leave."

"How in the world did you get home?"

"We just keep walking, Master, mostly at night. We hide in the woods sometime, and sometime we stay in the quarters of big plantations. People from the quarters give us food and a place to sleep. We keep asking how to get to Master Robert Carter plantation called Nomony Hall. At first, nobody seem to know where that be, but closer we get, the more folks know you. It good to be home. Master Carter, please don't send us away, even if you got to beat us."

They all looked into Master's face for an answer to that.

He rubbed his chin. "I was very angry when you left. You always managed to avoid the British before. Why did you let them catch you this time?"

"We out on the open water, Master. They see us. They have guns and swords."

"I am not sure if I believe you."

They looked at each other, fear in their eyes.

Master thought a long time. "Well, you are here. You certainly made an effort to get here, regardless of why you went away. And you knew you risked punishment coming back. I will let you stay if you go back to work."

Tears ran down George's face. "Thank you, Master. Thank you."

Master Robert sent me to Portsmouth, now in the hands of the Americans, to see about the others. He wanted them sold. He said he did not want to see them again because he believed they left willingly.

1782
Robert Carter

One day, six months after George and the others returned, I was at the fulling mill at Aries. Prue ran across the floor, waving her arms in the air.

"Master, Master," Prue shouted before she reached me. "I needs you to help me."

I stood still and waited for her.

Chest heaving, Prue took several breaths before speaking. "Master, Lemuel tell me that some people at Mount Airy hear my Betty be at a place in James City County, and she want to come home."

Prue's Betty was one of the Coles Point runaways. One that George said stayed behind with the British. When I sent Tom Henry to Portsmouth to check on the rest of the people from Coles Point, some were not accounted for, but they were not designated by name.

"What makes you believe she is there, Prue?"

"Somebody that visited that place told folks at Mount Airy he had seen her there—at a plantation that belong to a Master Musgrove. Will you get her back, Master? Please."

"If Musgrove bought her, Prue, there is nothing I can do. She belongs to him. I ordered all the slaves at Portsmouth sold."

"She don't belong to him, Master. She tell the man she be taken by Musgrove outta the woods, and she want to come home."

"She had a chance to come home, Prue, just like George and the others, and she chose not to do it."

"But, Master," Prue dropped to her knees and began to cry, "she didn't go on purpose. She wouldn't do that. She my only living child. Please, Master, see about her."

54

1781: James City County, Virginia

Tom Henry

I set off for James City County. I went first to Williamsburg. Though it was no longer the capital of Virginia, it was still the county seat of James City County. I went to the small brick courthouse on Duke of Gloucester Street. The clerk was not there, so I walked up along the wooden sidewalk until I reached Raleigh's Tavern.

The burley landlord hurried to the door in his apron, blocking my way.

"I have come with a letter from my master, Robert Carter of Nomony Hall, sir. I am seeking the whereabouts of a property owner named William Musgrove."

The landlord continued to look askance at me and would not permit me to enter the tavern, even the kitchen. "Let me see this letter," he said.

I handed him the letter, and his attitude changed substantially.

"I see," he said. "But the gentleman is not known to me."

"Can you tell me where I might find the clerk of the court, sir? He was not at the courthouse. Perhaps he can tell me where Mr. Musgrove's property is located."

The landlord continued to look at me in that strange way that white people do. I knew it was because of the way I talked, and I was used to it.

"How do you know that the clerk can tell you? You're a most unusual Negro."

"I have been fortunate to learn a good deal about government over the years. My master was a councillor before the war, and we lived here in Williamsburg."

"Well," he said, looking again at the letter, "as a matter of fact, the clerk is here having his dinner. I will tell him you seek him."

"I'll wait," I said.

I was still not invited to come inside, of course, but I could see through the window that the landlord spoke to an older gentleman seated near the fireplace. He looked up at the door.

I waited on the sidewalk until the clerk finished his meal and came out.

"Sir, are you the clerk of court?"

"I am. I understand you have a letter from your master regarding William Musgrove."

"I do."

I handed him the letter.

He gave me directions to Musgrove's home a few miles out in the country. I rode through the woods expecting to find a plantation, but when I came to the place the clerk had directed me to, it was a two-story clapboard farmhouse.

I stood on the porch and knocked on the door. Much to my surprise, the person who answered it was Betty herself. She was dressed in head-rag and apron. Working as a house servant, then. She took in a sudden breath.

"Lord have mercy. It be Tom Henry."

Rather than letting me in the house, she came out onto the porch and pulled me away from the door.

"What you doing here? How you find me?"

"Master heard you were here. He sent me to see about you. Your Mama heard you were in James City County at the home of William Musgrove. Master told me to find you and talk to Musgrove."

"I wants to go home, Tom Henry. I misses my Mama. Will Master take me back?"

"I don't know yet. Let me talk to Musgrove."

She led the way inside the house and left me standing on the worn wooden floor of the front hall.

The room was dimly lit, but I could see that the man who approached me was probably in his thirties, short of stature, with a round, red face. He was dressed in an open-necked linen shirt and oznaburg britches, a middling farmer. His manner was impatient.

"What do you want?"

I handed him the letter from Master Robert and waited for him to read it. The letter told him that I had been sent by Robert Carter of Nomony Hall and was directed by him to bring Betty back there, provided she wanted to go.

"What is the meaning of this?"

I decided not to beat around the bush.

"Betty is my master's property. She was taken by the British. He would like to know how she came to be here."

Hearing me speak, he gave me that long look white folks always did.

"I found her wandering in the woods—back in October after the skirmish at Yorktown. She was not under anyone's control. I am claiming her as spoils of war."

"With all due respect, sir, she has a legal master. The slaves found outside Yorktown are supposed to be returned to their masters."

"How do I know that this is true?"

"Well, sir, I suppose you could contact the American army at Portsmouth and ask for yourself."

"What if I refuse to return her? What you going to do about it?"

"In that case, I would have to go home and tell my master you refused to return his property, and then he would deal with it."

Musgrove raised his eyebrows. "Do you dare threaten me?"

I stood firmly where I was. "I mean no disrespect, sir. I am just telling you what I must do if I have to go home without Betty."

⟶

Betty told Master her story after we got home.

She was only sixteen or seventeen, and she shook uncontrollably as she talked. "George right," she said. She twisted the front of her skirt in her hands. "I stay with the soldiers when George and the others go. I afraid to sneak off. They take me to a town called Yorktown. They be lots of soldiers there, all in they red uniforms. They make the Negro men dig trenches in the ground. They call them 'trenchments.' The general he give the Negroes the hardest, dirtiest jobs to do. The women cook and wash and wait on the officers. Master Cornwallis promise after the war that then we get our freedom.

"But then the Americans and the French come. They make a circle all around the town, so nobody can get out. They was ships blocking the river, so they can't go that way. We trapped in there with the British soldiers and the people that live in the town. Then the Americans and the French start shooting they big guns, hitting buildings and everything, tearing up the town. I be mighty scared. It seem like a long time we be holed up in that town. Rations start getting scarce. Then Cornwallis, he told his soldiers put out the runaways—that what he call us—so they don't have to feed us. He say we got to fend for our ownselves. Inside the ditches be the British soldiers. Outside be the Americans and the French. We trapped any way we go, so I take off through the woods. I be cold and hungry and scared. One day, Master Musgrove find me. He take me home and make me his slave. I wish I never leave home. I wants to be home. Please don't make me leave, Master."

Master Carter relented, and Betty was safe.

55

1783: Lancaster County

Robert Carter

S am and I rode to Morattico Church at its building in
Lancaster County. The cool, clear weather and the easy
stride of the horses on the long ride lulled me into a reflection
of recent events.

A treaty had been signed between England and the
United States officially ending the war. The 1782 General
Assembly passed a law, finally, permitting the manumission
of slaves. I had read it. It set out particular—and difficult—
conditions under which it was to be done, all the expense and
responsibility falling on the slaveholder. Perhaps this year,
the Assembly would set up a path for freedom for all slaves.
Perhaps the Revolution would fulfill all its ideals.

I had turned fifty-five. I was still fairly lean and fit, but
my hair was gray at the temples, and I had slowed down a
bit. Fanny was thinner than she had been, and worry had
sprinkled her hair with gray also. She was frequently unwell.
Our seventeenth child, Julia, had been born this forty-fifth
year of her life.

So had little Thaddeus Henry. Rose seemed to match
Fanny child for child these days.

Our daughter Frances had married Thomas Jones from Hanover. It was a good match for her, and I gave her eight slaves as a part of her dowry, as custom demanded I do. I was uneasy at letting the people out of my control, not knowing how they would be treated, but I was learning I could not protect all my people forever.

Sam

Master been thinking all the way from Nomony, but he come back to hisself when we come up on the church building. It was small, built of wood, and it sat on a hill above the road through the woods. Lewis Lunsford built this church so folks have a regular place to meet. We get down from our horses and walk in the front door. The heat of the day lay heavy inside. There be no need to light a fire this day.

Master been elected clerk of the church. He have to write down what happen at the deacons' meetings, which be what was going on this evening.

The church was bigger and richer than it be when we got baptized. A lot of the money come from Master.

The head of the deacons let Brother John Wright speak first. Brother Wright a lanky, red-skinned little white man. He dressed like a farmer.

"I am asking that we remove Negro Tom, who is the property of Elizabeth Davis, from the congregation," he said. "He confessed to adultery."

Now, I was thinking it be hard for a Negro to commit adultery being as how Negroes ain't allowed to be married. I guesses it all in how you looks at it.

Anyway, Brother Wright look around and go on, gathering steam as he go.

"He is not the sort of person we want in our church."

Master write down what he say, but when they start discussing it, Master say, "I'd like to know more about this supposed adultery. I'm fairly certain Tom is not married. Was it the woman, then? Was she willing or are we talking about rape? That would certainly be serious. Is Brother Tom repentant? Has he asked for forgiveness? We have a duty to love him as a brother. Is this how we would treat a blood brother? Give up on him? I believe some sort of punishment is appropriate if he is guilty, but removing him from our fellowship is too strong a response."

Brother Wright straighten he shoulders and look around again.

"He'll give this church a bad name. I won't worship with him."

I see some white heads nod. Another man stand up and give Master a hard look.

"I say put him out!"

No one else speak up for Negro Tom, and he be put outta the church.

Brother Thomas Downing stand up. He some kind of shopkeeper from Kilmarnock. He be dressed up fancy in a cutaway coat, long in the back. He be one of the prosperous new members that start coming to Morattico.

Brother Downing say he hear Negro Solomon committed adultery, too, and he be looking into the matter.

Molly Bennett, a poor widow lady be reported to be a common swearer, and they start up another investigation about that.

Master look unhappy, but he write down everything they all say.

Finally, everybody stop complaining.

Master stand up. "Now that all that is behind us, there is something I would like to say. I have a letter from a James

Manning, president of a college established by the Baptist Church in Providence, the College of Rhode Island. Education is essential in a democracy such as we propose to live in. If we are to move away from control of government by wealthy families—like mine—then we must educate our children. This college is the first Baptist institution of its kind in this country, and they are asking for our assistance."

The deacons murmur about this awhile. The majority of the deacons vote to send some money to the college in Rhode Island.

"At least," Master say to me on the way home, "we accomplished one good thing this evening."

56

1784: Billingsgate Plantation

Robert

The afternoon sun slanted through the window onto my desk. I threw down the letter Tom Henry had just brought me. It was the third angry letter I had received complaining about an unpaid bill relating to Billingsgate Plantation. After the last such letter, I had sent for Bob. At that time, he told me that it was a mistake, and he would take care of it. However, I had heard nothing more. Now, this letter.

Tom Henry saddled my horse, and I set out for Billingsgate at a smart canter. Billingsgate was contiguous with Nomony Hall along the road toward Richmond Courthouse. Although Billingsgate was close to home, I had determined to leave Bob alone, to work things out in his own way. The more fool I.

I listened to the clopping of my horse's hooves as we entered the lane at a walk. The lane was set among native oaks and sweet gum and was lined with cedars, but I noticed it was full of ruts. The place looked unkempt and wild, weeds growing among the crops, the spaces between the cedars cluttered with underbrush.

The house, a modest two-story clapboard, came into sight, but *What is this?* The house looked deserted. Inside the furniture was carelessly set around. In the one used bedroom, the bed was disheveled and cold. No clothes were apparent anywhere. No slaves were about the house.

I should have come sooner. Whatever made me think Bob would handle the plantation without close assistance?

I tried to calm myself as I went on to the house of the overseer, Thomas Olive.

He was sitting on his porch, a wad of tobacco in his cheek.

"What is going on? Where is Bob?"

Olive did not get up, which did nothing to improve my temper. He spat tobacco before answering.

"He left here about a week ago, Councillor."

"Stand up when you talk to me, Mr. Olive."

He did so as if it required a great effort.

"Why did you not ride out immediately to tell me when he left?"

"Why, he told us you'd be about shortly, to tell us what to do. I thought you knowed he was leaving."

"How long did you propose to wait for me to come, I wonder. Never mind. I'll deal with you later."

According to Olive, Bob had abandoned Billingsgate and taken some money, saying he intended to go to England. And, he added, Bob said I would be taking care of any debts left behind.

When I went to the quarters, I saw people sitting around or puttering about in their own gardens.

I was met by Charlotte, the cook and general housekeeper at Billingsgate.

"Master, I think you never come."

"What's the trouble, Charlotte?"

She looked at me piteously, tears in her eyes.

"Before he go, young Master Bob done sold my Mary to a wicked man. Can you get her back?"

I remembered Mary as a pretty girl of twelve.

"Sold her? Why did you not ask leave to come tell me immediately?"

"I done told Mr. Olive."

I shook my head. In despair, I sat down on a chair left standing outside the kitchen door. I tried to collect my thoughts. No child of mine, no person, nothing in my life, made me feel more helpless than Bob. I loved him, always loved him, but so many of our encounters ended in anger. I resolved I would not tell Fanny the worst of it, but I had to tell her that Bob had gone to England. Bob's life, I supposed, was now in the hands of the Almighty.

Bob had always created gambling debts. I soon discovered that this time, he had outdone himself. I felt sick to think that he had stooped to selling a few young slave girls, because Mary was not the only one, to try to solve his financial problems. Only God knew what might happen to them.

He had also succeeded in ruining Billingsgate. The crop was of little value, and the place was worth considerably less than the total of his debts.

I sold everything of value on the place, trying to keep the land. The hardest thing was selling the slaves, keeping families together where I could. I was able to reunite Mary with her mother and sell them together. With a stab of conscience, I remembered telling Fithian I could take care of my slaves.

56

1785: Nomony Hall

I met Fanny in the hall as she was coming into the office. She was frantic.

"Anne Tasker did not come down to breakfast. She is not in her room, and I cannot find her. I've looked everywhere. I did think to send Tom Henry to the inn where John Peck is staying, and they say he is gone, too."

"I am very much afraid we both know what this means."

"Yes, it is a connection of which I do not approve, and I fear it will spell her ruin. Anne and John Peck both knew she was forbidden to see him."

We had noticed Anne Tasker's growing obsession with Peck and his willingness to take advantage of it. It had been a long time since we let him go as a tutor, and we forbad Anne to marry him, or even to see him. I barred him from Nomony Hall altogether.

"I cannot believe," Fanny said, "Anne would be so disobedient, and to take up with such a low character. I cannot believe she stooped to sneaking about with him." She started to cry.

All I could do was hold her and tell her everything would be all right even though I did not believe it myself.

I was so angry that I could feel the tension in every muscle of my body.

Then two days after their disappearance, Anne Tasker and John Peck were standing in my office. I could not help noticing what a pretty girl Anne had turned out to be, though she looked a little disheveled at the moment. She could not look me in the eye, nor did she look at her mother. She leaned on Peck's arm.

Peck, on the other hand, looked as if nothing untoward had happened, his handsome face relaxed.

Fanny sat beside me on a chair, her hands twisting in her lap. In contrast to me, she was exceedingly pale.

"Mr. Carter," said Peck. "I love Anne, and, because I am an honorable man, I have married her."

I wanted to strike the man. Honorable, indeed!

Anne Tasker instinctively moved between me and Peck.

"I know that you are angry, Papa, but John is a good man. You are wrong about him. Just give him time to prove himself and you will see."

"I do not know how you could do this, Anne, especially to your mother."

She had no answer.

To Peck I said, "Well, sir, what are your plans? How do you propose to support my daughter?"

"We thought we would stay here at Nomony awhile, until we can get on our feet."

"What have you been doing to try to get on your feet since you left here?"

"I have been trying, sir. I do a little tutoring."

"And after you were forbidden to see Anne Tasker or to set foot on this property, what makes you think you would now be welcome?" It was a rhetorical question, of course. I knew what he thought. I paused for breath and then turned to Anne Tasker. "You are married now. You have defied us and done what we forbad. You chose to go with Peck and trust your future to him in spite of all your mother and I told you."

Her head was down.

Turning back to Peck, I said, "You need to find yourself a permanent position and make a home for yourself and your wife. There are plenty of openings for tutors and clerks hereabouts."

The couple left with both Anne Tasker and Fanny in tears.

57

May 1785

"Come, sit in the shade, Bishop," Fanny said. "I'll fetch Robert."

To Sam she said, "Please bring this gentleman something cool to drink."

I was delighted to find the famous Methodist, Francis Asbury, sitting in my garden.

"I hope a stay at Nomony Hall will be a welcome reprieve from your travels."

I liked the looks of the man. He had the rough look of someone accustomed to being out of doors, but he had a compassionate face. Sam and I had heard him preach and I had given him an open invitation to visit Nomony Hall. Though I now considered myself a Baptist, I did not stop learning about other denominations. His visit presented a welcome distraction in our unhappy household, and Fanny was delighted with the company.

Asbury sat at the dining table long after supper and amused us the better part of the evening with his stories of the days he spent riding on horseback and preaching in the wilds beyond the mountains.

"I have traveled all over Virginia and all the settled—and not so settled—areas beyond. Sometimes people kindly allow me to stay in their homes. At other times, I find myself sleeping out of doors, in the cold and heat, rain and snow. I have come to know God's creation at close hand, and I am happy to say that Methodism is growing in Virginia."

"Like the Baptists," I said to Asbury, "the Methodists have reached out to all people, both Negro and white, slave and free, to come and worship together. It is one of the things I have most admired about the so-called Dissenters. However, I notice that, like the Baptists, as Methodism becomes more accepted by whites, it becomes less welcoming to Negroes."

"We have never abandoned our policy of racial acceptance and our antislavery position," Mr. Carter."

"In practice, though, I can see your congregations here on the Northern Neck becoming more and more dominated by whites."

"I am somewhat surprised at your concern, Mr. Carter. You will forgive me if I say it seems inconsistent with your being a slaveholder yourself."

"It is not as easy to cease being a slaveholder as one might think. It is not only the Negroes who are enslaved by the system but also the whites who find themselves responsible for the livelihood of great numbers of them. My slaves are encouraged to worship in whatever church they choose, and many of them worship in the same congregation that I do."

Asbury shook his head slowly.

"I am afraid that you are right, Mr. Carter, about the difficulty of freeing slaves. People are slow to change. Perhaps the Negroes feel more comfortable apart. They have begun creating their own congregations with their own preachers.

"In any case," I said, "you are certainly a man of your beliefs. I hope you will always look upon Nomony Hall as a place of respite whenever you are here."

"I shall be glad of it, Mr. Carter."

He held up his glass of cider (for he did not drink spirits of any kind) and made a toast.

"I find you to be a man who has the manners of a gentleman, the attainments of a scholar, and the experience of a Christian."

On Christmas Eve of that same year, Asbury returned to Nomony Hall and celebrated the holiday with us, much to Fanny's delight. But Asbury and the Methodists did not ease my mind about the continuing separation of Negro worshippers from the whites. I will say that when the Methodist General Committee met that year, they did declare slavery to be contrary to the will of God. Would that the General Assembly of Virginia felt the same way.

And what am I doing to help the situation? Asbury has pricked my conscience.

Anne Tasker came to Nomony Hall by herself this time. She looked agitated, and her eyes were red from crying.

I had relented, of course, and reconciled with Anne, fearing Peck's unwillingness to adequately care for her. She was, after all, our daughter, and we loved her. I gave them Billingsgate on which to live, the condition being that Peck manage it. I had felt compelled, also, to give Anne six slaves for a dowry, including her maidservant.

Anne Tasker sat down at my request and began to cry again.

"Papa, I am going to have a baby."

"Are you well?"

I sent Sam to get Fanny. I wondered why the coming of a child should be a reason for tears, although I did not view her pregnancy as a joyous event myself, under the circumstances. I was thinking, *At least she'll have the support of her mother through the next months.*

"John and I are moving to the North." Now the tears were flowing in earnest. "John feels he will do better there."

"Do you think that is wise in view of the coming child?"

"I do not want to go, Papa, but John says he knows people there, people who can help him find a suitable position. He will be happier there."

Fanny joined Anne crying at that point.

———

Tom Henry's usually placid face was clouded with anger. He approached me at the breakfast table, which was most unusual.

"May I speak, Master?"

"Of course, Tom. What is it?"

"There is something you ought to know, talk circulating among the slaves. I am afraid it is true."

"Yes?"

"It is John Peck."

I felt a very strong sense of foreboding.

"Now what?"

"He is taking Mistress Anne north, as you know."

"Yes, I know, and I am quite worried about her."

"But, that is not all of it."

"Oh, dear Lord, what else?"

"He sold all the slaves you gave Anne Tasker."

"Sold them? To whom?"

"Peck told me himself, when I asked, that he got a good price for them from a slave-trader in Richmond, and they are on their way south."

"Dear God."

Peck was taking my beloved daughter off to an uncertain future. And I had unknowingly consigned six slaves to be separated from their families and sent to a life of misery and toil hundreds of miles away. *What will become of them?*

58

1786

"Robert, it is time you and I were of one accord," Fanny said to me.

She looked beautiful this morning, dressed in a simple blue gown with a flowered bodice. Her color was good, too; she looked as if she felt well.

"What do you mean, dear? I always thought that we were of one accord."

"In most things, but for years I have continued to attend Cople Parish while you have ridden to your Baptist meeting. It is time we were together again in worship."

"Is this what you really feel? I know I have taken what society considers a radical step."

I was extremely pleased but still cautious. I had signed the Westmoreland Petition against Established Religion, not because I sought to destroy the established church, but because I believed it was important for people to worship according to their beliefs. I was afraid Fanny was doing this only to please me. I wanted it to be because she had a sincere desire to be a Baptist. Not only that, I had not yet expressed to Fanny the doubts I was beginning to have about the Baptists.

"I feel the need to be close to you these days, Robert. You know that I have never believed that any particular denomination had all the right answers. To me, they are different ways of seeking the same God, the same Christ who died for us. Is it not true that the Baptists believe that?"

"Yes, we believe in those things. We feel God's forgiveness and love. You must see for yourself what you think of the Baptists."

I teased her. "You know that you will have to submit to total immersion baptism if you are to become a Baptist."

Fanny kissed me on the cheek. "Well, I suppose if you can bear to see your wife publicly in such a bedraggled state, I can bear the immersion."

I hugged her tightly and kissed her. I could feel the softness of her body against me. I decided I liked the gowns women were wearing these days, without all the stiff underparts.

"I am truly happy that we will be worshipping together."

"Take good care of our sons," I wrote to James Manning at the College of Rhode Island.

It was the same Baptist college to which Lunsford's congregation and I had donated funds. It had a good academic reputation.

"You have our permission to be as firm as you need to be. We want them to experience a different sort of life than they have here in Virginia. We do not want them to continue to grow up under the system of slavery."

Fanny and I had talked about it for some time, but now we had made the final decision to send our boys, John, who was fourteen, and George, nine.

"It is such a hard choice," Fanny said.

"We have always tried to keep our children close, and I will miss them sorely."

"It is not too late to change our minds."

"No, we do not want them to follow Bob's way. Let them see a bigger world."

"Papa, this is not fair," said John. "I will miss the hunting this fall and winter. I wish to stay at home and learn here."

"Son, the world is changing. The future of this country does not lie in plantation farming alone, and I pray that it does not lie in continued slavery. I want you to know about the larger society in our country."

He stomped out of my office.

George, on the other hand, said, "I think it will be exciting to go see what the North is like."

I wore a heavy wool coat against the unusually cold weather as we boarded the *Betsy* for the trip to Baltimore. Slaves loaded her with boxes of the boys' possessions and clothing. I gave each of them a heavy coat also, expecting that they would need them in Rhode Island.

For a long while John stood on the deck and looked back to where we had come out the Nomini and into the Potomac. It made me sad to see him look back with such longing, and I prayed we had made the right decision. At least the two boys would be together.

Fanny was trying diligently not to shed tears in the presence of the boys, but I could see it took a great effort.

We sailed overnight. When we reached Baltimore in the morning, we all breakfasted together and then went to meet the public coach that would carry the boys to Philadelphia, Boston, and finally, Providence. George had a million questions about what they would see and who they would meet. John was wrapped in sullen silence.

"You must write to us, at least every week, and tell us what happens along your way," Fanny said to them. "We have never been to the places you are going."

I shook each of their hands as they turned to board the coach, then thought better of it and hugged each of them tightly. I was trying not to show my feelings.

"Take care. Study hard. Give my letter to Reverend Manning when you arrive. You must be men now."

Fanny could no longer hold back her tears. "We love you."

We stood and watched the coach until it was out of sight.

1787

Fanny could not stay warm. She was having another one of her weak spells. The paleness of her face contrasted sharply with her dark hair, now streaked with gray. She was trying to get up and be about the house, but she was straining to do so, trying to keep a smile on her face. She was not fooling anyone. Finally she gave up and went to bed.

It had been a year since the boys went away, and she saw them only when they came home at Christmas, but she wrote every day. Today, for the first time, she wrote from her bed.

Dr. Jones could never identify the cause of her spells. They were not like Ben's, which were accompanied by sweating and fever and that awful coughing. Tom Henry said she was just worn out. She was always working in the gardens right along with the slaves and directly supervising the keeping of the house. She could not be deterred from these tasks regardless of any amount of coaxing. The bearing of seventeen children, and the loss of five of them, had not helped her. She worried over Bob and Ann Tasker, and now George and John. Tom said she needed rest, and I knew he was right. My heart was aching.

On the morning of All Hallows' Eve, just as I finished dressing, Fanny sat up in the bed, smiling.

"Good morning, Robert. I feel so much stronger today. These two weeks past, you have been so kind to sit beside me and read to me."

She turned and fluffed up the pillows behind her.

"It is time I was up and about."

I was jubilant. There was color in her face.

"You look radiant," I told her.

"What shall I wear today? Something blue, I think."

"You are sure you feel well enough to get out of bed, then?"

"Oh, yes indeed. I feel like dancing ... and tomorrow we shall go to the All Saints service at Cople."

That took me by surprise. Fanny had not mentioned Cople, nor been there since her conversion to the Baptist Church.

Nevertheless, I said, "If that is what you want, then Cople it shall be."

I gave her a kiss on the forehead, which smelled of her lavender, and left her sitting up in bed, looking wonderful.

It happened I had to go to Richmond Courthouse that day. Full of joy and anticipation, I savored the ride in the late October sun. At court, I hurried through my business as quickly as I could, and, with a light heart, started the journey home. By the time I got home, Fanny would be up and dressed and waiting for me downstairs.

The horse carried me at a canter. *What a fine day it is.* I would go to Fanny—I could almost feel the softness of her in my arms and smell the scent of her lavender as I thought about it. She would make light of something and make me laugh, just as she always did. I could bear all the bad things life sent my way as long as she was by my side.

I rode up the poplar lane as I had so many times before, but as I reached the front of the house, I sensed something. I handed my horse to the hostler sent by Tom Henry and went into the house. Rose was standing at the top of the stairs, waiting for me.

59

1787

I was huddled in the chair beside the big bed in the room Fanny and I had shared.

I supposed I must look like a beggar, sprouting unaccustomed whiskers, my clothes disheveled and dirty. I didn't feel like changing them or being presentable in any way, for that matter. I wrapped myself in a blanket in the cold room and did not permit a fire to be set in the fireplace, nor a candle to be lit in the darkness. I even refused to let Sam in the room. What difference did any of it make anymore?

I wanted to be left alone in my misery.

I endorsed the funeral arrangements that Rose and Tom Henry suggested. I could not deal with them myself.

The day of Fanny's burial, the sky was suitably overcast and cold.

Sam was at the bedroom door. "Folks expect you to go to the graveyard. You want them to think you don't care about Mistress Fanny?" He refused to go away.

Finally, without dressing properly or shaving, I walked slowly across the top of the hill to the family plot. I spoke to no one. My face felt rigid as I watched her coffin lowered into the dark ground, and, as soon as the first shovel of dirt was thrown in upon her, I turned, ignoring everyone around me, and walked back to the house, to my darkened room. There was nothing left for me.

———

I could not stand to see the pity in Sam's face. For a month, only Rose came into the room, and then only to bring me meals, at which I picked. At first, Rose was gentle and understanding, but then one morning, she looked disgusted with me.

"Master Robert, "You got children that counts on you. They done lost they mama; now you taking away they daddy, too."

Rose was no longer a girl. She was more handsome than ever, full-bodied, still with her distinctive high cheekbones, smooth skin, and green eyes. At the moment, she was standing with her hands on her hips, just as she did whenever she really meant business. She was used to taking charge of five lively children and running the household staff.

"They will be fine without me, Rose. I am no substitute for their mother, poor orphans."

"You got plantations to run. We all gonna starve if you doesn't take care of things."

"The overseers can handle the plantations."

She let out a humph. "You knows you doesn't like the way they does things on they own. Shame on you, Master. You always talking 'bout Almighty God."

"What about Him?"

"You think He want you sitting around, feeling sorry for youself? He ain't done with you, Master. Doesn't you got something He want you to do?"

The next morning, I was up, dressed and clean-shaven for breakfast.

———

1788

Mr. Moyce was standing at the door, shivering, when I opened it. The cold and wind assaulted me. I had seen him from my office window riding up the poplar lane through snow blowing sideways. I went to let him in even before Sam could get to the door. At my invitation, he had traveled all the way from Philadelphia.

I led him into the office where a great fire was burning.

"You must have had a most unpleasant trip in this weather. I am very glad that you arrived safely."

"Truthfully, Mr. Carter, I am exhausted. And the fire is most welcome."

He held his hands out toward the fire while I called for hot tea spiced with lemon and sugar.

Then we sat on the wing chairs on either side of the fireplace, the planter and the missionary.

"I am so appreciative of your coming all this way to talk to me. I have read as many of the writings of Baron Swedenborg as I could get my hands on. My interest was piqued the moment I heard of him. I am impressed with the depth of his philosophy. I hope you can tell me more about his teachings and how the Swedenborgians function."

Moyce took a sip of the warm drink and savored it a moment.

"Actually, Mr. Carter, in many ways I perceive that the baron's experience and sensibilities are much the same as your own."

I could see that he really was not up to a long conversation.

"I know that you are tired. Let me suggest that you rest until supper and we continue our conversation afterward. Would that be acceptable to you?"

"That is most considerate of you."

After supper, we continued our conversation.

Moyce settled once again into a chair by the fire. "Swedenborg was the son of a Swedish Lutheran bishop who ministered to the Swedish royal family—an aristocrat. He was educated as a scientist and became distinguished in that field in his own country. However, in midlife, he began searching for what he called the true theology."

"That does sound like my own journey."

"Yes, I think so too, from what I know of you. Swedenborg came to believe that the scriptures are consistent with science and reasoning, not in conflict with them, as some followers of the Enlightenment believe."

"I certainly agree with that, and I see a belief in God underlying most of what the Enlightenment sets out to do."

"As a child," Moyce went on, "he was said to have certain psychic powers. He continued throughout his life to claim to have religious experiences, a connection with the 'other-world,' as he called it. Believing that he was divinely inspired to bring the word of God to his fellow man, he began writing pamphlets based on scripture to explain his philosophy."

"I claim to have no psychic powers, but I have had one or two religious revelations myself. I am afraid I do not claim that writing is the course to which God directs me, either. If you were to see my muddled expression on paper, you would agree."

Moyce chuckled.

"I wish to know what God is directing me to do. I have read many of the baron's writings, as I said, and I would not have asked you to come all this way if I did not find him very persuasive. Swedenborg was both rational and spiritual, if I understand him."

"Yes, yes, both rational and spiritual; that is correct. I understand that you had direct contact with the otherworld, also."

"I did have a gracious illumination that convinced me that God loved me and that what I did mattered to Him. It changed my life, but I have nearly lost my faith over the death of my wife. I have learned that I have no real power over the events of my life." I paused, lost in my thoughts for a second.

Moyce continued. "The role of the church in the community is an important aspect in the Swedenborgian church. The church takes no official stance on social issues, but rather encourages individuals to be active in them according to their own understanding of God's word. The idea is not only to teach spiritual truths but to teach and practice spiritual freedom, not only in purely spiritual matters but in social, moral, and political matters. In other words, it teaches people to study the scriptures to know what the spirit tells them, and then to act on it in the larger world. Swedenborg says that 'God is man' in that all that is truly human comes from God."

"Tell me this, Mr. Moyce, in Baron Swedenborg's philosophy, does one consider Negroes to be men in whom God is resident?"

"Most certainly. We are all creatures of God."

"How does one participate in this church?"

"Believers meet, read, discuss, and correspond. Where there are groups of believers, they usually meet at regular times. Most of all, they encourage each other to live according to their own beliefs."

"Where are such groups located?"

"There are several, mostly in cities. The closest group to you is in Baltimore."

I now lived alone at Nomony Hall, except for the people who served me.

Harriot Lucy was the third of my daughters to marry for love. I was extremely happy with her choice. He was a young lawyer named John James Maund, a bright, ambitious but good-hearted young man, and he was opposed to the institution of slavery.

I sent my three youngest daughters, Julia, Sophia, and Sarah Fairfax, to school in Baltimore while I tried to learn the practice of Swedenborgianism.

60

1790: Sam Harrison

M aster was sitting at his desk all piled up with papers. He sigh, then he pick up his quill, then he sigh again.

"You having trouble, Master?"

"Yes, Sam, the land here will no longer support any tobacco, and the other crops do not require the hand work that tobacco does. I have tried to develop trades like weaving and fulling, spinning and baking to employ people, but it is not enough. Like many of my neighbors, I have more people than I can use, but I refuse to sell my people south as some have done. It condemns them to a life of misery and separates them from their families. I cannot support all my people without using more of my western lands."

"That don't sound so bad, Master."

"Using the land is not what worries me, Sam. I have decided to move thirty slaves there to work the land now, but I will likely have to move more later."

"You still be in charge of them."

"Yes, but in the process of sending people west, I will be disrupting families. Look."

Master showed me a list of names and a map of his plantations.

"If I remove Mary and her baby from Old Ordinary, that will leave her mother and sisters here. Mary has never been separated from them before.

"Sarah, at Gemini must be moved too, but I need to keep her father here at Nomony.

"James is only thirteen, but he is a skilled mariner already. I need him out there, but I need his mother and father here.

"Mary from here on Nomony and her two small sons should be moved west, but her husband belongs to Fleet Cox. I offered to buy him from Fleet so that I could send them all together, but he won't sell him.

"Then there is George. He once gave me information about Betty Banks that caused me to send her to the Shenandoah. Now, I need him there too. I am uneasy to have them in the same place."

Master's eyes returned to his lists.

"I am trying to keep families together, and I can do that in many cases. James and Keziah will go along with their five children.

"Rachel can go with her daughters. Her husband died a few years past.

"Billy and Phoebe will be rejoining their family who went west last year. That's a good thing.

"Dorcas and John, the orphans, will be joining their grandparents.

"George Carey has disappeared, so I will not be sending him anywhere. And I will not have him pursued. Let him make his own way. I do not know what I'll do if he returns as he usually does.

"It is so hard. I continue to hope that the state will bring about an organized method for freeing slaves now that so many large planters have more slaves than they can use. The law permits manumission, but it can only be used at great expense to the landholder, and it offers little protection for the freed slaves." I shook my head.

"No, sir, it don't seem that the Revolution be for the Negroes."

Master look me hard in my eyes.

"Sam, are you happy?"

I doesn't know what to say to that. He look so serious and so sad.

"Oh, yes, Master. You takes good care of us."

"I try to do that, Sam, but aren't you disappointed that the Revolution has not helped the Negro?"

"Sure, I is, but I be happy here with you."

"But Sam ..."

It look like Master struggling, like some thought won't let him go. He drew a deep breath.

"Do you not really wish to be free?"

I doesn't believe I hear him right. I chokes up, tries to keep a happy face, but I feels tears coming in my eyes. I say, "I loves you, Master, has ever since we was little boys together. And I knows you loves me, too. But some things best left unsaid."

Master Robert's face growed pale, and he be mighty quiet. I doesn't know whether he mad or sad, and he never did say a word.

61

September 6, 1791: Robert

A sharp wind blew through the trees. I almost postponed the trip, but now that I had drafted the document to my satisfaction, I was anxious to file it. I bundled myself against the rain and invited Sam to go with me. I owed it to him.

The road was slippery under the horse's hooves, but I fancied every step I heard was a countdown. I did not speak to Sam—didn't know quite what to say. He seemed to respect my silence, sensing my mood, just as he always had.

We crossed Hampton Hall Creek while the wind blew at our coats. I still had hope that the Virginia General Assembly in its 1790 session would pass a law for gradual manumission of all slaves in Virginia, but instead they seemed to be moving in the opposite direction.

I looked over at Sam, beside me as he had always been in all things in my life. I decided that I was glad this had fallen to me personally after all, regardless of the consequences. I had not told Sam the purpose of this trip.

Some days ago, I took up quill and put my long-considered thoughts into writing:

"Whereas, I, Robert Carter of Nomony Hall in the County of Westmoreland and Commonwealth of Virginia, am possessed as my absolute property of many Negroes, mulatto slaves, whose number, names and situations, and ages will fully appear by a schedule hereunto annexed. And whereas, I have for some time past been convinced that to retain them in slavery is contrary to the true principals of Religious Justice, that therefore it is my duty to manumit them ..."

The law did not anticipate such a large-scale manumission; in this case the freeing of some five hundred slaves. The law did not spell out how it was to be done, either. I had to make it all up, but I was undaunted.

Sam and I arrived at Northumberland Courthouse, stamping to shake off the rain.

The clerk of court, Thomas Edwards, seemed surprised to see anyone on such an inclement day. He quietly received my document without reading it. He was accustomed to my filing papers in Northumberland, which was the repository for papers from that county, as well as from Westmoreland and Lancaster.

Edwards looked over his spectacles at me.

"What sort of document is this, Councillor Carter?"

"It is a deed of manumission."

Sam stared at me, mouth open.

"Manumission?" Edwards said. He looked up sharply. Then he read the entire deed while we waited.

The plan, spelled out in the document, was to free fifteen slaves each year, beginning with the oldest, to minimize the effect of the slaves' entrance into freedom. I also planned for any slaves under the age of twenty-one to be freed when they came of age, twenty-one for the men, eighteen for the women. Any children born to slaves on the list, who were born after 1791, were also to be freed when they came of age, so that the deed provided for people as yet unborn. It was meant to be a gradual manumission.

The state's law required that I guarantee a living to any slave over forty-five, and that I assure the ability of all the others to be able to support themselves. This I planned to do by setting them up or employing them in trades, or by renting them land for farming.

The deed applied to slaves now located on land owned by me, but occupied by my children, such as Priscilla and Ann Tasker (who had come back to Virginia with her worthless husband).

Finally, I went on to say that I did not wish the manumission to be of "disadvantage to my neighbors and the community at large."

"This is quite an undertaking, Councillor. Have you thought about what will inevitably follow?"

"Yes, I have, a great deal of thought,"

Edwards raised his eyebrows but copied the document as I watched and then affixed the recording information to the original. What a tremendous sense of relief I felt when I saw him inscribe his signature.

Sam watched with great curiosity.

When we had left the building, he asked, "Do this manumission be for me and my family, too?"

"Of course, Sam. After all, you are really the reason for it."

"What you mean?"

"You remember that day I asked you if you did not really want to be free? You said some things were best left unsaid."

"I remembers." He was silent for a moment. Then he said, "I always hope you come to freeing you slaves. Me and Tom Henry, we talk about it sometime, but now you actually done it."

"That's true."

It was true, but it wasn't going to be easy.

62

1791

"I will venture to assert," wrote a gentleman in the *Virginia Gazette,* in what he called "Open Letter to Robert Carter," "that a vastly greater number of slave people have passed or are passing now as your free men than you ever owned."

A letter that I received directly from a landowner adjacent to my land in Loudoun County said, "It appears to me that a man has almost as good a right to set fire to his own building though his neighbor's be destroyed by it, as to set free his slaves."

The response was worse than I had anticipated. Many of the neighbors I had lived and worked beside all my life would no longer speak to me.

Ann Tasker's husband, John Peck, who had already sold the slaves given to her in her dowry, now had the temerity to tell my people at Billingsgate (which they now called Bladensfield), where I allowed them to live, that he would no longer "clothe and victual" them.

"Send them to me," I wrote him, "along with a paper signed by you that you make no claim to them. I will take care of them myself."

I heard no more from John Peck on the matter.

⟜

May 1793

My musical instruments, clothes, and personal belongings were loaded into the *Betsy*. Tom Henry, now a free man, kindly agreed to bring my books over to me later.

Before walking down the road to the wharf, I walked across the hill to the family cemetery and sat down for a moment in the May sunshine, in front of the place where Fanny was buried.

"My dear Fanny, I have spent most of my life on this very land. Returning here in 1751 after all the unhappy years away was a great blessing. Then you came. I recall vividly the day you came home for the first time—beloved Fanny. Life is not the same without you. We refurbished a neglected plantation, and we worked hard to use all our holdings well. I believe we succeeded. We raised a large family, too, and I served Virginia while I could.

"Ah, well, my sweet, you are gone from this earthly place and free from the pain of your last days. Benjamin is gone. Bob is in England, lost to us. The older girls are all married. The two youngest are in Baltimore, and George is at the University of Pennsylvania in Philadelphia, an excellent school. John Tasker is here at Nomony, threatening to sell all the slaves on the place rather than see them go free. Do not worry, my dear; he cannot carry out that threat for he does not own them.

"There is nothing to keep me here now. I will find peace living among the Swedenborgians in Baltimore. Sam and Judith are now free, of course, and their children will live with them until their own dates for freedom come. They plan to move to Baltimore, also, though they will live in a separate house from me. And you, my dear, will go with me in my heart."

Priscilla approached me as I sat there. She was crying.

"Who will take care of your business in Virginia, Papa?"

"I have leased Nomony Hall to John Tasker. The rest I have left in the care of Benjamin Dawson."

"Are you sure those are wise decisions? John Tasker can be irresponsible, and Benjamin Dawson, though he purports to be a Baptist minister, is less than totally honest."

Priscilla had a sharp mind, especially for business, and a ready opinion, like her mother.

"I understand your concerns, my dear, but John Tasker deserves the same chance Ben and Bob had to prove themselves. If he fails, I will make other provisions. As for Dawson, he needs employment. He has collected my rents for many years, and he is quite willing to see to the schedule of manumission of the slaves, a hard task."

"Oh, I give him that credit, Papa. He cares more for freeing slaves than for life itself."

I held Priscilla and kissed her on the cheek. Then we walked together down the road to the wharf, and I boarded the *Betsy*.

I sailed out of Nomini Creek and into the Potomac, then overnight up the Chesapeake to Baltimore. The trip was uneventful, the weather being fine, with a soft wind blowing over the deck.

As we docked in Baltimore and I prepared to go to the house I had purchased on Green Street, a man approached.

"Be you Robert Carter of Nomony Hall in Virginia?"

"Yes, at least I was."

"I have a letter for you. It came from Hobbs Hole with instructions from the postmaster there to present it to you when you arrived."

I gave him some coins and took the letter. My hands trembled as I opened it because I could see that it was from London, and it was not in Bob's hand.

Inside was a letter from the coroner. He said that "Robert Bladen Carter died of wounds which had nothing to do with the sheriff in pursuit of him for gambling debts." Bob had died on February 22, 1793, at the age of thirty-four.

I sat down on a packing crate.

Perhaps, I thought, *he may be in heaven with his mother, finally at peace at last.* I hoped so.

63

1795: Baltimore, Maryland

A letter was delivered to my house on Green Street. I saw that the return address was Hanover County, Virginia, but the hand was not that of my daughter Fanny, who lived there. It was from her husband, Thomas Jones, and he wrote that Fanny had taken ill at their home and died at thirty-one years of age, leaving him with young children to raise.

"Please, God," I prayed, "do not let me live to see the death of another child of mine."

My daughter Sarah Fairfax had gone back to Nomony Hall to live with her brother, John Tasker, and not long after a letter from her informed me that she wanted to marry John Yeats Chinn of Richmond County. He was a doctor, educated at St. George and St. Thomas Hospital in London. He had been appointed a justice in Richmond County. I knew the Chinns to be a good family, and I was happy to support the marriage. They did marry in 1796 and settled on his plantation, Edge Hill. I did not give her slaves for her dowry, no longer having any, and I would not have done so in any case. I did give them a generous gift of money and wished them many blessings.

Sarah also told me that John Tasker was spending a lot of time visiting George Lee's daughter, Louisa.

<hr />

1796

The next letter I received was one from a distressed Ann Tasker, telling me that John Peck had died, leaving her with three small children. She told me that John had been so cruel to the slaves who lived on Bladensfield that they believed he haunted the place after his death. "Papa," she wrote, "what shall I do?"

I sent money and tried as best I could to console her. It was not long until she remarried, a gentleman named Hugh Quinlan. He seemed a good sort, far superior to his predecessor, and I had reason to hope Ann Tasker could be happy at last.

<hr />

1796

"His zeal in the cause of slavery," wrote Spencer Ball, the husband of my daughter Betty Landon, regarding Benjamin Dawson, "carries him beyond all bounds of justice."

Ball went on to say that Dawson was dishonest and kept a part of my rents for himself. My son-in-law, James Maund, and my son John Tasker also complained about Dawson.

That Dawson was not entirely trustworthy regarding the rents I had figured out long ago, and as I was sitting at my desk on Green Street, I was thinking about how to deal with the problem. I had put it off too long.

"I believe I have a solution to Benjamin Dawson and the rents," I wrote Ball, and I went on to explain to him what I intended to do.

Then I wrote to Henry Johnson, my attorney in Virginia.

"Engage William Garland to survey my lands in Virginia and have him mark off ten parcels of equal value. Once the parcels are marked off, I want you to number each parcel and then have each of my living children draw a number: John Tasker Carter, Priscilla Carter Mitchell, Ann Carter Quinlan, Betty Carter Ball, Harriot Carter Maund, Sarah Carter Chinn, Sophia Carter, George Carter, Julia Carter, and Thomas Jones, the widower of my daughter Frances Carter Jones. When that is done, please inform each child of what portion he or she has been allotted. If they wish to exchange parcels, that is up to them. Once the matter is settled, draw up deeds to each of them, retaining a life estate for me in each case. Provide that they are to pay rent of one dollar per year to me during my lifetime. At my death, the parcels will pass to the children outright. They shall have control over any of my former slaves on each parcel until, and only until, those slaves' turns come up to receive their certificates of freedom. Make sure that is a part of every deed. Benjamin Dawson will see to the slaves' appearance in court and to their certification as the times come."

To Tom Henry, now living on land rented from me, with Rose and his children, I wrote about the status of the manumission:

"Some of my people, not yet having received their certificates of freedom, will want to know what is going on. They all look up to you, and I want you to let them know that they are to stay on whatever plantation where they are now located until their court dates come. Assure them that they are not to be hindered from going to court and living wherever they choose afterward. If there is any problem, I will be grateful to hear from you so that I can address it. Benjamin Dawson will continue to arrange for their court dates at the proper time."

Harriot Lucy had drawn Nomony Hall as her parcel, for which I was thankful. Maund would manage it well.

Most of my remaining furniture and books were taken out of Nomony Hall and put into the care of my son George, who had drawn the plantation I called Leo in Prince William County.

I took away Dawson's power to collect rents, putting that into the hands of my attorney.

As for Ball's concern about Dawson's zeal in freeing slaves, I applauded it and gave Dawson power of attorney to continue. I provided him with money for his services and for the expense of getting my people to court.

64

1803

I heard a knock on the door at Green Street and hobbled as quickly to the door as my arthritis would allow.

There was Harriot, looking radiant in a blue gown in the new high-waisted style, and a straw bonnet with a matching ribbon. With her were John Maund and their baby daughter, Julia. The child smiled at me.

"What a beautiful child she is."

I reached to take her from her father's arms. She came without hesitation.

"What a delightful smile she has."

I winked at Harriot.

"I suppose she is as headstrong as her mother."

Harriot laughed.

I welcomed them into my house, modest compared to Nomony Hall but comfortable nevertheless. I showed my guests around. It suited my needs perfectly—an office, a sitting room where I welcomed guests and my Swedenborgian brothers and sisters, a bedroom for me, and a spare, a large dining room. Behind the house were a stable, a kitchen house, and a shed.

"Betsy, my free Negro housekeeper, and her husband, George, look after me. And Sam comes every morning to shave me and lay out my clothes. It is our little ritual. In the yard I have chickens and ducks and a vegetable garden—my little farm."

"Papa, you seem so happy. You never doted on us as you do Julia."

"I was always worried about you children—what kind of people you would become. Grandchildren are different. As for happiness, I must say that there are people I miss—most of all your dear mother—but I am content. I stay in touch with friends by letter, just as I do you children. I have finally accepted the fact that my plans and advice were never pleasing to the world. A person can only answer to his own conscience and to God."

"People do not always agree with you, sir," said Maund, "because you are ahead of your time."

Epilogue

1804

Tom Henry

"Tom Henry, Tom Henry!"

I saw Becky from Aries running across the field in my direction. She tripped and fell on the rough plowed ground but picked herself up and kept on coming.

I knew she had turned eighteen and was scheduled to go to court for her certification papers.

At fifty, I was gray at the temples, but I was still getting around very well, farming most days. I was held in respect by the Carter Negroes, slave and free. I farmed not only the acreage that I had bought but other people's land on shares. I doctored whites and blacks alike. In winter, I supplemented my family's diet with oysters from the river, deer, rabbits and turkeys from the woods, and geese from the air. In summer, I caught fish and crabs. I prospered.

This day as Becky ran across my field, I was walking behind my mule, cutting deep furrows in the dark earth. As she approached, I let go of the plow and took off my straw hat and wiped the sweat from my brow with the back of my hand.

"What seems to be the matter, girl?"

"Master Mitchell, he say we all in danger. Some folks never did like Master Carter man'mission, and Master Mitchell say now that Master Carter pass, we should go to his place for protection."

"Don't be foolish. You go back and tell all the folks you can that I said Mitchell has nothing to do with you all. When your time comes to go to court, you go on to court."

⟶

A wagon brought Robert Carter's body home to Nomony Hall to be buried. George had made the arrangements as his father requested him to do. Sam and Judith came with the body. Most of Mr. Carter's children were there to watch the casket brought up the lane from the wharf as a cold March wind blew. Several of Mr. Carter's former slaves and some of his neighbors were there, as well. We all watched as his sons and sons-in-law took the casket from the bed of the wagon and lowered it into the place dug for it next to the place where his Fanny rested.

I brought my whole family, which now included seven children. We all listened as a simple prayer was made by Harriot Lucy.

"Daddy," asked Henny, one of our twins, "was Mr. Carter crazy?"

"Yes, Daddy," the other twin, Oliver, said, "some folks say he was."

"The folks that say that don't like that Mr. Carter set his slaves free and gave up his plantation life. Without him, your mama and I, and you children, and all the other people who used to be slaves on his plantations, would never be free. Don't you ever forget that Robert Carter was a courageous man who did a great and generous thing. He was our friend. Someday folks will appreciate him."

George Carter went to court to fight his father's deed of manumission, but he lost. He later came to regret having bought new slaves himself to replace those freed by his father. Benjamin Dawson saw that the deed was carried out as long as he could. Robert Carter's other children helped carry it out as well. As late as 1852, his daughter Julia obtained the freedom certificate for a descendant of the Carter slaves.

In the census of 1810, there were no slaves at Nomony Hall, but in Westmoreland County alone, there were 621 free Negro men and women.

Printed in the United States
By Bookmasters